DEAD HANDS REACHING

DEATH'S LONG SHADOW

Marian Scott

DEAD HANDS REACHING

DEATH'S LONG SHADOW

Marian Gallagher Scott

COACHWHIP PUBLICATIONS

Greenville, Ohio

Dead Hands Reaching / Death's Long Shadow, by Marian Gallagher Scott
© 2015 Coachwhip Publications

Dead Hands Reaching, as by Marion Scott, published 1932.
Death's Long Shadow, as by Katherine Wolffe, published 1946.
No claims made on public domain material.

ISBN 1-61646-302-3
ISBN-13 978-1-61646-302-1

Cover: Hand shadow © Lensman2

CoachwhipBooks.com

CONTENTS

INTRODUCTION
Muses of the Mind: The Mystery Fiction of Marian Gallagher Scott

Curtis Evans

Detective novels are known for characters' uses of aliases, but the authors who write them often have employed them as well, in the form of *noms de plume*. (The most famous recent example is J. K. Rowling's adoption of the pen name "Robert Galbraith" for her newly-launched mystery series.) A crime writer still enshrouded in mystery today is Marian Gallagher Scott (9 October 1892–8 June1943), who, besides writing prolifically for the pulps, in a ten-year period published, under three alternating pseudonyms, four detective novels: *Dead Hands Reaching* (1932), by Marion Scott; *Tall Man Walking* (1936), by Katherine Wolffe; *The Moon Saw Murder* (1937), by Gail Oliver; and *The Attic Room* (1942), by Katherine Wolffe. Additionally, *Death's Long Shadow*, a final Marian Gallagher Scott mystery novel, was posthumously published in 1946, under the author's Katherine Wolffe pseudonym. Although Scott's second published detective novel, *Tall Man Walking*, received considerable critical praise around the world, the book was never reprinted in paperback and was soon forgotten, like the rest of her fictional work. The neglect of Scott's writing is especially unfortunate in the case of *Tall Man Walking*, one of the finest psychological crime novels produced by an American mystery writer in the 1930s.[1]

Maude Marian Gallagher was born to Benjamin James and Emily Amelia (Van Ness) Gallagher in the small farming community of Wilsey, Kansas in 1892, eight years after the town was founded as a stopping point on the Missouri Pacific Railroad. Shortly after the turn of the century Marian moved with her family to the Kansas state capital, Topeka, where her father owned a drugstore. (Marian's uncle, George B. Gallagher, was a Topeka grocer and her younger sister, Elizabeth Louise, later married a Topeka baker, Samuel E. Weirich.) Marian seems to have led a life in Topeka that, from what little we currently know about her, is not readily distinguishable from that of other young urban Midwest women of her era; yet her artistic muse must have insistently beckoned her even then, on the seemingly endless prairies of her native state, with the promise of a more brightly colored future.

Having graduated in 1910 from Topeka High School and Daugherty's Business College, Marian found employment for the next several years in the capital as a stenographer and court reporter. Although state auditing records list payments made to Marian Gallagher for clerical work done on behalf of the Livestock Sanitary Commissioner and the Kansas Senate, the ambitious young woman had hopes for a future that encompassed something more than mechanically recording the prosaic declarations of attorneys, businessmen and politicians. In addition to performing her workaday typing jobs, Marian regularly attended a class in dramatic expression. One day her teacher, praising Marian's acting ability, urged her to go study at the Lyceum Arts Conservatory in Chicago, under the tutelage of Elias Day, an influential figure in circuit Chautauqua: traveling shows arising out of the nineteenth-century lyceum educational movement that took place in thousands

---

[1] A 1939 American publisher's blurb claims that Marian Gallagher Scott in fact had "written six novels, published in this country, England, and France." My accounting above only lists three Scott novels, so it appears that there may be three additional, unknown Scott novels that were published, presumably under yet more pseudonyms (or perhaps serialized novels in pulps were counted in the tally).

of small town venues across America and included lectures, oratory, musical acts and performances of famous plays. "At its peak in the mid-1920s," notes a modern authority, "circuit Chautauqua performers and lecturers appeared in more than 10,000 communities in 45 states to audiences totaling 45 million people."[2] Inspired by her teacher's hopeful advice, Marian left Topeka and typing behind, moving to the Windy City in 1914 and enrolling in Elias Day's school.

Marian's greatest moment in life up to that time came the next year when Elias Day chose her to play the female lead in the school's staging of a renowned Shakespeare comedy, *The Taming of the Shrew*. The male lead was played by Earl William Scott (1891-1971), a recent graduate of Nebraska Wesleyan University and the Lyceum Arts Conservatory who was circuiting the country with fellow "characterist" Bob Mahoney, as the Scott-Mahoney Company. Marian and Earl became romantically involved and wed at the Methodist parsonage in Laporte, Indiana on May 21, 1917, when Marian was twenty-four years old. After their marriage the couple founded their own acting troupe, the Kenilworth Players (presumably named for 215 S. Kenilworth Avenue, Oak Park, Illinois, their street address at the time), which for a decade was a fixture in circuit Chautauqua. In the case of Earl and Marian Scott, the handsome pair over the next eleven years would give countless renditions of the perpetually-sparring Katherina and Petruchio, performing *The Taming of the Shrew* in such seemingly inhospitable locales as the roughneck central Texas oil boomtown of Caddo.

Marian Gallagher Scott, as she was now known, much later in life would evocatively detail her circuit Chautauqua experiences in a 1939 book, *Chautauqua Caravan* (published under the name Marian Scott), and readers of this introduction are urged to peruse this fascinating work of social history. However, only at the close of Marian and Earl's career in circuit Chautauqua—with the

---

[2] Charlotte Canning, "Traveling Culture: Circuit Chautauqua in the Twentieth Century," Records of the Redpath Chautauqua Collection, The University of Iowa Libraries Special Collections & University Archives, at http://www.lib.uiowa.edu/sc/tc/.

Marion Scott often made the
front cover of pulp magazines.

ascent of radio and the automobile the institution had entered a state of terminal decline—did the couple turn to the writing of pulp crime fiction as an alternative source of income. In *Chautauqua Caravan* Marian indicates that she and Earl enjoyed reading pulps while resting from circuits, specifically mentioning their happy discovery, in a cabin outside Woodruff, Wisconsin, of a "tattered copy of *Adventure* tucked back on a shelf," in which they read, much to their delight, a Stephen Chalmers' lost civilization treasure tale, "The Dance of the Golden Gods." Using the slightly disguised pseudonym "Marion Scott," Marian published her first known crime tale, "Folded Evidence," in the October 1927 issue of *Black Mask*. Under this pseudonym Marian would publish a total of three stories in *Black Mask*, while another seventeen tales would appear in this celebrated pulp magazine under the byline Earl and Marion Scott. Writing both jointly and separately, the couple over the course of the Twenties and Thirties published close to two hundred known stories in myriad pulps, including *Street & Smith's Detective Story Magazine, Detective Action Stories, Mystery Magazine, Clues, Gang World, Thrilling Detective,* and *Top-notch Magazine.*

For Earl Scott writing for the pulps seems never to have served as an impetus to novel authorship, but Marian Scott, following such recent successful examples as Dashiell Hammett and Raoul Whitfield, daringly sought to make the transition, publishing her first crime novel, *Dead Hands Reaching*, with Macmillan in 1932, five years after she had entered the pulp fiction mill. Rather melodramatic in tone and episodic in narrative yet undeniably eventful and exciting, *Dead Hands Reaching* to me very much seems to reflect, as the title suggests, Marian's apprenticeship in the pulps. She wrote the novel, which details the shocking events that follow actress Dallas Gentry's fateful return to Willow Valley to seek a divorce from her wealthy and tyrannical older husband, in Santa Fe, New Mexico, where the couple settled after leaving circuit Chautauqua and became, like a better-known crime writer, Dorothy B. Hughes, fixtures in the city's artistic community. Earl and Marian resided at the wryly-named "Crooks' Nook," a three-room

Marian Scott inscription to Harry Steeger of Popular Publications
(*Dead Hands Reaching*, Curtis Evans Collection).

adobe cottage on the Acequia Madre, and did all their writing at an office they rented on Sena Plaza. My copy of *Dead Hands Reaching* came from the library of Harry Steeger, founder of Popular Publications, one of the largest publishers of pulp magazines at the time, and is inscribed by Scott herself as follows: "To Popular Publications with all good wishes Marian Scott Santa Fe Aug 30 – 1932."

In addition to its drawing slightly on the author's extensive experience in circuit Chautauqua (Dallas Gentry, we learn, worked her way up to acting stardom from her beginnings in "Tom Willoughby's Repertory Company, touring the South and Middle West"), *Dead Hands Reaching* is of note for introducing New York City police detective Captain Courtney Brade, Marian Scott's series detective in three novels. Observing Brade for the first time, Dallas Gentry is immediately surprised by the cop's sophistication and sensitivity, in a passage that attempts to authenticate the sleuth's sterling credentials as a Golden Age Great Detective:

> Dallas didn't know much about detectives. . . . She rather thought they should be short, heavy men with thick red faces and blunt hands, who wore derbies and broad shoes. . . . Brade was almost as tall as Anthony . . . lean and looked in perfect condition. He was quietly and correctly dressed in gray tweeds. He had very thick, dark-brown hair . . . stained with gray at the temples. . . . He had the strongest, keenest, saddest eyes she had ever seen. They were a curious cloudy gray, rather long and habitually narrowed between crisp black lashes. He smiled and rested a hand on the table's edge. For no reason she could explain, Dallas looked at that hand. It seemed to her that every part of the man was distinctive, individual.
>
> "What a gorgeous ring," she thought, staring at a magnificent Oriental moonstone, set in a massive, hand-hammered, silver mounting. . . . "I wonder why a detective wears a ring like that?"

This crime investigating paragon—a suave study in gray sport-
ing a mysterious moonstone ring that holds, we are tantalizingly
told, "the story of Brade's greatest defeat and mightiest victory"—
would not appear again in another detective novel by Marian Scott
for a full decade. With Scott's second and finest detective novel,
Tall Man Walking, the author separated herself from her pulp past
by using a new author pseudonym, Katherine Wolffe. Although the
title of the book seems a play on *Dead Hands Reaching*, this ambitious and accomplished work is a non-series tale of a much different order from Scott's first detective novel. On the surface *Tall
Man Walking*, which was published in the United States in 1936
by Doubleday Doran's prestigious Crime Club, clearly belongs to
the American tradition of the so-called HIBK (Had-I-But-Known)
novels associated with the hugely popular mysteries of Mary Rob-
erts Rinehart. In the most typical examples of HIBK novels a
middle-aged spinster forebodingly narrates a recent course of dire
events, which might have turned out differently, had the narrator
but known the things she now knows. There has been a certain
male tendency to disparage the "feminine" HIBK novel as what
Julian Symons in his crime fiction study *Bloody Murder* dubbed
fiction written specifically for "maiden aunts" (Ogden Nash coined
the term HIBK in a humorous 1940 poem, "Don't Guess, Let Me
Tell You"), yet in fact the better writers associated with the HIBK
school, such as Rinehart, Leslie Ford, Mabel Seeley and Dorothy
Cameron Disney, enjoyed considerable popularity with both male
and female readers and reviewers and in the last fifteen years or
so an effort has been made within the academic world to revise
modern critical opinion of their work (see, for example, Catherine
Nickerson's 1999 monograph, *The Web of Iniquity*).

Forebodingly narrated by a fifty-four year old New England
village spinster, *Tall Man Walking* in this respect falls squarely
within the HIBK tradition, yet it takes readers into darker spaces
than is customary in this school of fiction. The spinster, local dressmaker Laure Hosmer, explains that she has been tasked with writing an account of the recent rash of murders that savagely struck
Wilromere, "a beautiful little village . . . named after our leading

family, the Rohmers." As described in an unconsciously amusing manner by the prim Miss Laure, Wilromere is a classic traditionalist village of the sort associated in many mystery readers' minds today with Golden Age English detective fiction:

> Somehow the tide of what is known as progress has pretty well passed us by and I for one am glad. A year ago last fall they oiled the main street and where used to be livery stables are now garages, and a big oil company put in a very nice station with dahlias and cannas blooming in the little square in front. Also the Congregational Church has been painted white. It was red when I was a small girl and I liked it best that way. . . . except for these things that I mention and few others equally unimportant, the town is like I always have known it. The people are old-fashioned, too. . . . I don't mean to imply that we are narrow in Wilromere. No indeed. We are really very up to date. Just last winter the Woman's Culture Club studied a huge book by James Joyce, and Stacey Madden, just back from a season in Europe, gave a lecture on the Art of the Vatican. All of the boys and girls of the wealthier families go off to college and sometimes travel abroad, like Stacey Madden, though she is no longer a girl, goodness knows. She's forty-six if she's a day and I'm sure, though I've never mentioned it to anyone, that her hair has been tinted.

Yet even Miss Laure realizes that, in writing this narrative of criminal violence, she must let her upright mind venture into the midnight alleys where murder lurks, even in old-fashioned villages like Wilromere:

> I closed my eyes, leaned back in my chair and just let my memory go. It was like when you drop a spool of thread and still hold onto one end. The spool rolls

away some place and the thread unwinds, becomes tangled, twisted, tied into knots. Then you're apt to find the spool anywhere. Under the sofa, behind the table, back of a chair. When you go in after it, you discover dust sometimes where you thought it was clean. Maybe you'll run into that coral pin you lost last winter. Perhaps you'll find hateful things like where the mice have been, or a spider has spun a web, so that your skin crawls and you want to back away real fast, not looking much.

That's the way it was with my memory. . . .

The lost spool of thread is a clever image that aptly conveys the unpleasant emotions that are unleashed in certain quarters of Wilromere by the June wedding of David Kaye and Wiletta Owens. When the hateful Wiletta is found stabbed to the heart in her wedding dress more than a half-dozen suspects can be discerned just within her own wedding party. Not for nothing is *Tall Man Walking* subtitled *Murder—with Music by Wagner.* (The subtitle also recalls how Marian Gallagher had once played the wedding march from *Lohengrin* at her friend Agnes Coulter's May wedding in Topeka a quarter of a century earlier.)

"Murder!" writes Miss Laure. "Who of us realized it fully? It was a word we had heard, that we sometimes used, but it was outside our real comprehension, like leprosy or the Black Hole of Calcutta." Yet the citizens of Wilromere come to realize to their mortification that hidden away within the village are its own black holes of hate and bile, which now stand to be exposed under the light of a murder investigation conducted by the novel's apparent detective figure: a mysterious sleuth of the mind, psychiatrist Kenneth Borden (the "tall man" of the title). As another character, Miss Laure's old friend Dr. Marc Wayne, retrospectively puts it to the spinster dressmaker, in the case of the Wilromere murders, the "physical clues weren't the important ones."

Tightly plotted and extremely suspenseful, *Tall Man Walking* twists and turns like an unloosed spool of thread. Part of the appeal of the novel is found as well in Marian Scott's compelling

portrayal of village life in New England, a region that had fascinated the author since she had met her future husband in 1915 and
he had regaled her in his letters with enchanting tales of his circuits with Bob Mahoney in the East. "I lived his accounts of the
snowbound New England villages," Scott recalled fondly in
Chautauqua Caravan. When she finally visited New England in
1922, she found that "the little villages with their quaint, dormer-
windowed houses, their neat squares and time-weathered churches,
were a constant delight."

Critics around the world were similarly delighted with *Tall Man
Walking*. "Why is it that mystery stories in which spinsters play
leading roles are almost invariably good?" queried Isaac Anderson in his highly laudatory review of the novel in the *New York
Times Book Review*. Hundreds of miles away in Middle America,
Todd Downing, himself an accomplished mystery writer, gave a
rave review to *Tall Man Walking* in the pages of the Oklahoma
City *Daily Oklahoman*, praising the novel as "one of the trickiest
and most intelligent yarns of the season, put over without fingerprints, broken cufflinks or rouge-tipped cigarettes in the way of
clues." The admiring Downing added that "Katherine Wolffe is a name
to be watched in mystery fiction." *Tall Man Walking* also was "warmly
recommended" by nationally syndicated book reviewer Bruce Catton,
who contrasted the novel's mature and superbly controlled narrative
with that of *Danger in the Dark*, a mystery by popular romantic crime
writer Mignon Eberhart that, according to Catton, was fatally afflicted
by the "complete brainlessness of the hero and heroine, plus the
author's breathless, awed style of writing." In Britain and the
Dominions, where the novel was published under the more lurid
(and rather silly) title *Bride of Death*, the critical response was
also extremely positive, with, for example, the *Melbourne Argus*
trumpeting: "As an exciting story of death and crime detection this
book is good; as a skillful study in suspense it is remarkable." In
1937 Scott, in collaboration with Philip Barber, a Yale University
professor of drama and New York director of the Federal Theatre
Project, adapted *Tall Man Walking* as a two-act play, but regret-
tably it seems never to have been performed on stage.

Perhaps daunted by the great critical praise for *Tall Man Walk-ing*—how does one, the author might well have asked herself, fol-low such a resoundingly huzzahed performance—Scott produced no new "Katherine Wolffe" crime novel for six years. Between *Tall Man Walking* and *The Attic Room* came another non-series mys-tery, *The Moon Saw Murder*, which Scott published with Macmillan under yet another pseudonym, Gail Oliver, and Scott's impressive non-fiction book, *Chautauqua Caravan*. By the time William Mor-row published the second Katherine Wolffe detective novel in 1942, less than a year before Scott's death, *New York Times* book re-viewer Isaac Anderson, despite having highly praised the author's *Tall Man Walking* six years earlier, pronounced in his notice of *The Attic Room*: "This appears to be Katherine Wolffe's first mys-tery story." After merely half a dozen years, Todd Downing's name to watch had become a name that time forgot.

It surely did not help Katherine Wolffe's fading reputation that *The Attic Room*, though entertaining, falls short of the high stan-dard set by *Tall Man Walking*. Evidently for her new novel Scott wanted to retain the sort of middle-aged New England spinster narrator figure that had served *Tall Man Walking* so well (in *The Attic Room* this figure is a fifty-six year old village postmistress, Martha Berry, though she is actually a longtime widow, not a spin-ster). However, the author shoehorned Courtney Brade, her Great Detective from the Marion Scott mystery *Dead Hands Reaching*, into the novel as well, making a somewhat awkward fit. Brade effectively steps into the shoes of the psychiatrist Kenneth Borden from *Tall Man Walking*, but as an individual personality he seems extraneous to the tale, despite references to his "cloudy gray eyes" and "gorgeous moonstone ring" (how the New York cop comes to take over a murder investigation in a New England village is not adequately explained). Moreover, the novel's non-series charac-ters are altogether more conventional than those in *Tall Man Walk-ing*. Nevertheless, the story is still an enjoyable one and the New England village setting again is well-conveyed.

A little more than a half-year after the publication of *The Attic Room*, Marian Scott died suddenly from a heart complication in

EARL AND MARIAN SCOTT

Hollywood, California, where the couple had moved about five years earlier. At her death Scott had completed more than two-thirds of a final novel, which her husband later finished and published in 1946 as a paperback original attributed to Scott's most successful pseudonym, Katherine Wolffe. The novel, entitled *Death's Long Shadow*, details the last known criminal investigation of Courtney Brade. It is, in my view, the best book in the Brade mystery series and a fitting tribute to the ingenuity of Brade's creator.

Like its two immediate Katherine Wolffe predecessors, *Death's Long Shadow* draws on a New England village milieu, yet it has a more modern feel, as though in its composition the Scotts had been influenced to an extent by the rise in American crime fiction of the hard-boiled style. The novel opens evocatively on a sleeting November evening at a soon-to-be defunct gas station in rural Minnesota, forlornly located by the Chippewa City-Minneapolis highway (I was immediately reminded of the 1940 Edward Hopper painting *Gas*), and then shifts to an isolated cottage where a mysterious hermit woman, Ann Regnas, has been done violently to death. Courtney Brade is soon on the scene—his appearance here is more plausibly explained than it is in *The Attic Room*—and, curiosity getting the better of him yet again, he manages once more to unofficially take over a murder investigation, this one leading to a long-buried past and some dark doings in Reddington, a stern and wintry Massachusetts town.

Marian Scott's depiction of Reddington may have drawn not on quaint New England villages, by which she always seems to have been quite charmed, but rather on her recollections of a dismal winter she spent alone not long after her marriage, when she was conducting a drama class in a small town in central Illinois, Earl being far away on a solo southern circuit. In *Chautauqua Caravan* Scott's memories of that central Illinois town, which she calls "Lovell," are imbued with bitterness over the social exclusion she suffered there:

> It was an old town, as our towns go, and its people
> were clannish, unfriendly, suspicious, to a new-
> comer. They were particularly skittish, where I was

concerned, because I was known to have some association with the stage. Also, although I had "Mrs." Before my name, which according to their lights should have automatically rendered me highly respectable, my husband was not in evidence. No one had ever seen him. With them, seeing was believing. So they stood back, reserved their judgment and some of them turned their heads the other way when I passed them in the streets. . . .

. . . . [I]n spite of [my landlady's] friendship and my class of interested youngsters, I was very lonely those cold, dark months. . . .

More than a year after I left Lovell and managed pretty well to erase it from my memory, I had a letter from the dignified and correct president of the Women's Club, who, during my residence there, had never been at home when I called. She invited me to return and coach a play for them. She was very cordial and pleasantly insistent, naming a handsome sum as compensation. I gathered from the letter that, after a sufficient time has elapsed, they had decided that I was quite harmless after all, and perhaps I did have a husband and was what was generally described in Lovell as a "good woman."

While I was, I trust, properly grateful for their eventual confidence in me, I did not go, and I recalled with natural resentment the only time I had attended one of their churches to be regarded with patent unfriendliness, not one of the large, satisfied congregation bothering to speak to me. . . . It . . . set before me vividly the extreme cruelty of which a small town may be capable.

In *Death's Long Shadow* Marion Scott devised a most engrossing swan song, providing readers a detective novel with both compelling human drama and clever criminal conundrums. Earl Scott, who probably wrote the last four or five chapters of *Death's Long Shadow*, deserves credit as well for so neatly disentangling the intricate plot threads in his wife's tapestry of murder. My only regret with *Death's Long Shadow* is that, the novel being the record of Courtney Brade's last recorded case, we will never learn the story behind the detective's mysterious moonstone ring (which in the novel he twirls with a flourish when making one of his dramatic revelations). The republication by Coachwhip Publications of *Death's Long Shadow* with three other Marian Scott mysteries, most especially *Tall Man Walking*, is an act of due historical recovery that should be applauded by fans of classic American crime fiction.

DEAD HANDS REACHING

CHAPTER ONE
RETURN

DALLAS WAS COMING back to Willow Valley after fourteen years! Returning in the hush of an autumn evening, when a purple haze lay softly over the hills and one bright star glittered coldly in the cobalt blueness of the sky. She sat stiff and straight on the edge of the dusty plush seat as the train approached the town, brown eyes stretched wide, face pressed against the grimy glass.

She was alone in the coach except for a tired-looking woman up front and the pale-faced man in the gray hat across the aisle, who had been staring at her with such insolent interest all afternoon.

Dallas was conscious of him even now as she leaned against the window ledge and watched Willow Valley growing closer. Her heart was beating swiftly and her whole body felt hot and tight.

She decided it was because the coach was stuffy and also because she had slept poorly the night before, due to the excitement of this approaching visit to the town she had run away from so long ago. Then, with a sudden shiver, she threw aside pretense and admitted that it was because she was frightened. Plain, everyday frightened. At the prospect that lay before her. At the thing she had come to do! Then she smiled faintly and shook her head.

Afraid? Of what? Whom? Who could hurt her now? Who could—reach her? She drew a deep breath, staring about the shadowy coach. The train lumbered along, swaying and pitching.

She leaned back against the dusty plush of the seat. She was tired, unstrung. She had been working too hard. Weeks of steady rehearsing bad beaten her down. She needed a rest.

Resolutely she turned toward the window again, eyes groping over the darkening landscape. There was the mill. Still like a ghost in the twilight. Arch Simmons had killed himself there because he couldn't pay the money he owed Jurden Keye!

"Oh," Dallas gasped faintly, and drew back from the window, suddenly sick. She had located the source of her dread, this thing that had been growing on her ever since she entered the train back in the city. She had put it from her as long as she could but now it had pounced from the gray shadows of the old mill where Arch Simmons had died, and gripped her terribly.

Jurden Keye!

After her rebellion, her struggles, her ultimate victory, she was still afraid of the tall, thin-lipped man at Willow Wilde. She had never been free from him. All these years he had held his dusty hands upon her. The narrow glitter of his eyes had followed her. The echoes of his dry voice had gone with her and at last—he had drawn her back.

She sat very still, fighting a rising hysteria. Why, Jurden Keye wasn't even aware that she was coming. Her visit would be a tremendous surprise to him. . . . Deep in her heart she knew better. He had dragged her back. Pulled at her with his dusty hands until she once more stood within his power. . . .

She looked up as the light came on, and her glance encountered that of the man in the gray hat across the aisle. He was staring at her intently and she could not read what lay back of his pale slanted eyes.

Why was he smiling? Why looking at her with that knowing secret triumph? He couldn't guess how unstrung she was. Slowly her glance went over him. He assumed a tremendous importance there in the rattle and dust of the little train. She felt that she must know him again—some time soon—be able to identify him.

He was a tall, very thin man, with an unhealthy white face that somehow suggested long confinement in dark, airless places and his ultra-stylish, expensive clothes could not conceal his cheapness, any more than his fixed smile could hide the cruelty and meanness of his lips.

Dallas wrenched her eyes away, turned again to the flashing landscape. Why had she come back to Willow Valley? Branson, her attorney, could have handled the whole thing. There were bound to be unpleasant moments. People in the town wouldn't have forgotten Dallas Gantry. Every time she turned her head, she would be remembering.

But she had loved it so, in spite of everything. The drowsy little town nestling in its leafy valley, encircled by the low knobs of lazy hills, the old town with its winding streets, its pleasant homes, its shaded ways had drawn her back. That was it. The town, not Jurden Keye, had led her here. She had wanted to see it again. Go back, retrace the old dead trails, meet old ghosts and lay them—all before she started life anew with Anthony.

At thought of him, Dallas' tense face relaxed and the longing to see him just then amounted almost to physical pain. He was safety! Security! He represented freedom from the strange cold fear. She began thinking very definitely about him. Memory of him was sanctuary. She recalled his thick, crisp sun-burned hair, with that one stubborn lock that would never stay in place. The way his eyes crinkled when he laughed. Anthony's eyes were blue, a violent intense blue, and his brows were like sharp black slashes above them. He had a lean, angular face, with high cheek bones, burned a ruddy brown. . . .

"Willow Vall—ey!"

The trainman's casual announcement jerked Dallas from her reverie. She jumped up, dropping her purse, stumbling over her traveling case, groping for her coat.

The conductor, whom Dallas remembered from the old days, but who evidently hadn't recognized her, grinned in a friendly way and picked up her luggage.

"I'll bring 'em, lady," he said, eyes frankly curious. He was thinking that he didn't often deliver such a passenger to Willow Valley.

Dallas thanked him breathlessly and ran down the aisle. The white-faced man in the gray hat blocked her way. He turned, eyes groping boldly over her face. Dallas drew back with a recurrence of the fear that had lessened with a mounting excitement at being really in Willow Valley again, then the stranger smiled and touched his hat.

"Pardon me," he said in a husky, unpleasant voice, and stepped aside.

Dallas hurried past him, eyes glowing with anticipation. The outer door was open and a gust of wind sucked through the stuffy coach.

"Oh," she cried softly, and stopped, sniffing hungrily. It was so very, very long since she had smelled air like that. Slightly damp, redolent of open fields where corn was drying in fragrant shocks, like Indian wigwams, with great yellow pumpkins dotting the brown stubble between; thick with the scent of woods, heavy with the fragrance of leaf fires.

She put out an unsteady hand and groped her way into the vestibule. At the top step she paused. In the early twilight the world before her was swimming in a delicate blue haze, through which the glow of lighted windows shone like winking eyes.

Everything was the same. The ugly red station, the board platform, the lumpy heaps of freight piled on squeaking trucks. Dry grass grew waist high in the ditch beside the sagging walk that led to the town nearly a quarter of a mile away. The road was rutted and thick with dust, blue-silver in the twilight. Far beyond the town she saw the hump of Elder's Hill where sumac and goldenrod grew in autumn and dogtooth violets in spring. . . .

A sob caught in her throat. Her eyes were suddenly dim with tears. She grasped the railing and descended the steps slowly. About her on the platform was leisurely bustle. Someone was leaving. A fat woman with a lunch basket on her arm, noisily herding three small, excited children. Dallas stared at her curiously. Did she know her? Would the woman recognize her as Dallas Gantry, who had married . . .

Dallas turned quickly. Her cheeks were hot. This wouldn't do. She must be prepared for recognition. She had no reason to come sneaking back to the town she had deliberately left. She was rich now. Famous. Happy . . .

"Hotel, madam?"

Dallas looked up with a little gasp. That pleasant courteous voice was so familiar, that pungent odor of good cigars. A tall man in a long, careless dark raincoat stood before her. His hat was in his hand and the fading light touched a great unruly shock of silvery white hair. Beneath it his face was lean and copper-hued, heavily marked with slashing lines that could not mar its queer beauty. He had fine dark eyes.

Dallas stared at him blankly. Who was he? She ought to know. She should remember that face. But something about it was so different. . . .

He was regarding her with equal interest, bending slightly forward so she caught again that fresh pleasant odor of good tobacco that clung to the rough wool of his coat. They stood there, groping for recognition while people strolled casually around the platform, gossiped, wrangled, laughed, then—

"Gregg MacFarlane!" Dallas cried.

"Dallas!" MacFarlane said sharply. "Little Dallas Gantry!"

She extended her hands. He grasped them in his that were firm and very strong. "Dallas," he repeated, and again: "Dallas!"

Then a woman said from somewhere back of MacFarlane.

"What is this? Who are you talking to, Gregg—"

Dallas whirled, eyes shining. "Oh, Faith!" she cried. "To think of seeing you and Gregg, the very first thing—"

Faith MacFarlane stared at her a moment in astonished speechlessness, then her arms were around Dallas and they were laughing and crying all at once. Gregg watched them, chuckling softly. Then Faith stepped back, held Dallas at arm's length.

"My dear," she said unsteadily, "you're so—beautiful! But the same Dallas—just the same—"

Dallas was finding it very difficult to speak. Gregg and Faith MacFarlane had always been bright memories for her when she thought of Willow Valley. They had come to town the year before she left. They had been present at her wedding. Gregg, tight-lipped and a little grim. Faith, lovely Faith MacFarlane, like a small bright bird. . . .

Dallas recalled it all so vividly. The long bleak parlor at Willow Wilde. The gleaming brass chandelier, newly installed, the stiff shiny chairs arranged like soldiers around the walls. . . .

That had been an autumn night, too, and rain had slashed against the windows, dead leaves drifted before the wind, and old mad Margery had predicted unhappiness for a bride of storm. But the MacFarlanes had been there and Dallas' cheeks flushed in the cool dark now, recalling her husband's eyes on Faith.

"I can't believe it, Dallas Gantry," Faith MacFarlane was saying in that low rich voice of hers. "It's like—spring—just seeing you again—"

"We've missed you a lot, Dallas," Gregg cut in. "But we've followed your career. We've been so proud of you."

Dallas' eyes blurred with tears. There had been few enough to be interested in those first bitter footlight years.

"It's wonderful to be back," she told them. "It's been such a long time—I had—to—come." She stared at them, wide-eyed. Their charming, friendly faces stood out clearly in the gray dusk. She was so fond of them. There would be many pleasant hours spent in the homelike security of the little inn which they owned and operated. She told herself all this, but it did not slow the excited beating of her heart, or banish that chilling premonition of trouble just ahead. She realized that they were regarding her curiously and forced herself to speak casually.

"I've always loved the sleepy old town," she said.

"Of course," Faith agreed, smiling.

Gregg nodded with his grave courtesy. Dallas drew a deep breath, studying Gregg, wondering what about him was so very different.

Then Faith said, "Of course, you're stopping with us, Dallas, or are you—?" she hesitated, and Dallas smiled, sensing her confusion.

"Thank you so much, Faith," Dallas' voice was a bit unsteady, "but you know I have a house here. I think I should like to remain there during my stay."

"It will be rather run down, Dallas," Gregg reminded her. "You won't be very comfortable, I'm afraid."

"I suppose not, but I'm going to try."

"To-night?"

"To-night." She nodded definitely. "I just want to—Gregg."

He smiled. "You'll let us drop you there. I have the car here. Faith just came with me for the ride."

Dallas shook her head. "I want to walk, Gregg," she confided. "All day I've been thinking about—walking—home—in the twilight." Her voice broke slightly. "If you'll arrange for someone to bring my things."

"Of course. And you'll come to see us soon, won't you, Dallas?"

"In the morning, I expect. It's been wonderful to meet you both. The old town about the same?"

Faith laughed softly. "Willow Valley doesn't change, Dallas. A few have died. Some are married. There are some new babies, but it doesn't change."

Dallas nodded, laughing through tears. "No excitement, then?"

"No excitement," Gregg cut in. "Oh, yes, we have a show troupe here but they're closing to-night—" He stopped abruptly, glancing away. "Just a barnstorming bunch," he went on lamely. "You wouldn't care about them."

"I've put in my time barnstorming," she told him. "It's all in the game."

"I suppose so." He lifted his hand in an unconsciously gallant gesture. "Good-night, Dallas."

She waved back. "Good-night, dear folks." Then impulsively, "Here are my checks. You'll see about the baggage, Gregg?"

"Certainly."

She turned, drawing a deep breath, and came face to face with the white-faced man who wore the gray hat. She stopped abruptly, eyes slowly widening. *He* was stopping in Willow Valley, too! The train was already pulling out. Again he stepped from her path with that knowing secret smile, and Dallas saw his companion, a small thin-chested man in an exaggerated plaid raincoat, a long peaked cap pulled down over one eye. He held himself with an undeniable swagger, but his narrow sharp face was furtive, his eyes uneasy.

Dallas started on, then turned impulsively for one more glance at her friends, and stopped, frowning, to see the two strangers, heads bent, edging near the hotel car driven by Gregg MacFarlane. There was something so dangerous in the look of the two, such a suggestion of hidden evil, that Dallas hesitated, fighting an impulse to hurry back and warn the MacFarlanes of some danger, which she could not name, then she shrugged and went on, marking the feeling down to unstrung nerves.

That meeting with Gregg and Faith had done much to steady her. She had become very friendly with them in the days before the crash that ended in her leaving Willow Valley. They were such quiet, charming people. There was a suggestion of strength about them, of something conquered and subdued. She stopped abruptly, glancing over her shoulder.

"It's his hair," she said softly. "That's what makes him different. Gregg's hair is—white."

She frowned, and went on along the sagging boardwalk with the dry grasses rustling against her skirt.

Well, after all, why shouldn't Gregg MacFarlane have white hair? He must be—she pursed her lips—he must be near—fifty. But so very, very white, as if something had blighted it.

She was walking swiftly now, head up, eyes starry. The old ghosts were being crowded back by the sense of friendly things about her. It was getting too dark to see much, but the place smelled—familiar. There was Widow Huston's house! Dallas had learned to make currant jelly in the widow's kitchen. She began humming softly. She wondered if she'd remember about currant jelly now. Maybe Anthony would like her to make some when they were married. All men liked currant jelly. She laughed under her breath, then paused.

A few cars passed her on the way back to town. She heard a bunch of boys and girls laughing boisterously. Wistfully she looked after them. They would likely be planning a Hallowe'en dance.

She turned sharply to the right, drawing her coat closer. A chilly breeze had lifted. There were a few scudding clouds across the sky. The spire of the Congregational Church stood out starkly, faintly touched with the gold of a rising moon. It looked bleak and cold. Behind it was the graveyard. There were towering pines, low furry cedars and many, many lacy-fronded willows. The graves were mostly well tended, but in the old portion there were some with sagging headstones, stained with moss and lichen.

Her house was just beyond. Next door to the burial ground. She hadn't minded in the least. Still didn't. She had loved to stand by the darkened window on a winter's night and watch the black shadows of the pines against the snow. Dallas didn't fear the dead. She had known many who now rested endlessly there beside her house. Patient, gentle women, bent with toil, mute with many sorrows, yet intensely kind and human. Big-boned men, with shambling steps, slow speech, strong convictions. Children whom one day Dallas had seen skipping by to school—the next quiet forever. Old, old people whom she used to talk with as they sat on vine-covered porches, watching the twilight creep into the valley, exhausted with life, content to wait patiently for death.

She wondered if she would ever be like that. If the surging, clamorous joy of life within her would ever be silenced. If one day, when she had lived too long, she would welcome death.

She stopped, lifting her head and letting her eyes, that were oddly somber, wander over the darkening world around her. Moonlight was growing about the church spire. Wind whimpered through the rustling maples. Sere leaves eddied stealthily about her feet. Somewhere a dog set up a mournful baying. She shivered and snuggled closer inside her coat. It was very lonesome here. The light had gone and the cold moon on the silent church tower looked bleak and forbidding. There was the hint of winter in the sobbing wind. The world was dying and all about her was the dead.

Why had she come back? What mad impulse had brought her to Willow Valley after fourteen years? Why hadn't she let the old ghosts rest? There came upon her again that cold premonition of

trouble. Death! Tragedy! She had a quick longing to race back for
the station, catch a train to the city—and Anthony—then she remembered there was no train till the next morning. And by that
time the sun would be shining. The purple haze would rest over
the crimson-tinted hills—there would be old friends to greet. . . .

She jammed her hands in her pockets and started on resolutely,
unconsciously quickening her steps. Gregg had said her place was
run down. It wouldn't be comfortable. Well, she had known that
but she wanted to see it. Her eagerness grew until she was running, high heels tapping lightly on the warped boards of the walk.
There it was, a white blur through the trees. There was the old
picket fence with the woodbine crawling over it. The bed of myrtle
was just beyond. And the lilac bush where she had buried Tiger
Eyes, her kitten. . . .

She jerked open the gate, ran up the walk, heart hammering a noisy
tattoo against her ribs. In the shadowy darkness of the porch something stirred. Dallas stopped with a low gasp. Then a figure came down
the steps, paused at the foot, looking at her. A woman's voice said:

"Hello, Dallas, sort of surprised to see me, ain't you? It's Opal,
honey, Opal Garth."

Dallas gasped and her stiff body relaxed. "Good heavens," she
said, "how you frightened me. Opal Garth? Where on earth did you
come from?"

Opal came toward her. Dallas caught the white blur of her face,
the heavy odor of cheap perfume that swept over with such terrific
force of memory. Bleak wind-swept stations where trains were
always late. Frigid hotels. The dusty clatter of cheap dressing-
rooms in wretched small-town theaters. Heat that sucked life and
breath. Noise. Clatter. Blare of bands. Crying children. Sweat of
humans. All the mad, glamorous, horrible back-ground of small-
time trouping—and always that nauseating odor of Opal's perfume!

Opal said: "I been playin' here. Tam O'Shannon's gang. Hot
dump, I'll say." She laughed shortly. "Well, ain't you glad to see
me, Dallas, or are you too upstage to remember old pals?"

There was a hidden venom in the tones. The unfailing jealousy
of the incompetent for the gifted person who succeeds by sheer
hard work and sacrifice.

Dallas replied slowly, ignoring the thrust:

"What do you want, Opal?"

Opal shrugged and buried her hands in the cheap fur of her sleeves.

"Why don't you ask me to come in?" she countered.

Dallas glanced at the blank, dead windows of the house. "Come in, certainly, if you wish, but it will be cold and very uncomfortable. I just arrived—"

"I know. I was at the station and seen you come. I knew this was your place. Everyone in town points it out to you. Where Dallas Gantry lived! The great and famous Dallas Gantry." The thin, high voice tightened with passion. "Why was it that you shoulda' made good out of all that old bunch?" she demanded indignantly. "You wasn't any smarter than the rest of us. You ain't any better lookin' than—I am. I don't see—"

Dallas broke in, suddenly very tired of the other's whining. "If you want to see me about anything in particular, Opal, get it over with. I've got a lot to do to-night. To-morrow might be better—"

Opal turned swiftly, putting her face close to Dallas'. "Don't kid yourself, baby," she said harshly. "I wanta see you *to-night*. Let's get inside."

Dallas returned her venomous stare coolly, and without a word stepped past her, drawing a key from her bag, inserted it in the rusty lock and threw back the door.

A gust of dead air eddied to the rush of wind, Stirring old dust, ancient smells, all the strange, impalpable odors of a house long closed. It caught Dallas by the throat and held her motionless on the threshold. How could she go in? How enter the place where she had been so happy—especially with the hateful presence of Opal Garth beside her?

Then she threw notions aside, stepped across the sill, snapping on a small flash. "It's dreadfully cold," she said, "but there should be wood in the box. I left some when I—"

Her voice died away into another room. Opal stood just inside the door, staring around her curiously. There was the bulk of furniture, the shadowy white of walls. She could hear Dallas fumbling around in the kitchen. Presently she returned, dumped an armful of dry sticks on the floor, scratched a match and lighted a candle. She had opened a rear door and the fresh cool air sucked hungrily through the place.

She tore up an old magazine, stacked the wood above it in the fireplace, lighted it. It burned fiercely, throwing a warm ruddy glow over the room. Opal looked it over avidly.

"Huh," she grunted. "So this is where you lived. Gee, I thought you'd have somethin' swell—"

Dallas dusted her hands. "Get it over, Opal," she snapped. "I'm tired and want to rest. What do you want?"

Opal stepped over and closed the door, then leaned against the wall and faced Dallas. "I'm broke," she stated flatly.

Dallas eyed her coolly. She had never liked this cheap common girl who was now a cheaper, commoner woman. Their association had been one of necessity. Dallas was naturally kind and it was not in her consciously to sense her own superiority. She adapted herself to whatever condition she occupied at the moment. So she and Opal Garth had roomed together in the old days when they had both been insignificant members of Tom Willoughby's Repertory Company, touring the South and Middle West.

"How much do you want?" she asked crisply.

Opal scowled at her. She was pretty in a cheap, showy way, though the freshness of twelve years ago was entirely gone. In its place was a hard sophistication, a sullen resentment at the fate which had kept her still in cheap companies, playing small parts. She displayed the same bad taste in clothes, Dallas reflected. That imitation leopard coat, now. Those silly, ungroomed pumps with the red heels. The cheap froth of grimy lace showing through her coat front.

"I don't want any of your charity," Opal said thickly, a dull red burning in her thin cheeks. "I'm shot all right." She began to tremble and Dallas looked at her more closely. "We've had a hell of a season and now that old fool has shut us up—"

"What old fool?" Dallas asked with a queer detachment.

Opal glared at her under heavily mascaraed lashes. "Keye," she snapped, "Jurden Keye." Then she smiled and licked her hot dry

lips with a thin, red tongue. "He ain't so bad—to meet," she said.
"In fact"—she glanced away from Dallas' flaming eyes, then went
on sullenly—"he's on the City Council and he revoked our license.
Said we wasn't the right kind of influence for the town," she laughed
shrilly. "God, that's good," she choked. "Influence! Say, baby, what
I know about him."

Dallas was fumbling in her bag. She was prickling hot all over
and the air of the place was choking her. That horrible perfume!
"Here is some money," she said. "Take it and go, Opal. I'm sorry
for you. I want to help you but I can't—stand—this—please go—"

Opal's short thick fingers clutched at the bills. She was smiling
with her fat, red lips, but her eyes were haggard. "Yeh," she said
softly, "take some money and get out—wanton! That's what you
think about me, ain't it? Well, listen, kid, I ain't goin' so easy. You
and me used to be pals. I was good enough for you then, and I'm
good enough for you now, if you have played on Broadway. What if
I have got the low-down on your hubby? What if I do know plenty
about him? That ain't no reason for—"

"Opal!" Dallas cried and unconsciously jerked off her small
smart hat as if the pressure were crushing her. The dull gold of her
hair caught the light and glowed like polished metal where it lay,
thick lustrous waves around her vivid face. "Opal," she repeated
hoarsely, "won't you please leave—me? I can't help—what—my
husband does. He isn't my husband—really—I haven't seen him—
for—"

"Why don't you get a divorce?" Opal demanded suddenly.

Dallas locked tense fingers together. "That's what I'm here for,"
she said and immediately regretted it. Why should she tell this
woman her affairs?

Opal grinned. "I thought so," she said. "Y'see, I met a girl that
used to work for you. Gee, it must be swell havin' a maid!" Her flat
blue eyes darkened angrily. "This girl, she told me about how you
was sweet on a swell bird in the city. Regular top-notcher, the Jane
says and how you two was figurin' on gettin' married. Well, I knew
you couldn't, bein' already tied up to some fat daddy in a small
town some place, then when I come here and found out everything,

and seen you come in to-night, I just figured you'd be down to see about gettin' free." She paused, groping for a cigarette in her cheap, bulging purse.

Dallas stood silently by the fire. She was sick all through. There was something so—contaminating, about hearing her love for Anthony Gordon discussed by Opal Garth, who had heard of it from a maid discharged for theft. She supposed it was already all over town. She could imagine how tongues would be wagging.

"Lemme tell you somethin', Dallas," Opal said with sly confidence, "you ain't gonna' get your divorce."

"*What?*" Dallas stiffened and her eyes went wide, then she relaxed. "Is there anything else, Opal?" she inquired politely.

Opal's face whitened. She looked at Dallas and laughed. "Don't like bein' chummy with me, do you?" she mocked. "Well, that's all right, only get this, baby. I had a little talk with Keye about you and he said out flat he wasn't lettin' you go. What do you think of that?"

Dallas couldn't even think. There was a tightness in her throat and she felt suddenly nauseated. It would be like Jurden Keye to discuss her with—Opal Garth! But Opal's words had struck her with the force of a solar plexus blow. Not grant her a divorce! Why, how could he help it? There wouldn't be any kind of law that would permit him to keep her tied to such a travesty of marriage.

Opal went on. "He meant it, too, Dallas, so that's really what I come to see you about. I got a plan." She sat down, resting skinny elbows on her knees, glancing up at Dallas from her flat blue eyes. "Mebbe you won't like it very well," she went on, "but it'll sure work, honey. I'll come right out and give you the dirt. Keye's sweet on me." She smiled with a widening of her fat lips. "He's been—entertainin' me now and then up at the house. Oh, he's mighty secretive about it. That's the kind of a daddy he is. All pure white on the outside but—sheer filth underneath." Her face twisted furiously.

Dallas looked at her and nodded slowly. For a moment there was a trace of kinship between them.

She said: "He is, Opal, you're right about that. Now what is it you want to suggest?"

"A way for you to get the low-down on him."

"The what?"

"The dope for your divorce. 'Course, Dallas, it will cost you somethin'. Say a grand, but it ought to be worth it."

Dallas was staring at the girl in open bewilderment. "What are you getting at?" she asked.

Opal nodded confidentially. "You'd be surprised," she said slyly. "I'm goin' up there to-night after the show, see? He's lettin' us give our last performance to-night. We had the tickets sold. So I'll be up there spendin' the evenin' with him. All nice and comfy, just the two of us. Well, s'pose you manage to drop in at a certain time. Bring a witness along. You must have a friend or two here. Bring someone with you. Wing my act. It'll be good. You won't have any trouble gettin' loose then and you can marry your rich Johnny—"

"Oh, my God," Dallas cried in suddenly stricken tones. "Get away from me. Get out of my sight. I never want to see you again. Leave me—go—"

Her voice had risen until she was half screaming. She was so completely sickened that she went suddenly faint and pressed shaking hands across her eyes. "Get out!" she cried hoarsely. "Go! At once! I'll—kill you if you—don't—"

A sudden clamor sounded in the rear of the house. Someone stumbling. A crash. A muffled curse. Both women whirled, staring at the door, then a large-footed, shock-haired boy appeared, grinning fatuously.

"S'cuse me, Mis' Gantry," he said, "I brought your truth and things and stumbled gettin' in, but there they are. Mr. MacFarlane sent me."

"All right," Dallas said. "Thank you. Here's some money."

The boy pocketed the coin, his small bright eyes traveling from one face to another with a queer animal eagerness. "Yes'm," he said again and backed out, still staring.

Dallas had regained control. She faced Opal Garth, quietly now.

"What you suggest is impossible, of course," she said curtly. "And I don't want to talk to you any more. Go at once."

Opal was backing toward the door. She was trembling violently. Her voice was hoarse with fury. "All right, I'll go," she chattered, "and I'll see you fry before I offer to help you again. You'll be sorry for this, Dallas Gantry. Damned sorry. I know a lot of things you'd like to know and I'll get even with you if it's the last thing I ever do—"

Dallas was close behind her when she went out. She shut the door on her yammering, turned and slumped inertly in a dusty chair before the fire. She buried her head on her crooked arm and her slim body jerked with the force of angry, shamed sobs that tore her.

"Beast!" she choked. "Filthy—beast! Oh, I hate him—I hate him—so—"

Then she sat up slowly, staring at the fire which was already dying down. Before her was the dust and desolation of her old life, the one she thought she had forgotten, only to find that it was surging around her with all its old fury and vehemence.

She stared at the room with stricken eyes. Then she leaped up, opened doors and windows, letting the fresh cold air whip through, sweeping before it dust and memories and the dreadful odor of Opal Garth's perfume.

She dug candles from a box in the kitchen, lighted them all over the place. They guttered in the wind, but she did not mind. She stripped muslin covers from the chairs. Found a battered broom, ripped up rugs, dumped books into a heap in the center of the room, yanked the mattress from the bed. She worked with a fury that left little time for thought. She wanted the place clean, fresh, sweet. To-morrow she'd get someone to scrub and wash windows. She'd put up fresh curtains. She'd paint the woodwork; but to-night, it all had to be different.

When, nearly an hour later she dropped exhausted onto the sofa in the living-room, the place was cheerful and bright, and Dallas was completely exhausted. There was dust on her hands, grime on her smart frock, her shoes were skinned, her hair tumbled. But her eyes were bright, her cheeks were flushed and she had nearly forgotten Opal Garth and Jurden Keye.

The moment she sat down and lighted a cigarette the whole ugly thing came back to her and being the sort of person she was, she did not try for diversion again but leaned back, frowning at the fire, and faced her problem.

The first thing to do was to see her husband. It had to be done. Just drop in on him at Willow Wilde, meet him pleasantly and naturally, tell him she had come to get his agreement to a divorce, granted quietly and without publicity. She shivered a little, thinking of what Opal had said and also remembering Jurden Keye, but surely, surely, he couldn't refuse such a reasonable request? He had always—hated her. Why had he married her? Simply because she had been so terribly young and eager and he was already dusty and exhausted, and she had struck him in the face like a riotous spring wind.

But he couldn't conquer her, so he had tried to break her and when she ran away. . . .

Dallas got up, went into her bedroom and began removing her dress. She heated water over the bed of coals in the fireplace, creamed and washed her face and hands, then she set about deciding what she should wear for this momentous interview. Common sense told her to wait till morning but a terrible unrest was on her and she could not be quiet. She wanted to know that Opal was merely talking when she said Jurden would not grant the divorce. She wanted to face the matter and find out where she stood.

In the middle of her toilet, there came a knock on the rear door. She jerked on a kimono and ran out. It was the shock-headed boy again, grinning foolishly. He had overlooked one of her bags. Here it was. Dallas thanked him and was closing the door when a notion struck her.

"Wait a moment," she said. "I want you to deliver a note for me."

She hurried back to the bedroom, took out her writing case and scribbled a message. The boy followed her into the living-room, stood there, gaping wide-eyed. He had heard of Dallas Gantry, who was the wife of old Jurden Keye, and had run away a good many years ago to go on the stage. Dallas Gantry was a tradition around Willow Valley. Mention of her name could start a neighborhood row any year. Some called her wanton, worthless, flighty. Hadn't she left her husband's home? Hadn't she deserted the wealthiest man in Willow Valley, an elder in the Methodist Church, member of the City Council, the prop and support of all worthy civic ventures?

That was one side. The other said Dallas Gantry was a lovely girl without evil in her, and who could blame her for running off from old Keye, and he wasn't as white as he was painted, and . . .

She came out just then, holding the folds of the heavy golden satin negligee around her. Her hair matched the garment and her lovely brown velvet eyes were very bright. She smiled at the boy, gave him a dollar and a letter in a thick-looking gray envelope.

"This goes to Jurden Keye," she said. "You know where he lives?"

The boy nodded eagerly. He couldn't keep his eyes from her. He had never seen a woman just like this. One thing bothered him greatly. He had once heard his aunt, old Ma Witherspoon, the town gossip and shrew, refer to Dallas Gantry as a crimson woman. Buddy Witherspoon had always remembered that phrase. Now he looked at Dallas Gantry and she was golden, not crimson.

"Yeah, I know where old man Keye lives," he said, jerked his cap on and went out. In less than half an hour all of Willow Valley knew that Dallas Gantry had returned and that she had sent a note to Jurden Keye. Immediately old scores were forgotten and the town *en masse* fell to the discussion of this new and startling development. It brushed away all minor subjects. Such, for instance, as what Gregg MacFarlane would do when he found out that Jurden Keye had sent Faith, his wife, a gorgeous bunch of American roses from a florist in the city, and that he had waylaid her outside the Farmers' Bank no later than this afternoon and forced her to walk a way with him. For fifteen years, ever since, in fact, the MacFarlanes had arrived in Willow Valley from where, no one rightly knew, the town had watched with avid interest Jurden Keye's untiring effort to interest Faith MacFarlane.

Chapter Two
Who Screamed?

DALLAS APPROACHED the house slowly. When she was a small child, Willow Wilde, home of Jurden Keye, had been the finest residence in Willow Valley. She had regarded it with awe and never dreamed that one day she would be mistress of it, in name, at least.

It was a large, three-story white house, tall and rather severe, with narrow porches and many arched windows. There were green wooden shutters to the windows and the top story had jutting dormers that looked like rather wicked, half-closed eyes. There was the tiny railed balcony, halfway between the second and third stories. Dallas had always loved that spot with the view it offered on a clear day.

The house stood in the center of an acre and a half of grounds and there were many tall trees around it. Maples, elms and the lovely lacy willows which gave the place its name. The house looked rather dilapidated, Dallas noticed. Even viewed under the moon, the paint had cracked and the porch was sagging slightly.

The grounds had been allowed to go to seed, too. The winding graveled paths were narrowed down by the encroachment of tall, unkempt grass. Shrubs had gone out of bounds and there was a carpet of rustling dry leaves over the lawn.

She tilted her head and set her lips firmly. The fear that had gripped her on the journey down, the sickness and fury that had shaken her after Opal Garth's visit, had pretty well gone. She had had a cup of tea, she was rested and refreshed, sure of herself and in possession of her normal, jaunty spirits. The coming interview wouldn't be exactly a delight, but she would get it over as quickly as possible.

She mounted the steps and pressed the bell. In the silence of the porch she heard her heart beating thickly and she had to gulp three great breaths before the door opened and old Mrs. Maybrick faced her. Dallas settled her shoulders and confronted her ancient enemy.

"Good-evening, Maybrick," she said. "I have come to see Mr. Keye. He's expecting me."

Mrs. Maybrick's short, thick body stiffened. Her small head shot out and her little cold eyes flared wide with surprise.

"Come in," she said stolidly, and stepped aside to allow her former mistress to enter. "He's in the parlor," she said tonelessly, and closed the door.

Dallas' eyes flashed over the well-remembered hall in quick survey, then she looked full at Maybrick. "Thank you," she said sweetly and stepped across, opened the door of the great gloomy apartment, called the "parlor," and went in.

The room was dimly lighted by a shaded lamp on the table. A fire was smoldering in the grate, filling the room with a faint acrid smoke. Dallas sniffed distastefully, recalling that fireplaces at Willow Wilde had always smoked.

The high, narrow windows were draped in stiff white lace curtains. There was a huge brass bowl containing a giant fern. Dallas wondered oddly if it were the same one she had tended.

She paused, still clinging to the knob, wide eyes going slowly over the room, then she heard a well-remembered voice, her husband's, saying:

"There's one way out for you, my dear. I can fix everything—"

A low feminine gasp stopped him. Dallas looked around the room curiously. There was no one in sight, then she caught movement in the small alcove over beyond the fireplace. There was a hurried protest, her husband's quick exclamation, the opening and closing of a door, then Jurden Keye walked into the room, hands swinging by his sides in that way she knew so well.

He came slowly toward the table, eyes narrowed on Dallas, still standing by the door. He was older, much older. Hair thin and nearly white. Face harsh and lined. Lips more like a trap than ever. Shoulders bowed and minus their old uncompromising squareness but the secret sly cruelty of his deep-set eyes was the same, there was the same nervous jerk to his thick sandy brows, the old, compelling, dangerous smile on his lips.

Dallas stood very still, staring at him, wondering at the fear she had felt on the train. Who was this ugly old man that she should be terrified of him? Why had she thought his hands had power to hold her?

"Good-evening, Dallas," Jurden Keye said in his dry, dusty voice. "This is indeed a pleasure I hadn't anticipated."

"Didn't you get my note?"

"Yes. Naturally your being in town was a great surprise." He coughed raspingly, crossed to the window behind the desk and a little to the right, lifted the green shade a bit and raised the sash some six inches, then he came back, stood again facing her. "Your note said nine o'clock," he stated. "It is now a quarter past ten. I had given you up."

Dallas gasped, glanced at her wrist, frowned, remembering she had smashed her watch crystal against an iron railing there at the station, given it to Anthony to be repaired. She had depended on her traveling clock.

Her cheeks began to burn and her eyes lowered. That beastly failing of hers about appointments. And she hadn't dreamed she had put in so much time going through that old trunk in the attic. And, as always, Jurden Keye had put her in the wrong. She felt the same childish fear of him she had experienced so long ago, that same desire to run and hide, but instead she lifted her head, looked straight at him and said:

"I'm sorry about being late. I can wait until tomorrow. I interrupted you—"

He made that motion of brushing something aside. "It is of no importance," he said, and Dallas, watching him, shivered. He would speak like that if some one's life hung in the balance. That was Jurden Keye's way of handling human problems. Brush them aside—smile with his thin lips: "They are of no importance," he would say.

She came toward him, walking with that strong, graceful stride of hers, hands locked lightly before her, eyes narrowed into the dimness. She wore a careless suit of deep brown that matched her eyes and clung to her lithe vibrant body like an embrace. Her hat had been especially designed for her. It emphasized the line of her cheek, the jut of her chin, intensified the sweep of her brows, left one broad wave of dull gold hair to show against her face. She was lovely and knew it. She was more than that, a splendid, fully developed woman, who had known tragedy and conquered it, faced destruction and been victor. Assured. Confident. Serene.

"You look—well," her husband said thickly, dark blood surging over his dusty face.

"Thank you. And now, let's get it over. I want a divorce."

His hand clenched around the chair arm as he dropped into it. "Won't you sit down?" he inquired. "Shall I have Maybrick bring you—refreshments?"

"Thank you, no." She accepted a chair, opposite his, across the long heavy table. She was smiling and there was a wicked glint in her eyes. Here was where he used to summon her for his frequent chidings, lecturing her as if she were a child, which she had been. She waited, sitting very still.

He continued to study her under lowered lids. She could see how his skin had wrinkled and thickened. There was a scum of white beard showing beneath it as if he had not shaved to-day. A vein beat thickly in his temple.

"A divorce?" he said. "You know how I feel about such things, Dallas."

She said in a level, even voice. "How you feel, Jurden, is not of the slightest importance to me. I married you because I—didn't—know any better. We were desperately unhappy. There were two alternatives facing me. Dumb acceptance of an impossible situation resulting in complete effacement for me. Rebellion and release. I chose the latter. For fourteen years we have been separated. Our ways have grown apart. We have no interest in each other now. I want my freedom—legally. I am asking you to give it to me, quietly and—decently. Will you do it?"

Jurden Keye picked a long-bladed Damascene knife from a pile of papers on the table before him, turning it slowly between shaking fingers. His eyes were blazing with a restrained passion. He spoke thickly, gaspingly. He said:

"No. I will not give you a divorce!"

Dallas did not stir. A darkness swept before her eyes for a moment and she thought she was falling through terrific space, then everything cleared and she was smiling at him, confidently, rather insolently.

"Don't be a fool," she said crisply. "You—can't—hold—me. You can be disagreeable and cause me trouble, but you can't—hold me."

"No?" He tossed the gleaming knife to the table. "Let us consider, Dallas. You left my roof of your own free will. Absented yourself from my home without due cause. I did everything in my power to get you to return—"

"You—what?"

He nodded. "I can furnish copies of advertisements which I ran in leading newspapers in the personal columns, asking you to come back, promising forgiveness for your—madness. My home has at all times been open to you should you care to return. I have held myself ready to receive you, place you in your rightful position. I have, in short, done everything that a husband could be expected to do." He spread his hands. "You have ignored my efforts and now you ask for divorce. I do not believe in legal separation of husband and wife. I refuse."

He paused, shifted slightly in the chair, the look of mock sanctity on his face deepened, but behind his hateful eyes lurked savage triumph. For *this* he had waited patiently—for fourteen years! He asked almost gently: "What can you do? Where is your case? On what grounds can you gain your freedom—as you call it?"

Dallas' cheeks were very white. She asked, trying to keep her voice steady: "Why are you doing this, Jurden? You don't—want—me—"

He laughed, deep in his throat with a greasy chuckling sound. "No," he said, "I don't—want you. You are very lovely but—you do not interest me. Why am I doing it, my dear? Simply because I want to make you unhappy. Cause you all the trouble I can. Because I know you are in—love with some one else"—his face twisted—"ready to give to another man what you never gave to me, because I know you well enough to guess that if you can't go to him legally you'll go illegally and I want to ruin your soul. I want to make you—wanton—do you understand?" His voice rose shrilly, he was leaning forward staring at her with dilated, red-rimmed eyes. "I want to know that you are—smirched. That when you die—there will be—hell fire waiting for you—a fallen woman—a—"

She leaped up. She was trembling so the cluster of diamonds at her breast glittered like angry eyes. Blood pounded savagely in her brain until it hummed like a giant dynamo.

"You—damned—hypocrite!" she flung at him. "*You*—talk about—wantonness! Smirching my soul!" She stopped because a thickness grew in her throat and she could scarcely speak. Jurden Keye was watching her tensely, crouched forward, hands clenched on the table's edge. His eyes were stretched wide, so the yellowish white showed around the faded iris and Dallas, staring at him through the fog of her sick fury, suddenly realized that he was afraid!

It came to her like a long draught of heady wine. He was afraid! Of her! Of the girl he had bullied and tortured—their positions were reversed. *He* was cringing now. She leaned forward swiftly, thrusting her face across the desk, into his.

"Smirching?" she cried thickly. "Smirching my soul! When the months I lived with you, you degraded me through your association with other—women. You thought I didn't know. That I was only a dumb little fool. But you were wrong. You're wrong now. I know about Opal Garth—she's coming here to-night. She's been here—she's—here—now—"

Dallas' eyes flashed to the alcove. "She was here when I came in, you shunted her outside for this interview—"

"No," Jurden Keye said with curious clarity. "No. Opal Garth isn't here. She hasn't been here—"

"You lie," Dallas panted and surged forward, closer to him. "You associate with that—cheap—"

Jurden Keye said harshly, "I won't listen to you any longer—"

"Oh yes, you will. You'll hear everything I have to say. All the things I wanted to say—so long ago, the things I didn't have the courage to say. You'll hear them all—then we'll see—"

"Get out," he cried shrilly. "Get out of my house!"

Dallas was laughing. Brokenly, unsteadily, and back of the laughter was all the agony of disillusionment, heartache which she had endured as his wife. The long-curbed flood of hatred suddenly broke its barriers, and swept down, engulfing her, and out of the turmoil, reared one stupendous realization. *She longed to kill Jurden Keye!* Crush him. Destroy him. As she might a poisonous reptile.

She heard his harsh cry as from a great distance. Glimpsed his white writhing face through a fog. He was saying over and over:

"Put that down! Put it down! Get out—of—my—house!"

And Dallas, rousing dully from the stupor that held her, followed the glance of his distended eyes and saw her own gloved hand clutching the handle of the long-bladed Damascene knife!

On the other side of the door, in the cold, draughty hall of Willow Wilde, Mrs. Maybrick hunched on her stiffened knees, one eye glued to the narrow opening of the keyhole. Her thick body was rigid. Her lips worked soundlessly. Voices reached her muffled through the heavy door. Her range of vision was limited, but her senses were keyed high. Abruptly she surged backward, one hand pressed across her lips. Her fleshy face went gray, then she heaved forward again, hands fumbling toward the knob, that turned abruptly as she touched it. The door was jerked back. Dallas Gantry halted in her headlong flight, gazed unseeingly at the crouching woman, then with a choked sob, she crowded past her, jerked the door to behind her, reached the outer door in a swift, desperate plunge, opened it and disappeared into the night. Only then did Maybrick rouse from her trance, rise to unsteady feet and stumble after her. She was trembling and her breath came in panting gasps. She leaned heavily against the outer door, groping at the dusty lace curtain covering the glass, pressing her face against the dark oval.

"Come back," she cried thickly. "Come—back—"

Dallas stood for a moment in the shadow of the porch, breathing deeply of the cold, fresh air. Her fingers were icy. Her cheeks like fire. The night was suddenly terror-filled. Gaunt trees bent before a rising wind. A pallid moon rode high. She stumbled down the steps, broke into a run, racing through the darkness to lean exhausted against the old rusted iron gate.

Then, over the whispering of the leafless trees, the myriad small noises of the night, one sound rose with terrible solidity. A shrill, stabbing cry, high with terror!

Dallas whirled, crouching back against the gate, staring at the house, glowing a cold dead white through the leafless trees.

"What's that?" she whispered of the night and the wind. "Who—screamed—"

CHAPTER THREE
DAMASCENE STEEL!

THEN SHE WAS RACING back for the house, groping up the steps, fumbling at the knob, opening the door. Firelight confused her. The hall was filled with gray shadows. Somewhere was a terrible choked moaning. A man's voice saying something she could not understand. She reached the door of the parlor. It was partially open. She stood there, frowning at the room.

The first person she saw was Gregg MacFarlane, standing silent and pale by the table. As she stepped into the room she caught a whiff of that pleasant tobacco odor that hung to him and was poignantly reminded of the moment there at the station when he had greeted her.

Then she saw old Maybrick on her knees beside him, fingers twisting in her gray hair, rocking back and forth, moaning. Jurden Keye was slumped forward across the desk, one arm hanging limply, head half over the edge, almost as if he had bent down to examine the contents of the open drawer at his hand. Blood dripped monotonously to form a bright red pool on the dusty floor.

Gregg MacFarlane turned, met Dallas' eyes, flinched slightly. "Keye's dead," he said flatly. "He's been stabbed—"

Dallas was just across the table now. She was staring at the handle of a knife buried to the hilt in her husband's back. She had one curiously clear thought. "It is," she said to herself, "the Damascene knife which I gave him for his birthday the year I left. Odd I didn't recognize it—"

Then old Maybrick roused from her wailing, turned and saw
Dallas. Her face twisted, her bloodshot eyes narrowed. She pointed
a thick, shaking finger.

"She done it," she screamed. "She—that—woman! She murdered
the master!"

Dallas sat down abruptly. "Oh," she said softly, "so that's it.
How odd."

Gregg MacFarlane ran unsteady fingers through his strangely
white hair. "Be quiet, Maybrick," he said curtly. "Go upstairs and
stay there until you're sent for." He picked up the telephone. "Give
me Tom Gary," he said to the operator.

Dallas extracted a cigarette, lighted it, drew smoke into her
lungs. She saw Maybrick heave to her feet, clump out of the room,
rubbing at her swollen eyes. Dallas had always wondered at the
old housekeeper's devotion to Jurden Keye. She was very glad when
Maybrick left.

Then she heard MacFarlane's voice, steady, rather tight:
"Jurden Keye, Tom—yes—dead! Stabbed. No, of course I don't
know. You'll notify Doc Monery? He's coroner—Yes, I'll wait."

He set the phone down carefully, dusted his hands. His face
looked very white and strained. He smoothed his hair. "You're all
right, Dallas?" he inquired gently. "You don't want to lie down?
You won't—"

She shook her head. "I won't faint, Gregg," she said. "The death
of Jurden Keye isn't such a blow to me as that. I think the world
will be cleaner now he's gone."

MacFarlane's thin lips tightened. "I quite agree with you, Dallas, but I suggest that you don't make that statement public."

She met his glance, frowning slightly. "No? Well, it isn't very
good taste, is it? But otherwise— Oh," she said with a faint gasp. "I
understand. You think—I—did this?"

MacFarlane shook his head. "Of course I don't, my dear. But
others might. You were the last one to see him—alive—"

"Gregg! That sounds terribly official. I don't understand—"

"Listen, Dallas," he said and came around to stand before her.
"This is bound to be very unpleasant. I'm so devilishly sorry you
were here. Why did you come?"

She was plucking absently at her gloves. Gregg, watching her closely, caught the pulsing of a vein in her long white throat.

She said, without lifting her head: "I came to ask him to give me a divorce. I want to marry—Anthony Gordon."

"And he, Jurden, what did he say?"

She met his glance, wide-eyed. "Why, he said—that is, he—refused. He tried to prove to me that I couldn't get loose from him—that I could never—marry—Anthony—"

"Dallas!" he said blankly. "Oh, Dallas."

She nodded slowly. "That would be motive, wouldn't it, Gregg?"

"Yes, Dallas, that would be excellent motive." They were silent for a time and each was terribly conscious of the other. In that little space of quietness, the isolation of the individual was sharply defined. It came to the man and to the woman how meager is the real knowledge one may have of another.

Dallas thought: "Who is Gregg MacFarlane really? The proprietor of Willow Inn? Surely, but who else? Where was he born? Where did he spend his youth? Where did he live before he came to Willow Valley? Who is—he—beside Gregg MacFarlane? Of what real significance is a man's name? He might be Tom Jones or Jim Smith and he would still have that tragedy in his eyes—that look of something conquered—that blighted hair—"

Then she hunched lower in her seat and set her lips hard to still the chattering of her teeth. "How did he happen to be here?" she asked herself. "He wasn't here when I left. Where did he come from, to be standing there beside Jurden's body?"

And Gregg MacFarlane thrust crowding ideas from his mind. "Who is Dallas Gantry, really? A terribly vital, high-strung woman, who fought her way to liberty, who loves someone called Anthony Gordon, who came back to ask for legal freedom, who, when it was refused—" He turned, staring at the knife in Jurden Keye's back.

"You know that knife, Dallas?" he asked hoarsely.

"Yes," she replied. "I gave it to him. There was a party—you and Faith—were here—"

He nodded. "Dallas," he said, "I want you to wire the very best attorney you know of. Get him on the job and until he comes to advise you, say absolutely nothing. It may save you a lot of trouble."

She crushed the cigarette out absently. Her eyes, strained and dark, were on his face. "Of course, Gregg, I'll do that if you think I should. But how could anyone actually think—that I murdered—"

Gregg MacFarlane sighed. It was not the first time he had encountered that total inability on the part of individuals to realize the way the law is going to look at things. Only too well he knew that personal conviction as to innocence didn't mean anything. Before he could answer, Dallas said:

"Get the station, Gregg. I'm sending a wire."

She sent the message to Harley Branson, her attorney, stating briefly what had happened, asking him to come down at once. As she set the phone down her eyes clouded with quick tears. Anthony! Oh, how she longed to see him. What would she give for his courage, his wisdom, his comfort. But she wouldn't involve him in this nasty mess. It was her own problem. She'd handle it alone. For one flashing moment she sensed what it was going to mean. Merely as a matter of unpleasant publicity. "Dallas Gantry Involved In Murder Of Husband." She saw the headlines screaming across the country. "Star of 'Blue Heaven' Named In Murder Investigation."

A car stopped before the door with a scream of brakes.

Tom Gary had been constable of Willow Valley for fifteen years. He was a big quiet man with large lumpy hands and deep-set, patient eyes. His hair was gray and his shoulders bowed. His duties were mostly nominal. There certainly had never been anything during his term of office to approach the importance of the murder of a prominent citizen. He brought Jimmy Arnold, his nephew, with him. Jimmy was a bright boy and the business at Willow Wilde was rather in the nature of a holiday for him.

Tom Gary stood a long time staring at the body of Jurden Keye. He whistled soundlessly between his teeth. At last he said:

"Hm, case for the coroner, all right. He'll be along quick as he gets home off a pneumonia case over Bently way—hm. Stabbed, huh? Who did this, Gregg?"

Gregg smiled faintly. "I don't know, Tom. You'll have to decide that, I guess."

Tom's glance went slowly over the room, rested a moment on the slightly lifted window behind the desk and to the right, then he looked at Dallas.

"It's a long time since you been around here, Dallas," he said. "How'd you happen to come back to the Valley?"

Dallas shrugged helplessly and looked at Gregg. He had told her not to talk until her attorney arrived. Vaguely she realized that it was good advice. But Dallas was naturally honest and straight-forward. It was not in her to employ subterfuge and she had known Tom Gary since she could remember. Why shouldn't she tell him the truth? It would have to be told sooner or later. All of it. . . .

She said: "I came back, Tom, because I wanted Jurden—my husband—to give me a divorce."

Tom grunted. It had almost passed from the mind of Willow Valley, that Dallas Gantry, the well-known theatrical star, was still married to Jurden Keye.

"Well, you got it fixed up all right, I s'pose," Tom said. "There wouldn't be no sense in Jurden holdin' onto you."

"No," Dallas told him, avoiding Gregg's eyes. "He refused—flatly."

"Yuh don't say." Tom frowned at the dead man. "Like him," he muttered under his breath. "Well, what then? What'd you do?"

Dallas gazed at him from wide, desperate eyes, opened her lips to speak, hesitated, then: "I—left—" she said faintly. "I—just—left." She caught her breath sharply, eyes on the body of the murdered man. "That's all," she whispered, "and—and—when I got outside—there by the gate—I heard someone scream—I came back—"

"Yeah? And what'd you find?"

Dallas motioned with a slim hand. "That," she said. "Jurden—dead. Gregg and Maybrick—were beside him. It was her cry I heard—"

"No," Gregg cut in, "she didn't scream! It couldn't have been Maybrick!"

They both looked at him, startled. Tom's eyes narrowed slightly. "Where do you fit into this picture, Gregg?" he asked. "Where'd you come from?"

Gregg was staring at the floor. A muscle in his left cheek twitched. He said: "I came up this evening to borrow a book Jurden told me about, Tom. I knocked and no one answered so I just opened the door and came in. There in the hall I heard voices in this room—" He paused, shifting uneasily.

"What kind of voices, Gregg? Angry? Excited?"

"I—don't know. I didn't listen. I just heard two people talking. A man and a woman. So I went over and sat down on the sofa out in the hall. Presently Mrs. Maybrick came downstairs. She didn't seem to see me and I started to speak when she tip-toed across and crouched down before the door, listening. Just about then Dallas jerked the door open, pushed past Maybrick, said something to her and went out."

"And what'd you do?"

Gregg smiled. "It's a curious thing, Tom," he said slowly. "I just sat there. I don't know why. I should have spoken, stood up, done something, but I didn't. I just stayed where I was. Maybrick ran after Dallas, looking through the curtain in the front door. I don't know how long it was—before I heard that cry—in here—"

He paused, wiping sweat from his forehead. "Then we both tumbled in, Maybrick and I," he said. "It was—like this—: Maybrick began sobbing. Dallas came back. I called you—"

"This window's open," young Jimmy Arnold said suddenly, and they turned to see him in the alcove, wide-eyed with excitement. Tom stalked over. Dallas followed him. The deep embrasure had three long narrow French windows. The center one swung idly on its hinges. Jimmy jerked out a flashlight, stepped to the window, leaned out, raking the ground with the beam. Suddenly it stopped, focused. Jimmy squinted into the dark.

"Hey!" he yelled. "Hey, you—" In a long-legged leap he was through the window, bounding down the incline after a fleeing figure that darted and ducked like a startled rabbit, to disappear in the fringe of trees at the end of the grounds.

Dallas gasped faintly. "It was a man," she cried. "I saw—his face."

"Yeah?" Tom was through the window after Jimmy. She heard them crashing around in the bushes, then their low, excited voices dying away.

Gregg was staring at her curiously. "You recognized that chap?" he asked.

She frowned. "Yes," she said slowly. "I saw him at the station to-night. He was talking to a man who came in on the train with me. He's a little fellow in a big plaid raincoat, with a cap—"

"Alden," Gregg said suddenly. "Clay Alden. Character man with the show troupe that's here. He's the only one in town who dresses like that." Then he looked at her sharply. "This other chap, the one who came in on the train, what was he like?"

Dallas described him accurately, recalling that weird conviction she had experienced that soon she would be called upon to do this very thing. She was frowning all the time at Gregg MacFarlane, remembering how the stranger and Clay Alden had stared at him there on the station platform.

Gregg nodded as she finished. "That boy's registered at the hotel, Dallas," he said. "They rode up with me. His name's Fredricks, Samuel Fredricks."

"What does he want here?" Dallas asked curiously.

Gregg MacFarlane shook his head. There was a troubled look in his eyes. "He didn't give any explanation. Said he'd only be here a day or two. Might leave in the morning."

Tom Gary climbed through the window, puffing. "Got away," he said, mopping his face. "Either of you get who he was?"

Gregg told him of Dallas' recognition of the actor, Clay Alden.

"Huh!" Tom grunted "We'll pick him up, all right." He turned again to the window, whistled shrilly. "Hey, Jimmy," he called. A distant voice answered him and Jimmy pounded up beneath the window. Tom spoke to him in a low voice and Jimmy sang out a cheery: "Sure thing, Tom. I'll get him," and went off whistling.

Tom Gary came slowly back and stood there glaring down at the body of Jurden Keye.

"I don't reckon it could be," he muttered. "Naw, I guess I'm just dreamin'." He turned to MacFarlane. "Jurden Keye put that show bunch on the blink," he said. "Revoked their license and got the mayor to order 'em otta' town. The boss, that Shannon fellow, was plenty sore. You don't suppose that guy bumped him off to get even, do you?"

MacFarlane shook his head. "It strikes me as a slim motive for murder, Tom," he said, "but you never can tell. Might not be a bad idea to talk to him; check up on him a bit."

Dallas gasped sharply. They both looked at her. She said uncertainly: "Oh, it's nothing—nothing at all—it's just that—"

"Better let us hear it, Dallas," Gregg said. "Information's what we want."

"Someone was in the room with—Jurden—when I came in," Dallas said.

"Yeah?" Tom Gary took off his hat and scratched his grizzled hair. "Well, who was it?"

"I don't know. Maybrick told me Mr. Keye was in here. She evidently thought he was alone or she wouldn't have sent me in. I supposed he was expecting me, so I just opened the door and came in. At first I didn't see anyone, then I heard Jurden speaking—" She paused, frowning at the alcove.

"All right," Tom Gary said, voice sharp with tension. "What did Jurden Keye say, Dallas?"

She was frowning at him as if her mind groped for something she could not catch. "Why, I didn't really listen—that is, I just heard him say: 'There's one way out for you, my dear. I can fix everything—'"

She paused, eyes troubled. "He was talking to a woman," she said bluntly.

"You didn't see her?"

"No. She must have seen me or at least realized that someone had come into the room, for I heard a sort of gasp, someone moving, a door opening and closing—"

"What door?"

"They were in the alcove."

Tom glanced over his shoulder. "Musta' been the French window," he commented. "All right, go on."

"Why, that's all," Dallas said. "Just what I've told you. He was talking to a woman there behind those curtains. He said what I've repeated. I didn't even hear her voice except for that little gasp she gave, so I knew it was a woman, then the door or window opened and closed and he came out—"

Tom Gary was paring blunt nails with a huge knife. He didn't somehow want to look at Dallas Gantry. He had lived in Willow Valley for forty-seven years and he had known Jurden Keye as long as he could remember. It was not the first time he had heard intimations that the French windows in the parlor at Willow Wilde were used for other things than air and sunlight.

"Well," he said slowly, "we'll have to check up a bit. Mebbe we can find out—"

The hall door opened. Mrs. Maybrick came in. She wore a purple, knitted jacket over her dark dress and it intensified the swollen redness of her face. Her eyes were hard and bright as marbles.

"You told me to wait till I was sent for," she said flatly, "but I guess when the master's been foully murdered, I got a right to be down here and to tell what I know." She paused, tear-filled eyes on the body of Jurden Keye. "A better man never lived," she said unsteadily, "and I for one ain't gonna rest until them that killed him is punished. You, Tom Gary, I got plenty to tell you and it's your duty as an officer of the law to listen."

Tom bit off a chew of Granger Twist. "Listenin' is the best thing I do," he said calmly, "but I'd like to ask you a question or two first. Did you know Miss Gantry was comin' up here to-night to see Jurden Keye?"

Mrs. Maybrick's face flushed dully. Her small bright eyes flashed hate at Dallas, came back to the constable.

"Yes," she answered shortly. "He told me a while before she come. He came into the kitchen where I was parin' potatoes for to-morrow and he said: 'Maybrick, my—wife—is in town and will call on me this evening. When she comes, show her into the parlor.'"

"Uh huh," Tom grunted non-committally. "And he didn't say nothin' about anyone else comin'?" Tom persisted.

"Who did come?" she countered. "I didn't admit anyone else."

"Well, there's other ways to get into this room than through the front door," Tom said. "We do know that someone was in this room with Jurden Keye when Miss Gantry came in. It was a woman—and I want you to try and figure out who it coulda' been. What lady friends has he been entertaining—"

Mrs. Maybrick's eyes flared wide. "That's a lie," she choked. "He never had no one else here. They say terrible things about him but they wasn't true— he was the kindest—grandest man—"

"Sure, I know," Tom soothed. "But what I want to find out—"

"What you want to find out," Maybrick began defiantly, then paused, jaws sagging. Her high-colored face went a mottled, sickly white.

"Look," she whispered. "Look! There—behind—you! There in the window—" She stood silent a moment, then with a gasp she slumped to the floor unconscious.

CHAPTER FOUR
BRADE TAKES CHARGE

DALLAS HAD BEEN THINKING curiously that there must have been some good in Jurden Keye to hold Maybrick's unqualified allegiance all these years. The notion was wrenched abruptly from her mind. She rose slowly, facing the window in the alcove. Gregg MacFarlane and Tom Gary were beside her, but she scarcely saw them. Her startled eyes were focused on the figure that stood there clinging to the dusty drapes in the archway, head drooping, blood smearing one side of the face.

Dallas said faintly: "It's Opal. Opal Garth!" and she thought with sudden clarity, "It *was* Opal who was in the alcove when I came in." Then immediately her mind rejected the notion. "If she had been here there would have been that terrible perfume—Jurden told me Opal Garth was not here. He said she had not been here. I believe him! It was someone else!"

Tom Gary was leading the half-conscious woman to a chair. "Get some brandy, there on the sideboard, Gregg," he directed, and began sopping at the bruised cut on Opal's left temple. Mrs. Maybrick had regained consciousness, was sitting up, breathing noisily, sharp, startled eyes on Opal.

"My land," the housekeeper gasped, getting unsteadily to her feet. "It did give me that much of a turn. Just a'seein' her standin' there like a ghost with blood all over her face—" She approached cautiously, hands on her ample hips, staring curiously. "The show girl," she said. "Well, now I never."

61

Opal Garth opened her eyes, gazed around her blankly, then she saw the grim figure by the table and she began sobbing, huddling into the chair, hands writhing at her throat.

"Take him away," she chattered. "He's dead! I'm afraid of the dead! Oh—my God—there's a knife in his heart!"

Tom rubbed his grizzled hair. "What kind of a knife is it, ma'am?" he inquired politely. "Tell us in your own words just what sort of a weapon you see?"

Opal was fumbling at twitching lips. She seemed unconscious of the blood which trickled across her white face. "It's got a brass-colored handle," she said thickly. "There's engravin' on it. It's a terrible long knife. Take it away!"

Tom grunted. "You got an uncommon good description of that there knife," he said slowly, "uncommon good, 'specially considerin' that you can't no ways see it from where you're sittin'!"

In the moment of tense silence that followed his quiet words, Dallas turned. Tom was entirely right. Opal could not see the knife from where she was sitting. She had certainly been too near oblivion to get that clear picture of it when she first came in.

Opal was staring at Tom from wide, hard eyes. The girl was terribly frightened. Fear relaxed face muscles so her cheeks sagged and her mouth hung open. Yet transcending even her panic was the suggestion of some definite purpose that gave her a grim control.

"What you gettin' at?" she asked hoarsely. "Tryin' to pin this thing on me? Well, you're barkin' up the wrong tree." She paused, breathing unevenly. "Gimme another drink of that stuff," she demanded, and gulped the brandy thirstily.

She was bare-headed, Dallas noted, and underneath the imitation fur coat, she wore a gaudy, spangled dancing costume. It was of crimson-colored stuff with an overskirt of fluffy crinoline, drooping sadly from long wear and the damp night air. There was a long jagged tear on one side. Opal's face was scratched. A damp, brown leaf clung in her hair. The soles of her dancing pumps were stained with wet. Make-up lay in thick chunks on her face and her lashes were heavy with mascara.

"Never mind what I'm barkin' at, young lady," Tom advised grimly. "It's up to you to say what you're doin' here to-night and how you got your head hurt. Better make it snappy or you'll find yourself in the jail along with that fellow actor of yours—"

Opal glanced at him quickly. Beneath the make-up, her face paled. "Who you talkin' about?" she asked sullenly.

"Clay Alden. We found him sneakin' around out here and I sent my deppity"—Tom unconsciously expanded over that word—"to bring him in. He's likely in the jug by now."

"My God," Opal whispered and crouched lower in the chair, eyes darting frantically over the room. They were easy to read. Terror, suspicion, frenzy, the groping for a way out, and always that gleam of purpose.

"What was he doin' here?" Tom asked.

"I dunno," she admitted. "I guess he was lookin' for me."

"Yeah? And what were you doin' here?"

She looked at him slyly under heavy lashes. "I had a date with Mr. Keye," she said.

Dallas turned to the window, cheeks hot with shame, remembering Opal's hateful proposal. Then she heard the girl speaking again.

"It was this way, Mr. Policeman. Mr. Keye and me, we been friends ever since he come to the first show we give here: 'Troubled Waters,' it was, and I played the innocent little country girl—"

"Yeah I remember," Tom said dryly. "Go on now and make it in a hurry."

"You needn't try to rush me," Opal cried angrily. "I got plenty to tell and I'm gonna take my time about it." She squared back, placed her skinny, none-too-clean elbows on the chair arms and glared defiance at Tom. Her attitude said as plainly as words: "This is a swell break for me. I'll get my pictures in the paper. I never had a chance like this before. Watch me make the most of it."

Tom waited philosophically. He was not a trained manhunter. He had never worked on big cases. But he had a hard, practical common sense and he judged people swiftly and accurately through intuition and the homely knowledge acquired in close to thirty years of observation.

"I had a date with him," Opal went on slowly. "I was to drop in after the show—" She paused, twitching at the spangles of her skirt.

"Well, you dropped in, I guess," Tom said.

"No," she snapped. "He wrote me not to come."

"When?"

"About six o'clock, it was, I got the note."

"What'd he say in it—exactly?"

She fumbled in a pocket of her coat, drew out a crumpled piece of paper, extended it to Tom. It was heavy white, with a small plain monogram in blue in one corner. The writing was cramped, tight, secretive, the wording stilted, old-fashioned. It said:

> "Dear Miss Garth:
> "I regret that a pressing matter of business will prevent my keeping the appointment with you this evening at the time agreed upon. Please do not come as I shall be unable to receive you. I will get in touch with you to-morrow.
> > "Very truly yours,
> > "Jurden Keye."

Tom Gary grinned as he folded up the missive and stuck it in his pocket. That formal phraseology didn't fool him a bit. It was like Jurden Keye to so word the note that there would be no comeback, but Tom was willing to bet that Opal knew exactly what he meant. Tom looked at Dallas.

"What time did you send your message, Dallas?" he asked.

"It must have been about seven-thirty," she said, recalling the unpleasant interview with Opal which had delayed her.

"Hm, then Jurden couldn't have canceled the date with this young lady because you were coming," he said. Then to Opal: "Well, if Keye told you to stay away, what in time was you doin' snoopin' around here?"

"I got suspicious," she admitted.

"Of what?"

"I dunno. I just wondered why he told me to stay away, so after the cabaret scene in the third act where I do my toe dancin' turn, I beat it up here." She glanced down at her stage costume. "I didn't come in the front way, bein' afraid he'd get sore, but I wanted to see what he was doin' that was so important, so I sneaked in across the lawn to the window—" She looked away and had the grace to blush. "I've come in that way before," she admitted sullenly.

No one said anything. Tom Gary leaned easily against the table, watching her. Gregg MacFarlane stood back in the shadows and his eyes were on Dallas, dark with pity. Mrs. Maybrick hunched down on a stool by the fire which was only a bed of gray ashes now. She was watching the girl avidly.

Dallas had her back to the group. She was staring with a curious lack of emotion out over the moon-white world before her. Subconsciously she heard all that was said, quivered to every admission Opal made, but with the active part of her mind she was re-living the days of her youth here in Willow Valley. Recalling happy autumn tramps over the hills, jaunts after violets in the spring—Christmas eves when the snow wrapped the world in white—that day she promised to marry Jurden Keye. . . .

Opal Garth's voice reached her again. "I come up," Opal went on, "and the window was unlocked, so I didn't think it would do any harm to take a peek inside. I heard him talkin' to a woman. They was—quarrelen' terrible. I listened, thinkin' I'd go every minute but bein' too interested."

Tom Gary opened his lips to ask a question, closed them again, like a steel trap. Sooner or later he'd have to get the name of the woman who had quarreled with Jurden Keye but he wanted to put it off as long as he could.

"Go on," he said curtly.

Dallas' eyes lifted to the dark sky where stars glittered frostily. Somewhere up there was a low, faint drone. The night mail, she supposed. She and Anthony had decided on a long plane trip after they were married. . . .

"Then," Opal was saying, "I heard Jurden Keye get to his feet. He said somethin' like: 'Get out of my house—this minute—' and the woman laughed and said somethin' I couldn't catch, then I heard a sound like someone was strugglin' and he cried real sharp: 'Put that down—' Then he gasped low and terrible—and I heard a chair overturned and the sound of someone runnin'.'"

She was leaning forward, eyes wide and black, fixed on the fireplace. The room was very quiet. Only Mrs. Maybrick's panting breath disturbed the silence. Dallas turned slowly, hands clenched tight in the folds of the lace curtain. She ought to take some interest in this thing.

"I peeked out," Opal said huskily. "I had to see what happened. And so help me God, I seen him, there, like that—and I thought first he was asleep or—somethin'—and I took a step nearer and seen the knife in his back—and"—she jerked up, staring at them, frenzy in her eyes—"I screamed," she said. "I yelled plenty."

Gregg MacFarlane was on his feet beside her. "All right," he demanded. "What did you do then? Go on."

"I ran," she said. "I went back through that alcove, out the window—and then ran into a—tree—it put me out for the count and I don't remember any more until I woke up and heard someone talkin' and I came in."

Gregg was bending over her. His hands were clenched into hard fists. "It's all a lie," he said savagely. "You killed him yourself! You—"

"No!" Opal choked. "I didn't. Let me alone—don't touch—me—"

Tom Gary pushed Gregg aside. His harsh face was grim.

"Shut up," he snapped to the girl. "Who was the woman in this room? Did you see her face? Recognize her voice?"

Opal dabbed futilely at the drying blood on her face. Her lips opened, closed gaspingly.

"It was her," she said clearly. "Her! Dallas Gantry! She killed him. I saw her!"

"She's right," Mrs. Maybrick agreed bleakly. "The girl's right. Dallas Gantry murdered the master—I saw it—through the keyhole—I saw her pick up the knife and stab him—she's the murderer—she—"

A loud pounding came on the front door. Tom Gary said slowly: "See who it is, Mis' Maybrick," then he looked at Opal Garth again. "You been sayin' plenty, ma'am," he grated. "You're accusin' a woman of murder! Do you realize that—"

"She done it! She done it," Opal insisted frantically. "I stood there in the alcove and seen her—"

The door opened. A breath of fresh night air sucked through the room, dispelling momentarily the thick atmosphere of death, then Dallas exclaimed sharply, stumbled forward, suddenly sobbing as if her heart would break.

"Anthony!" she cried. "Oh, Anthony—darling—" And she was in his arms, head buried on his shoulder. He was holding her tight, while his stormy glance went sweeping over the room.

"That's all right, Dallas," he said very low. "Don't you cry, little one. I'm fixing things all right. You listen to me. Everything's going to be settled in short time. Branson was out of town and his man phoned me—I got a plane and came fast—I brought"—he released Dallas gently, turned to a man who stood quietly just inside the door—"Dallas," he said, "this is Captain Courtney Brade from the city detective bureau. I kidnapped him and brought him along."

Dallas looked at Courtney Brade. She was so shaken by the unexpected arrival of Anthony Gordon that the world was swimming hazily before her eyes and she had a wretched feeling that she was going to faint. It had taken the sight of Anthony's face to make her realize how terrible all this business was, how unspeakably frightened she had been ever since she first looked at the body of Jurden Keye.

Now she stepped forward, stopped directly before Brade.

"How do you do," she said and extended her hand.

Brade enclosed it in his own and Dallas' eyes flared wide. It was as if an electric current had flowed through her, from the pressure of that strong, vital clasp. He smiled.

"How do you do, Dallas Gantry," he said. "Your 'Queen Anne' was the loveliest thing I have ever seen."

"Oh, thank you," Dallas gasped, eyes suddenly blinded by tears. "I'm so glad you came. I need someone to help me—so badly."

Anthony interrupted her by a hand on her arm. "Dallas, let me introduce Captain Brade to—"

Dallas looked up and saw Tom Gary standing almost at her elbow. There was a quiet, whimsical smile on his lips.

"Hello, everybody," he said. "I'm Tom Gary, the constable here. Seems like I heard Captain Brade's name mentioned. I sure 'nuff hope so, if he's come to lend me a hand. I don't mind sayin' I'm in over my head."

Brade shook hands with him. Dallas told Tom that Anthony was the man she was going to marry and blushed rosily when she said it, then her glance flashed to the figure of her husband by the table and she closed her eyes, suddenly faint. For the first time since she rushed blindly into that room at sound of a scream, she realized fully what Jurden's death was going to mean to her. She was free! Free to marry Anthony! Jurden couldn't stop her now, couldn't hold her.

She paused, staring wide-eyed at the grim dead form. Couldn't he? Couldn't he still—hold her? Still keep the touch of his dusty hands upon her, blighting her happiness. . . .

"Dallas," Anthony Gordon said with his charming one-sided smile. "Don't stand there like you're seeing a ghost. Captain Brade's time is valuable. He only came because he's the next to the best friend I have and he admires you immensely. Catch hold of yourself, sweetheart, and let's get this over."

Dallas roused as from a trance. The feeling of horror had been so strong upon her that she seemed to be coming back from another world. She slipped her hand in Anthony's arm, pressed it. They walked slowly toward the center of the room.

Brade was standing beside the body of Jurden Keye. The light in the room was dim but its reflected rays struck his face and Dallas studied him curiously. She supposed he was a detective. Dallas didn't know much about detectives. She read stories about them sometimes but to the best of her knowledge she had never seen one in real life. She rather thought they should be short, heavy men with thick red faces and blunt hands, who wore derbies and broad shoes.

Brade was almost as tall as Anthony, who stood six feet in his socks. Brade was lean and looked in perfect condition. He was quietly and correctly dressed in gray tweeds. He had very thick, dark-brown hair. It was stained with gray at the temples. Dallas thought he would be about thirty-nine. She wondered why his hair was gray when he was so young.

Just then he lifted his head and his glance met hers. He had the strongest, keenest, saddest eyes she had ever seen. They were a curious cloudy gray, rather long and habitually narrowed between crisp black lashes. He smiled and rested a hand on the table's edge. For no reason she could explain, Dallas looked at that hand. It seemed to her that every part of the man was distinctive, individual.

"What a gorgeous ring," she thought, staring at a magnificent Oriental moonstone, set in a massive, hand-hammered, silver mounting. "It's—glorious," she repeated to herself. "I wonder why a detective wears a ring like that?"

And Dallas had no way of guessing that she had inwardly voiced a question which most of Brade's world would have given a great deal to have answered. Which not three persons besides himself could have answered, holding as it did, the story of Brade's greatest defeat and mightiest victory. Then she heard him speaking to Tom Gary:

"You understand," Brade was saying, "that I'm here in an unofficial capacity, merely at the request of Gordon, who is a friend of mine. I'll be glad to assist if I can—"

Tom Gary sighed hugely. "Captain Brade," he said, "official or otherwise, I'm mighty happy to have you here. I'm goin' to need assistance and plenty of it."

"All right," Brade said crisply, "let's get to work—"

Suddenly Dallas cried: "Gregg! Where is Gregg MacFarlane? He's gone—"

Brade glanced at her sharply. "Gregg MacFarlane?" he asked. "Who is Gregg MacFarlane?"

Dallas was suddenly shivering so she could not reply. She clung to Anthony's arm. Tom Gary answered Brade's question.

"Gregg MacFarlane runs the Willow Inn. He, with Mrs. Maybrick here, the housekeeper, discovered Keye's body." His eyes went carefully over the room, rested on the open French window. "He was here a minute ago," he muttered.

Opal Garth said hoarsely: "He went out that window! I saw him! When these others came in, he ducked."

There was a moment of strained silence. Brade's glance passed slowly from face to face. Dallas Gantry? He had admired her work for a long time. *She* wouldn't commit murder! Brade smiled very slightly. He didn't judge people by their appearance. He had to know what was inside of them. How their minds worked.

The girl in the dancing dress? He hadn't heard her name yet, didn't know where she fitted the picture but he recognized her type. Cheap, common, vindictive. Scratching like an angry cat when cornered, yet capable of stubborn adherence to an idea.

Maybrick? Ordinary enough from outward appearance but with a stolid venom behind her small, bright eyes. Had she murdered Jurden Keye?

The phone rang. Tom Gary picked it up. "Hello," he said, then he sighed faintly. "Oh, hello, Gregg. Been wonderin' where you disappeared to." He listened in silence a moment. "All right," he said, "we'll be lookin' for you." He put the instrument down.

"Gregg went down to look after his wife," he explained. "Was afraid she might have heard and would be worried sick. Heart ain't any too good. He's comin' right up—"

Chapter Five
"A Man Had Died!"

Steps sounded in the hall. The door was pushed open. Jimmy Arnold entered, dragging a man after him. Jimmy was grinning broadly. "Got him, Tom," he said. "This is the egg that we saw hanging around here—"

Opal Garth gasped faintly. "Frosty!" she said, then clamped her lips shut hard. Brade glanced at her quickly, back at Jimmy's prisoner. He stroked his chin, strolled forward, stood looking down at the man.

"Frosty," he said reflectively. "Frosty—"

"My name's Alden," the man declared sullenly. "Clay Alden. I belong to Shannon's Stock Company and I—"

"Frosty. Frosty," Brade repeated, not heeding him. "That sounds very familiar somehow." He caught Alden beneath the chin, jerked his head up. "Seems like I ought to know you, guy," he muttered and frowned. "Well, what's your line?" he demanded. "What were you doing around here tonight? Speak fast. I don't like your looks."

Clay Alden was shivering and hair clung in damp streaks to his forehead. His eyes darted furtively over the room, avoiding Brade's. He squirmed in Jimmy's uncompromising hold.

"Jimmy," Tom began, then stopped. "Captain Brade," he said, "this is Jimmy Arnold, my nephew. He helps me out now and then."

Brade shook hands with Jimmy. The boy's eyes were round and reverent as they met the Captain's. Jimmy had heard of Courtney Brade.

71

"Where'd you get him, Jimmy?" Brade asked, nodding at Alden.

"In his room at the Inn, packin' for a flit. He showed fight and pulled a gun on me so I just cracked him down and when he comes to, he was willin' to come along peaceable."

Brade grinned at Jimmy Arnold. If the man calling himself Clay Alden was who Brade thought he was, Jimmy had taken his life in his hands when he casually cracked him down. Brade thought he'd like to have young Arnold in his department.

He said to Alden: "I'm waiting to hear what you've got to say. My time's short."

Alden wet his lips. "I ain't done nothin'," he whined. "Opal there, she's—my—girl," he glowered angrily. "I knew she'd been foolin' around with this Keye bird and I got sore, so when she beat it after her act to-night, I come along to see what was what."

"Yeah? And what'd you see?"

"Nothin'," Alden said grouchily. "I was just hangin' around outside when all of a sudden the window opened up and someone shot a flash on me and I beat it. I didn't know about anyone bein' croaked till this guy," he glowered at Jimmy, "picked me up."

"No?" Brade asked. "Didn't know a thing had happened, eh? That's why you beat it back to the hotel and started packing in a hurry, isn't it? Just because you didn't know anything had happened. You'll have to do better than that—Frosty."

Alden cursed and tried to jerk loose from Jimmy. "Lemme alone," he snarled. "I ain't done anything. You ain't got a thing on me. I just happened to be here—"

The outer door slammed. Brade's head lifted. Footsteps sounded in the hall. The door was jerked wide. He saw a tall, lean man with strange dead-white hair and deep-set black eyes, holding very gently to the arm of a small pale woman in a gray cape. Gregg MacFarlane paused in the door, eyes flashing over the group in the room, then he smiled slightly, pushed the little gray figure gently behind him and stepped in.

"I tried to make Faith stay away," he explained, "but she—"

Faith slipped under his arm, darted across the room and put her arms around Dallas. "You poor child," she sobbed. "You poor,

poor child—" then she looked back over her shoulder at Captain Brade. "Dallas Gantry is an old friend of mine," she explained. "I had to come."

Gregg MacFarlane was staring at Brade. His dark face was pale and sweat gleamed on his forehead. He stepped forward. "I'm Gregg MacFarlane," he said quietly. "I didn't mean to run out on you. You're Captain Brade, I suppose—"

Brade's head was lowered. He was frowning hard at Mac-Farlane. Telling himself he was getting funny notions, becoming too impressionable. Just because that egg calling himself Clay Alden reminded him of someone was no sign this dark-faced white-haired man. . . .

He extended his hand and a quick, charming smile touched his lips. "I'm Brade," he said. "Glad to meet you, Gregg MacFarlane.

"Now," Brade went on, turning back to the table, "I want to get at the bottom of this thing quickly. A man has been murdered and we've got to find out who committed the crime. Constable Gary has asked me to help him. At present, I know absolutely nothing about the case aside from the fact that Jurden Keye is dead by violence. I want to get the story in my own way. It isn't very pleasant for any of you here in this room. Mrs. Maybrick, where can the folks here wait while I ask some questions?"

She looked at him sullenly. "The library is across the hall," she admitted. "It's big but there ain't any fire."

"Well, we can remedy that. All of you," his eyes went slowly over the group, "with the exception of Frosty—"

"Don't call me that!" Alden grated. "You know my name, mister."

Brade smiled. "Oh, yes, of course. Mr. Alden, isn't it? Excuse me. Very well, all of you except this young lady, you see I don't even know your names—"

"Opal Garth," the girl snapped.

"Thank you. Opal Garth and Mr. Alden, I want to talk to you first. I sighted what I thought was an excellent spot as I came in. A small room under the stairs—"

"That's the mornin' room," Mrs. Maybrick volunteered. "Opens into the main dinin' room."

"Excellent. Excellent," Brade agreed, "but we won't need the dining room. Opal Garth and Alden step into the morning room. The rest of you try the library. Wait until I call for you. Constable Gary will keep you company. Let's go."

They went. Brade leaned against the mantel and watched them. He studied their faces, watched their walk, the way they carried their shoulders, the movement of their hands. Nervous, yes. That was natural. Indignant, some of them. Frightened—furtive.

He smiled rather wearily. Up to to-night they had been normal human beings, going about their own affairs, involved in their own problems. Then a man had died, and they immediately became tense, watchful, suspicious, lying to save themselves, to incriminate others, darting like frantic mice caught in a trap; baring their teeth at him because he represented the law that sought to exact an eye for an eye.

Opal Garth stood before him, hands fumbling at the sequins on her waist. "All right," she said. "What you want, mister?"

Brade looked her over carefully. Her thin, worn face flushed under his scrutiny. "Aw, go on and gawp," she spit at him. "I know I ain't pretty. I ain't—anything. But I didn't do the old boy in, and you can't prove I did."

Brade extracted a cigarette, tapped it against the moonstone in his ring, lighted it, looked at her through the smoke. "Your beauty, or lack of it, Opal," he told her, "has nothing whatever to do with your guilt or innocence in this matter, and I can't recall saying that I thought you murdered Jurden Keye. You see I know nothing at all about the case—"

"No?" Her lip curled. "Huh! First time I ever seen a copper that didn't know everything right off the bat. Huh!" She slapped a hand to her hip and gazed at him insolently through sticky lashes. "What you want me and the boy friend to do?"

"Go across to that room," Brade said sharply and the girl backed away, paling. When the door of the morning room had closed behind Opal and Clay Alden, Brade said over his shoulder:

"You, Jimmy, come here."

Jimmy Arnold stepped up smartly.

Brade's eyes were still on the closed door. "Know this house pretty well? All right. Any chance for a getaway from that morning room?"

Jimmy scratched his touseled yellow hair. "There's a row of windows on the west. No doors goin' outside."

"Good. Now you shag out and plant yourself under those windows, see? If anyone tries for a getaway, why just"—he looked at Jimmy and grinned—"crack 'em down," he finished.

Jimmy nodded, touched his cap and went out. Brade leaned against the hall door and smoked reflectively. There was a grim humor in the depths of his somber eyes. The house was very still. Wind crept about it like a stealthy prowler. Occasionally, a voice sounded from the library, to stop abruptly as though the burden of conversation were too much. Brade tossed his smoke away, shoved his hands into his pockets and walked swiftly and silently down the hall, glanced around him curiously and finally opened the second door on his left. According to his calculations this should lead to the dining room. It did.

The room was dark, but he drew out a pocket flash and shot it around. It was a big cavernous apartment with high, narrow windows and a long, meager table down the center. There was a massive old sideboard against the far wall. A glass dish held a heap of ruddy apples. They filled the room with a pleasant fruity odor. Brade closed the door behind him, stood there, with the flash off, listening. His eyes caught a narrow band of light under a door at the far end.

He slithered over, paused, frowning at it. It should lead into the morning room where Opal and Alden were waiting his questioning. Waiting, nervous and tense, wondering what he would ask, figuring out their replies. He was anxious to see how his little experiment would work.

He leaned against the wall, ear pressed to the panels of the door. His wrist watch ticked loudly in the silence. The odor of the apples was heavy in his nostrils. Beyond the door someone moved. A chair creaked. A match was scratched. Tobacco smoke drifted through the crack. Then Opal said:

"Aw, fer Pete's sake, gimme a smoke. My nerves are shriekin'."

The man grunted. Paper rustled faintly. A second match gritted. "Gawd!" Opal said huskily. "That's better." Silence, again. Brade's lips were tight. His eyes were on the panels as though he would force his vision through them.

"What in hell'd you crash the party for?" the girl asked suddenly.

Sullen silence, then Alden growled. "Yeah, you would ask that. What'd you mean hornin' in on our deal?"

"Your deal? I come because I was checkin' up on Keye. He invited me to spend the evening with him, then sends me word not to come. I don't take second place for anyone. As for it bein' your deal, didn't I tip you off to Leo and that stretch—"

"Shut up! Where's that damned dick? Thought he was comin' to quiz us."

The voices stopped. Minutes ticked loudly. Brade remained immovable. It wasn't written that the two within the morning room could remain alone for a length of time without talking. He had lots of patience.

Alden said suddenly: "Say, kid, what's the low down? You was here first. What really happened?"

"How do I know?" she demanded and stopped abruptly.

"No?" he queried, voice nasty. "Did poppa get fresh or somethin'?"

"You're bein' dumb. Think I can't take care of myself?"

He laughed. "I damned well know you can, baby. That's why I think mebbe you knifed—"

"Button up your lip," she hissed frantically. "Someone's likely to be listenin'."

They were silent for a time and Brade could almost feel their hard, suspicious glances creeping over the room. But they had to talk. They weren't the kind to stand silence.

Alden said in a hoarse whisper: "What'd Keye say the last time you talked to him about—everything?"

"He said to leave it to him. He'd take care of things. He knew a way—" She paused, then she said: "I wonder what he meant, he knew a way."

"We was fools to spill it to him, baby. You and me and Leo coulda' cleaned up without him. It was your hunch draggin' your sugar daddy in—"

"I didn't want to cool my Enna Jetticks in stir on a blackmailin' charge," she defended herself. "I figured with a—leading—citizen behind us, we'd—be playin' safe. I still think it was a swell hunch."

"Yeah, and what a swell hunch it turned out to be," he mocked. "Say," he said suddenly, "how'd you get that bloomer on your pan? Poppa crack you down?"

"I—stumbled—into—a tree."

"Yeah? Baby fall and cut her little headdy—"

"Well, that's what I did—I fell—"

"Where?"

"None of your business!"

The voices stopped but the air was heavy with conflict. Brade could sense it through the door, almost see the two of them, facing each other, angry, frightened—groping.

Alden said very low: "I think you're holdin' out on me, kid. You got somethin' on your mind—"

"No—no—no. Let me alone."

"Don't try for no double cross. We're in this together. There's still a chance at some sweet pickin's."

"I'm through. I won't—play with you."

"No? What you figurin' on—somethin' on your own?"

"Oh, no," she cried on a high shrill note that abruptly died. "No," she said again in a voice that shook. "I ain't got anything, Frosty, I ain't holdin' out."

Brade wondered how he was so sure she was lying. Alden said savagely:

"You played hell spillin' my name when I come in there. Where's what passes for your brains?" She laughed, low, insolent.

The man cried: "Shut up or I'll spill a few things to that dick."

"Do it and I'll tell him somethin' too. If he knew you was Frosty Rivet—"

Sound of a blow. A smothered cry. A muffled curse.

Brade nodded grimly. Frosty Rivet, eh? That was sweet. A small-time crook, pickpocket, a carnival con man, wanted right now for a job up state. . . .

He straightened, shot on his flash and slipped quietly from the room. He called Tom Gary outside the library, held a hurried conversation with him, gave him his instructions and went back to the dining room to again take up his vigil.

Brade had told the truth when, on his arrival, he said he knew nothing about the case aside from the fact that a man had been murdered. He did know that Dallas Gantry was Jurden Keye's wife, legally. That Dallas had come to Willow Valley to see about getting her divorce. Anthony Gordon had told him that on the way down. But of all the myriad interwoven, tangled threads that had gone into the weaving of the pattern of murder, he was ignorant.

He could have questioned these people in the regulation, orthodox way and for his pains he would have received a tissue of lies, a mass of statements, innocently and intentionally misleading, and he would have been just where he started. His little experiment in psychology was bearing fruit. He knew that one of the suspects was a wanted criminal. Not a killer, as far as the police knew, but certainly the stuff of which killers are made.

He knew that Opal Garth had been friendly with Jurden Keye. That she was to have spent the evening with him. That he had sent her word not to come. That she had come anyway, probably on fire with jealousy—that Opal, Frosty Rivet and someone named Leo had been in on a blackmail scheme which the girl had insisted on sharing with Jurden Keye. That Opal certainly was holding something back—some scheme of her own.

He let the matter rest there. He was going in for a bit more eavesdropping. Opal and Alden were in the library with the explanation that Brade wasn't quite ready to talk to them yet, and two more people were coming into the morning room—two more who might unintentionally give to the grim, quiet man standing there in the dark, further insight into the death of Jurden Keye.

A MAN SAID: "Cold, sweetheart?"

Brade's head lifted. He stared hard at the panels. Faith MacFarlane answered, "A little, dear. I hope we won't have to wait too long. Why should this man, this— What is his name?"

"Brade. Captain Courtney Brade. He's from headquarters in the city. I've heard of him before. A top-notcher, Faith."

"He looks it. I wonder why Captain Brade wants to talk to me?"

"Mere formality, I suppose. Better let me go for your cape."

"No, he might not like it. He won't keep us long."

"Cigarette?"

"Thank you."

A little silence, then she said in a voice that shook slightly: "You're wonderfully good to me, Gregg."

He laughed low in his throat. "Good to you?" he echoed softly. "Faith, little sweetheart, if I lived to be a hundred, if I spent every minute of every twenty-four hours serving you, loving you, I couldn't pay you—"

"Gregg," she said with tears in her voice. "Gregg! That you should speak of pay—"

Brade's cheeks were hot in the dark. There was a muttered curse in his throat. At times he wished he were a ditch digger, a garbage collector, a street sweeper, anything but a policeman. He felt somehow as if he had crashed, in a drunken swagger, into a cloister, as if something holy had been desecrated.

Faith said softly: "He's dead, isn't he, Gregg?"

"Yes—he's—dead—"

"Do you think he knows—now—who killed him?"

"Hush, little pigeon; don't talk like that."

"But I wonder—Gregg."

"I—don't—know—Faith. I hope—not."

"Why, Gregg?"

Gregg MacFarlane said with restrained fierceness: "Because I honestly believe, Faith, that Jurden Keye would come back from—beyond—to make his murderer pay. I don't think the grave could hold him—"

"Then you don't think—he's—really—gone? Just because he's dead—he isn't really—through— Oh, Gregg!" Her words ended in a gasp of sheer terror, then she said: "That's better, Gregg. I love to feel your arms around me. They've always—shielded me—they always will, won't they, dear? You'll never take your arms from around me, will you, Gregg?"

"Never, Faith."

Presently she said: "I wish Captain Brade would come. It's so quiet in here."

"Yes, but we're not afraid of silence, Faith. We've lived with it a—long—time."

"And been happy, Gregg."

"Very happy, sweetheart."

After a while he spoke. He said: "I'm worried for Dallas, Faith."

"Oh, Gregg! You mean?"

"Jurden refused to grant her a divorce. I think he was beastly to her to-night—"

"But she—couldn't—do it."

"Hush, Faith, don't get excited. What we think Dallas could or couldn't do won't impress Brade. You understand that?"

"Oh—yes—policemen are terrible, aren't they, Gregg?"

"Rather terrible, Faith. But some of them, Brade, for instance, I don't think he enjoys it, really."

"But, Dallas—about her?"

"Well, you see, that actor girl, that Opal Garth, she said she saw Dallas kill him—"

"Oh, Gregg!" The words were an anguished cry.

"Hush, or I won't talk to you."

"I'll be quiet. We've got to help Dallas. There isn't anything I wouldn't do for Dallas Gantry. What else?"

"Maybrick confirmed the Garth girl's statement. She said Dallas killed him—that isn't so good. She had plenty of motive if you want to look at it that way."

Silence again, then Faith MacFarlane said in a low, tight voice: "Gregg, why did you come up here to-night?"

He didn't answer for a long moment, then: "I came to borrow a book, Faith."

"Gregg," she pleaded, "don't lie—to—me."

"Faith!"

"Tell me why you came?"

"I've told you."

"What time did you get here?"

"I don't know exactly—I think about ten-thirty."

"And he was killed at—ten-forty."

"Was he? I don't remember."

"I wish Brade would come."

"He will. Be patient."

"What shall we tell him?"

"The truth."

"But someone might think that—you—"

"That I killed Keye. Yes, they might. They know I hated him because of the way he's always—looked at you—"

"There'll be gossip."

"The town's buzzing with it now. That shock-headed Buddy Witherspoon is careening all over town blatting about the note Dallas sent up here—"

Brade slipped from the room, down the hall, tapped on the door of the morning room, entered at Gregg MacFarlane's low summons.

The place was cold and cheerless. Dust lay thickly over everything. The wallpaper looked moldy. The furniture was massive and depressing. Faith MacFarlane sat on a low stool before the cold fireplace. She was hunched down, arms encircling her knees. Gregg stood over her grimly protecting, as though he had just risen from beside her. They regarded Brade quietly.

Brade strolled toward them.

"Chilly in here, isn't it?" he asked.

Gregg MacFarlane nodded. Faith smiled at Brade through her lashes.

"Beastly," she admitted.

Brade studied her without seeming to do so. The MacFarlanes were interesting people. Faith was so tiny. She scarcely reached her husband's shoulder. Brade had never admired small women. He did not have that natural, common instinct of protection toward them which doubtless has its origin in the feeling of power and superiority which it affords the male animal. He liked women who could look well on a level into his eyes. But oddly enough, though he saw clearly that Faith MacFarlane was not five feet tall, she did not seem small. She was so strongly made, so poised, somehow so perfect, that it was simply impossible to compare her with her surroundings.

She rose now, folding her arms for warmth. She stood like a soldier, straight and steady. From the soles of her little feet, to the crown of her honey-golden hair that was like a cloud around her head, there was a rhythmic co-ordination, a subtle flowing strength that seemed to make of her something tall and stately. She had large blue-gray eyes, deeply shadowed by long curling black lashes. Her mouth was wide and rather pale. Sensitive, passionate, but somehow terribly strong. She smiled at him.

"We're anxious to help you, Captain Brade," she said. "What is it you would like to know?"

Brade smiled back at her. "Who killed Jurden Keye?"

She shivered and for a moment her eyes closed. Then she put a hand on her husband's arm. "What can we tell you?" she asked.

"Everything you know about the matter. You, MacFarlane, you discovered the body?"

"Mrs. Maybrick and I together. I opened the door. She pushed past me."

"Why were you here?"

"I came to borrow a book." He looked straight and hard at Brade.

Brade tapped out a cigarette. "Mind if I smoke, Mrs. Mac-Farlane?"

"Certainly not. I'll join you—" He extended his case. As she took the cigarette, her hand touched his. It was cold and steady as a rock.

"Please talk to me in your own way," Brade requested. "Just tell me what happened—all along."

MacFarlane said: "I came up to borrow a book. I knocked and no one answered. Thinking Maybrick was busy at the back and Keye in the library I opened the door and came in. There was no one in the hall. I was about to tap on the library door when I heard voices across the way in the parlor. I sat down and waited—"

"Whose voices did you hear?"

"Keye's and Dallas Gantry's," MacFarlane said savagely. "And I'll tell you the truth because you'll find it out anyway. Dallas isn't trying to hide the fact that she and Keye were quarreling."

"I see. About—the divorce?"

MacFarlane glanced at Brade sharply. "Yes. Keye refused to free her. He was rather—beastly. As soon as I caught the drift I got up, intending to leave but just then Maybrick, the housekeeper, came down the stairs and without noticing me back in the shadows of the hall, she squatted down outside the parlor door and listened. She hadn't been there two minutes when Dallas jerked the door open and surprised her. Dallas was very angry and went out quickly. Maybrick got up, waddled over to the main door and stood there peering through the glass after her. My position was rather uncomfortable. I didn't know just what to do so I stayed where I was, hoping Maybrick would leave so I could get out unobserved."

"She didn't?"

"No. Just then someone screamed there in the parlor. I don't know just what the two of us did, but the next thing I remember is opening the door and feeling Maybrick push past me into the room, and when I followed I saw Keye—then in a few minutes Dallas came back. I called Tom Gary and—you know the rest."

Brade studied his fingertips. The two watching him could not tell what he thought. He said presently:

"You have known Jurden Keye a long time, MacFarlane?"

"Since I first came to Willow Valley, fifteen years ago."

"You have been friends?"

MacFarlane's lips tightened. Faith's head lifted. They stood there defiantly looking at Brade.

"I do not believe," Gregg MacFarlane said slowly, "that Jurden Keye had one real friend in the entire world. We have been acquaintances. We were entertained at his home. He visited us. He and I met in a business way."

"There had never been any unpleasantness between you?"

Gregg shrugged. "There was unpleasantness between Keye and every single person in town with whom he came in contact—"

"Nothing special, I mean. You had no reason to—dislike him?" Brade was leaning easily against the wall, arms folded, head lowered. His eyes were like sharp bright instruments, probing, exploring, dissecting. Gregg MacFarlane tried very hard to escape that regard, but wherever his glance went, Brade's was there. The man was like an intangible force, permeating every corner of the room.

MacFarlane said through tight lips: "I hated Jurden Keye like hell. He was an evil, slimy, hypocritical old devil. I have higher regard for the open-and-shut criminal, the robber, the murderer—" He stopped, panting. There was dull color in his face. He was trembling.

Faith was pale as death. She held both steady hands pressed hard against her heart. A gray pallor spread gradually over her whiteness. Her eyes went wide and blank. She stood so terribly still that the clashing glances of the two men unlocked and went involuntarily to her.

Gregg cried out in such mortal agony that Brade straightened with a muttered exclamation, then Faith MacFarlane took an uncertain step forward and crashed heavily to the floor. Gregg was beside her, white to the lips; Brade knelt and laid a steady finger on her wrists. Across the rigid body the eyes of the two men met and Brade had all he could do to hold his glance steady before the savage pain in MacFarlane's.

"You've done this!" MacFarlane cried hoarsely. "You, with your damned prying—your probing—you've killed her—"

"Let's get her to the fire. Does she often have spells like this?"

He slipped an arm under Faith's body, but MacFarlane pushed him roughly away, lifted her gently, holding her so tight and hard against him.

"It's her heart," he said thickly. "She's been through—a lot—"

Brade opened the door. Mrs. Maybrick was passing down the hall. She stopped and her little hard eyes widened.

"Another?" she gasped. "Another—dead—tonight?"

"No," Brade snapped. "Mrs. MacFarlane has fainted. She's coming out now—" He glanced at the fluttering lids in the still white face. "Lead us to a bedroom where it's warm and quiet. Snap into it."

"There ain't any warm rooms here, mister," she said sullenly. "They're quiet enough, though."

"Then show us one and make a fire."

The woman turned and went upstairs. MacFarlane followed and Brade came after him. They laid Faith on a great cold-looking bed at the front of the house. Like the rest of the place it was huge and bleak. The bedding felt damp to the touch. She was conscious now, though still desperately white, but she smiled at her husband.

"I'm sorry, Gregg," she said so faintly that Brade hardly heard her. "I'll be all right now. Let me rest—I'm very—tired—" The small voice broke on a sob.

Brade turned away. Gregg MacFarlane was on his knees beside the bed. He looked like a man kneeling before an altar. He held Faith's hands very gently. His shoulders were shaking. He said over and over: "Forgive me, Faith—please forgive me. It was my fault. I should not have said it—I might have killed you—forgive me—"

Then Faith MacFarlane lifted weakly on an elbow, leaned forward and touched her husband's face. Her strong little hand rested on it like a benediction. Through tears her eyes sought his, clung pathetically.

"Forgive?" she whispered. "Oh—Gregg—" She fell back. Gregg stood up, pulling a blanket over her. Mrs. Maybrick had a fire going in the grate. It threw a ruddy glow over the funereal black furniture. She dusted her hands together and turned toward the door. Brade said curtly:

"Stay with Mrs. MacFarlane, Maybrick. We are leaving."

MacFarlane turned swiftly. "You're wrong, Captain Brade," he said. "I am not—leaving—my wife."

Brade stepped close to him. "All Mrs. MacFarlane needs is rest, quiet, and a stimulant which Maybrick can bring. I need some information from you which is to help solve murder. How about it?"

MacFarlane's hand clenched, but Faith spoke from the bed. "Do as Captain Brade wishes, Gregg," she urged. "Please—for my—sake."

He turned to look down at her. Brade watched from the shadows. There was angry indecision in MacFarlane's glance. Pleading in Faith's and something else, a very definite warning.

The two men went out. Brade gave Maybrick her instructions. She was to fetch some brandy from below stairs, hot-water bottles, extra blankets, and she was to stay with Mrs. MacFarlane until she was relieved. She agreed grouchily.

CHAPTER SEVEN
ONE SHOT!

BACK IN THE MORNING room MacFarlane faced Brade again. "Let's get it over," he said. "What else do you want to know?"

"The real reason for your coming here to-night."

"I've told you."

"No. Your statement was untrue."

Hard and bleak, Brade's eyes. Hot and furious, MacFarlane's. They faced each other like two wrestlers, stripped for battle. About them was the same tense wariness, the same professional appraisal of the opponent, the alertness for advantage, the obvious determination to battle to the death. Faith MacFarlane's going had removed the last barrier.

MacFarlane laughed. "Liar, eh? That's me, Brade?"

"Yes, if you persist in your story about coming up to borrow a book. Why did you come?"

"To borrow a book."

"All right. Let it ride at that. I don't believe you, if you're interested in my reaction."

"I'm not."

"That's okay by me, too. How many times, in the course of fifteen years, do you suppose you've come into this house by the front door?"

"I'm not a mathematician. Hundreds, I suppose."

"Exactly. I've only entered once, yet if I should come again, I would ring the bell, not knock. Why didn't you ring?"

"I don't see what you're getting at."

"You can understand my question. Answer it."

MacFarlane straightened a corner of the rug with his shoe tip. "No," he said, "I can't answer it, because I don't know. I just walked up the steps, crossed the porch and knocked."

"Instead of ringing?"

"Instead of ringing."

Brade smiled. "I'll tell you why you did it, MacFarlane," he said. "Because you didn't want anyone to answer that door at your summons. You knew that no one would hear that tap. You wanted to come in unannounced, which you did. You didn't want your visit advertised. A man doesn't when he comes to talk to another man about unwelcome attentions to his wife."

MacFarlane's lean dark face whitened. His somber eyes flared wide, flashed hate at the detective. Then he said thickly:

"You're being a damned cad, Brade. You've met my—wife—talked to her. How can you—drag her name through the mud like this? Suggest—"

Brade shook his head gently. "Mrs. MacFarlane was not to blame for what Jurden Keye did, MacFarlane. Isn't it true that he'd always—admired her—"

"Admire! That beast! His admiration, as you call it, would be an insult to any decent woman."

"Yes? Pretty bad, wasn't he? All right, and you quite naturally resented his—admiration for your wife. I don't blame you. I'd have likely called on him, too, especially as people were talking about his forcing her to walk out from town with him yesterday afternoon—"

"Who told you that?"

"Never mind. And as she had just received a rather expensive gift of roses from a florist in the city with his card."

"I wouldn't have him sending her—gifts." MacFarlane said hoarsely.

"Quite correct in that, I think. But this story about a book, it doesn't go down well, not with relations what they were between you and Jurden Keye. Better come clean and admit that you came up here to-night for an understanding with him—that—"

MacFarlane turned abruptly to the window, jerked back the curtain and stood there staring out into the night. Brade lighted a cigarette and waited. There was a grim, satisfied smile on his lips. He knew people. Men and women. MacFarlane, with his passionate reverent devotion to his wife, his archaic chivalry, would not take Jurden Keye's attentions to her easily. Part of what he had told him, Brade had guessed at. The facts he had gleaned from a swift conversation with Tom Gary. He inhaled smoke and waited.

MacFarlane said over his shoulder: "All right, Brade, you win. I came up to tell Jurden Keye that if he ever so much as looked at my wife again, I'd smash his rotten face for him. I didn't even knock. I didn't want it known I'd been here. I didn't want Maybrick gossiping all over town. So I looked through the glass, saw the hall was deserted, opened the door as softly as I could and came in. The rest is exactly as I've told it."

"Thanks," Brade said. "It always helps when people tell the truth. And now—"

There came a knocking on the door. Brade opened it. Tom Gary stood there, extending a piece of crumpled white paper.

"Jimmy Arnold found this in the grounds, Captain Brade," he said. "And in the excitement and all it slipped his mind until just now. He brought it in to me. I thought you'd want to see it."

Brade took the paper, stepped back into the room, leaned under the light, frowning at it. Tom Gary followed him. Gregg MacFarlane turned from the window. The paper was a thick heavy white with a small blue monogram stamped in one corner. There was a message written on it, unsigned and unaddressed. The writing was small, cramped, tight looking. Brade read:

> If you want to avert complete disaster, come to see me to-night at ten o'clock. I mean business and I will do everything I say. Also, I can save you if you will listen to me. I'll expect you.

"In the grounds, you say, Gary?" Brade asked absently, smoothing the paper.

"Yes, sir. Over by the northeast corner. He was shootin' his flash around lookin' for tracks and he saw this. What do you make of it?"

There was a gleam of excitement in the constable's eyes. He glanced past Brade to Gregg MacFarlane, who had been bending over the note as Brade held it.

Brade looked at MacFarlane. The man's face was twitching. It shone with sweat for all the room was unpleasantly cold.

"Recognize that writing?" Brade asked whichever one of the two men could answer.

Tom Gary started to say something, stopped as MacFarlane cut in. "Yes, it's Jurden Keye's. That's his monogram there at the top, too."

"Yes? And there was no envelope, Gary, nothing to indicate who received it?"

The constable shook his head. "Just that, Captain Brade. It looks like someone dropped it."

"Yes," Brade said slowly. "Someone who came to keep the appointment, who lost the note as he left." He frowned thoughtfully. "It might have been the Garth girl—she said he invited her to come, then canceled the engagement—"

"Dallas?" Gregg MacFarlane asked. "It couldn't have been addressed to Dallas?"

"How did it get where Arnold found it?" Brade asked. "You said Dallas left by the front door—of course she might have come in across the grounds."

"I think not," MacFarlane said. "She told me she sent Jurden a note asking to see him. She sent it by a village boy who sometimes runs errands for me. Buddy Witherspoon. I know she did because he's been telling about it all over town—besides I don't think Jurden Keye knew his wife was in Willow Valley until he received her message."

Brade ran mentally over the people involved in this matter. Dallas Gantry. Opal Garth. The man, Frosty Rivet, who called himself Clay Alden. Gregg MacFarlane. . . .

None seemed to fit the picture. It didn't sound like a note Keye would send to a cheap little actress with whom he was temporarily amusing himself. It couldn't have been Dallas if what MacFarlane said was true. He glanced obliquely at MacFarlane, who was frowning at the note spread out on the table.

He recalled what Opal and Frosty Rivet had said about a blackmail scheme in which one Leo was involved and which Opal had shared with Jurden Keye.

He hooked his thumbs in his vest pockets and continued to stare at MacFarlane. The man was handsome in a queer, exhausted way. He had a fine head. A lean, forceful jaw. A strong grim mouth. His eyes were splendid. That queer white hair—what had seared MacFarlane's hair like that? Almost as if it had passed through fire. . . .

He wondered why he was staring at MacFarlane so intently. What there was about the man that intrigued him. Was it a hint of familiarity? That had struck him at the moment MacFarlane came in downstairs, earlier in the evening. He had decided he imagined it. Had he? He wished MacFarlane's hair was some other color—black, say, or very dark brown. How would he look then?

MacFarlane lifted his head, met the detective's intent gaze, colored faintly, straightened. "Do you mind, Captain Brade," he asked, "if I go to my wife for a few minutes? I'm worried about her."

Brade said: "Just a moment, MacFarlane, I want to figure something out." And he continued to study the man until the silence in the room grew oppressive and Tom Gary stirred uneasily. Wind rustled round the windows, scattering sere leaves to crackle against the glass. It whistled down the empty fireplace chimney, sending out a faint gray dust of dead ashes to float eerily round the room.

MacFarlane smiled: "Do I help you to concentrate, Brade?" he inquired politely. "If so, I'll stand perfectly still. You've been staring at me for five minutes."

Brade nodded. "Sorry," he said. "I was—thinking." He rumpled his thick hair. "Say you've lived here fifteen years, MacFarlane?"

"Yes."

"How'd you happen to pick this little place? I get funny notions about folks," he added in a pleasantly conversational tone, "you, now, I'd pick you as a city man."

MacFarlane said evenly: "I have lived in cities, Captain Brade. Maybe that's the reason Willow Valley appealed to me. There are advantages, you know."

"Yes? I wonder." Brade turned the massive silver ring thoughtfully. "Such as—" he asked.

"Quiet. Peace. Friendliness. The beauty of out-of-doors easily accessible. To be specific, I came here because of my wife's health. She is very strong really, but a—bad attack of pneumonia a long time ago left her with a weak heart. The doctors advised fresh air and lack of excitement. Willow Valley seemed to offer both. Anything else?"

Tom Gary, watching uneasily from the shadows by the door, thought he had never seen two men so tense and yet so easy-looking. The constable sensed the conflict between them. He didn't quite get it. They both smiled frequently. Their voices were low. Their manner pleasant—yet he wouldn't have been surprised to see them suddenly leap at each other's throats. MacFarlane's hands were clenched by his sides. It was the only outward sign of tension about him. Brade's left leg was extended slightly as he leaned against the wall. Where the cloth of his trouser was jerked tight about it Tom caught the flexing of a long muscle.

"Anything else?" Brade repeated MacFarlane's question. "Yes," he said slowly. "There's one other question. When you've answered that, MacFarlane, I'll be through with you to-night. You may do what you like."

MacFarlane bowed. "Thanks," he said, "and the question?"

Brade's lips opened, but no question came. From somewhere in the great silent house came the sharp crack of a shot!

CHAPTER EIGHT
WHAT MAYBRICK SAW

GREGG MACFARLANE kicked over a chair as he lunged for the door. Brade was close behind him and the constable followed, but MacFarlane was already up the stairs before they reached the foot.

As Brade streaked up, the hall door behind him opened and he heard a man's voice saying something excitedly but he did not pause. He rounded the newel post into the upper hall of Willow Wilde and rushed head on into someone standing there, clinging to it.

"Oh," he said breathlessly, "I'm sorry, Miss Gantry. What's happened? There was a shot—"

Dallas Gantry turned slowly to look at him. "Yes," she said. "Opal's been hurt—shot, I think. You can see—there she is—"

"Dallas!" Anthony Gordon called and stumbled to a pause beside her. He was bare-headed and his face was flushed as if he had been walking rapidly in the night air. Dallas put out a hand toward him.

"She's—been—shot, Anthony," she gasped. "You can see her—there—on—the floor—"

Brade was trained in the valuable art of observation. His mind was keyed to catch every small detail of a scene with startling clarity, while he registered the more salient points. So that when he bent over the crumpled figure on the floor there in the hall of Willow Wilde, he knew that Opal Garth was dead, that she had been shot behind the right ear and lay face down, arms outflung—pointed toward the stair well.

93

He saw all that as he noted that Gregg MacFarlane had disappeared into his wife's room which was three doors down the hall, that Maybrick, the housekeeper, was standing in the open door of that room, clinging to it for support, and that Frosty Rivet was sneaking along the hall away toward the rear stairs.

"Rivet!" Brade snapped.

He leaped up, hand bulging his pocket. Frosty Rivet stopped with a low whine of fear and rage, turned, glared at the detective and sulked slowly back. The man's face was working and his slanted, red-rimmed eyes were feverish.

"I didn't do it," he chattered. "Let me go. I ain't done anything."

"Get him, Gary," Brade directed quietly, and as the big constable collared Rivet, Brade asked slowly: "How does it happen that you're all up here? I thought I told you—" He frowned at Gary. "I gave you the job of keeping them quiet, Gary," he said.

Gary swallowed. "And I did, Captain Brade," he explained. "Then when Jimmy brought that note in I thought you ought to see it and I—"

Brade nodded. "I see," he snapped. "And the minute you left they all scattered." His eyes went coldly round the group. "Who knows why Opal Garth came upstairs?" he demanded.

No one answered. Brade shrugged, jerked the covering from a couch near the wall and spread it over the body. His eyes went swiftly round the hall, searching for a gun. There was none that he could see.

"Well," he said, glancing at the covered body, "she can't speak for herself—can any of the rest of you tell me why you're up here? You, Anthony! Where have you been?"

"Out for a breath of air," Anthony said clearly. "I was walking on the path before the house when I heard the shot."

Brade was studying him curiously. "All right," he said, "and you, Dallas Gantry?"

Dallas had removed her little hat and her dull gold hair lay in thick moist waves around her white face. Her eyes, like brown pansy leaves, were strained and bright.

She said: "When I heard that Faith was ill—"

"Who told you?

"Why—why—Maybrick. She came in to get some liquor from the sideboard. She said Mrs. MacFarlane had fainted—that she was up-stairs—and when Tom went out I just had to see her—so I came up—"

"All right, then what?"

Dallas lifted tired eyes to look at him. She wondered dully why this man with the cloudy eyes, the firm, sometimes gentle mouth, the gray-stained hair, why Captain Courtney Brade should be so interested in murder. Why he should be here like a lean greyhound continually on the scent.

She said slowly: "I didn't know where Faith was. Which room, I mean. I thought it might be the old guest room, down there—" She motioned to the far end of the hall on the other side of the stair well. "I opened many doors but did not find her. I was in that room," again the gesture behind her, "the third from the stairs, when I heard a door slam—"

"Where?"

"I don't know, exactly. Up here some place."

"Hear anything else?"

"Yes. I heard Opal say—"

A sharp cry cut her short. It came from the open door of the room where Faith MacFarlane had rested. Gregg's voice sounded: "Faith! Faith! Lie still, be quiet—Faith—"

But the agonized cry came again and Faith MacFarlane stumb-led into the hall, face as white as that of the dead woman, one hand pressed against her breast. She took half a dozen blind, uncertain steps, stopped, leaned heavily against the wall. Gregg was just be-hind her, arms hovering over her. She was sobbing brokenly and her eyes were fastened on the covered body of the dead girl.

"Oh, I heard her," she moaned. "I heard her, but I couldn't rouse. I must have been in a stupor of some sort. It was like a nightmare—"

"What did she say?" Brade demanded sharply, to break through her rising hysteria.

Faith looked at him dazedly, shook her head. "I heard her plead-ing with someone—not to kill her—over and over she was saying: 'Don't shoot me. Oh, for God's sake don't shoot me—I didn't mean it—I won't tell—' You see, Captain Brade, I heard that so clearly, but I couldn't move. It was terrible—" She pressed shaking hands across her eyes. Gregg put an arm around her, drew her close.

"Hush, Faith," he soothed in a voice that trembled. "You can tell them later—please—Faith—"

But for once Faith pushed her husband's arms away. "Let me go on," she choked. "I've got to tell it—get it off my—mind—it's driving me mad."

Brade caught her fluttering hands, held them tight and quiet in his, looked down into her suffering eyes and said very, very gently:

"Easy, Faith MacFarlane, take it easy. Where's your courage now? That strength you've kept with you all these years? This is the time to use it. Steady. Quiet. It will all be better after a while—" His voice was low, monotonous, almost hypnotic.

Under its spell, Faith gradually quieted. The shaking of her body passed. Her lips became steady again, her eyes clear and strong. She still hung hard to his hands as though she would absorb his splendid vitality for her own need, and slowly she nodded and then smiled faintly into his eyes.

"Thank you, Captain Brade," she said. "I'm all right now. I don't usually let go like this."

"I know. Don't bother to explain. Bring her a chair, MacFarlane. That's better. Mrs. MacFarlane, do you want to talk to me now or would you rather—"

"Now," she said clearly. "I'll talk now though I think I've told you all I know. Just that I seemed to be in a stupor, bound hand and foot, unable to stir but with my mind terribly clear, and I heard this girl—pleading with someone not to kill her. She wasn't talking very loud, or so it seemed to me, but her voice penetrated to me distinctly. And still, I was unable to stir until I heard—the shot— then something snapped inside me and I didn't know anything until Gregg lifted me from the bed—" She shut her lips hard and Brade saw her eyes flare wide.

"Thank you," he said. "There is nothing else you can tell?"

"Nothing," she said.

He turned to Dallas. "You were saying—" he suggested.

Dallas pushed heavy hair from her eyes. "I heard the door slam and Opal say: 'Don't kill me—I won't tell—' then there was a shot and she screamed."

"You don't know to whom she was speaking? You didn't hear another voice?"

"No. Only what I've told you. I was—paralyzed—for a moment—I couldn't stir out of the room—"

"Not until the shot? That brought you out?"

She nodded. "Yes," she said, and stopped at the sound of a low, grating laugh.

Brade turned quickly. Mrs. Maybrick was standing flat and square against the wall, hands firmly planted on thick hips. Gray hair had become disarranged and fallen into her eyes. She said, looking at Dallas:

"Why don't you ask what *I* saw, Mr. Policeman? I was up here, you know."

"Yes," Brade said. "You were up here and where were you? If you had obeyed my instructions, you would have been with Mrs. MacFarlane, you would have heard the girl's pleading, you might have been able to tell me something."

"Oh, I can tell you plenty," Maybrick said dryly, and she never took her eyes from Dallas Gantry's face. Watching that heavy red countenance, those small, venomous eyes, Dallas' lips went gray, she took an uncertain step backward and Anthony slipped a protecting arm around her, angry glance on Maybrick's face.

"I can tell you plenty," Maybrick went on, "and here it is: I left Mrs. MacFarlane sleeping, and went to get an extra blanket. Down there," she pointed to the shadowy hall behind her. "There's the linen closet and there's where I went. I had the door open and I was inside when I heard someone talking out here in the hall. I looked to see who it was. It was this girl"—she pointed at the shrouded figure on the floor—"and—her." A thick, accusing finger was leveled at Dallas. "Oh, you needn't look so sick, my lady," she snapped. "I seen you, all right, and I heard you."

"You heard me talking to Opal?" Dallas gasped. "Why, I never saw her, I didn't know she was up here—"

Maybrick's dry lips curled. She disregarded the interruption. "That—woman"—she nodded toward Dallas—"she was talking to Opal, and all of a sudden she jerked a gun and that's when Opal began beggin' for her not to kill her. I was that overcome I couldn't move," she said to Brade. "I couldn't believe my eyes, and Opal turned and started to run toward me, and that—woman—shot her, then she ran the other way and into a room—and you all came."

Anthony Gordon set Dallas aside and reached Maybrick's side in three long strides. "Every word of that is a lie, and you know it," he snapped. "Why should Dallas kill her. Why?"

Maybrick glanced at him through puffy lids. "Because the girl knew that she had stabbed the master," she declared bluntly. "And that she would go on the stand and tell about it."

Anthony's face whitened. Brade laid a hand on his shoulder. "Let me handle this, Anthony," he ordered quietly. "Look after Dallas." He faced the housekeeper. "Mrs. Maybrick," he said, "please step into this room," he opened a door on his right. "You have furnished me valuable testimony and I wish to get further details—in private."

Maybrick glared at him suspiciously, then with a triumphant grin she marched into the room. Brade said to Tom Gary: "Take these people downstairs and see that they stay in one place this time. I'll join you soon."

"I say, Brade," Anthony called excitedly, "you aren't swallowing what that woman says about Dallas, are you? You aren't going to—"

Brade stopped him with an uplifted hand. In the dim glow of light from the overhead fixture, his face was grim set and very hard.

"Anthony," he replied, "it is my duty to find the murderer of Opal Garth. This is not a time to let personal feelings interfere. Please do as Gary directs."

And he went in, closing the door very definitely on the stricken faces in the hall, blurring Faith MacFarlane's choked sobbing.

Dallas stood head high, eyes very bright, staring at the closed door. Anthony laid a hand on her arm. She pushed it gently away.

"Anthony," she said in a hard, tight voice. "This Captain Brade of yours evidently thinks I am a murderess. He doesn't know how terribly Maybrick always hated me, how she'd literally sell her soul to ruin me—"

Brade, on the other side of the door, had one ear pressed against the panels. At Dallas' words, a queer little smile twitched his lips, but Maybrick was over by the window and did not see; when she faced him, he was very serious.

"Now, Mrs. Maybrick," he began in that charming way of his which made his listener, even a fat unlovely old woman like Maybrick, suddenly feel honored and important, "I want to ask you a few questions, then I'll permit you to retire. The night has been trying for you. You must be exhausted."

To his immense surprise, Maybrick stared straight into his unreadable eyes, and her thick red face began to quiver like jelly, and down her roughened cheeks tears rolled in big bright globules, to lose themselves in the heavy folds of her chin.

"It's been terrible," she choked, "terrible, what it has. With that—woman—comin'—that—" She checked herself on the hateful word she longed to utter. Something in Brade's face warned her. She dabbed her eyes, sniffed audibly. "The master's goin'," she sobbed, "it hit me hard, Captain Brade." And Brade, studying her through narrowed lids, could not doubt her sincerity.

"He was a good—master, Maybrick?" he asked gently.

She nodded. "He was—wonderful, sir. Wonderful! There's them that said he was hard, and maybe he was. They said he—he wasn't all he should be but to me he was—" She stopped, grinding heavy knuckles into her eyes.

"Yes?" Brade urged. "He was—to you—"

She lifted her head, gazed at him unseeingly for a moment and in that moment Martha Maybrick came very near beauty. Something deeply buried within her glowed to life and the glory of it transfigured her thick, ugly body, her heavy common face, until she stood there, suddenly radiant.

"He was—everything to me," she breathed as if she were speaking in confessional, and Brade marveled anew at the unending miracles of human nature.

"You had been with him a long time?" he asked.

"Since I was a girl," she said. "You mayn't think it, sir, but I was uncommon pretty at eighteen when I came to work at Willow Wilde. I was slim," her glance shot down over her shapeless body, "I was young. I had red cheeks and I was white as milk. My hair was brown and it reached below my waist—" She sighed heavily. "I was uncommon pretty," she repeated. "And I could 'a' had my pick of the young 'uns around the countryside but—" She stopped, frowning at a distant corner, and Brade watched her, wondering what shattered dreams she saw, what bright and shadowed days she was reliving, then she dried her eyes and looked at him. "Now I'm ready," she stated. "I'll tell you anything you want to know."

Brade nodded, smiling slightly. He rather thought she would, especially if what he wanted to know promised the destruction of Dallas Gantry.

"You were in the linen closet, is that right, when you heard voices in the hall?"

"Yes, sir."

"Did you recognize those voices?"

"I recognized that—"

"Just refer to her as Miss Gantry," Brade suggested.

"That ain't what I'd like to call her, but I recognized—Miss Gantry's voice. I wasn't sure about the other until I looked."

"All right, and how were they standing? Think carefully now. This is important."

"The Gantry woman was facing me," Maybrick said flatly, "that's how I got such a good look at her. The other girl had her back toward me."

"Yes? And then Miss Gantry pulled the gun, and Opal Garth started to run—which way?"

"Toward me," Maybrick said, the creases deepening in her forehead. "She turned and started to run toward me."

"And Dallas Gantry was still facing you so you could see her clearly with the gun in her hand?"

"Yes."

"Then she fired and Opal fell in her tracks, didn't she? With a wound like that—"

"She fell like a rock," Maybrick said solemnly. "She stopped like something had hit her, threw up her hands and down she went—"

"Did you see what Miss Gantry did with the gun?"

Maybrick's eyes flicked. "She had it in her hand when she ran—"

"She ran the other way, past the stairhead, into that room on the other side?"

"She did that. With the poor girl lyin' there in her own blood, dead by the same hand that killed—"

"Just a moment, Mrs. Maybrick," Brade's voice snapped like a pistol shot. He was leaning forward a bit and the light glinted on his eyes, suddenly hard and bright as polished metal. "Just a moment," he repeated. "I want to ask you one more question."

Maybrick's thick body stiffened as if she sensed approaching doom. She hunched back into the chair, hands clenched in the folds of her bright knitted jacket.

"What is it?" she said hoarsely. "What is it you would ask?"

"Why—do you hate Dallas Gantry so completely that you would lie with this much thoroughness in order to send her to the electric chair for a crime she did not commit?"

Maybrick's face went patchy white. Her lips sucked in with the force of her strangled breathing. "I ain't lyin'—" she gasped. "I seen it—I seen her shoot—that girl—I—"

Brade shook his head. "Human observation is notoriously undependable," he said more to himself than to her. "I covered the body when I first came on the scene. You should have looked more carefully, Maybrick, used your senses more effectively. By your own words you have condemned yourself, proven yourself a vicious liar—" He reached her side in two long strides, stood there, implacable, over her cringing, shivering body.

"You had Dallas Gantry face toward you in this fanciful story so you could swear to her identity. Your mind worked logically when you had Opal Garth turn, to run from threatened death. It is what you would have done. What I would have done. What ninety-nine out of a hundred would have done—but you made one grave mistake. Opal Garth was shot as she ran the other way, toward the stairhead and not toward the linen closet where you claim you were standing. With a bullet entering the brain from the rear as it did, she would fall forward, which she did, and her head is pointed toward the stairs. Now"—Brade bent lower over the cringing woman—"what did you see when you stood there in the linen closet? What is the real story behind the shooting of Opal Garth?"

Mrs. Maybrick wiped sweat from her face, lifted her head and looked straight and hard at him. "Captain Brade," she said in a flat level tone, "you're a very clever policeman. You can twist the words of an old woman any way you like but you might as well know this. When this case is tried in the courts of this land, I'll go on the stand and I'll tell my story, and my story will be that I with my own two eyes saw Dallas Gantry shoot Opal Garth to death in the upper hall of Willow Wilde and I defy you or any smart lawyer to prove me a liar."

She nodded definitely, and behind her sunken bloodshot eyes was such a tremendous force of savage determination, such a controlled weight of hate for the woman she swore to destroy that Brade had a momentary feeling of complete helplessness, as though he stood face to face with a granite mountain which he had to move with his two bare hands.

"You may go," he said.

She got up, walked stiffly toward the door, without a backward glance.

CHAPTER NINE
THE BRONZE CLUE

BRADE WAITED UNTIL she had disappeared, then he tapped out a cigarette, set it between his lips and stopped in the act of striking a match. Somewhere was a low, subdued sobbing! It was muffled and faint, but through it ran such an undercurrent of grief that Brade stood there motionless, eyes fastened on the blank expanse of a tall, narrow door, communicating with the next room. Swiftly he calculated. That would be the room where Faith MacFarlane had gone to rest. . . .

He stepped close to it, listening. Just that strangled, broken sound of agony. He could almost see her crouching against the bed, face buried in her hands, small body shaking with the force of her grief. A door opened, closed. The crying stopped abruptly. Gregg MacFarlane said:

"Drink this tea, Faith. It will strengthen you. I want to take you home, little pigeon. This is too much for you."

And to Brade's astonishment, Faith answered in a clear, almost cheerful tone, devoid of tears, "Thank you so much, Gregg. And I think we'll be allowed to go home very soon. It's nearly morning, isn't it?"

Brade went downstairs. He walked soundlessly past the door behind which MacFarlane and his wife waited. They wanted to go home? He smiled grimly. Well, they wouldn't—for a while. In the lower hall the coroner had arrived. He had come to Willow Wilde immediately upon reaching home from a long, hard country trip.

Dr. Monery was a wrinkled little gnome of a man with sharp bright eyes and very strong, beautiful hands. He had been physician, counselor, friend to most of the people in the county since he was a young man. He had guarded them through sickness, helped them in financial difficulties, attended their weddings, their funerals, brought their babies into the world. He looked rather tired, the little doctor, and there was a crease of anxiety between his bushy gray brows because of the tragedy that brought him to Willow Wilde.

After his examination of Keye's body, Brade requested the knife which he wished to send to his department in the city for finger printing. Then he took the doctor upstairs where Opal Garth lay under her shabby, dusty covering. The doctor shook his head.

"This is bad, Captain Brade, very bad," he said. "Jurden Keye was a hard man, he lived two lives, and in his passing he has taken others down with him."

Brade nodded somberly, wondering how many more would be sucked into the maelstrom of death and destruction into which Jurden Keye had vanished. The doctor gently rolled the body of the murdered woman to one side, the pucker of anxiety between his eyes deepening, then he bent down, lips pursed in a soundless whistle.

"Look here, Captain," he said softly. "Have you examined this?"

Brade dropped to a knee beside him. "I didn't touch things," he said. "Oh, what have we?"

He was staring at a heavy bronze object that had lain concealed under Opal's body. It glistened dully in the light and Brade saw that it was one of a pair of book-ends, the beautifully modeled figure of a dancer, lithe body bent backward, metal hair a flame of brightness, slim arms following the curve of the body.

He rumpled his hair thoughtfully. "Now where did that come from?" he muttered.

Dr. Monery was squatting down, frowning at the thing. "She might have picked it up, somewhere—" he suggested.

Brade glanced at him quickly. "Someone threatened her life," he said. "I have that from the testimony of witnesses. Suppose," he constructed slowly, "when she first realized her danger, she grabbed this thing as a weapon of defense, still clung to it when she ran for her life along this corridor and when she fell with a bullet in her brain, it dropped here where her body covered it."

"I think it quite reasonable," Dr. Monery said. He pulled excitedly at his sharp little goatee. "This ought to narrow things down for you," he went on. "Find what room this came from—"

"I don't know that it was a room. Dallas Gantry said she heard a door slam, but the incident which ended in Opal Garth's murder might have occurred here in the hall." He raked its shadows with sharp hard eyes. "Besides," he went on, "which room the book-end came from won't prove too much. None of the rooms are occupied up here, legitimately, that is. Still, I'd be glad to know—"

He got up, crossed to the first door on his right, opened it and snapped on the light. A quick survey showed him there were no book-ends there. No books, in fact.

Two more yielded the same results. In one of the bedrooms stiff volumes were held in place by bookends of painted wood. He paused outside the room where Faith MacFarlane was resting, tapped lightly.

Gregg opened the door. His face was haggard. His eyes bloodshot.

"Excuse me," Brade said with his usual courtesy, "I'd like to take a look round if I may."

Gregg stepped aside. Faith was lying on the bed, eyes closed.

"She's asleep," MacFarlane explained, "will you be as quiet as you can?"

"Certainly. I just want to find out—" Brade was walking slowly round the room, eyes busy. He completed the circle, came back to the door. "Thank you," he said, "that's all. I was looking for the mate to this." He extended the book-end which he held very carefully by the extreme tip of the base. "I see that the books in this room are stacked on the lower shelf of the table."

He went out. "Maybrick ought to know," he said to the doctor. "Where's her room?"

"Around the bend in that far corridor. I've been to see her once or twice."

Brade left the doctor finishing his examination and walked quietly down to the housekeeper's door, tapped and waited. She was a long time opening. When she saw him, her face hardened. She had on a thick cotton flannel night dress under a lumpy-looking bathrobe. Her gray hair was braided in a thin pigtail down her shoulders.

"What do you want?" she demanded.

"What room did this come from?" Brade extended the book-end.

She asked defiantly: "What you want to know for?"

"That," Brade assured her, "is none of your business, but I don't mind telling you that it was found beneath Opal Garth's body. I think she grabbed it up in an effort to protect herself. Now—where did it come from?"

Mrs. Maybrick leaned forward, staring hard at the book-end. Brade was looking down on the top of her head, on the quarter-sized spot where the hair had thinned and the pale pink scalp shone through. He couldn't see her face, but he did see that little scrap of skin go a bright red, then she lifted her head, gazed at him stolidly.

"I don't know," she said.

Brade set the book-end carefully on a small table beside the door, shoved his hands into his pockets and grinned down at her. The grin wasn't exactly pleasant.

"Mrs. Maybrick," he said, "you're a woman of reasonable intelligence. You are, I should say, at risk of mortal offense, right next door to sixty. By your own statement you came to this house when you were eighteen. That means you've been here better than forty years. And yet—" he went on slowly, "you insult my intellect by standing there and telling me you don't know from which room in this house an object is taken. Now let's start all over again and see if we can't get somewhere. That bookend belongs in Willow Wilde, I suppose?"

She was glaring at him. Her lips twitched. "Yes," she said hoarsely. "It belongs here. It belonged to that—Gantry woman— the master married. She would have an—indecent—thing like that around. I'd have thrown it away but he wouldn't let me

"I quite understand your antipathy to it," Brade assured her pleasantly. "But what I'm trying to find out is where it stood. Which room contained it. And don't waste any more time pretending you don't know. You took care of this house. You dusted and swept and arranged. Where was the pair of bronze book-ends? Where did it stand? Which room? Come alive now. Speak snappy."

He longed to twist her thick, stubborn old neck. She stood there so stolidly defying him. He knew that she knew where the thing had come from. It didn't make sense that she couldn't remember. She knew and she wouldn't tell because it didn't fit into her pattern of hate and revenge against Dallas Gantry. Brade reflected luridly on the advantages of torture.

Mrs. Maybrick raised her eyes and regarded him blandly. There was even the hint of a secret smile somewhere about her. "I'm terribly sorry, Captain Brade," she stated, "but I just can't tell you which room that book-end came from. You see, the house has been rearranged so much, I tried to keep it fresh and pleasant, the thing was first one place and another. I just couldn't say."

Brade seized the book-end and stalked away, leaving her standing there by the door, talking after him. His cheeks were hot and his eyes blazed. A fat unpleasant old woman in a small stupid town far from the whirling city had completely routed Captain Courtney Brade, headquarters division, Metropolitan Police.

Maybrick watched his tall, erect form out of sight around the turn and closed the door of her room, chuckling to herself.

As Brade stepped into the main corridor from which the body of Opal Garth had been removed, he came face to face with a man he had never seen before. Brade stopped abruptly, head lowered, frowning at the stranger.

"Hello," he said, "who're you?"

The man had paused uncertainly by the stairhead, now he stood nervously turning a soft dark hat in his hand and regarded Brade with mingled surprise and timidity. He was a tall man, very thin, and he wore a long black overcoat of rough-looking material, with a collar of Astrakhan which must once have been fine. Now it was badly worn, there were bare patches on it, the coat itself was shiny at the seams. The man's shoes were carefully blackened, but the covering could not prevent the cracks from showing. He had a delicate, handsome face, seamed with many fine lines. His eyes were rather faded and entirely hopeless. His sensitive mouth smiled easily. He had fine teeth. His hair was thick and iron-gray.

He said: "I'm Tomlinson Shannon, better known as Tam O'Shannon. I'm owner and manager of the show troupe which has been showing here and I'm looking for Captain Brade."

"Yes?" Brade was studying Shannon curiously. Tom Gary had confided to him his theory that the showman might have murdered Jurden Keye as reprisal for Keye's activities in closing the stand. "Well, I'm Brade," the detective said. "How did you get here and what can I do for you?"

Shannon smiled apologetically. Everything about him, in fact, was slightly apologetic, as if he had been hit so hard and so often, kicked and cuffed so relentlessly, that most of his spirit was gone.

He said: "I just opened the door downstairs and came in. I didn't meet anyone but I heard voices behind one of the doors and I listened. I wanted very much to get in touch with whoever was conducting the investigation up here, without attracting attention. So when I heard your name mentioned as having the matter in charge, and also that you were somewhere above stairs, I just came up. Could I have a few words in private with you?"

Brade opened a door to his left, snapped on the light. "Come in here," he invited and stood aside for Shannon to enter, then followed, closed the door and leaned against it. "All right," he said. "What's on your mind?"

Tam O'Shannon was standing uneasily in the center of the big bleak room. His eyes flitted nervously from object to object. He moistened his lips, said in a very low voice:

"Mr. Keye was murdered, wasn't he?"

"Yes. What do you know of it?"

"Oh! Nothing! That is, not actually. I heard about it. It's all over town and I got to thinking of something and it was hard to make up my mind, but I finally decided it was my duty—"

"It certainly was," Brade said crisply. "And what do you know?"

"It may not be of the slightest importance, Captain Brade," Shannon said slowly, a certain new dignity in his bearing as he found himself in the familiar position of stage center, "but I understand that one of my men, a chap from my company, also a girl, are somehow implicated. Clay Alden, Opal Garth. Is that correct?"

"Very much so."

Shannon breathed deeply, took a fresh start. "What I have to tell you, sir, is merely a conversation which I overheard through the walls of the theater dressing-room no later than to-night, last night I guess it would be now. The conversation took place between Miss Garth and Clay Alden."

"All right. And it was?"

"I won't attempt to repeat it to you *verbatim*. I shall merely give you the gist of it. They had recognized someone in this town as—being somehow very important—"

"How do you mean that? Important?"

"I don't know exactly. Except that they expected to get some money from this person."

Brade's eyes narrowed. Blackmail! There had been something about blackmail in that conversation between Opal and Frosty which he had arranged to overhear.

"Did they mention the person's name?"

"Not exactly. I think they referred to him as Andy—"

"All right, go on."

"It seemed to be a question of identity, that is, of proving the identity, and I gathered that Alden, at the advice of Miss Garth, had sent for a former associate of the girls, who for some reason they thought could furnish the necessary identification."

"Did you get his name?"

"Leo. That is all. They kept talking about Leo. Leo, it seems, arrived in town to-night. Alden had met him at the station. Leo apparently had seen the person in question and unqualifiedly confirmed their suspicions. So the stage was set."

"For what?"

"The culmination of this blackmail act. I regret, Captain Brade, to have to use such harsh language, especially about people in my employ, but I considered it my duty—"

"That's right. Let's go on. What then?"

"I gathered," Shannon said diffidently, "that Opal Garth had disclosed the facts in this case to Jurden Keye." The old actor glanced away uncomfortably. "Jurden Keye," he said stiffly, "insisted on the closing of my show, claiming it had a bad influence on the community, then in secret he was—"

"I know," Brade said grimly. "I know quite a bit about Jurden Keye. You say Opal had told Keye. And what was the result of that?"

"Keye, oddly enough, had insisted on handling the thing himself. Alden was very angry about it, but Opal thought it wiser that way. Keye had told Opal that he would take care of the arrangements, naming the price for their silence and so on and that he intended doing it to-night. I thought—"

Brade nodded briefly. He was remembering that note picked up in the grounds, the note Jurden Keye had written to someone. Threatening in tone: "If you want to avert complete disaster come to see me. . . . I mean business and I will do everything I say. . . . I can save you if you will listen to me. . . ."

He stared thoughtfully at Tam O'Shannon, reflecting that if he knew to whom that note was addressed, he would have the solution to two murders. "What else?" he asked.

"That's about all, except that the Garth girl and Alden ended up in a furious quarrel, the subject being this man Keye's interest in her. Alden used some very dangerous language, sir."

"Such as?"

"He—he—" Shannon turned his hat nervously. "He actually threatened to kill Mr. Keye! He said: 'I'll bump that bozo, so help me God, if you don't stay away from him—' Then Opal tried to quiet him by telling him that Keye had written her not to come to the house to-night as they had previously planned, and Alden finally went away grumbling. Opal left the opera house after the conclusion of her part in the show. She was seen slipping out the stage door still wearing her costume—then Alden disappeared shortly after—I can only suppose he came here."

"He did," Brade agreed, then he said slowly: "Opal Garth has been murdered too!"

Shannon's faded eyes opened wide. His face went a dull gray white. He stood there trembling visibly for a moment. "My God," he whispered. "Alden—he did it! I know he did; he—he swore to kill Keye—he—"

Brade said, "We have too many conflicting clues at present to form any definite conclusion, Mr. Shannon. I thank you for bringing this information to my attention and I will have to ask that you stay on hand for the inquest."

Shannon nodded, turned toward the door. He was still very white and shaken. Brade watched him curiously as he crossed the narrow hall, walking with a conscious, almost mechanical grace, and disappeared down the stairs. Men like Tam O'Shannon belonged to a class that was fast disappearing; their place taken by a new type that had its origin in the necessity for actors developed overnight. Younger, flashier, smarter men who would never be able to give to the grandest profession on earth that blind devotion, that desperate battle against long odds, that gay, courageous abandon that the old trouper offered as homage at a shrine he worshiped.

CHAPTER TEN
JIMMY OPENS A DRAWER

BRADE CLOSED THE DOOR and stood a moment, thinking. What Shannon had told him confirmed his own investigations. Namely, that Opal Garth, the man calling himself Alden, Frosty Rivet, one Leo and Jurden Keye, had entered into a combination of destruction against someone in Willow Valley.

Who? Whom had one of the actors seen and recognized? Who, that it was of sufficient importance to import Leo someone-or-other for purpose of identification? When he knew that. . . .

Swift-running steps approached and Brade turned to see young Jimmy Arnold pounding down on him from the other end of the hall. The boy's face was flushed with excitement and he paused, panting noisily.

"I been lookin' everywhere for you, sir," he said. "Y'see, I heard the shot and I came in the house, but stuck around mostly downstairs just in case any one should try to make a sneak—"

"Good boy, Jimmy," Brade praised. "You know what's happened up here then?"

"Yes, sir, I got it all from Tom. He's guardin' that actor chap and the others are in the library, but that ain't what I want to say—"

"All right, what is it?"

Jimmy heaved a great sigh. "I always thought I'd like to be a detective, sir," he explained rather diffidently and Brade noticed that he kept his hands carefully behind him and that he was actually quivering with the desire to tell something and at the same time make as much of it as possible. "I don't know very much about

112

it," Jimmy went on, "but I've read some books and—but here's what I want to tell you. I heard all about everything and what Maybrick said about Miss Dallas killin' the girl and then runnin' down to that there room"—he nodded back along the hall—"and so I just thought I'd look around some. So I went in and I found— this!"

He paused dramatically, looking at Brade with very bright eyes, then very slowly and impressively he brought a hand from behind him and extended it, holding a tiny blue-barreled Colt's automatic by his fingertips!

Brade's lips tightened. He stepped closer, staring at the weapon, but not touching it. ".25," he muttered, "ugly little brute; do plenty of damage at close range. You found that in the room where—"

"Where Miss Dallas said she was when the shot was fired," Jimmy explained breathlessly. "It was hidden too, sir. Clear at the back of a dresser drawer. I had to hunt a long time for it. Do you suppose—"

Brade wasn't exactly listening to young Arnold's suppositions. He was remembering Dallas saying she was in the third room from the stair well when the shot was fired. Hearing Maybrick's harsh voice in answer to his question:

"What did she do with the gun?"

"She had it in her hand when she ran—"

He took the weapon from Jimmy's careful grip. "All right, Jimmy," he said crisply, "you made an important discovery. Best keep quiet about it for the present. I'll send the thing along to be printed with the knife. Maybe that will tell us something."

Jimmy drew a deep breath. "Do you think, sir, that is—would Miss Dallas—"

"Jimmy Arnold," Brade said, wrapping the gun in a linen handkerchief, "if you're interested in becoming a detective the first thing you must learn is not to—think!" He smiled at the boy's wide-open astonished eyes. "By that I mean," Brade explained carefully, "you must learn not to form definite conclusions from fragmentary bits of evidence. In a crime of this sort, my son, in every crime, unless it is the work of a homicidal maniac and consequently unmotivated, unless it is committed by the professional killer, there is bound to be a clearly defined, sharply marked motive—clear, that is, once you can find it.

"You or I may not consider that motive sufficient warrant for killing. That has nothing to do with the matter. It was sufficient for the killer at the moment of commission of the crime. Once you find that motive your work is half done. Follow it intelligently and it will usually lead you to your criminal, but you must then build up an edifice of proof sufficiently strong to hold him.

"Consequently, it is your business as a detective to collect every bit of evidence you can, file it away, consider it, sort it and try your damnedest to keep your mind uncluttered with preconceived ideas. It is a difficult thing to do.

"Consider this case before us: Jurden Keye is stabbed. Opal Garth said she saw Dallas Gantry kill him. Dallas had a motive. Maybrick, the housekeeper, further strengthens Opal's testimony by stating that she also saw the murder through the medium of a keyhole. Opal Garth is killed. Again Maybrick says she saw the crime committed. Again Miss Gantry has a motive. To close the lips that could testify against her. Substantiating all this, you find the gun with which, no doubt, the second crime was committed, in the room where Maybrick claims to have seen Dallas disappear after the shooting, where it might be assumed a frightened, desperate woman would attempt to hide it."

Jimmy was hanging open-mouthed on the detective's words. His eyes were bulging and he nodded emphatically to every point Brade made. Brade, himself, was using this opportunity of arranging certain facts clearly before his own mind. He spoke quietly, clearly, concisely and behind him somewhere a door opened very slightly. He heard the click of the lock, checked his natural impulse to turn round and continued to build up his case against Dallas Gantry.

"Then you think," Jimmy gasped, "you really think Miss Dallas did it, sir?"

Brade smiled. "Jimmy, my boy," he said very low, "haven't I already told you not to—think? Now come along with me. I've got a job for you."

Jimmy followed eagerly. At the head of the stairs, they met Gregg MacFarlane carrying a tray with a freshly filled pot of tea.

"How is Mrs. MacFarlane?" Brade asked as he passed.

MacFarlane shook his head. "Badly upset," he said. "This is—actually dangerous for her, Captain Brade. When may we go home?"

Brade looked hard at him. "Try to be patient," he advised, "two people have been killed, you know."

Gregg nodded wearily and went on. Brade's glance followed him absently, then he carefully set the bronze book-end on the flat surface of the newel post.

"Jimmy," he said, "I believe that this is the object which the Garth girl seized from some convenient spot in an endeavor to save her life. Then she ran, still holding onto the thing, and when she was shot she fell on it. If I can find from what room she carried this, I stand a chance of getting some place. I have gone over all the rooms up here and I cannot find the mate. Why?"

He gazed at Jimmy through narrowed lids. "Because I think the murderer concealed it, when he realized he couldn't get the other one back. Now, I want you to go out in the grounds with a flashlight and search carefully along the front of the house and see if you can find the thing. I believe the murderer would naturally step to a window, jerk it open and throw the book-end out. What do you think?"

Jimmy nodded sagely. "I'll try, sir," he said. "I'll get right on the job. If it's there I'll bring it in."

"You'll do nothing of the sort," Brade snapped. "If it's there, you'll leave it exactly where you find it and get me. Then maybe we can form some opinion as to where it was thrown from."

Jimmy got the idea and clumped down the stairs. Brade stood up from his leaning position on the railing, ran fingers through his hair and stretched his long, strong arms above his head. He was physically tired, but mentally he was keyed high.

Brade responded to knotty problems. They stimulated his keen, high-powered brain to white-hot efficiency. Outwardly he was ice and steel, inside he burned with the intensity of the chase, the necessity of concentration, the constant driving of the intangible.

He shoved his hands into his pockets and frowned at the shadowy hall. He tried to train his subordinates in the business of logical deduction. He endeavored to convince himself that he followed it, in his work. He did, in minor matters, such as the business of the book-end. But in every case on which he had worked in his long years of police service, there was one moment on which he could definitely place a finger, when there came to him a blinding flash of comprehension, when, with a queer, uncanny instinct, he reached out, figuratively, and laid a hand on the murderer's shoulder.

Following that, there were sometimes days, weeks, months, when he plodded steadily on, building up his case, seeking hidden clues, deeply buried motives that would eventually culminate in open accusation and arrest. But all the time, down inside, he knew. There was that hateful, heavy knowledge in his mind. . . .

He scratched his chin. Did he know now who had murdered Jurden Keye? Opal Garth? Had the moment of illumination come? He shook his head. He'd have to keep on plodding, disregarding the suffering of those about him who were innocent, remaining adamant to the claims of friendship, the promptings of chivalry, forge on inexorably until the moment came, until the hand went out—

Downstairs a woman cried out sharply!

Brade whirled, making for the stairhead. Halfway down he paused, peering over the rail. He saw Dallas leaning weakly against the wall, eyes fixed on the body of a man, face down on the floor, in the shadows under the stairs.

"Tom!" she gasped. "It's Tom Gary! That—man—has killed—him!"

The library door opened and Anthony ran out, stopped suddenly. "Good Lord!" he said. "Got him sure—"

"Just a minute," Brade cut in. "Tom's only out for the count. See, he's breathing." He bent over the constable, laid a steady finger on the thick wrist. Tom's gray hair was stained with blood which tricked sluggishly across his cheek from a nasty cut over the left ear. At Brade's touch he stirred, groaned, opened his eyes.

"Get him," he said hoarsely. "He's beat it—knocked me out—got loose—" Then he struggled to a sitting position and Brade saw the steel of handcuffs dangling from his wrist.

"You had Alden cuffed to you?" he demanded.

Tom nodded. "Yeah, and he wanted to—go—to the bathroom—I took him there—on the way back—I don't know exactly what happened. He said something real quick and sharp, pointed. I looked, and he crowned me plenty. The key was in my vest pocket, I don't know anything more."

"What's his chances on a flit?" Brade snapped. "Any trains out to-night?"

"No." Tom was groaning dully. "Nothin' till ten in the morning."

"Garages? In the village?"

"All closed. He'd have to break in a garage, steal a car or—"

Dr. Monery came slowly downstairs. Brade said: "Look after the constable, doctor," and raced for the door.

Calling to Jimmy to cover the east side of the grounds, Brade took the west. He came back panting—sweat streaking his face, and without discovering a trace of the fugitive. Jimmy stumbled up just then to report similar lack of success.

Brade mopped his face, told the boy to go on with the hunt for the book-end, then he, himself, went in the house and picked up the phone. It took him about ten minutes to set the machinery in motion for the apprehension of Frosty Rivet.

First he notified the state police, giving Frosty's description, the reason for wanting him and the information that he was a known crook. Then, when he had the Sergeant's assurance that all highways would be patrolled and crossroads combed, he got his own department in the city.

It gave him a feeling of relief to hear the strong cheery voice of Sergeant Terry Shanolosky over the wire. Brade had wished more than once during the hours he had been in Willow Valley, for the presence of his friend and subordinate.

Brade gave his message, heard Terry's confirmation, then he said:

"On the job late, aren't you, kid? What's the idea? Town on fire or something?"

He heard Terry's groan over seventy-five miles. "Naw," Terry grumbled, "it's just that some dumb cluck claims to have seen a boy that's wanted pretty bad some place and the Lieut's kept me up all night, checkin' up on his record."

"Oh, I see. Well, don't work too hard."

Terry grunted in disgust. "A copper never does," he said. "By the way, the boy I'm checkin' up on is Andrew Stillwell. Ever hear of him?"

Brade frowned at the mouthpiece. "Stillwell?" he repeated. "Oh, sure, but I can't remember a thing about him. Come from our district?"

Terry chuckled. "I should say not. Oregon! Well, S'long, Chief. Anything else?"

"Nothing, Terry, only I may send for you."

"Wish to pat you would. I'm tired of—"

The remainder of Terry's complainings were lost in the whir of the wire as the connection was broken. Brade stood up, rumpling his hair. Andrew Stillwell! The name was vaguely familiar and suggested tremendous possibilities, but as he told Terry, he couldn't tie onto one single fact definitely. He put the matter from his mind and went back to the hall from the library, whistling soundlessly.

Dr. Monery was just completing a neat white bandage on the constable's head. Tom looked rather sick and avoided Brade's glance. Brade paused, grinning down at him.

"Don't take it too hard, old man," he said with that consideration which made his men worship him. "We'll pick up the little grifter before daylight, then we'll get something out of him. He'll get a stretch for assaulting an officer, if nothing else. Leaving us, Doctor?"

The doctor was placing his hat on his head with great care. "My work is done for the present, Captain Brade," he said quietly. "I sincerely hope I shall not be summoned to Willow Wilde again soon." He went out, closing the door gently.

Chapter Eleven
"I—Killed—Them!"

Dallas sat on the settle near the cold fire, Anthony beside her. Brade lighted a smoke, faced Gary. "Get Frosty's story?" he asked.

"Yeah, but I don't believe it. He claimed that he thought Opal Garth was in danger because she knew who bumped Keye and when she sneaked out of the room, he went after her, but took a route through the parlor there and up the servants' stairs."

"What'd he see, according to his own story?"

Tom pressed his throbbing head. "He says when he was half-way up the stairs, he heard voices. Thought they were women's. He started a sneak then, goin' slow and easy. Then the voices got louder. Opal was beggin' with someone not to kill her. That slowed him up even more, he says. Then he heard a shot and topped out in time to see Opal fall and—" Tom paused, blinking owlishly at Brade.

"The fellow claims that he saw Maybrick, the housekeeper, streakin' across the hall from somewhere on the other side and duck into the linen closet, then Miss Dallas appeared from somewhere and we all got there. Sounds fishy to me. I'd sooner think he bumped 'em both. Keye, because he was jealous of his noticin' this Garth girl; the girl, because—"

"Yes?" Brade asked. "Why did he shoot Opal?"

Tom lifted his head to stare at Brade. "I dunno," he admitted. "These crooks is always quarrelin'."

Brade studied his fingertips, recalling the conversation he had overheard between Opal and Frosty earlier in the evening. Fragments sounded in his ears, the voices of two people who had suddenly crossed his path, in the shadow of murder, one of them dead now, silenced forever, the other a fugitive from justice.

He heard Opal say: "What in hell'd you crash the party for?"

Frosty's husky voice: "What you mean hornin' in on our deal?"

"Your deal? Didn't I tip you off to Leo and that stretch—"

And again, Frosty asking: "What'd Keye say, when you talked to him about—everything?"

"Said to leave it to him—he'd take care of things—he knew a way—"

"—we was fools to spill it to him—you and me and Leo could 'a' cleaned up without him—"

The ghost voices rose in clamorous confusion until they filled the silent hall for him and he was not conscious of the three persons before him. The voices made a network of sound, mocking, gibing, shrilling—defying him to read their meaning, untangle the snarl. . . .

"How'd you get that bloomer on your pan?"

"I stumbled—into—a tree."

"Where?"

"None of your business."

Then Frosty Rivet's voice lifted stridently from the jumble: "—You're holdin' out on me."

"No—no—no."

"Don't try for a double-cross . . . still chance at some sweet pickin's—"

"I'm through—through—"

"Figurin' on somethin' on your own—"

"No—no—no—" screamed the ghost voice of the girl who was dead, and Brade remembered that conviction he had had that she was lying. That she was figuring something of her own. That deep in her shallow, evil mind Opal Garth had even then held the key to the murder of Jurden Keye, that she was crouching, furtive and on guard, waiting her opportunity, breathless for the chance to play her cards.

And while she waited . . .

"Dallas Gantry," Brade said suddenly, "did Opal Garth hate you?"

Dallas looked up with a smothered exclamation. Then she nodded wearily. "Very much, Captain Brade. I knew Opal many years ago, we were in the same road show, I think she always—hated me—"

"Had you seen her to-night before this all happened? Did you know she was in town?"

Again Dallas nodded, cheeks flaming hot. "She was at the station when I came in," she said, trying to make her mind stretch over the dreary eons of time since the moment she had stepped from the train and been so happy. "She went to my house, was waiting for me when I arrived—"

"What did she want?" Brade asked. "Tell me as clearly as you can."

Dallas stood motionless, slim shoulders taut. It was hard to do what he asked, relate that beastly conversation with Opal Garth, then she came over and stood before him, looking up into his eyes with her own that were dark with strain, but level and strong just the same.

"I'll tell you what she wanted," she said, and went over again the proposal Opal had made. It took courage and poise to go through with it. Dallas was inwardly quivering with shame, her hate and loathing for the dead man and the dead woman who had the power so to humiliate her.

Brade listened, not taking his eyes from her face. "Stout fellow, Dallas Gantry," he applauded in his mind; "take it standing. It isn't your fault that Jurden Keye—was—what he was; that Opal Garth was—Opal Garth. It isn't making us think any the less of you, all this dirt. Anthony is loving you more every moment. Look at his eyes. . . ."

"That's all," Dallas finished quietly. "I sent her away. I didn't see her again until the moment she staggered in that window."

"Thanks," Brade said curtly. "Have a cigarette?" He extended his case.

He had what he wanted for the moment. Proof satisfying him, that Opal Garth, while she hugged her own hidden schemes, would take time out to ruin the woman she hated. Just as Maybrick. . . .

"How about Maybrick?" he inquired casually. "She doesn't love you either, does she?"

Dallas smiled slightly. "I never realized before, Captain Brade," she said, "how many enemies I had. Maybrick has hated me since the hour I came into this house. There was something almost interesting about her dislike of me, that is, if I could have reached a state of detachment sufficient to allow me to enjoy it. As it was, it only made me miserable. Why, I think," Dallas said slowly, eyes on the dead fire, "that Maybrick would have killed me back in those other days—I remember one time when I sprained my ankle and the pain put me out for a time, when I wakened to such agony as I hope never to encounter again, she was—twisting my foot! Standing there by the bed, bending those ligaments and muscles that were so badly wrenched—that's how much she hated me, to the point where it was necessary to inflict physical pain."

"Dallas!" Anthony called sharply. "Stop it! You're torturing yourself." He put an arm around her, drew her beside him, angry eyes on Brade. "Is this necessary, Court?" he demanded. "Can't she—rest—now? It's going to be beastly to-morrow."

"I'm sorry," Brade said quietly. "Murder's—murder."

"But Dallas didn't do it! Dallas couldn't—"

Brade bowed gravely. "We shall hope that proof is forthcoming to satisfy the law that she did not," he said.

Anthony stared at him blankly a moment, while his mind struggled with the conviction that his friend, the man with whom he had played poker, gone duck hunting, attended musical reviews, old Court, jolly old cuss, actually thought, believed, that Dallas was a—murderess.

"You're crazy," he said thickly. "I'd like to smash your face for that! You ought to know—"

Dallas interrupted him wearily. "Don't, Anthony. Captain Brade isn't to blame."

He did not heed her. "You think, I suppose," he cried passionately, "that because Maybrick said she saw—"

"Look here, Anthony," Brade cut in quietly, "let's talk this over a bit. And I do wish you'd get it out of your head that I'm a savage-minded devil rampaging round, seeking whom I may destroy. I don't enjoy it. I don't like hunting—people down! I'm just a human being like yourself. Damn it, man," he cried, suddenly angry, "someone's got to guard you. Someone's got to look after—you—and by you, I mean the public at large. You're like a bunch of muddle-headed kids, getting yourselves tangled up in one mess after another, running your heads into danger, getting killed and wounded and—"

He stopped with a slight shrug. It wasn't often that Brade allowed himself the luxury of anger. He said very quietly: "It's this way, Anthony. My job is crime. Any man, if he's—decent, tries to do his job as well as he can. Mine's different, in that when I do it, someone's bound to be hurt.

"But I can't help it. If your mother, your sister, your best friend—your—Dallas, suppose one of them had been murdered? Wouldn't you want something done about it? Wouldn't you be howling for blood? Well, now listen to me. When I agreed to come down here, I came to do my job and that job is to discover the murderer of Jurden Keye and later Opal Garth. I'm doing it to the best of my ability and if someone gets hurt—"

He stopped, breathing unevenly, then he went on. "The case against Dallas Gantry is bad. She had motive for the killing of Jurden Keye. She had opportunity—"

"He was alive when I left," Dallas said in a dull, listless voice.

"That's what you say," Brade told her curtly. "There were two witnesses, only one now, who tell a different story. In a court of law, two prime requisites are motive and opportunity. You had them both—in both killings."

"Opal? That girl! Why should I kill her?"

Brade smiled mirthlessly. "The simplest, most intensely human reason in the world," he said, "self-preservation. She held your life in her smudgy little hand—if we are to accept her story. She was an eyewitness to your killing of Keye—"

Dallas broke loose from Anthony, once more stepped before Brade and stood there staring up at him. Her face was like white fire and her brown eyes glowed with a restrained passion.

"All right," she choked with difficulty. "Go on. Go on and prove it. One of your witnesses is dead. The other hates me like poison.

That man—Alden—or whatever his name is, said Maybrick ran to the linen closet after the shot was fired; maybe she did it. She'd kill anyone who interested Jurden Keye."

Brade was studying her through the crisp blackness of his lashes.

"Jurden Keye was dead," he reminded her. "Opal Garth—no one could interest him—then."

"No, but Maybrick's hate would go on. I know her, I tell you. She'd kill—gladly—"

"We're getting off the subject," he said. "Why, exactly did you go upstairs?"

"I've told you. To find Faith MacFarlane, who is a very dear friend, who, I heard, was ill."

"And you couldn't guess in which room she might be resting? You had to go groping all over the place trying to locate her. Here in your own home—"

"My home!" she flung at him. "This isn't my home. It never was my home. I haven't seen it for fourteen years."

"You went up there because Opal Garth had gone. You wanted to try and bribe her into silence. You met her in the hall, when she wouldn't listen you drew a gun—"

"No. I never had a gun."

"You drew a gun, she snatched up a bronze bookend, tried to strike you with it, then she lost her nerve before that automatic, turned and ran and you stopped her with a bullet. You raced back for that room at the other side of the stairs, threw the bookend from the window, hid the gun in a drawer—"

"My God," Dallas gasped faintly, "you're mad. Stark mad."

Brade was leaning toward her. His face was a cold, bleak white. His eyes gleamed like polished metal. His lips, tense and hard, were parted over his strong white teeth.

"Didn't you throw that book-end out of the window?"

"I don't know what you're talking about."

"It was a bronze piece, a dancing figure it was—yours."

She shook her head dumbly. "Hush," she whispered. "Hush—you're mad—"

He jerked something from his pocket, held it before her straining eyes. "This," he said softly, "this is your gun! You hid it in the
drawer. It was found."

Dallas backed from him, eyes on the gun. The front door burst
open. Jimmy Arnold rushed in, eyes bright with eagerness. He took
no notice of the tense group in the hall. His thoughts were all on
his job.

He said breathlessly, "I found it, Captain Brade. Found the
bronze book-end. It was on the lawn, under the mulberry tree and
the mulberry tree is on a direct line with the window of that room
where I found the gun—where Dallas Gantry—"

He stopped, breathing hard, eyes groping over the staring faces
before him.

"Hear?" Brade asked softly. "Hear, Dallas Gantry? *The book-
end was thrown from the window of the room where you hid the
gun!* Where you ran for refuge after you shot—Opal—"

There was a rush of feet on the floor above, a smothered cry,
then a choked, distorted voice—

"Stop! I can't stand it any longer. Dallas didn't do it! I did it! I!
I! I! I—killed them—both—"

Chapter Twelve
"How Many Times Can A Man Die?"

THERE ARE MOMENTS that rob individuals of conscious thought. When, on the peak of Brade's accusation of Dallas, on the crest of his summing up the evidence against, that voice sounded from the stairhead, the little group in the hall below were paralyzed, mentally and physically. Even Brade!

All his instincts were against considering Dallas Gantry as the murderer of Jurden Keye and Opal Garth. He didn't want to think that she was. Because she was a charming, beautiful woman, the future wife of a very good friend of his, because down underneath Courtney Brade had an Old-World chivalry toward women and if his experience and knowledge had permitted it, he would have liked to think them all pure and stainless creatures, without sin and without evil.

That was Brade, the man. Brade, the policeman, knew perfectly well that a fair face and gentle manners are no guarantee against crime. He knew that slim white hands could pull a trigger, grasp a knife, as efficiently, as savagely as any.

Mistaken loyalty, jealousy, hatred, fear of consequence were swaying every individual in the Keye murder case. The same intangible, devilish ring that surrounds and baffles the investigator in every mystery. A vicious circle that sooner or later must be broken to achieve results.

Did he, Courtney Brade, think beautiful Dallas Gantry guilty of the killing?

That was beside the point. With the evidence in hand she was the most likely suspect. Brade had been keenly conscious of the furtive eyes of watchers, surreptitious closing of doors, pad of guilty footsteps at almost every turn. His every move was watched. The walls had ears.

His baiting of Dallas Gantry was not purposeless cruelty. He believed that if he could beat through her defenses, get her at bay, back to the wall, fighting with primitive fury to save her own life, with all barriers down, some furious sentence, some heedless gesture of hers, or some nerve-fagged listener might point the finger or place his feet on the right path. The ruse had worked. The circle had cracked.

Faith MacFarlane was coming down the stairs! She walked stiffly, head high, eyes wide. She was deathly pale. There was no color anywhere about her. The soft gray of her dress faded to neutrality, burned out by the whiteness of herself. She rounded the stairs, came over and stopped, standing a little apart from them. She looked straight and hard at Brade.

"This has gone far enough," she said clearly. "I killed Jurden Keye! I killed Opal Garth! I am ready to make full confession as to motive and method, then I am prepared to take what comes."

Gregg MacFarlane stumbled down the stairs. "Faith!" he cried brokenly. "Oh—Faith, what have you done?"

She did not heed him. "I did not think, Captain Brade," Faith went on, "that you would pick Dallas as a suspect. I thought the crime would remain unsolved. That no one would suffer. When I killed Keye I had no notion that I would have to kill again, that all these developments would arise. As it is, I cannot stand by and see a woman I sincerely love and admire, one who has the prospect of a long happy life before her, suffer for my crime. Do you wish to ask questions?"

Gradually they were coming to life, that little frozen group of people there in the cold hall of Willow Wilde. Tom Gary was leaning forward, unbelieving eyes on Faith MacFarlane. He was thinking that such a tiny fluff of a woman could never have buried that knife in Jurden Keye's heart. Jimmy Arnold was leaning weakly against the door, eyes bulging. Anthony stood silent, unable to look away from the woman who claimed murder. Dallas had dropped to a chair. Her head was buried in her hands. She rocked softly to and fro.

Brade was himself again, in full possession of his faculties, recovered from the shock of the thing. He put a foot carelessly on the railing in front of the fireplace, rumpled his hair and said:

"Do you understand, Mrs. MacFarlane, that it is not necessary for you to talk now? That you are entitled to advice of counsel before—"

"Oh, my God, yes," she cried in a suddenly frantic voice and her fluttering hand pressed hard round her throat. "Don't—bother with—technicalities, please, Captain Brade. I have killed. I am guilty. Do you think I care—about counsel?"

He nodded briefly. "Very well," he said. "Tell me about it. Why did you kill Jurden Keye?"

Her frozen white face came to life with a sudden convulsive writhing. "Because he was a—beast!" she said thickly. "He—had made life miserable for me—ever since I first saw him. I couldn't escape him. There was no way but to kill him."

"Why, specifically, did you come here to-night?"

She was silent a moment, and Brade got the feeling that she was mentally collecting herself, arranging certain facts logically. She said at last: "Jurden Keye sent me flowers two days ago. That, in itself, may seem insignificant. It was not, considering what Jurden Keye was. The implication he managed to put into his gift was an insult. So yesterday afternoon, uptown, in front of the bank, I met him. I tried to tell him what I felt. He grasped my arm and forced me to walk a ways with him. He said if I would come to his house to-night and talk with him a while that perhaps he would agree never to annoy me again."

She paused, glance groping slowly over the faces before her, avoiding her husband's, stopping on Brade's. There was a queer veiled look in the detective's eyes which she could not fathom.

She went on. "It was a foolish thing to do. I see that now. But I was so afraid—if matters went on that—Gregg would do something—

rash—so I came in by the French window as I had agreed. We were talking there in the alcove, when Dallas entered the room. He let me out the window—I waited on the balcony. I heard what he said to Dallas, and I thought of all the evil this man had caused. Of how—unspeakably wicked he was—and something grew hot and searing inside me, told me to kill—"

Her voice died away. There was no sound except the creeping wind outside, the sob of Gregg MacFarlane's labored breathing, then Faith went on:

"And when Dallas left I had come back into the alcove, was peering through the curtains and I saw her go, I stepped into the room, confronted Jurden Keye and told him what I thought of him. I think he knew I would kill him, for he kept opening and closing his lips without saying anything, then he turned and I saw the knife—and—I only remember my fingers closing round the hilt—and the swing I gave when I struck him—"

She lifted one hand, pushed the soft hair off her forehead. "That is all, I guess," she said wearily. "I went home and got into bed. Gregg came and told me that Keye was dead and that Dallas was accused of the crime. Then I began to realize what I had done, that not only Dallas but my—husband—might be suspected—"

"And Opal Garth?" Brade asked. "What about her?"

Faith started and her eyes flared wide. "I—don't know—" she gasped. "I guess—I think—she must have been there—somewhere—she came upstairs and told me she had seen me commit the crime—and so I killed her—"

"You didn't see the girl when you left by the French window after stabbing Keye?"

"I don't—know—I don't remember. No—I didn't see—her—"

Gregg MacFarlane placed his hands on his wife's shoulders and gently but firmly lifted her aside. "Stay there," he said without looking at her, then he stepped before Brade.

"Captain Brade," he said, "I have often read that murderers return to the scene of their crimes and I have never believed it. I thought if I killed a man I would never come back, but I have found that I was wrong. To-night I stabbed Jurden Keye because of certain—

things—which he said about my wife in an interview I had with him—then I went out the French window and got safely away, but I could not remain away. I came back to the front of the house and entered the hall—"

"It isn't true," Dallas cried suddenly as if it were impossible for her to keep silent longer. "You're mad, Gregg, you couldn't have done it any more than Faith. You forget that I was in that room, that I had not been gone more than five minutes before Opal Garth screamed—"

Gregg smiled. "I was behind the curtains in the alcove, Dallas," he said. "What my wife has told is, of course, ridiculous and is prompted by her unstrung nerves and her desire to save you, my dear. She did not come to this house to-night until I brought her here after Captain Brade's arrival. She was home and in bed and I can prove it. I was the one who came to Willow Wilde and I came to smash Jurden Keye to bits. We quarreled, of course. I had stepped into the alcove preparatory to leaving and he followed me. Dallas came and I went out the French door, but I did not close it. When she left I came back in, picked up the knife which was lying on the table and killed him."

"Did you also shoot Opal Garth?" Brade inquired politely. "If I remember correctly, you were with me in the morning room at the time."

Gregg's eyes narrowed. "No," he said. "I did not kill Opal Garth any more than my wife did. I believe *Maybrick killed her.* I saw the housekeeper bending over her body when I came up the stairs. She still held the gun. She did not see me and she ran for the linen closet. I've kept still about it because I realize we've all been under a terrible strain here and under those circumstances one has delusions, sees things crookedly. I thought there might be some logical explanation for Maybrick's movements. But I'm convinced I was wrong. My wife said she killed Opal Garth, but she did not tell a very good story."

Dallas began laughing. The sound was low, quiet, almost gentle. She sat there with her hands clenched tightly in the folds of her skirt, not looking at any one, and laughed. There was something rather terrible about it and Anthony dropped beside her, caught her hands, shook her roughly.

"Dallas," he cried. "Dallas! Stop it! Dallas, what ails you?"

"It's so—horrible," she choked, still laughing. "I never knew anything could be so—horrible. Maybrick says *I* killed Jurden. Opal said *I* killed him. Faith says *she* killed him. And now—*Gregg*. Oh, we couldn't *all* have done it. How many times can a man be murdered? You ought to know that, Captain Brade? How many times can a man die—"

Brade said sharply: "Take her upstairs, Anthony. Get Maybrick to put her to bed. Go! At once!"

Anthony lifted Dallas, unresisting, and led her to the stairs.

Brade said to Tom Gary: "Better get along, constable, and see if any word has come in about Frosty Rivet. Then get some rest. I'm going to need you to-morrow. Jimmy—" he frowned at the wide-eyed boy.

"I'm not a bit tired, Captain Brade," Jimmy said hopefully. "Couldn't I—"

"Yes," Brade decided. "You stay here. Go into the library and wait until I call you."

When they had all left and there was only Faith MacFarlane, Gregg and himself, Brade drew up a chair, tossed wood into the fireplace, thoughtfully tore a paper to bits and lighted a match. "That will be better," he said conversationally. "It's getting cold in here."

Faith MacFarlane was sitting on the divan. Gregg stood beside her. Brade glanced up at them obliquely, smiling slightly. "It's awfully decent of you two," he said, "to try and settle this matter so early in the game, but I'm sorry you couldn't have thought up better stories. If you had gone into conference on the subject, decided which one was to be sacrificed and thus avoided conflict, it would have been better."

Faith gasped faintly. "I have told you the truth," she said slowly.

Brade lighted a cigarette. "What did you hope to gain by coming to see Keye to-night? You say you were afraid your husband would do something rash if Keye's attentions to you continued.

How could the situation have been bettered, if MacFarlane had learned of your visit?"

Faith shook her head. "I can see I was mad," she said faintly. "Looking back, it is all clear to me. But then—then it seemed different, Captain Brade."

"And, knowing that your husband resented Keye's interest in you, you further risked trouble by consenting to visit Keye surreptitiously, entering that room through the window?"

"Yes, yes, I can see it now, but not then. I thought—"

"This is absurd," Gregg MacFarlane said harshly. "I killed Keye and I had a good motive. Faith is merely trying to—"

Brade lifted a hand. "We aren't getting any place," he said. "MacFarlane, take your wife upstairs and see that she gets some rest. I'll talk to you to-morrow."

He waited quietly by the fire until they had gone, then he crossed over to the library where Jimmy Arnold waited. Jimmy was round-eyed with interest.

"Gosh, Captain Brade," he gasped, "think of Mis' MacFarlane doin' all that. Such a little thing—"

"This book-end," Brade interrupted. "Bring your flashlight and show me where it is."

They went out into the windy dawn where light clouds scudded across a cold gray sky. Willow Wilde looked grim and bleak in its park of leafless trees, with its high turrets, its blind windows, its air of desolation and mystery.

"Here it is, sir," Jimmy said in a hoarse whisper and shot his flash on a sodden patch of withered grass. Brade took the flash and knelt down. The book-end lay just at the edge of a clump of bushes. Its sharp base was buried a good half inch in the damp, soft soil. He studied it a moment, then he stood up and his eyes went in a slow appraisal over the front of the house.

"That window," he asked, pointing, "that is the room where you found the gun?"

"Yes, sir. And the room where Miss Dallas—"

"Wait a minute, Jimmy. Let me think this over a bit." Absently he lighted a cigarette without taking his eyes from the broad expanse of the house. Back and forth his sharp glance went, measuring, calculating, judging, then at last he said, without looking at the boy beside him:

"Almost a direct line—almost direct." He walked forward a dozen paces, stood frowning up at the window, glancing back at the piece of bronze. "Almost direct," he repeated. "*At the same time it could have come from any one of three or four windows*. Jimmy," he said abruptly, "I want you to stick around out here and watch that thing, see that it is not touched until I can get a photographer. Up to it?"

"Oh, gee, yes," Jimmy said reverently. "Sure, I'm up to it, sir, and I won't go to sleep either."

"Good," Brade clipped and turned back toward the house.

Jimmy's hushed voice stopped him. "We're workin' on this together, ain't we, Captain Brade?" he asked.

Brade grinned. "Sure thing, Jimmy. It's you and me for it. We've got to straighten it out."

"Then you wouldn't think me nosey if I asked something. Of course, you told me not to think but it's awful hard and I'd like to know if you believe that Mrs. MacFarlane really killed Mr. Keye, if you honestly think her story is true?"

Brade was stirring a drift of wet leaves with the toe of his shoe. In the dull morning light he looked white and tired. The gray stains at his temples seemed brighter. There were unexpected lines in his face. Jimmy decided that he was older than he had thought, then Brade said slowly:

"I overheard Mrs. MacFarlane tell her husband, Jimmy, that she would do anything to save Dallas Gantry from serious trouble. I think she is the type that would gladly sacrifice herself to save someone she loved. She was listening up there in the hall when I built up a fairly good case against Dallas. She was upstairs in the hall there just at the last when I was ragging the poor girl again. Her outbreak and subsequent confession came on the heels of my definite accusation against her friend. What is your opinion?" Brade regarded his young assistant gravely.

Jimmy pulled his left ear till it was very red. "She didn't do it," he declared explosively. "I knew she never done it. She's sayin' she

done it just to save Miss Dallas and Mr. MacFarlane says he done
it to save his wife—"

"Also," Brade interrupted, still speaking very slowly, as if he
were carefully considering his words, "Mrs. MacFarlane's story is
obviously false on the face of it. She says that after Dallas left she
stood across the desk and told Keye what she thought of him, then
she grabbed up the knife and stabbed him. That is false, Jimmy,"
Brade said, *"because Jurden Keye did not die from the blow of
that knife! He died from a bullet and I think we will find that it
came from that open window behind him—so whoever plunged
the knife into his heart, buried it in a body already dead!"*

He left Jimmy too overwhelmed to speak, and as he slowly re-
traced his steps toward the door he reflected grimly that Dallas
Gantry had guessed better than she knew when she said Jurden
Keye had been murdered twice.

Chapter Thirteen
Dallas Runs Away

THE DOUBLE KILLINGS at Willow Wilde touched a spark to a powder train and literally set the community on fire. It was odd, Brade reflected, how death loosens tongues. Sometimes to mouth fulsome praise of the departed; again to shrill hate and slander. And so it was in Willow Valley, as if those who talked realized the subject of their tirades was gone beyond the power to retaliate. Brade wondered rather grimly how quickly the ugly chatter would change to cringing flattery if gaunt, evil old Jurden Keye could suddenly come to life and face his traducers.

But the detective, trained in unpleasantness, kept silent and let the town talk. Perhaps out of the muck he would pick up something. Some neglected thread that, when carefully drawn from the ugly tangle, would lead the way to the solution of the crime to which two persons had already confessed.

Brade kept those confessions to himself. Swarms of newspaper men and women descended on the quiet little town, engaged the best rooms at the Inn, reveling in the fact that the proprietor of the hostelry and his wife were already involved in the mystery. The detective met them, talked to them, made general statements, sent them away as nearly satisfied as a reporter can ever be. The business at Willow Wilde intrigued the press as it interested the country. There had been, one enterprising city editor decided, entirely too many urban crimes. People were fed up on gang fights, murders following hold-ups which came as the result of the depression. They were also rather tired of love-nest exposés and the killing of

135

a night-life queen by any one of her myriad admirers; accounts accompanied by photos of her over-furnished boudoir had also ceased to boost circulation.

What the public wanted, the press decided, was a nice, wholesome murder in a rural setting, something with a largish dash of mystery, of course, a bit of romantic background, one or two good-looking principals to photograph, a picture of the village church where the deceased had helped trim the Christmas tree and attended box socials, a hint of scandal, a bit of naughtiness, that, indeed, was the ideal recipe just now. And in the murders at Willow Wilde, they had it with a vengeance, along with the added lure of a nationally famous actress, one about whom, up to this time, no hint of luridness had been attached, and the man she hoped to marry, wealthy, socially prominent, famous for his speed-boat record, noted for his racing stables—Anthony Gordon, in short, than whom there could have been nobody better.

So the press sharpened its pencils, pinned back its ears and went to it. Amateur detectives appeared as if by magic with demands to be allowed to solve the mystery. The usual number of crank letters were received and carefully read in the ever-present hope of really finding that one contained something worth while, and through it all, Frosty Rivet continued to elude the efforts of police and state constabulary to catch him. Also, the white-faced man with the gray hat, who had arrived on the same train with Dallas, registered at the Willow Inn under the name of Samuel Fredricks, had completely vanished from the picture.

Some time during that hectic night when news of the killing of Jurden Keye and Opal Garth swept the little town, Mr. Fredricks had packed his classy Gladstone, strapped up his obviously new brief-case and departed for parts unknown. Brade considered gloomily that it was entirely his fault for not scenting the importance of Samuel Fredricks and grabbing him. But Brade had long ago learned the futility of worrying over barn-doors left unlocked, so he got the best description he could of the man and set the country to looking for him. After that, he squared back and again took up the problem before him.

DALLAS WAS RUNNING away! She was wrapped in a soft brown coat of fur, there was a small brown hat pulled low over her hair, her hands were wrapped in the sleeves of the coat and she was running.

All around her was evening. A dull, stormy nightfall following a day of threatening rain, with a high quarrelsome wind that stripped the few remaining leaves from the trees round Willow Wilde.

It had been a day of unmitigated horror for Dallas. Even Anthony's presence, his unfailing good humor, his quiet optimism could not dispel the clouds for her. Brade had kept them all at Willow Wilde. Loathing it as she did, Dallas was almost grateful for its protection, for the shelter of Brade's tightlipped personality, the seeming ease with which he dealt with reporters and the horde of curious that besieged the place, yammering for a sight of the inmates.

So she had remained pretty much in her room, slumped down in a chair before the fire, lost in her own unhappy thought, tortured by the seemingly unsolvable mystery around her, filled with a shivering dread of something lurking in the background to destroy her. In the hours of that long day of agony, Dallas had come very much to doubt the possible consummation of her happiness. Then, about five o'clock, she could stand it no longer.

She had started up, jerked on her coat and hat, scribbled a note to Brade and, watching her chance, escaped from the house by the side door, slipped across the dreary sodden grounds and out into the road. Perhaps, she considered, as she slowed her steps somewhat, if she had gone to Brade, explained how she felt and asked permission to take a walk, he would have permitted it. But she had not dared put it to the test. She was really very much afraid of Brade.

As twilight deepened and chances of recognition lessened, she slowed to a leisurely walk, breathing deeply of the clear, cold air, heavy with threat of snow, filled with the indefinable hint of approaching winter.

Gradually a degree of normalcy returned to her. The tight lines around her mouth relaxed. A dash of color warmed her white cheeks. She lifted her head, let her eyes wander over the familiar scenes and a dreary pleasure came to her. She was walking along the winding road that led toward the old schoolhouse which, as a child, she had attended. There were many familiar landmarks for her. Houses of old friends in which now she would be a stranger. The bridge, over the small riotous stream, where she and little Polly Martin used to play at exploring. On past the house that mad Willoughby Crane had built, where his mad mother had put in the last years of her life, carving the woodwork into intricate, beautiful designs. To the small Dallas it had always seemed a fairy palace set on a hill. A place of romance and mystery, terribly alluring, yet banded round with a wall of fear which kept her out. Now she saw it as a rather small, entirely shabby story and a half dwelling of dingy white with green shutters. The grounds, which had seemed so magnificent, were just a lumpy expanse of bare black soil. The trees looked dwarfed, insignificant. There was a feeble light in the uncurtained window and she saw numerous small heads bent over something on the table. Dreary. Commonplace. Ordinary.

She climbed the slight rise and turned west. At the end of the street lay open country and the gentle hump of Elder's Hill which she knew now was just a mound and not a mountain. Her thoughts, which had been ranging far afield, returned to the immediate present with a disagreeable jolt. Someone was following her! She quickened her steps, her heart making an uncomfortable thumping in her side, then she decided she was foolish and slowed. Who would follow her? And why? If it was Brade, who had discovered her truancy and set out after her, he would just call to her, tell her she must come back. . . .

She glanced over her shoulder. A dark figure was just emerging from the lane of maples before the old Stearns place. A man, hands shoved in the pockets of his long raincoat, hat pulled low, head bowed. But the sight did not reassure her. Somehow she knew that the man walking behind her was not a native of Willow Valley. There was to her sharpened senses a certainty of the city about him. She drew her coat closer and walked faster. The unrelenting steps behind quickened.

Dallas, lashed now by a strange terror, hurried on past the last house on the street and felt the damp soil of the open road beneath her feet. Too late she realized that this was a mistake. She should have crossed the street—gone back along—

"Pardon me, please."

She jerked up at the low, unpleasant voice, turned.

The man had caught up with her. He was breathing unevenly and there were spots of color in his thin, white cheeks. He had narrow, slanted, light-colored eyes that regarded her boldly through sandy lashes. He wore a pale gray hat! It was the man who had come in on the train with her! The man for whom the entire country was looking. . . .

"Oh!" Dallas gasped faintly. "What do you want?"

She was regarding him with wide, fear-filled eyes. Looking back, she remembered the terror that had gripped her there in the coach as the train approached the station. This man had been part of it. He had somehow managed to permeate her thoughts, insert his personality into her consciousness. She thought now, staring at him, tense with a panic she could scarcely control, that this man with his thin, knowing smile, his pale, unreadable eyes, held in his hand the solution of the murders at Willow Wilde!

"What do you want?" she whispered again through dry lips.

He stepped close to her, slipped a hand round her arm, held her with a tight, cruel grip, still smiling at her.

"Just to talk to you," he said. "I've had a lot of trouble finding you alone. I was up at the place half an hour ago. I saw you leave. I followed. I merely want you to walk a little distance with me. I have something I wish to discuss with you. Believe me, it is to our mutual benefit."

And Dallas, suddenly powerless in his grasp, felt herself propelled gently along the wet, lonesome road, away from the town, from Anthony, from Brade and the law he represented, out into a void of nameless terror, from which there seemed no returning.

Chapter Fourteen
The Gray Envelope

BRADE WAS WHISTLING softly beneath his breath. He was bare-headed and the rising wind of evening lifted his heavy gray-stained hair. He was on his knees on the wet ground, hunched down over the well-defined imprint of a shoe in the soft soil beneath the window of the parlor at Willow Wilde.

"Give me the flash, Jimmy," he directed his young assistant.

He began whistling again, while he measured, calculated, studied the track. "A man stood here," he said at last. "Stood here last night. It rained a bit just after daylight, you recall, Jimmy. It's been cloudy all day. The track is very wet."

He lifted his head, frowning at the window which was open about six inches. Then he stood up and, carefully avoiding the track, peered into the room. A grim satisfaction settled around his lips.

"If you were in that chair, Jimmy," he said, "and I should stand here and fire a bullet—"

"Oh, Captain Brade," Jimmy breathed, "you'd kill me."

"You said it, kid. I sure would. Plenty. If you were seated before the desk, back to this window, the bullet would hit you about here." He whirled the boy round and jabbed a long, strong forefinger at a spot just under his left shoulder blade. "There's where it would land, Jimmy, and if it were a small bullet it would not make much of a hole where it went in, there wouldn't be a great deal of blood right there, and you, my son, would pitch forward on your more or less handsome face across that desk—"

140

"Gosh, Captain Brade," Jimmy said, "you mean that's the way Mr. Keye was killed, really?"

Brade looked at the boy and nodded soberly. "I know it, Jimmy," he said. "The bullet got him first. The knife wound did not bleed. It was dim in that room, you will remember. Tom Gary did not make any extensive examination of the body when he arrived. Keye was dead! There was a knife in his back. Wasn't that enough? Fact is," Brade admitted frankly, "I didn't get it myself at first. Of course, a strong light showed it up, but I kept still and let the doctor make his own deductions. Now what we've got to find out—"

He frowned, rumpling his hair. "The window was open," he said, "I recall the draft. I wonder if Keye opened it himself or if—" He turned back toward the side door. "Dallas might be able to tell me," he said. "Let's find her, Jimmy."

He went into the house, which was unspeakably dreary and chill. The great high-ceilinged rooms seemed continually filled with a faint gray mist that was part of the growing night outside and even more a part of the shadow of death that hung over the place.

He met Maybrick coming toward him along the hall. The housekeeper had grown taciturn and sullen. She accepted the extra duties thrust upon her by the augmented household without complaint, merely brought in a girl to help her, but she marched through the house in dignified, angry silence, and there was continually, in her small bright eyes, a hint of knowledge and triumph that annoyed Brade. Just now she was smiling and her full face was deeply flushed. She was going on past him without a word, but he stopped her.

She stood there, glaring up at him and her heavy bosom rose and fell spasmodically. Sweat gleamed on her upper lip. Her thick fingers worked at the folds of her skirt.

"Where have you been, Mrs. Maybrick?" Brade demanded. "I wanted you half an hour ago and you were no place in the house."

She glanced at him sullenly under lowered lids. "I got a right to attend to my duties, ain't I?" she countered. "I went to the village for shopping. You can't keep me prisoner—"

"I can slap you in a cell and then we'll see how much shopping you do," Brade told her sharply, annoyed that he could not conceal his dislike and suspicion of this fat, stubborn old woman who really played such a small part in the scheme of things. "Where's Miss Gantry?" he asked.

Maybrick's eyes shifted. She wet her lips. "How would I know?" she mumbled. "I ain't seen her since morning. Mooning around in her room, I suppose, or—" she looked at him slyly, grinning.

"Yes, or what?"

"Or else she's gone," Maybrick said. "I wouldn't put it above her to sneak out on you, sir, seein' as she's already killed two people and—"

He turned angrily and ran up the stairs toward Dallas Gantry's room. Jimmy tagged dutifully at his heels. Brade tapped, received no answer, tried again, then opened the door. The room was warm and held a faint elusive fragrance of sandalwood. A chair was pushed back before the fire as if someone had risen suddenly.

Then he saw Dallas' brown dress hooked over a chair, her slim high-heeled pumps beside it. A closet door was open. There were two empty coat hangers. Dallas had had her trunks brought to Willow Wilde.

He paused, frowning at the room and a pucker of perplexity grew between his eyes. That fat, old woman hated Dallas. She would suggest that she had run away. Brade didn't pick Dallas Gantry as the sort to run away from anything—but just the same—where was she?

Downstairs, Maybrick stood immobile until the detective's steps had died away. Then she began chuckling softly and evilly to herself and, stepping into a corner of the dim hall, she drew a slim gray envelope from her pocket, opened it and extracted a single folded piece of paper. It said:

> "Captain Brade:
> "Don't think I'm running out on you. I just can't stand the house any more and I'm afraid you wouldn't let me go for the walk I simply must have.

"I'm going down the old Mill road through the west side of town and swing around past Elder's Hill and back to the house. I'll be gone about half an hour, I expect. If you're too angry, send Jimmy after me and I'll come peaceably.

"Dallas Gantry."

Mrs. Maybrick, still grinning, padded back to her own domain in the kitchen where an apple-cheeked girl was making biscuits. A hot fire roared in the old-fashioned range. Maybrick stepped up to it, made a pretense of adjusting dampers, then lifted a lid and laid the gray envelope on top of the glowing coals, and stood there watching it curl into nothingness, while the satisfied smile deepened on her lips.

She knew Dallas Gantry hadn't run away. She wouldn't gain much by destroying the note which she had found on the hall table, addressed to Captain Brade in a hand she recognized. But she would make Dallas out a liar and, Maybrick hoped, succeed in shaking Brade's faith in her.

Then, after giving Minnie Lee further instructions about the evening meal, she dusted her hands and went out of the kitchen. She had a certain very important matter to attend to. Maybrick had gone shopping all right, but shopping was not all that had occurred in that forty-five minutes of absence from Willow Wilde.

What had happened had shaken the housekeeper to the roots of her being and changed her from a merely vindictive old woman into a compact bundle of avarice and determination. She didn't see why she shouldn't gain a little too. She had worked hard all her life and she doubted if Jurden Keye had remembered her in his will. She faced a dreary prospect of old age with only her meager savings between her and actual want. If she could turn an honest penny, so much the better. She smoothed her apron, put back a strand of gray hair and defiantly mounted the stairs.

Chapter Fifteen
Beneath the Balcony

It took Brade some little time to believe that Dallas Gantry really was missing. A careful search had disclosed that she certainly was not in the house. Anthony glanced over the closet and said that her mink coat was missing, also the little brown hat with the orange feather which she usually wore with it

Brade kept calm and decided she had gone out for a bit of air and would soon return. He told Anthony not to worry, that Dallas would be back shortly.

The MacFarlanes were downstairs in the library. Faith was lying on a divan and Gregg was reading to her. Brade dropped in on them and temporarily forgot his search for Dallas Gantry. He stopped abruptly in the center of the room and for once his remarkable control was completely shattered. His eyes opened wide, his lips sagged. He said hoarsely:

"For God's sake, MacFarlane, what's hit *you?*"

Gregg MacFarlane laid down the book, looked straight at the detective and smiled. He looked as if he had slipped down into hell and come back for a brief respite. Brade thought even his hair was whiter. His lean, dark face was wounded by searing lines. His lips were colorless. They looked as though they would always be gray blue like that, like the lips of the dead. And his splendid dark eyes were dead as cold embers.

He said: "Everything, Brade! Everything's hit me. I didn't know so many things could hit one person. You wouldn't think there would be room enough." He laughed a little and lit a cigarette with steady fingers. "It's nothing to worry about," he went on, puffing strongly on the glowing cylinder. "But when— Oh, well, you ought to be able to understand—"

Brade glanced at Faith. She was lying inertly with eyes closed. She looked so frail and gentle, lying like that. The strength seemed to have gone out of her.

She said without looking up. "It's all been pretty terrible, Captain Brade. You can't expect us to be happy."

"No," Brade agreed. "Have either of you seen Dallas?"

There was silence for a moment, then Gregg MacFarlane asked: "Isn't she back yet?"

"No, where did she go?"

"I don't know. I broke parole myself and went out for a breath of air in the park. I saw Dallas slip out the east door. She had on her hat and coat and cut off cross the lawn and into the road. I didn't say anything because I thought I knew how she felt about getting away for a bit and I knew she'd come back."

Maybrick's harsh voice sounded at the door. "I made the tea you asked for, Mrs. MacFarlane. I served it in your room. Thought you were there."

"Oh, thank you," Faith said. "I think I will go up. You don't want anything else just now, Captain Brade?"

"No, Mrs. MacFarlane, only don't you leave." She smiled faintly. "I'll stay," she promised and followed the housekeeper upstairs.

"What time did you see Dallas leaving?" Brade asked.

"About five, maybe a few minutes later."

Brade looked at his watch. "It's ten to seven now," he announced curtly. "That's two hours. A brief constitutional shouldn't last that long."

"No," MacFarlane agreed. "What are you going to do?"

Brade didn't know what to do. He couldn't forget Mrs. Maybrick's hateful insinuation about Dallas running out on him. He told himself he had been several kinds of a fool not to put everybody connected with the case under lock and key. Just because folks were aristocrats, like Gregg MacFarlane and Dallas Gantry, was no reason to think they wouldn't look out for themselves if they got the chance. He glanced around impatiently, wondering where Anthony Gordon had gone.

He went into the hall, jerked wide the door, stepped outside. It was settling down for a nasty night. A cold wind whipped the tall trees around Willow Wilde. Black clouds raced across a leaden sky. A fine mist was already falling. It would be snow in an hour, Brade thought.

He stood there a time, glowering out into the darkness. He was angry and disturbed. His usual cool mastery of people and events seemed missing in this case. He told himself disgustedly that that was because he had allowed the personal element to creep in. Because he liked Anthony Gordon a lot, because he sincerely admired Dallas Gantry, was intensely interested in the MacFarlanes, because he thought with all honesty that Jurden Keye had been an unspeakable cad and that Opal Garth. . . .

He turned savagely, ramming his hands into pockets and went back into the house. This wasn't any way to solve the mystery. By getting interested in the principals in the case. Brade knew that to his bitter satisfaction.

There had been one other time, a great many years ago, when Courtney Brade had allowed his emotions to interfere with the performance of his duty—for a time. In the end he had won out and his allegiance to the uniform he wore had remained unbroken, but he had paid a price and would continue to pay as long as he lived or thought or felt.

He paused in the dim light of the hall at Willow Wilde and let his somber, tired eyes rest on the cloudy beauty of the moonstone on his third finger. That ring was the tangible evidence of his defeat and his victory. It was never absent from his finger. There were times when, like this, he felt his very human emotions involved, that he took time out to stare at the ring, to remember that night in Italy, on the shore of moon-white Lake Como, when to snap the bright steel of handcuffs on a pair of slim, appealing wrists threatened to call for more strength than he had.

Dallas Gantry had been gone almost three hours! One of two things had happened. She had deliberately cut and run or something very serious had happened to her. Brade picked up the telephone, set it down at sound of a light step behind him.

He turned to see a plump, red-checked girl in a gay pink ging-
ham dress, which lent a note of unaccustomed brightness to the
dim old hall, staring at him. Her eyes were very wide and bright,
and she twisted one foot uncomfortably.

"All right," Brade said impatiently. "What is it, my girl? You
want to see me?"

She nodded diffidently. "Jimmy, he told me—that Miss Gantry
was gone," the girl said very low.

"Yes, she is. You're the youngster who came in to help the
housekeeper, aren't you? Minnie Lee, isn't that your name? Do you
know anything about Miss Gantry?"

"I came in to help Mis' Maybrick and my name's Minnie Lee,"
the girl answered dutifully and chronologically. "I don't know anything really about Miss Gantry and if Mis' Maybrick finds out I
told you that she burned the letter—"

"What letter?" Brade's voice snapped.

Minnie Lee backed hurriedly. "Why, a letter that Miss Gantry
left for you, sir, there on that table there. I was coming downstairs
and I saw her put the letter there. She had on her hat and coat and
she went out through the library and—"

"Well, where is the letter? How do you know it was for me?"

"Because I—looked," Minnie Lee confessed guiltily. "I came
right on down and as I went by I looked and your name was on it.
And later I saw Mis' Maybrick put it in the kitchen stove."

"The devil you did! When was this?"

"About half-past six, I think. She had come in from her shopping, told me about making biscuits, then she went upstairs to see
about changin' the linen and when she come back she went right
over past me, fooled with the dampers on the stove a bit, then lifted
the lid and laid the letter on the coals. I was standin' by the table
and I could see right over her shoulder and I saw your name on the
envelope just as plain as plain—"

"All right, Minnie Lee," Brade said grimly. "That's a good girl.
Don't say anything about this to Mrs. Maybrick. Where is she, by
the way?"

The girl shook her head. "She took Mrs. MacFarlane's tea upstairs a while ago. I ain't seen her since."

Brade took the stairs in half a dozen strides. He was white-hot mad and there was a dangerous glint in his eyes. From now on the housekeeper at Willow Wilde was going to get a taste of real police routine. She had stalked her sullen way through the tragedy, confusing the issue by lying and trickery and she had forged the final link in her chain with the destruction of Dallas Gantry's letter, explaining, no doubt, her absence and the Lord only knew how much else. She might have stumbled onto some important bit of evidence and been foolish enough to try and run it down herself. Brade had known things like that to happen. She might have left word for him to meet her some place. She might have written one of a dozen terribly important things and that hateful, fusty old woman had. . . .

He paused on the upper landing and he was trembling with anger. His eyes flashed over the long, quiet hall with its rows of blank, closed doors.

"Mrs. Maybrick," he called. "Mrs. Maybrick!"

The echo came back to him in mocking cadence. "Mrs.—May—brick—May—brick—"

He stood there, hands clenched, staring at the silence. The emptiness. The drabness. Then a door opened.

Faith MacFarlane looked out. "Mrs. Maybrick isn't here, Captain Brade," she said. "She left some time ago, after serving my tea. Is there—anything—"

From somewhere at the front of the house sounded a hoarse yell. A high, startled cry, that was picked up by the wind and tossed away. Brade and Faith MacFarlane gazed blankly at each other, then the detective leaped down the stairs again, just as the front door was thrown open and Jimmy Arnold stumbled into the hall.

The boy's cap was gone and his face was white, with big frightened eyes stretched wide. He stopped, leaning on the newel post, staring up at Brade, lips opening and closing without forming words. Brade sensed Faith behind him, clinging hard to the bannister. Vaguely he wondered where Anthony and Gregg MacFarlane were, then Jimmy said in a broken, choked voice:

"It's her, sir! I stumbled over the body. She's dead! I found her—"

Brade leaped the bannister, landed beside the boy, seized his shaking shoulder. "Who?" he cried hoarsely. "Who are you talking about? Whose body?"

Faith gasped faintly. "Dallas!" she sobbed. "It's—Dallas!"

"No," Jimmy Arnold stuttered, "no—not Dallas! It's Maybrick! Mis' Maybrick! She's lyin' out there under the balcony. She must'a' fell off—she's—dead—"

And, as Brade followed the boy out the door and bent over the crushed and broken body of the housekeeper of Willow Wilde, the one thought that remained clearly in his mind was that with her had died the knowledge of what Dallas Gantry had written before she disappeared.

Chapter Sixteen
The Shack on Elder's Hill

DALLAS LEANED BACK against the stiff, uncomfortable chair and closed her eyes. She was shivering with cold and fear, and the bonds that held her wrists cut deeply. Her hat was gone but she still wore her fur coat.

She remained like that for a time, eyes closed, body tense, mind alert with a terrible clarity. Slowly, carefully, she went over the events that led up to her finding herself a prisoner in the old deserted shack on the shoulder of Elder's Hill.

She had run away from Willow Wilde. From Anthony and Brade, and the fear of death that hung over the house. She had only intended to take a swift, bracing turn and come back and she had left a note addressed to Captain Brade, in plain sight on the hall table, where he would find it and know that she was not running out on him.

Then she had discovered that someone was following her and the man in the gray hat had seized her arm. Dallas moaned and twisted her head frantically from side to side. That horrible man! His pale face, his narrow white eyes, his terrible fingers on her arm, that moment when he had paused and confronted her there at the entrance to the old lane, when he had said:

"I know who murdered Jurden Keye and Opal Garth! I can prove it and save you, get you off clear, straighten out the whole mess and I will do it if you will pay me twenty thousand dollars!"

Dallas opened her eyes, stared dully around her. Why was she here? Did he mean to kill her? Why hadn't he done it before? Where was he now? She was alone in the shack, there was a candle guttering in a rusty tin sconce on the far wall. The place was unspeakably ugly. There were cracks in the boards and the whistling wind sucked hungrily at the tiny flickering flame, even pushing the sconce out from its hanging, setting it to swinging gently.

The candle did not illuminate the entire room. The far corner was in thick shadow. She thought there was a bunk there. She could just make out the ragged end of what looked like bedding. There were some empty food cans tossed to the floor. A battered pan sat on its neat little frame above a can of solidified alcohol. Someone had been living here, cooking and sleeping.

Dallas' mind went back to the lane and the words of Samuel Fredricks. "Twenty thousand dollars," she seemed to hear him say again. "It's cheap, Miss Gantry, to get you free from all this mess. I know you've got it and plenty more. If you haven't Gordon will help you and you'll come in for old Keye's estate—"

That was the way it had gone on while he stood there holding tight to her arms, and her terror grew until it filled the night about her and sang on the wings of the rustling winds, crept up at her out of the sere brown fields where corn was standing in shocks like wigwams and golden pumpkins glowed between.

And it had reached a point where she could not stand it any longer and she had screamed and fought against his hold, crying over and over: "Let me go! Let me go! You are the killer—you— murdered them—I know you did it—!" and then something had crashed on her head, cutting through the felt of the little brown hat, seeming to split her brain in two and that was the end until she opened her eyes and watched the guttering candle, the swaying sconce—heard that movement in the corner!

She surged forward against her bonds, dry lips parted in a soundless sob. There wasn't anyone there! She was alone! Much as her aloneness had frightened her a few minutes ago, now the thought of other occupants of the shack seemed infinitely worse. She shook her head to get the hair from her eyes and strained into the darkness.

A hoarse voice said: "Hey, lady—can you hear me?"

Consciousness left her for a moment. There was blackness all around her, the hooting wind, the stealthy pattering of feet, then she groped back and the man said again:

"I ain't gonna hurt you, lady. I'm tied up too. I thought mebbe between us we could get free."

"Who are you?" she whispered.

He did not answer for a moment, then: "I'm Frosty Rivet," he said very low. "I lammed on that killin' back in town, didn't want to be mixed up in it, and Leo double-crossed me and—"

"Leo! Who's he?"

"That guy that brought you here. What's his lay?"

"His what?"

"What's he plannin' to do with you? You're Dallas Gantry, ain't you?"

"Yes, I'm Dallas Gantry. I don't know what he's planning to do with me. Kill me, maybe—"

Frosty considered this in silence a time. "Not unless you got the low-down on him," he said. "Not unless you're wise that he really bumped Keye."

Dallas gasped, eyes flashing over the place, groping for sight of the man called Leo. "Did—he—was he—the one who stabbed—"

"Keye wasn't stabbed," Frosty said sullenly. "He was plugged! Leo done it. Standin' outside the window there in the dark. He plugged Keye in the back, then someone else planted that knife in him. I don't know why."

Dallas stared at him, wide-eyed, shocked into immobility by this news.

"How do you know that?" she demanded at last. She could make out the man now, huddled back on the rumpled bunk.

He was disclosed in the light of the melting candle as it leaped up before the wind, and he disappeared as it died down, only to leap out at her again, his pale blood-stained face, his disheveled hair falling in lank damp strands over his forehead. He was huddled down with his arms behind him. His feet were bound with ropes. There was something eerie about his appearances and vanishings, as if he were a weird Jack-in-the-box, popping out unexpectedly.

His eyes were terribly bright. They glittered like the eyes of a cornered animal. A rat! Yes, Frosty Rivet made her think of a rat she had once seen caught in a trap.

"How do you know," she repeated, "that Jurden Keye was shot?"

"Never mind," he replied huskily. "I know. But don't let's talk about that. How we gonna get out?"

"I don't know. Where has this man—Leo—gone?"

The bright, restless eyes avoided her. "I dunno," he said. "He's cookin' up somethin'. He brought you in, dumped you in that there chair and tied you up, then he went out. I dunno where he went. Won't be gone long. He left that candle—"

The eyes of the two prisoners involuntarily went to the candle. "Geeze," Frosty husked, "it's gettin' low, ain't it? Be dark in here pretty soon."

"I'd rather it would be dark than have it blow like that. It's dangerous—suppose it—"

She stopped on a faint gasp. The cheap little tin container banged merrily against the wall, the rusty nail which supported it slipped from its ancient moorings and the whole thing clattered to the floor! For a moment Dallas thought the flame had been extinguished, then in the sudden darkness a little red tongue licked hungrily at an oiled bread paper, devoured it, flickered, died down, leaped up at a sudden gust of wind, and laid hold of a piece of greasy-looking cloth against the leg of the table.

"Geeze!" Frosty whispered. "It's climbin'. Can you put it out—"

Dallas was writhing against the ropes that held her to the chair. "I can't get them loose, can't you—reach it?"

The man was cursing between set teeth. Sweat stood on his livid face. His eyes grew brighter as they watched the creeping flame. He surged against whatever it was that held him locked to a heavy wooden stanchion of the shack.

"Tip your chair over," he choked. "Fall on the floor—mebbe you can—get to it—"

Dallas' feet were tied to the lower rungs of the chair which was a heavy crude thing, handmade of stout oak. Her arms were drawn backward and fastened behind the chair back.

For all her desperate struggling, she could not move the thing. There was no purchase anywhere. Nothing she could touch, catch hold of. She closed her eyes a moment, breathing in great gasping breaths of the air that was already getting hot. She could hear Frosty Rivet floundering around like the tortured rat she had seen in the trap.

She rested there, quietly, not thinking of this thing that had happened to her. Not looking into the immediate future. It all seemed so foolish and futile to her. She was an individual. A personality. She had mind and body, touch and smell and sight. Why should she die like this? Roasted to death in a wretched little shack on Elder's Hill?

"Cripes!" Frosty yelled frantically. "It's climbin'! It's catchin' the table—"

Dallas opened her eyes. The fire was certainly gaining headway. The old shack was dry as tinder. There was a boisterous wind whooping over the hill.

"Leo!" Frosty screamed. "Leo—help! Help! Aw—fer—"

His babblings reached Dallas from a great distance. She was so very, very tired. She had tried too hard for everything. She had loved life when she married Jurden Keye! She had left him and found herself in her work. She loved the theater. Smell of grease paint. Tang of canvas. Glitter of lights. Blare of orchestra—crowds! People! Milling in! Crowding out! The creak of the curtain as it lifted, the crack as it hit the floor boards.

She jerked up, staring at the bellowing flames. They had eaten up the side wall, caught the newspapers that covered the window. They made a dry crackling sound, like autumn leaves, like Jurden Keye's hands when he rubbed them together, when he looked at her and said:

"No! I will not give you a divorce!"

She kept her thoughts on that meeting with her husband there at Willow Wilde. That way she could shut out the sound of Frosty Rivet's mumbling screams as the flames licked hungrily at the musty coverings of the bunk, she could partially forget the heat that was torturing her. . . .

She had gone into the old parlor, leaned against the door, staring at the room, remembering terribly. There had been no one there, at first, so she had thought, then that stirring in the alcove, Jurden Keye's voice saying:

"There's one way out for you, my dear. I can fix everything—"

Fix—everything? Fix what? What could he fix for anyone? Who was he talking to? Who stood beside him there in the alcove before the French windows? There had been no voice but his, or had there? Had someone said something, gasped a name—had she, Dallas, caught that tone, buried it in her subconscious until this moment, when pain and a terror that had ceased to lash her brought it out? Was the voice she heard that of. . . .

A lusty hail sounded outside! Something crashed against the door. It swung in, and with it came a sweeping breath of wind that sent the flames leaping ceilingward in a driving sheet. Dallas saw a man stagger back, caught the black outline of him as he crouched there, one arm crooked over his face, then he came on, he fought through, calling her name over and over:

"Dallas! Dallas! Where are you?"

She had no consciousness of answering but she must have, for presently she felt hands groping at the bonds around her ankles, she heard sobbing, panting breath, then someone seized the back of the heavy chair, jerked it round and started dragging it backward toward the door.

When the blessed air struck her face, she looked up to see Gregg MacFarlane, bare-headed, the flames making his dead white hair red like blood, and she moaned faintly and, closed her eyes, then she heard Frosty Rivet's hoarse yell and saw Gregg disappear again in the flaming caldron of the shack on Elder's Hill.

Chapter Seventeen
Shattered Crystal

Captain Courtney Brade straightened from beside the body of Mrs. Maybrick. He held Jimmy Arnold's flashlight in a steady hand and he was playing it carefully over the front of the house and the ground around the woman's body. Then he sent it up, creeping over the turreted windows, the scaling paint, coming to rest, finally, on the bulging roundness of a small, railed balcony protruding from the house between the second and third stories.

"What is that?" he asked Jimmy.

"It's the Look-Out spot," Jimmy said breathlessly. "You go up a short stairway from the second floor, and a door opens onto the balcony. You can see all over the country—"

"Poor soul, poor soul," Faith MacFarlane was murmuring over and over as she bent beside Maybrick's body. "How could it have happened? Why did she go out there? As long as she has lived at Willow Wilde . . . that she should fall from the balcony—"

"When she left you," Brade asked, "she was normal? Nothing out of the ordinary happen to upset her as far as you knew?"

Faith met his eyes calmly. "Nothing so far as I know, Captain Brade," she replied. "No, I noticed nothing wrong with her."

Brade said: "You had better go in the house, Mrs. MacFarlane," and knelt again beside the body of the dead woman.

Faith MacFarlane stood up, drawing a hand across her eyes. In the reflected light of the flash which Jimmy held, she looked very white and tired. There were deep purple stains beneath her eyes. Her lips looked gray. She cried suddenly:

"Oh, I can't stand it! I can't go on living like this! So much death! Death all around me. I'd like to—die—too!" Then she turned abruptly and went into the house, walking very straight with that queer sense of height about her, of strength, of terrific control.

Brade was examining something he had picked up from the ground. It was a small piece of glass, very thin, slightly concave. He turned it curiously.

"Watch crystal," he muttered, then his probing eyes went over the scene again, and from a tangle of dried grass he lifted a bit of black leather with two perforations neatly made, one end torn and whitish.

"Huh!" he grunted again. "Strap for wrist watch! See if you can find—" he said to Jimmy; then with a muttered exclamation he dived forward and from a nick of leaves he drew out a thin, octagonal watch of white gold! The crystal was missing. The leather strap was torn off near the bar, the hands were bent and ruined.

Brade turned it curiously and a strangely troubled light grew in his eyes. He glanced up at the balcony, at the body of the dead woman and in his mind there grew a reconstruction of the scene that might have taken place there on the balcony in the still of the chilly autumn evening.

Maybrick standing there with someone. Talking. Arguing. Deaf to entreaties. Quarreling finally. Nerves strained to the breaking point, guiding suddenly tense clawing fingers to grapple with the woman, to clutch at her thick body, to push her nearer and nearer the edge, bend her back over the railing, her cries lost in the soughing wind and the choking grasp that strong fingers held on her throat. Then, as she felt herself bent farther and farther, felt her feet slipping from the floor of the balcony, her own hands outcurled, claw-like, searching madly for support, for something that would save her from certain death on the wet, slippery red clay below, clutching at her assailant's arms, slipping down, fastening at last on a wrist, hooking into the stout leather of a strap, holding, tightening, breaking it at last as she plunged over, taking with her the shattered proof of her murderer's identity.

Brade stood up. "Bring something to cover the body, Jimmy," he said quietly, though his lips were white. "Then phone Dr. Monery. I'll be busy in the morning room for a while."

He went quickly toward the house, carrying the watch in his hand. In the hall he met Anthony Gordon. He looked pale and worried.

"I say, Court," he began, "can't we do something?"

"Come here," Brade said, and opened the door on his right.

Anthony followed him, startled eyes on his friend's face.

"What's wrong, Court?" he asked, then suddenly tremulous, "It isn't Dallas? You haven't heard—that Dallas—"

Brade smoothed his rumpled hair. He was breathing unevenly. He kept one hand in his pocket. He said: "Mrs. Maybrick has been murdered, Anthony."

"Good God! You don't mean—that someone—has—"

"Exactly. She was thrown from that balcony and was instantly killed on the ground below. Seen her lately?"

Anthony shook his head. His eyes were blank and he was obviously trying to adjust himself to this new tragedy.

"Not lately," he began, and stopped, suddenly rigid. "No, I haven't seen her," he mumbled and turned away to light a cigarette with fingers that trembled.

"What time is it, Anthony?" Brade asked gently.

Anthony's left hand lifted involuntarily, his eyes flashed to his wrist. Then the hand dropped. He looked up, met Brade's eyes, smiled with a queer recklessness.

"Sorry, Court," he said. "My watch is in the repair shop. Smashed a crystal."

"Yes?" Brade's hand came from his pocket, laid the remnants of the octagonal watch on the table. "Recognize that?" he asked.

Anthony Gordon stared at it as if he were suddenly blind. All the color went out of his face and before Brade's hard, level eyes little dots of moisture broke through the skin and gleamed there wetly. He didn't say anything. He just stared and the muscles in his lean jaw tightened. Then his glance lifted, met his friend's eyes.

"No," he said clearly. "I have never seen it before."

Brade leaned forward with a quick, controlled movement, lifted the watch, turned it deftly and inserted a thumb nail under the back cover, flipped it out. Staring back at him were three words engraved on the polished metal. They read:

"Anthony from Dallas"

"Mrs. Maybrick stuck to her story about Dallas murdering Jurden Keye," Brade said. "She claimed to be an eyewitness to the shooting of Opal Garth by Dallas—"

Both men whirled toward the window. A voice reached them, harsh, commanding. "Halt!" it said, and again, "Halt!" Its echo was drowned in the roar of a heavy automatic.

Chapter Eighteen
The Marks On The Knife

BRADE'S FACE went grim as granite. He said, "Wait here, Anthony. Something's wrong." He turned swiftly to the door, opened it and disappeared.

Gordon remained standing by the table, eyes on the closing door. Suddenly he began trembling. Shaking all over like a man with ague, then deliberately he picked up the watch, strode across to the fire that blazed in the open grate and threw it in. He stood there wiping his hands on his trousers and the clicking of his teeth sounded clearly in the silent room.

Brade stopped on the veranda, staring out into the dark through narrowed eyes. Somewhere in the grounds were sounds of muffled voices, pounding feet, but he could not locate them.

"Hello," he called. "Hello, out there. What's wrong?"

A voice answered him from considerable distance. "All right, Captain Brade, we got him. Be right in."

Brade ran toward the sound. He had snapped on the porch light and by its aid he saw two men struggling toward him, hanging on hard to a third, who cursed and groaned alternately. Then he saw Jimmy Arnold, Tom Gary. Their prisoner he did not recognize.

"What's the row?" he demanded, shooting on his flash. "Who is this fellow? Wounded somewhere in the chest, isn't he? What happened?"

Jimmy mopped sweat from his face. Tom clicked handcuffs on the prisoner's wrists. Jimmy said: "I had just covered Mis' Maybrick's body like you told me, sir, and was turnin' back toward

160

the house when I saw this guy sneaking through the grounds. I called to him and he started runnin'. I went after him. He fired at me and—"

Tom Gary took up the story. "I happened along just then, Captain Brade, and I winged him. I think we want him bad."

Brade stepped closer, peered down at the white twisting face. A tight, hard grin twitched his lips. "Hello, Wyche," he said. "What in hell are you doing here?"

Tom Gary asked abruptly: "You know him, Captain Brade?"

"Yes," Brade said grimly. "Leo Wyche, about as clever a crook as it's been my pleasure to meet up with. Not quite clever enough though," he commented, eyeing Wyche's bloody shirt front. "Well, bring him in. I'll have a word with him. Leo, I deduce, is the lad who came down here to meet Frosty Rivet and Opal Garth on some little private business of their own. Registered at the Inn, then lammed when the trouble broke up here. We'll have to have a little heart-to-heart, Leo."

Wyche set his thin lips and glared at Brade. His soft gray hat was gone, his expensive suit was rumpled by the rough handling he had received. There was a long bloody scratch across his cheek where a branch had torn it.

Tom Gary spoke suddenly. "There's been trouble out on Elder's Hill, Brade. That's what I was comin' to tell you. The old hunting shack out there took fire. Dallas Gantry and that man called Alden were prisoners in it."

Brade whirled. "Dallas!" he snapped. "Frosty Rivet! Get them out?"

Tom nodded. "Mr. MacFarlane did. Don't know how he happened to be there. Some of the folks livin' near the edge of town saw the blaze and by the time they got there, Gregg had the two out. They're all pretty bad off."

"Where are they now?"

"Dr. Monery's bringin' 'em up in his car," Tom said. "He's patched them up a bit. They ought to be here any time."

As the little group stepped into the hall, the phone rang. Brade said: "Take Wyche into the library, Tom. I'll join you in a minute."

He picked up the phone. "Hello," he said, "Captain Brade speaking."

A smoothly professional voice said: "Hold the wire, please. Long distance calling."

Brade grunted. This call might be important. Then he heard Terry Shan's voice: "Hello, Court, ready for an earful?"

"You said it, kid. Spill the works." Brade's fingers tightened on the receiver. There was a tremendous confusion in his mind, a medley of disassociated ideas that, for the moment, he could not sort into intelligent pattern.

"You know that knife you sent up to be printed? Well, get a load of this. It's got the digit marks of a boy we been lookin' for. That bird I told you about over the phone last night. Andy Stillwell. What do you think of that?"

Brade's straight black brows were drawn down in a tight hard line. He was thinking furiously. "Andy Stillwell?" he questioned. "Andy—" Then he said again: "Sure of that, Terry? No reflection on the Department, of course, but it's devilishly important."

"Sure as sunrise," came the carelessly professional voice over the wire. "What's more, the tip we got that kept me up nights checkin' up was that this same Stillwell had been seen in a little town called Centerville, which is just twenty miles from Willow Valley. Looks like he's been in that neck of the woods, all right. Thought you'd want to know."

"I'll say. What else? The gun—"

"Got a mess off that, but the sheets you sent haven't arrived yet and we can't hook 'em up with anything here at H. Q."

"All right, Terry. They ought to be in any time. Sent 'em special. Everybody here at the house except one. He was out of the picture when I made the printing and I didn't wait. His will come along later. Anything else?"

"Nothin' except we got a tip that Leo Wyche headed down for Willow Valley last night on an important job of some kind. Seen him?"

Brade grinned. "Yeah," he said. "I could see him now if the library door was open. I got him, Terry, with a hole in his middle."

"Good work, Captain," Terry sang out. "S'long till next time."

"Wait a minute, Terry. This Stillwell boy. What's he wanted for?"

Silence a moment, then Terry said: "I'm sendin' his dossier down by special messenger, Court. It's too complicated to spill over the phone. It ought to be there pretty soon."

Brade hung up the receiver and leaned against the wall. Now what did this mean? That Andy Stillwell, and for the life of him Brade couldn't connect on that name, had been in the vicinity of Willow Valley on the night that Jurden Keye was murdered. He had been seen in Centerville, twenty miles away, seen and recognized, and someone had tipped headquarters.

Terry had set to work to check up on his record and when the knife that had been buried in Keye's back was examined, it contained Stillwell's prints. But who had shot him? And why had Stillwell stabbed him—

Brade looked up at sound of a car stopping. He opened the door and saw a silent little procession mounting the steps of Willow Wilde. Dallas Gantry came first. She walked carefully as if she were not exactly sure of her footing. Her lovely gold hair was rumpled and disheveled. There was a long black streak across her cheek. Her left arm had been bared to the shoulder and was heavily swathed in surgical dressings, showing beneath her coat. Her face was stark with pain.

She came up the steps and stopped before Brade. "I didn't mean to run out on you," she said in a flat mechanical voice. "I left a note. You got it, of course?"

Brade looked hard into her eyes, shook his head. "Your note was destroyed, Dallas," he told her, "or we might have come to your aid. Go in now and I suggest that you go at once to your room and lie down. I'll come and talk to you later."

She went past him without a word, mounted the stairs and disappeared. Then Brade saw Dr. Monery supporting a shivering wreck of a man and even the hardened officer involuntarily looked away.

Frosty Rivet had been badly burned. His head was wrapped in bandages and his arms protruded stiffly in their multitudinous swathings. Only his eyes shone with a terrible brightness and he moaned and mumbled dully.

Dr. Monery said to Brade: "This man must be put to bed at once, Captain. I would have left him at the hotel but I understand he is an important witness and there were not adequate facilities to guard him."

"That's right, Doctor," said Brade. "I'll take care of him." He turned to Tom Gary, who had stepped into the hall. "Tom, take Frosty upstairs somewhere, put him to bed and"—Brade added slowly—"watch your step. We're going to need him."

Tom Gary nodded grimly as he seized one of Frosty's bandaged arms not too gently and propelled him up the stairs, then Brade turned and saw Gregg MacFarlane. His eyes went over him slowly, appraisingly; he smiled slightly.

"Bad hurt, MacFarlane?" he asked.

MacFarlane managed to smile back with white pain-twisted lips.

"Not too bad, Captain," he said gamely, then he drew his hands from behind him and Brade's eyes went hard and cold. Gregg MacFarlane's hands had not been bandaged! "I was anxious to get back here," he explained quietly. "The doctor can take care of them here."

Brade stepped closer, bent down, looking hard at the terrible things that had once been human hands. He remembered that Gregg MacFarlane had possessed remarkably fine hands. Long and strong, with sensitive, sentient fingers, powerful, slow moving, beautiful things.

He said rather uncertainly: "How did it happen? Tell me while the doctor fixes you up, will you?"

"Of course." MacFarlane followed Brade into the hall. The doctor went back to the car for his equipment. MacFarlane said rather low: "Faith! I hope she doesn't see—until—they're fixed."

"She's in her room, MacFarlane. Let's go in here."

He opened the door into the parlor where Jurden Keye had been killed. The room had quite naturally been shunned by the inmates of Willow Wilde. Now it was bleak and cold and there was a heavy dead air about it that chilled the marrow. Brade kindled a fire while

Dr. Monery spread out his bandages and ointments and went calmly about his work. Gregg MacFarlane sat motionless, like a man of stone, staring at his hands.

"Bad, aren't they?" he asked at last, as if he were commenting on the roads.

The doctor grunted, looked away, suddenly very busy with gauze. Brade came and stood beside the table. He did not look at MacFarlane, he looked at MacFarlane's hands.

"When you're through, Doctor," he said, "there's another case for you across the hall. Man with a hole through his chest, I think."

The doctor looked up with a quick widening of his patient, kindly eyes, shook his head and clipped surgical tape into long strips.

"There," he said at last, "that will do for the moment. Feel better, Gregg?"

Gregg nodded. "Better," he said tonelessly. "Thanks, Doc."

The doctor went to look after Leo Wyche. Brade lighted a cigarette, sat on the edge of the table. Gregg dropped weakly back in his chair. Brade studied him a moment, then he lighted a second smoke and placed it between the injured man's lips.

"Sorry I can't make it a cigar," he said. "You'd prefer that, I take it."

The other smiled. "This will do nicely," he said.

Brade continued, "What caused that fire up there, MacFarlane, and how did Dallas happen to be there? Get any dope?"

"Yes. This man Samuel Fredricks, you've been looking for him—"

"I know," Brade said. "His real name is Leo Wyche and he's a bad actor. Go on."

"He—kidnapped her. Was hanging around the place here, saw her leave, followed her, cracked her down and tied her up in the cabin."

"Why?"

"I don't know. She was too—upset—to talk much. I only got a few details. Clay Alden—"

"*His* name is Rivet. Frosty Rivet. Another crook."

"All right. He was there, too. Fastened by a piece of baling wire to an upright. That's how—" MacFarlane paused, glanced at his hands, looked away. "I had a devil of a time getting him loose," he explained. "Dallas said that Samuel or Wyche or whatever his name is, went off and left them while she was still unconscious. There was a candle on the wall. The wind blew it down. That started the fire."

"I see." Brade was studying his fingertips. "Lucky you happened along in time, isn't it?"

"My God, yes." MacFarlane's eyes went suddenly wide and dark. "They'd have been—"

"Of course. Now, Gregg, how did it happen, exactly, that you were on the spot? I missed you here—"

"Right after you told me Dallas was gone? Yes. I went out to find her."

"I see. And how did you do it? What clue led you to that lonely spot on Elder's Hill so soon? I might have hunted half the night."

Gregg MacFarlane was leaning back in the chair, with eyes closed. The light touched his ravaged face, his pain-whitened lips. Brade got the feeling just then that MacFarlane was past caring what happened. That in his life there had been so much tragedy, so many bitter jolts, that nothing much mattered. Brade and the law behind him could hammer as much as they wished. Gregg MacFarlane would take the buffeting, keep his feet as long as he could and when he finally went down, it wouldn't matter to him. There was a curious air of detachment about him, and Brade felt it. It was as if he questioned a man already dead.

MacFarlane said: "I don't know how I found her, Brade. Isn't it sufficient that—I—did?"

"Possibly. Did she tell you where she was going?"

"No. I didn't talk to her there in the grounds."

"Yet when the report reached you that she was missing, you went directly to her. There must have been something."

"I heard Mrs. Maybrick talking to Leo Wyche."

"Eh? What's that?"

"Yes. There under the lilac hedge. I came on them unexpectedly. Listened in. He told her he was occupying that shack on the hill. He wanted to get in touch with Dallas."

"What else did he tell her?" Brade's voice was so soft it sounded like a purr.

MacFarlane shook his head, there was a gently stubborn smile on his lips. "That's all," he said.

Brade tapped ashes from his cigarette. "Of course you're lying," he said.

"Of course," MacFarlane agreed. "What are you going to do about it?"

Brade considered this gravely. "If you would tell me what Wyche told Maybrick," he said slowly, "I might be able to figure out why she was murdered here in this house an hour ago."

MacFarlane leaped to his feet, stood there swaying drunkenly, then limply he collapsed. "Murdered!" he whispered. "Maybrick murdered!"

"Yes. Someone pushed her over the balcony. She had something on her mind. What did Wyche tell her?"

"I suppose medieval torture had its advantages," MacFarlane commented. "You could boil me in oil if that practice still persisted. If you did," he added conversationally, "I still wouldn't tell you what Wyche and Maybrick talked about. If there's nothing else just now would you mind if I got some rest?"

"No," Brade said. "You may go to your room. Of course, if you attempt to leave the house again you will be shot instantly." He stood up. MacFarlane got to his feet unsteadily.

"I won't attempt to leave," he said. "Thank you."

"Just a moment," Brade said. "I received an interesting bit of information from headquarters to-night. That knife, you know, the one that was found in Keye's heart, well, the prints on it are those of a man who has been wanted by the police for a long time. A chap named Stillwell. Andy Stillwell! Ever hear of him?"

MacFarlane was staring at the rug. There was a pucker of perplexity between his brows. "That's odd," he said. "How should his prints be found on the knife? You mean—that—this—Stillwell stabbed Keye?"

"Looks like it. Ever hear of him?"

"Seems like I have," MacFarlane said, "but it's a bit hazy in my mind. What's he wanted for?"

"I can't remember either," Brade admitted. "Something rather important, I should say. Thought maybe you could give me a tip. You used to live out West, didn't you? Well, this chap hails from Oregon. I'd hoped you remembered the case."

"Sorry," MacFarlane said seriously, "it eludes me. I almost get it, but it isn't there."

"That's just the way it is with me," Brade confided, then he added, "You know, MacFarlane, it's unfortunate that you were out of the house to-day when I printed everybody, isn't it? I was in a rush, so I shot the sheets off without getting your fingerprints. It's going to be a time now before anything can be done about it. Too bad, isn't it?"

Gregg MacFarlane looked straight at the detective from his haggard, suffering eyes and laughed. Softly, triumphantly, "Isn't it?" he agreed and walked quickly from the room.

Somewhere a door clicked shut very, very softly. Brade whirled, eyes busy. There was no one in the room. He stalked over to the alcove, examined the fastenings on the French window. They were intact. He stood there glaring at the room. He was mortally sure someone had listened in on his conversation with MacFarlane, but where?

"Oh, ho," he said and ducked toward a small door partially concealed by heavy red drapes in the far corner of the room. It was through this door, he reflected, that Frosty Rivet had found his way upstairs last night, before Opal Garth was murdered.

Brade opened it. The narrow stairway was empty, chill, thick with dust. He drew out a pocket flash, shot it around, bent lower, and a grim satisfaction mirrored in his eyes. There on the step was a tiny, crumbling fragment of red clay! He stared at it a while, then his glance went up the stairs to the door at the head which led into the upper hall, and slowly he stepped back into the room and let the thick, dusty drapes fall into place.

Chapter Nineteen
Brade Should Wear Brown

BRADE STOOD BESIDE the bed staring thoughtfully down at Leo Wyche. The man was badly hurt. Tom Gary's bullet had come dangerously near the lung. Dr. Monery had said Wyche was not to be questioned. There was a chance that he would recover. An even better one that he would die. Brade had heard this verdict and nodded shortly.

"All right, Doctor," he said, "and just in case he's going to pass out, I'm talking to him now. Understand? Now!" And at the little doctor's sudden flaring of professional protection, the detective had said:

"Leo Wyche is a criminal. A killer. An ex-convict. A thoroughly bad egg. If he recovers and gets off from complications in this business, he will immediately take up his life of crime again. There's nothing good about him. He's a parasite. A menace to society. All right. There stand, in the shadow of serious suspicion of murder in this house to-night, several people who are Wyche's exact opposite. Constructive, rather than destructive. Wyche knows something about this mess. It's my duty to try to get what he knows. If I endanger his life in doing it, well—" He shrugged. "I've got to save the innocent if I can. How about it?"

And the doctor had looked hard at him and slowly nodded. "Go to it," he said, and so Brade stood now beside Leo Wyche in the north bedroom at Willow Wilde, looked down at the flushed face and wondered what the man could tell.

"Wyche," he said suddenly and the man's eyes opened, blank with pain, yet containing something of their old insolence.

169

"What you want?" he muttered.

"Is Andy Stillwell in Willow Valley?"

For a moment Wyche's eyes held a normal light. He glared at the detective suspiciously, then he twisted, moaning with pain. "Find out," he gasped.

Well, Brade reflected, he hadn't thought it would be easy. "That's what Frosty and Opal got you down here for, isn't it?" he persisted. "To identify Andy Stillwell? Wasn't that it?"

"Don't you wish you knew?" Wyche snarled. "Get to hell outta here, copper, I ain't spillin'."

Brade rumpled his hair. "Oh, all right," he said. "Suit yourself." He began whistling and half turned away. "I think you're going to croak," he told the sick man. "I hope you don't, Leo, I'd like to see you burn for the murder of Keye—"

A stifled curse stopped him. He glanced back over his shoulder. Leo Wyche was struggling to sit up. "Keye!" he choked. "I didn't bump him. That lousy little rat of a Rivet did it, then he come sneakin' to me for protection and—"

"And you nabbed him? What for?"

Wyche sank back. "None of your business," he said, looking at the detective through narrowed furtive eyes. "I got dope you'd like to have, though," he went on, then laughed with a horrible twitching of his white lips. "I'll see you in hell before I spill," he added, and turned his head away.

"Thanks, Leo. The same to you." Brade leaned against the wall. "It's quite natural that you'd accuse Frosty of Keye's murder. Of course, that won't get you any place, my lad. I've got the record of that print I found under the window through which Keye was shot and I can prove that you—"

"Say, looka here," Leo said thickly. "If you'll send one of your low-brow dicks to general delivery in the city and ask for a package addressed to Louie Brown, you'll find that it contains a gat. You'll find that the bullet which killed Keye came from that gun and you'll find little Frosty's name engraved on the stock. Now see where that gets you."

Brade's eyes were very bright. "Oh, yes?" he said softly. "Well, toodle-oo, Leo, and thanks a lot."

He went quickly downstairs, called headquarters and gave the necessary instructions about collecting the package addressed to Louie Brown at general delivery. Then he went to Dallas Gantry's room. Anthony was with her and he rose quickly when Brade entered, standing there, head high, eyes defiant.

"Mind leaving us a moment, Anthony?" Brade said pleasantly. "I want to talk to Dallas if she feels up to it."

Anthony glanced at Dallas. She was stretched out on a lounge near the fire. She nodded slightly. He went out without a word. Brade waited until the door had closed, then he drew up a chair, rested his elbows on his knees and grinned at Dallas.

"Hard life, isn't it?" he inquired.

She choked a sob. "It's terrible, Captain Brade—terrible. What are we—what shall we do—this can't go on."

"Never you mind, my girl," he said grimly. "It's going to end one of these hours. How're you feeling?"

She just shook her head, looking at him with bright feverish eyes, dimmed by tears. "All right," he agreed. "Don't go into it. What did Leo Wyche want with you?"

She closed her eyes a moment and he saw her white face twitch, then she said: "He told me he knew who had killed Jurden Keye and Opal Garth, and that he could prove it. He offered to fix the whole thing up so I wouldn't be implicated if I would pay him twenty thousand dollars."

"Oh—I—see," Brade said softly. "That was his game, eh? And what proof did he give you, if any?"

"None. I didn't give him a chance. I was so—terrified—I thought I knew that he had somehow done it and I started screaming and tried to run and he struck me and when I regained consciousness I was in that shack and that man—you call Frosty— was captive there too."

She stopped, breathing unevenly. Brade watched her somberly. It was all very complicated.

Suppose he proved that Frosty Rivet or Leo Wyche killed Jurden Keye? Killed him with a bullet through that open window. What did that get him? It didn't explain who had plunged that knife into Keye's heart? It didn't tell how the fingerprints of a man named Andy Stillwell happened to be on the handle. It didn't clear up the matter of Opal's death, of Mrs. Maybrick's murder—of who had listened there in the stairway when he talked to Gregg MacFarlane.

He thought he saw through Leo's plan. If what he said about the gun he had mailed to himself in the city was true, he certainly had proof that Frosty Rivet had murdered Keye. He had also held Frosty Rivet a captive in the shack on Elder's Hill, ready to turn him over, when a sufficient cash incentive was offered him. He had tried his scheme on Dallas, figuring her frantic and desperate, fighting, back to the wall, for her own life and liberty, an easy victim to his plot, then when she proved obdurate, afraid to let her return, he had struck her down, tied her up and returned to Willow Wilde—why?

Brade pondered that a time. Why had Leo Wyche come back to Willow Wilde? Whom was he looking for? Whom did he wish to talk to? Dallas was lying with eyes closed, but through the fringe of her lashes she was watching him. She was wondering what she ought to do, what she should tell him about that terrible conviction that had leaped up there in that moment of terror and pain when the flames. . . .

"What is it, Dallas?" Brade asked gently.

Her eyes flared wide. She tried to draw back from him. "Nothing," she said through white lips. "Nothing."

"What's on your mind? Better tell me. It will be easier all round."

"No, no," she cried, suddenly frantic. "I won't tell you, I can't—it's nothing, I'm tired. Go and let me rest. I can't stand this—"

"I know. Murder's never pleasant. The murderer has to be punished—"

She sobbed brokenly. "There ought to be a difference. Some people deserve—murder."

"Why?"

"Because of what—they are—of the pain they cause others. Because everything about them is stained and ugly and—evil."

"And you mean they should be murdered as punishment? Deprived of life because they are evil?"

"Yes, that's what I mean."

"You think, to lose one's life, that is the greatest punishment, Dallas? There is nothing so bad as being—dead?"

She stared at him wide-eyed. His face was close to hers and she could see the lines in it, the twitching of his strong mouth, the cloudiness of his eyes, and suddenly the cloudiness was swept away as a fresh breeze dispels sea fog, and she looked into the heart of the man, gazed in terror at his loneliness, his tragedy. She began crying soundlessly, tears overflowing her eyes and running down her cheeks. Crying as she had seldom cried before, because suddenly all of life seemed so sad and she realized fully what he meant, and then his voice reached her, gentle, kindly, comforting.

He said: "Don't cry, Dallas. Please don't, my dear. I hope you will never learn that there are worse things than—being—dead! That there is a loneliness greater than that of the grave, a grief—"

"Oh!" she cried. "Oh! that you should say that—you, a policeman. I never thought a policeman— would be like—you—I never thought they—"

"They were human?" he finished for her, and there was such wholesome natural mirth in his voice that she looked abruptly and saw to her amazement that he was laughing.

"You never thought them human, did you, Dallas?" he repeated, still with that suggestion of wholesome laughter in his voice. "Well, I don't blame you, my girl. But you know policemen actually enjoy the things other people do. I knew one who liked to fish, and there's another who's quite demented over the radio and I've even known them to be interested in the color of their ties and—"

Dallas cried suddenly: "Oh, Captain Brade, how can you? Talk about hunting and—radio—and ties—now! Radios don't seem very important, and—ties—"

"There are some very terrible ones," he assured her gravely. "My pal wears 'em green. He's Irish. Would you guess it? Now I

think this one is nice—" He leaned forward, extending the fold of
silk. "It's moiré, isn't that the word? And the salesman assured me
it was very becoming—"

"I think you should wear brown. Your hair is brown. Still, your
eyes are gray." She put her head judicially on one side. It is hard
for a woman, regardless of circumstances, to lose her innate desire to select ties for mankind. "Brown or gray," she decided. "And
if your shirt were dark, I'd say something bright—"

"Orange?"

"Good heavens, no! Men have such taste. There are so many
delightful shades of brown. Russet. Leaf brown. Cocoa—loads of
them." She took hold of the tie, examining it critically. Brade's eyes
lowered swiftly, rested on her slim white wrist, on a dull stain that
marred its smoothness.

"Hurt yourself?" he asked casually. "Your wrist there?"

She hardly glanced at it, she was studying the tie, frowning intently. "No," she said. "That's the mark Anthony's watch made. I
broke mine just before I came down here and he insisted I put his
on last night, but it grew too heavy and I removed it before I went
out—that's really a very nice tie. Well tailored—"

"I'm glad you like it. I hope you'll lend me the benefit of your
judgment the next selection I make. What did you do with
Anthony's watch when you took it off? Give it back to him?"

She lifted her eyes, staring at him curiously. "Why, no," she
said slowly, "I loaned it to—"

There came a sharp knocking on the door, and Jimmy Arnold
stuck his head in. "Message for you, Captain Brade, just arrived by
special messenger from the city. Marked very important."

Brade was on his feet, glaring across at Jimmy. He wanted to
wring his neck. Then he looked down and saw that Dallas Gantry
had crumpled forward against the cushions of the lounge. Her eyes
were closed. She had fainted!

Chapter Twenty
Frosty Talks Some

"Frosty," Brade said, "I know that you killed Jurden Keye! What I want you to tell me is—"

Frosty's parched lips curled back from his teeth in a snarl. His pinched blue-white face stared out from the cap of bandages that covered his head. He said huskily:

"You're coocoo, Brade, I didn't plug him. Leo done it—"

"No," Brade said patiently, "*you* done it! That track under the window fits your shoe. Your fingerprints are on the sill! I have the gun"—this was not quite true—"with which you shot him. The bullet taken from his body came from that gun. It has your name on the stock—"

Frosty cringed back, wetting his lips. "Go to hell," he choked. "I ain't talkin'."

"Oh, all right," Brade agreed wearily, "but it won't make it any easier for you when you come to trial, my lad. If you would unbutton your lip and spill a few—"

"What's it gonna get me?" Frosty demanded. "What you givin' me if I squawk?"

Brade met the eager pleading of the feverish eyes with a cold, hard stare. "I'm not bribing you to talk," he said flatly. "I'm not holding out any reward, understand that. You killed Keye, I can prove it, and you'll pay for it, but if you can help me out on a few points I won't be forgetting and I'll do anything I can to make it easier for you."

175

Frosty crouched lower in the bed and closed his eyes. He was shivering with pain and fear. His sick mind reeled from the quiet deadliness of the detective's words. He was desperate, cornered, frantic to save his puny meager life. . . .

"What do you want to know?" he gasped.

"What you saw when you stood outside that window?"

Frosty's lips shut hard. He made one last defiant stand and capitulated.

"I seen Jurden Keye—in there—talkin' to someone—"

"Who?"

"I don't know."

"What time was this?"

"A little after ten-thirty, I think. I left the theater about ten-twenty, soon's I found out that Opal had beat it."

"You trailed her here?"

"Yeah. Didn't see her. But I knew she'd come." The injured man's face jerked spasmodically. "I knew she was playin' round with that old devil," he choked. "I thought a lotta Opal, Brade," he added almost timidly. "I been a lousy bum mosta my life, I guess, and I ain't ever had anything very decent to hang onto. I thought— Opal—" He groaned and writhed on the pillow. "I thought—she— was—decent. I wanted her to marry me. I was ready to cut loose from the racket, settle dlown somewhere and live straight. Yeah, if Opal had played the game with me, I'd 'a' given the racket up."

Brade regarded him stoically, a faintly cynical smile on his lips which was too slight for Frosty to catch. The detective knew so well that old, old determination. That resolution to "quit the racket." He had heard it expressed so very many times. Seen it tried out. And he knew with a hardened weariness how very, very seldom it worked. He knew that crime and the commission of crime is like a virus in the blood. That it takes hold like a stealthy disease, permeates the system, eats into the brain and it is a malady for which, as yet, modern science has not discovered a cure.

He said: "Sure, Frosty, I know how you feel. Opal meant quite a lot to you, didn't she? And you were pinning a lot of hopes on her, then she up and double-crossed you. She started playing around with Jurden Keye and—"

Frosty nodded grimly. "She wouldn't listen to me," he grated. "I tried to tell—her—things, but it wasn't any go. She claimed she had to see him. A matter of business—"

"What business? What were you and Opal and Leo and Jurden Keye working on, Frosty?"

Brade's heart was beating rather swiftly as he asked that question. A great deal depended on it. If Frosty would talk. . . .

But Frosty wouldn't. Some queer secretiveness sealed his lips. Whatever the plot had been it had promised great reward. It was muffed for the moment, everything was in a mess; Frosty himself stood in the shadow of the chair—it was beyond all reason to think that he could still profit, but that queer, distorted egotism that is an integral part of the make-up of every habitual criminal hinted that there *still* might be a chance. If he spilled to this dick, everything was over. If he kept still. . . .

He grinned furtively. "I ain't spillin' about *that*, Brade," he said. "You might as well write that down."

Brade accepted temporary defeat philosophically. "You followed Opal up here," he said, going back to the original question, "and you started sneaking around seeing what you could see. All right, what *did* you see when you looked in that window there in the parlor?"

"I seen Keye sittin' by the desk," Frosty said sullenly.

"What was he doing?"

"Chinnin' with someone."

"With whom?"

"I dunno. I couldn't see who was in the room with him. His back was toward me mosta' the time. Once or twice he turned half-way round and I could see he was talkin' but that was all."

"Then what?"

"Pretty soon he got up and I didn't see him any more for a while. Then that girl—that Dallas, she came in from the door to the hall. She just opened it, stepped in, shut the door and leaned against it,

lookin' around. Then Keye came out from over in the corner somewhere and they started talkin'. I heard what they said, for he come
over and opened the window. They was talkin' about a divorce she
wanted. Cripes, that guy was—lousy!"

The words came involuntarily from Frosty's lips. Even Frosty,
a hardened criminal, held himself better than Jurden Keye. He
went on, talking monotonously, not looking at Brade, almost as if
words were a relief.

"Then she got up and went out," he said, "and Keye jumped up
like he would go after her, then he flopped down and leaned forward with his elbows on the table and it was then—"

"Then you shot him?" Brade prompted, voice very low.

Frosty was staring at the wall and there was a dull, hypnotized
look in his eyes. He nodded mechanically. "I shot him," he
breathed. "And I'm glad I did. He'd taken my girl away from me.
I'd figured quite a lot on marryin' Opal, when I thought she was in
there with him, I plugged him—"

Brade turned the moonstone ring slowly. "What made you think
she was in there?" he asked.

"Huh?" Frosty stared at him blankly. "Why, I dunno—I just
thought—"

"You didn't hear her voice?"

Frosty puckered his sandy brows. "No," he said at last, "I didn't
hear her—voice—"

"All right," Brade said, "go on. What'd you do then?"

"I beat it, mister, beat it hard. I ran until I nearly croaked, then
I got to thinkin' that after all Opal had gone there and mebbe she'd
be mixed up in it, so I came back, sneakin' along, walkin' careful,
and I got an awful scare when someone bumped into me—"

"Who?"

"I dunno. It was dark as hell. Someone just slammed into me
and knocked me outta the way into the bushes and grass and went
on and I couldn't see a thing. I got up, heard whoever it was scram-
bling through the fence, then I come on up to the house and that's
when some bird opened the window and shot a light on me—"

"This person you ran into, Frosty, could you tell whether it was a man or a woman?"

Frosty scowled at the floor. "It was a man," he stated flatly. "I felt the rough cloth of his coat and it smelled like a cigar factory. Course, a Jane might smoke a lot," Frosty reasoned, "but not Havanas—usually pills. Opal used to—" Frosty's husky voice quivered, he twisted over a moment and buried his face in the pillows. Brade could see the fringe of light thinnish hair showing below the bandages against the dry skin of his neck. His shoulder blades showed plainly through his shirt. Murderer or not, just then Frosty Rivet looked pathetic.

"I know, Frosty," Brade said almost gently. "And this cigar odor was plain about this chap, eh?"

"Yeah," Frosty said thickly. "It smelled plenty plain."

"All right. Now let's go on. When Opal was murdered," he made the statement brutally frank on purpose, "when you came up the stairs there—"

"I'll tell you about that," Frosty said savagely. "We was all sittin' in the room there and that old fat girl, Maybrick, she come in, got some hootch offa' the dresser and said that Mrs. MacFarlane had had a bad spell. Then she went out and pretty soon Opal got up and slipped out the door. Didn't say where she was goin' or anything. Right after that Dallas Gantry beat it. I thought the croakin' of Keye was gonna be pinned on Dallas and that since Opal claimed she seen her do it, mebbe Dallas would try to bump her off er somethin', so I went out, too, through that room where Keye was bumped—"

"Yes, I know, and when you came out upstairs there, what did you see?"

Frosty stared at Brade owlishly. "I seen," he stated, "that housekeeper jane bend down beside Opal's body and pick up a gun! Then she beat it back to the linen closet and right away you all came."

Brade stroked his chin. Things were ironing out. Not too much, but a little. Mrs. Maybrick, with her poisonous hatred of Dallas, if she hadn't actually killed Opal Garth herself, must have witnessed the killing, and had stolen the gun to plant it later where it would be sure to be found and throw heavy suspicion on Dallas.

"And now, Frosty," he said, "when you cracked Tom Gary down and escaped, what did you do?"

"I went to Leo, the dirty lousy double-crosser," Frosty growled. "I spilled the works to him and he promised to help me. He said if we beat it for town, we'd be sure to be collared and that he had been trampin' over the hills and found a place where we could hide out till things quieted down and he could hook up with—"

Again Frosty's lips closed stubbornly. He would talk freely of his own share in the killings of Willow Wilde but he wouldn't disclose what it was the band of them had been planning. Brade didn't urge him. Frosty continued:

"I was fool enough to fall for his line and when he got me out there, he smacked me down, tied me up and told me he was gonna sell me out to Dallas Gantry for twenty grand." The white face convulsed with helpless rage. "He was gonna turn me over as the guy that done the croakin' and he tied me up and took my gun and—"

Brade knew the rest, but he let Frosty tell about Dallas' coming, about the fire and the subsequent rescue by Gregg MacFarlane, then he said:

"Thanks, Frosty, you've helped a lot. I'll remember it."

He went out, closing the door softly. Another night had descended on Willow Wilde, bringing with it a storm that was swiftly gaining force and strength. Wind whooped around the tall turreted house. Rain slashed the windows. Tall trees bent before the fury. There in the hall it was dim and quiet. Behind closed doors were unhappiness, anxiety, agony and guilt!

Brade nodded grimly.

He had solved the mystery of the first of Jurden Keye's murders. He had died from a bullet from Frosty Rivet's silenced gun, victim to his own uncleanness, his hypocrisy, his ruthlessness. Frosty had, in the moment he pressed that trigger, assumed a new dignity, a certain fineness, as he avenged in the only way he knew what he considered the despoilment of all he held dear.

But who had plunged the knife into a dead man's heart? What mixture of fury and despair had prevented the eyes of the second killer from discovering that Jurden Keye was already dead, who was it in a rough overcoat, strongly scented with tobacco, who had run into Frosty Rivet there in the darkened, wind-swept grounds at Willow Wilde? Brade didn't know—for sure.

Chapter Twenty-One
The Dark Coat

JIMMY ARNOLD ROUNDED the turn in the corridor and came toward Brade. The amateur detective looked the worse for wear. There was a new seriousness in his eyes and some of his exuberant spirit was gone.

Brade beckoned him over. "Jimmy," he said, "I'm going out for perhaps a half hour. You and Tom are to keep things in hand here. Can you do it?"

"Sure, Captain Brade," Jimmy answered seriously. "We'll take care of things."

"Every one," Brade went on, "connected with this case is at present in their rooms, I think." He glanced down the hall. "Dr. Monery is with Leo Wyche and will stay there. Mr. and Mrs. MacFarlane are in that room there." He nodded across the corridor. "Miss Gantry is there. Mr. Gordon—"

Anthony came up the steps just then, stopped when he saw Brade, stood there glowering. Brade smiled. "By the way, Anthony," he said pleasantly, "what did you do with the watch I picked up from beside Mrs. Maybrick's body? I left it on the table in the library when Leo Wyche was shot. It isn't there."

Anthony strolled over, hands in his pockets, stopped, facing the detective. His blond hair was rumpled and there was a light of savage determination in his heavy, bloodshot eyes.

He said carefully, "Sorry, old man, I don't know what you're talking about. Must be thinking of some one else. You didn't show me any watch."

Brade looked hard into his eyes. "No?" he said softly. "That's odd. I wonder who could have thrown it into the fire there in the library. I fished it out a while ago, rather dilapidated but still capable of being identified. Well, see you later."

He turned toward the stairs. "By the way," he said, turning to look back at Anthony. "I'm going out for a short time. I'm asking you to keep to battery area, if you get what I mean."

Anthony nodded shortly. His pale face was deeply flushed. Anthony Gordon didn't lie well or often. "I get you," he said. "I'm going in to see Dallas."

To Brade the quick walk through the cold stormy night was very refreshing. The wind had died. The rain had changed to snow, which fell silently in great white flakes, like feathers, in the darkness. Already the trees were whitened with it, and it made a soft carpet that deadened the sound of the detective's feet.

The little town looked very warm and bright behind its lighted windows. Brade saw pleasant family groups gathered around glowing pot-bellied stoves. Somewhere a radio was playing and the music sounded cheerfully in the darkness. A few pedestrians passed him silently, muffled in long coats, heads lowered.

He breathed deeply of the fresh wet air. It was a relief being out of the house for even a short time. And now that he was out, away from the strongly conflicting personalities at Willow Wilde, he could think more clearly, and more definitely arrange his facts.

And as he walked, his face hardened, lines deepened in it, his eyes grew somber. It wasn't going to be easy, what lay before him. The special messenger from the city had brought the *dossier* of Andrew Stillwell, wanted by the police in Portland, Oregon, and, accompanying the papers, was a photograph. It flashed before Brade's eyes now, standing out with startling clarity, gleaming bleakly against the snowflakes.

Andrew Stillwell had been a handsome man. Thirty-two, the identification said. Height, five feet eleven and a half. Weight, one hundred and seventy-two. Hair: black. Eyes: black. Clean shaven. Mole behind left ear.

All the usual things that go to make up police circulars. Brade sighed faintly. Andrew Stillwell! Professor of foreign languages at Oregon University. Author of a brochure on "The Language of Vanished Civilization," co-author with. . . .

Brade paused, staring around him curiously. He had walked faster than he realized and now the brightly lighted windows and cheery front of Willow Inn gleamed before him.

He mounted the steps slowly, somehow reluctant to enter. Willow Inn was a low, pleasant structure, covered with woodbine and clematis. There were two great spreading maples before it. He sensed a large lawn to the right, dotted with snow-covered bushes. There were arbors and wooden benches, the outlines of flower beds, with gaunt dead stalks of flowers sticking up starkly. He wondered if Faith MacFarlane tended them. He thought she would love flowers. She made him think of flowers. Old-fashioned posies in a shaded garden, with pleasantly winding paths and birds singing in blooming apple trees. Andy Stillwell's wife had disappeared with him, the information stated. Neither had ever been heard of since. There was a reward of ten thousand dollars. . . .

He opened the door and stepped in, Mrs. Mumford, the housekeeper at the Inn, was managing it during the absence of the MacFarlanes. She was a large, pleasant-faced woman, with scanty gray hair pulled back into a flat little biscuit at the back of her head. She wore a gray percale dress, with an old-fashioned apron tied round her ample middle. She blinked at Brade curiously from her position behind the cigar case in the lobby.

Brade took off his hat, slapping snow from it against his thigh, and smiled at her. She smiled back because she thought him a very handsome man and the pleasantest person she had seen for a long time.

He said: "I'm Captain Brade, Mrs. Mumford, and I've been trying to find out who killed Mr. Keye and that unfortunate girl at Willow Wilde. I wonder if you would help me?"

Mrs. Mumford put her thick, ruddy arms on the cigar case and leaned toward him. "I certainly will, sir, if I can," she answered, "but whatever would I know about it?"

"You can never tell," Brade said thoughtfully. "By the way, Mr. MacFarlane wanted me to bring a coat back with me. He described a thick dark overcoat, I believe—"

"Yes, sir," she said. "The one he always wears in cold weather. He went off without it the other night and he said he couldn't think what had become of it." She went swiftly up the stairs, talking over her shoulder, and Brade stepped to the radiator, holding out chilled fingers. He stared at the floor and whistled soundlessly until the old lady returned, carrying over her arm a coat, such as he had described. "This is the one he wants, I guess," Mrs. Mumford said, extending the garment.

"Thank you," Brade said, tossing it over his arm. "By the way, what time did Mr. MacFarlane return for his wife that night? Do you remember?"

"Yes," she said slowly. "I certainly do. I was sittin' here crochetin'. And that took control," she added gravely, "'cause I'd already heard of what had happened and I'd gone up to tell Mrs. MacFarlane, but she was that sound asleep

"You couldn't waken her?" Brade finished, when she hesitated, frowning.

"That's it," she said. "I knocked a dozen times when I thought, well, let her rest, she'll know soon enough."

Brade stayed about twenty minutes talking to Mrs. Mumford, then he thanked her and left. He paused on the porch, out of line with the window, and slowly, carefully, he examined the coat.

It was thick, expensive-looking wool tweed, in a dark pattern. It smelled strongly of good tobacco, especially in the clear, cold air. He ran sensitive fingers over the pockets, hesitated, inserted a hand in the side one and drew out a thick white envelope. His heart was beating heavily as he stepped nearer the light from the window, and read the superscription in that small, crabbed, pinched writing he knew so well, then he put the envelope in his own pocket, hooked the coat over his arm and started back for Willow Wilde.

In the darkness his face was rather white. There was a shocked surprise in his eyes. He knew at last to whom Jurden Keye had written that note which had been picked up in the grounds the night he was murdered.

CHAPTER TWENTY-TWO
DEAD HANDS REACHING!

THE FIRST THING Brade did on reaching Willow Wilde, after his trip to the Inn, was to call Terry Shan. His conversation was brief and enlightening. The prints Brade had made of the inmates of Willow Wilde had reached the city department, been classified and checked. As Terry gave him the dope, Brade studied a memorandum he had made of the sheets, and when he hung up the receiver he knew whose prints had been found on the gun that was used to kill Opal Garth. The knowledge didn't tend to lessen the pain in his eyes.

Jimmy Arnold sat stiffly on a straight chair in the hall, busy about his business of guarding. "Everything's all right, Captain Brade," he explained. "Tom's been keepin' an eye on things upstairs. The doctor's still up in Wyche's bedroom. That boy's pretty sick, I guess. Been groanin' a lot."

"Okay, Jimmy," Brade replied absently. "Where's Gregg MacFarlane?"

"In the room with his wife, I think. Want to see him?"

Brade nodded somberly. "I sure do, Jimmy," he said softly. "And how!"

He started upstairs, met Tom Gary coming down.

The constable's eyes were bright and sunken. There were red fever stains on his weathered cheeks. He looked sick. Brade eyed him thoughtfully.

"Head bothering you, Tom?" he asked.

"Yeah."

186

"Better have the Doc look you over first chance you get," Brade advised.

"Maybe so," answered Tom, shivering. "Right now I'm headed down to stoke the furnace."

He went on downstairs. Brade mounted slowly, walked down the hall, pausing outside Dallas' room. He could hear her low voice, Anthony's deep and troubled.

He knocked softly. Anthony opened the door. "May I come in?" Brade inquired.

Anthony stepped aside. Brade strolled over to the fire, holding out his hands. Dallas gave him one swift, frightened look and turned her head away. Anthony stood behind the couch on which she lay, glowering at Brade. Brade smiled.

"I'm not exactly welcome, I see," he said.

Dallas did not reply. Anthony said savagely: "You've made a hell of a mess of this thing, Court."

Brade laughed, though he did not look exactly happy. "That phrase has a curiously familiar ring, Anthony," he stated. "Seems like I've heard the Commissioner employ the same words." Then he sobered and his eyes passed slowly from one flushed, frightened face to the other.

"I'm sorry, Anthony," he said. "I know you brought me down here for one purpose and one only. To free Dallas from implication in the murder of Jurden Keye."

"Of course I did," Anthony rapped. "What else?"

"Well," Brade said thoughtfully, "there is that thing called justice, you know. My job was, in reality, not to free a woman you loved, but to find the real murderer. I've tried to make you understand that. Apparently I've failed."

Anthony didn't say anything. He continued to stand there tensely, watching Brade. Brade said, not heeding him:

"Dallas, our conversation was interrupted a while ago. Shall we finish it? To whom did you loan Anthony's watch when you removed it from your own wrist?"

Dallas shivered and her fingers bit into the covering of the couch. Anthony bent forward slightly, as if he thought Brade might strike her, then Dallas turned her head, looked full at Brade and said:

"I'm sorry, Captain Brade. I cannot answer that question."

"I see," Brade commented, "All right. I don't really need the information. Just like to tie up loose ends. Well," he waved carelessly, "*adios*. See you later." He went out jauntily, conscious of hot, hostile eyes that followed him.

"Damn him!" Anthony muttered. "He hasn't any—feeling."

Dallas smiled faintly. "You're wrong there, Anthony," she said softly and shook her head. "Very, very wrong."

"Huh!" Anthony snorted. "Women always fall for Court. I don't know what there is about him that gets 'em—"

Outside in the hall, Courtney Brade was standing very still, eyes fixed somberly on the floor. His face was gray with weariness and the lines in it made him look very old. In the thick warm silence of the hall, sound of the snow came softly as it rustled against the windows, piling in high white pyramids against the black glass. He turned at last as if something were dragging him, and went down the hall to the MacFarlanes' door.

Faith answered his light tap. She looked considerably better. There was a faint flush of color on her white cheeks. Her eyes were clear and calm.

"Oh, it's you, Captain," she said, holding the door open. "You wished to see me? Or Gregg? Won't you come in?"

"I want to see Gregg," Brade said quietly. "If he will come with me—"

"I'm sorry," she said, glancing back over her shoulder at the portion of the room Brade could not see. "Gregg has gone out for a bit of air."

Brade's cheeks flushed with anger. "I told Gregg MacFarlane—" he began.

She smiled at him. "Don't be annoyed, Captain," she pleaded. "It's really my fault and he hasn't gone out—really. He just stepped out there on the balcony for a few minutes. Shall I tell him you wish to see him?"

"Never mind," he told her shortly. "I'll find him." He turned away quickly. The door closed behind him. He went down the hall, climbed the little flight of some half dozen steps that led to the balcony, opened the door and paused, head lowered against the sudden fury of the storm. The temporary lull had passed. Wind whipped fiercely around the high turrets of Willow Wilde. The night was a pit of blackness and whirling snowflakes eddied in a stiff current round the exposed balcony. A fine place for a bit of air, Brade reflected grimly.

"MacFarlane," he called shortly. "Hello, MacFarlane!"

He thought he caught a quick movement, though it might have been merely the rustle of the wind. He peered into the blackness, stepped out. Snow crunched under his feet. The air was bitterly cold. He had come without hat or coat. His eyes were blinded by the snow. He groped for his flash, remembered disgustedly he had left it in his overcoat pocket downstairs, then he started forward at a sudden rustling sound somewhere to his right on the narrow platform—

"MacFarlane," he said softly. "If you're there, better speak. The game's up! I have you covered!"

A giant maple limb swept across his face as he moved cautiously forward, its heavy snow-laden branches sent him stumbling back. He threw out a hand in a sudden gesture of defense, let it fall, realizing that the sound he had heard was only the scraping of branches.

Dashing the snow from his eyes he stared around. There was no one there. His glance dropped to the balcony floor. He stooped. There were no foot prints in the virgin snow! It was a ruse. Gregg MacFarlane hadn't come to the balcony! Had Faith lied, or the husband?

Stepping to the rail he sheltered his eyes against the pelting sleet. The grounds were a wind-swept torrent of darkness.

Was that movement below? He strained forward, peering. The light railing, against which he leaned, swayed dangerously. He heard the split of cracking wood. Pivoting, he clawed at the empty air. He had a terrible sensation of helplessness as his body toppled. . . .

Brade kept his head in that moment. There in the darkness and the wail of the howling gale he saw death grinning at him, glimpsed fleetingly the terror of destruction, then he thrashed forward, fighting with everything he possessed to overcome that balance of gravity that was dragging him backward to oblivion.

He heard his own voice in a hoarse, startled yell, then he was staggering forward toward the dimly lighted door that, before his straining eyes, went suddenly black!

He cried out sharply! There was the rush of feet below him in the darkness, a man's startled cry, footsteps on the stairs, crack of a shot, a terrible choked scream.

Silence. Blackness!

Brade crouched there, hanging onto the door, trembling. What had happened? His mind reeled in a monstrous confusion. He had gone onto the balcony to find Gregg MacFarlane, and instead he had all but found death. One thought remained clearly in his mind. *That railing had been tampered with!* He had examined it after Mrs. Maybrick plunged over it to death, and found it made of stout strong wood, yet the light pressure of his body against it. . . .

Almost at his feet someone was moaning. There was sluggish, heavy movement. A man's choked, panting breath—then another sound penetrated to Brade's consciousness, above the tramp of pounding feet, as Jimmy Arnold and Tom Gary stumbled up through the darkness from the lower hall.

Standing there, momentarily incapable of movement, Brade heard a woman sobbing. There was something in the sound that turned the detective sick. He straightened, drew a shaking hand across his face that was wet with sweat, then light speared the darkness. Jimmy pounded up, flashlight darting.

"What's wrong?" he gasped. "Lights went out all over the place! Brade! Captain Brade—"

"Hold her steady, Jimmy," Brade said, and his voice was flat with a queer lack of emotion. "Hold the light steady, I'm coming down—"

The light in Jimmy's shaking hand flashed in the detective's face, lifted, lowered, circled, settled on a limp dark form, sprawled halfway down the short flight of stairs, on the stooping figure of a woman crouching beside it. The light steadied there in a bright beam of terrible revelation and Brade saw Faith MacFarlane huddled beside the body of her husband.

As he stared, Gregg MacFarlane lifted his head that seemed to droop under the weight of the strangely white hair, looked straight into his wife's eyes:

"Faith!" he whispered. "Faith, little pigeon—"

Brade groaned suddenly between set teeth. Then MacFarlane's eyes, dull like worthless gems, found the detective's face. "Brade," he said, with a queer clarity, "I—killed Jurden Keye! Opal Garth! Mrs. Maybrick! I killed them because they knew—"

Faith cried out chokingly. Her hands fumbled for him, like terribly vital little animals, groping over him, touching his hair.

"Gregg!" she sobbed. "Gregg—speak to me—"

For answer, he lifted his heavy head again, looked into her eyes and smiled. Then he dragged up one limp arm, put it across her shoulders in that old gesture of protection, shivered once convulsively and died!

Brade stood up. "Mrs. MacFarlane," he said, "your husband's dying confession was a splendid piece of devotion. But it is useless. You and you alone—have done this thing. All of it! All!"

She looked at him from a gray-white face, smiled with colorless lips. "Yes," she said. "Gregg was innocent. I don't think he even suspected me until there, at the last. He—he—must have been down the hall—heard me send you to the balcony—followed you there and—"

She paused, frowning impatiently. "You see, I had to kill you if I could," she explained. "I stood on the stairs and heard you talking to Gregg—after the doctor had dressed his hands this evening and I realized then that you knew—what for so long we have—kept secret. So I got a meat saw from the kitchen, watched my chance, went out on the balcony and hacked the railing nearly through. I intended to ask you to come out there and talk to me, then to push you against it—but it was not written that way." Her voice had grown even quieter. One hand fluttered toward her heart.

"Gregg had gone to the doctor for some morphia tablets when you came to the room," she went on. "So I told you he had gone to the balcony and I thought—perhaps—"

Brade shivered in spite of himself, remembering that terrible moment when he had leaned against the railing.

"I hoped," she went on, "that in the darkness and storm you— might—still—" She shrugged faintly. "When you didn't," she continued, "when I heard your voice there in the door, I knew I had failed. Gregg's gun was in the pocket of his coat over the chair—so I shorted the lights and shot at you—I could see you—outlined against the snowy night—"

She stopped just there, sinking fingers in her hair, rocking gently to and fro. Dallas was standing, white-lipped, staring at her. She made a slight movement forward, but Brade warned her back.

"Gregg took the bullet meant for me," Brade said. "You killed the man you—loved—"

She looked up at him and smiled. "Loved?" she repeated. "Don't bother to speak of—love. You wouldn't understand. No one knew but—Gregg—and I—murdered to save him. What did I care for life— other than his?" She made a curiously expressive gesture. "When Frosty Rivet thought he recognized Gregg, when he and Opal Garth brought that man, Wyche, down to Willow Valley to identify him, when Jurden Keye stopped me before the bank yesterday afternoon and told me what he knew and held their knowledge over me, why, what could I do?" She gazed at the detective questioningly. "I killed him!" she went on monotonously. "I was in the alcove when Dallas came in. He put me outside, but I returned, leaving the French door ajar. I heard them talking. When she left, I came out. He was sitting there at the desk with his head down, hunting for something in the drawer, I guess. It was dim in the room, but I saw that—knife—I picked it up and buried it in his heart—"

"You wore gloves?" Brade asked.

She nodded. "Yes. Then I ran—Opal had slipped in through the window. She was hiding in the alcove when I came out. I didn't see her. She stepped into the room, saw Jurden and screamed. I heard that cry and knew that the thing was discovered, though I didn't know by whom. Opal told me about it—afterwards. She ran from the room and struck her head against a tree—"

"Then," Brade broke in, "everything that she told me was a lie. All about what she overheard between Dallas and Keye?"

"Yes," Faith agreed. "All of it. She wanted to hurt Dallas and at the same time she thought she could blackmail me—"

Brade asked suddenly. "Mrs. MacFarlane, why did you wear your husband's coat when you came to see Jurden Keye last night?"

She shivered. "It was warm and dark," she said, "and so—big— it hid me. I thought the chances of recognition would be less. I ran into someone out in the grounds as I was leaving—it didn't seem to mean much to me. I went home, got into bed—Gregg came. I returned with him. Only then I saw what it was—going to mean— that he—or Dallas—might be—involved."

She was sitting on the lower step, one hand across Gregg MacFarlane's body. She was not looking at anything, it seemed. Her pale honey-colored hair made a bright cloud around her head. She spoke very low.

"You see," she went on reflectively, "I had to kill Opal too because she knew everything. She came to me up there in the room— and told me what she knew. About my killing Keye. About—Gregg—"

"And the revolver Mrs. Maybrick found by Opal's body was yours?" asked Brade.

She nodded. "I've had it for years. Ever since we left Oregon. Gregg never knew I carried it. I brought it back from the Inn when he came after me."

Suddenly Faith MacFarlane lifted her eyes and looked at Brade. "Captain Brade," she said, "I want you to know this. I did not kill Opal because she knew that I had killed Jurden Keye. I did not push Maybrick over the balcony edge because she had seen me shoot Opal from the open door of my room as the girl ran down the hall. Those were not the reasons. I killed them because they knew the truth about—Gregg. For myself, I did not care. You see," she said and smiled a little, "I told you I had done this thing and you would not believe me."

"You did not tell me all the truth," Brade said gravely. "You told me you spoke to Jurden Keye before you stabbed him and I knew that when the knife was plunged into his heart, he was already dead!

She lifted haunted eyes. "Already—dead!" she whispered. "Keye was—"

"Yes. Dead from a bullet in his heart. Frosty Rivet killed him. You didn't have to do it, Faith, it was—wasted murder!"

She did not speak for a long time, then simply: "I did not know," she said, and repeated dully, "I did not know. I thought it would make a better story," she added, "and of course I could not tell you the real motive for wanting to kill him. I had to lie about that. I did not make a very good—confession."

Brade said slowly: "You made a perfect confession, Faith MacFarlane, very early in the case, but I was not wise enough to catch it. You said in your conversation with your husband, there in the morning room—yes, I listened in on it, you said: *'Jurden Keye was killed at ten-forty.'* Just like that. Not a question. A definite statement. I should have wondered how you *knew*. It returned to me later, of course, but the issue was obscured by—"

"By Gregg?" she questioned. "Of course, when you learned the truth about Gregg"—her voice broke slightly—"you thought he had done it. It seemed more logical, didn't it?"

"Much more," Brade told her, "though I should have learned long ago," he said almost to himself, "that murder is seldom logical."

"Gregg would not have murdered to save himself," Faith said. "He would have murdered—gladly—to save me." She shivered, huddling lower on the step. "I wouldn't have killed—for myself. But for Gregg—many times. Can you understand that, Captain Brade?" She lifted her lovely tired eyes and gazed at Brade. "Can you understand that?" she asked plaintively.

Brade studied his fingertips. His lips were hard set and there were deep lines between his eyes. His glance traveled down the length of his strong, fine hand, rested a moment on the glorious ring he wore. He caught breath sharply, looked across the body of Gregg MacFarlane, into the eyes of Gregg MacFarlane's wife.

"Yes," he said very low. "Yes, Faith MacFarlane, I can understand that."

She sighed deeply as if with relief. "I am glad," she said simply. "And now—I think—I'd—like to—rest—" Her voice broke. She stood up, clinging to the railing, swayed slightly a moment and slipped to the floor.

Dr. Monery, his kindly old face twisted with emotion he could not hide, reached her side swiftly, laid a finger on her wrist. He stayed that way for a long minute, not looking at Brade, then when he lifted his head his faded eyes were dim with tears.

"Her heart," he said thickly. "It has been bad—a long time. I'm—almost glad."

And Brade, bending over the lifeless body of Faith MacFarlane, was glad too.

Chapter Twenty-Three
Faith

"There was the matter of the book-end," Brade was saying, sitting across the table from Dallas Gantry, Anthony Gordon, Tom Gary and Jimmy Arnold in the morning room at Willow Wilde. "I found the place on the table where it had rested in Faith MacFarlane's room. The outline of the base was clearly marked in the dust. The books were piled hurriedly on a lower shelf of the dresser. Lying where it did, out in the grounds, it could have been thrown from any one of three of the upper windows.

"That remark of Faith's about the hour that Keye was killed kept recurring to me, though I unconsciously associated it with Gregg, at first. The watch I found beside Maybrick's body," he glanced with grim humor at Anthony, "I traced first to Dallas. But she would not tell me—"

"I gave it to Faith," Dallas said faintly, "she wanted to keep a check on the hours for her medicine. Of course, I knew then—"

Brade nodded. "That was rather conclusive," he said. "Was it the first time you had suspected her?"

Dallas gazed at him thoughtfully. "No," she said. "There in the cabin on Elder's Hill—I suddenly got it—all. Whose voice it was that I heard in that startled gasp, the night I came in—and Jurden was in the alcove. Oh, I couldn't believe it. I wanted to forget it—I couldn't believe—" she began crying softly.

Brade said quickly. "Frosty Rivet threw me off when he said he bumped into a man in the grounds, described the coat and that odor of tobacco. I immediately thought of MacFarlane. I got his

196

coat from the Inn and in doing so discovered that Faith had been absent from there the night Keye was killed. I also found the envelope in the pocket of the coat addressed to her. Then I knew that she had worn her husband's coat—"

"But," Anthony broke in suddenly, "what's it all about. Who was—Gregg MacFarlane?"

Brade shook his head slightly. "Twenty-two years ago," he answered, "Gregg MacFarlane, then Andrew Stillwell, was sentenced to death by the state of Oregon. He escaped from the death house in one of the most spectacular breaks for liberty in the annals of the West Coast. Escaped and disappeared. From that day to this, no trace has been found of him, until a woman whose husband sat on the jury at his trial, saw him in Centerville, two weeks ago. Then, in the illogical way things happen in real life, Frosty Rivet thought he recognized him here in Willow Valley. The MacFarlanes were wealthy. Frosty and Opal Garth cooked up a blackmail scheme and imported Leo Wyche, who was in prison at the same time that MacFarlane was, to identify him. They took Jurden Keye in on the deal and he—"

The detective stopped. After all, it was no use dilating on what Jurden Keye had tried to do, before the woman who had been his wife.

He said: "We found Stillwell's prints on the knife in Jurden Keye's body and that was hard to figure for a time. Looking back now, knowing that Faith MacFarlane wore gloves, I can only assume that MacFarlane, when he came in that room involuntarily grasped the hilt to draw the knife out, then realized that Keye was dead and let it stay." He frowned at the fire.

"For twenty-two years," he went on somberly, "Gregg MacFarlane had lived in the shadow of death. Gregg and his wife, Faith. Her real name wasn't Faith," he added gently. "I wonder why—he called her—that?"

The little group was silent. Snow sifted softly against the pane. The fire burned cheerily in the grate. Why had the small, golden-haired wife of Andrew Stillwell come to be known as Faith? There wasn't one in the room but was able to see the connection, and Dallas cried suddenly:

"Oh, poor Gregg, I don't wonder his hair was white."

Brade nodded gravely. "He killed the man who tried to black-mail his wife," he said slowly. "It was a sensational trial and he would not give his reason for the crime. That would have defeated the end for which he had killed, but it might have cleared him. He kept silent and took the death sentence unflinchingly. They loved each other," he ended simply and in those four words, unwittingly he voiced the legend that was graven onto the double headstone that came to stand guard over the graves in the quiet, tree-shaded graveyard in sleepy Willow Valley.

It was not for Brade to decide as to the right or wrong of the motive that had prompted Faith MacFarlane to murder. No court in the land was called upon to pronounce judgment on the results of her devotion to her husband. Three persons had died violently that Gregg MacFarlane might have a chance at life. It is written on authority that may not be questioned:

"Thou shalt not kill!"

And man has evolved a system of judgment and punishment for those who transgress that law. Brade was one of its many expo-nents. He saw his job and did it. Brade, the policeman, condemned Faith MacFarlane in the light of the law he represented.

To Courtney Brade, the man, was given the ability to under-stand much that is hidden from eyes less used to sorrow.

DEATH'S LONG SHADOW

Highway Incident

When the dreary pelting of November rain assumed a harsher quality against the filling station windows, Arnie Lund tossed aside the crumpled page of comics and scowled out at the brooding dark.

Few cars had rolled the Chip' City-Minneapolis Highway in the past hour and none of them had stopped.

Arnie's flat freckled nose lifted, sniffing. "Snow," he muttered, "or I'm a mink."

Well, let it come. Snow, hail or rain. He'd seen his last day in the joint. Had already tacked his notice on the door. It said:

> This Place is Closed
> *Alaska—or bust.*
> *Arnie.*

He rose, stretched leather jacketed arms and gave a prodigious yawn. So this was it. He'd greased his last chassis and booted his last casing for anybody. The company truck would siphon out the tanks in the morning and he—well he'd be rolling toward the Twin Cities.

Scuffing to the pot-bellied stove he closed the drafts, straightened and zippered up his jacket. As well lock up and go home. Business was over.

Seizing the knob he swung back the door and paused, eyes narrowing on two bobbing lights rocking toward him from the Woodvale cutoff. Wallowing up out of the ruts, the car swung onto

201

the pavement, quartering around. It hesitated a moment, radiator steaming, then wheeled across in a wide arc to pause beside the pumps.

It was a big coupe with foreign pads. From inside a muffled voice called, "Fill 'er up."

Arnie sighed resignedly, unhooked a hose, rounded the bumper. As he unscrewed the gas cap the dome light blossomed inside the car. The pump bell donged off seven gallons and Arnie went forward to check the motor.

"She's pretty hot for cold water," he called. "What you say, mister?" His eyes searched the mud-spattered window.

The glass lowered a few inches and the driver said, "Give it some anyhow." He was hulked over the wheel in a bulky overcoat picking at his bare right palm with a small pen knife. Bright beads of blood showed on the gleaming blade. He muttered, "Damn," and his white face puckered up with pain.

Arnie shrugged and went back to his work.

The oil gauge registered full and he slapped down the hood cover. Noting the wipers were still working he didn't bother with the windshield, and called out, "One forty-three, mister," swabbing his hands on the cleaner cloth.

The dome light died—the motor came to life, and a pudgy hand extended exact change.

Arnie said, "Thanks," and stepped back as the car leaped away. Spinning tires showered him with gumbo and he thumbed his nose at the disappearing taillight.

"Nice pleasant guy," he muttered, running a sleeve across his face. He made for the pumps.

The rain had already turned to sleet.

CHAPTER ONE

THERE WAS A LOUD demanding knock on the front door. Stacy stood up, heart pounding. The knocking continued. A man's voice called something.

She thought, "Well, it's what I've been wishing for, isn't it?" and shut her jaws hard to stop the clicking of her teeth. "But he needn't pound like that. Loud enough to . . . to wake the dead."

She began laughing, a tight hurtful sound that jerked her face muscles, brought tears to her eyes. Then resolutely she picked up the small automatic from the table and went into the hall.

The insistent knocking persisted.

A man called, "Hello in there. Anybody home?"

Stacy's hand rested over the stout chain that held the heavy door. "Who is it?" she demanded. "What do you want?" and knew comfort in the thought that he couldn't get in if she didn't admit him. The house was like a fortress.

He stamped impatiently. She caught his disgusted exclamation.

"Stalled on the road. Car ahead of me. Can't get past."

Stacy loosed the chain, opened the door, automatic steady. Snow whipped in, wet smell of the night. The man came with it, head lowered, gloved hand brushing moisture from his eyes. He kicked the door shut and blinked at the light, glance flicking over her and resting on the gun.

"Lord!" he gasped. "What a sweet one this is."

Then he looked straight at Stacy. Stacy looked back at him. His eyes, blurred between snow-clogged lashes, widened slightly.

"Hello," he said. "Who're you?"

She lowered the gun thinking, "I might ask *you* that," but she said, "Stacy Lane. That's my car in the road. Out of gas."

"I'll have to tell him," she thought desperately, "about Ann up there in the chair." Then she found herself saying automatically, "There's a fire in the kitchen. Better come out."

He grunted, stamping caked snow from his shoes, followed her. She felt the muscles siding her spine rippling like a cat's when you touch it lightly.

The kitchen was largish, low, plain and painfully clean. An old-fashioned cook stove, a dish cupboard, work table, fragments of lettuce wilted on its top. Stacy's chair had been hastily pushed back beside the stove, when she had risen to answer his knock. A battered coffee pot simmered pleasantly and there was a cup which she had used.

The man took it all in with one swift glance and held numb fingers to the fire. "Say, this is good! Do I smell coffee?" His eyes crinkled pleasantly. "That would make things perfect."

"Yes, there's coffee," Stacy assured him, thinking, "If it were only as simple as that. Coffee to make things perfect!" The cup she had lifted slipped from her trembling fingers, breaking brittlely against the stove.

The man said, "Hope there's another. Hate to miss the coffee," and jerked off his soaked felt, showing thick, dark hair liberally stained with gray at the temples. It was like snow had fallen there and stuck.

She cried suddenly, "It's terrible! I tried to get out right after I found her. My car was stalled. I thought I could make it in hers. She had a good one. A Ford coupe . . ."

"You didn't get out in that!"

"You're right, I didn't. It's been . . . the barn, garage, it's all been destroyed by fire. I tried it on foot then. It's only three miles to Woodvale, but I had to come back. The snow was blinding. There isn't any real path you can follow, just that rutty dirt road. No one lives near here, no one came by . . ."

Her voice trickled to silence. She heard the sweep of snow, purr of the fire, the strong, even sound of the man's breathing. The outline of him blurred before her: a big man in a wooly overcoat, dark hair, while stains like pressure of blighting fingers at the temples. She was suddenly conscious of his hands, loosely clasped before him holding the soaked felt. Fine, lean hands with long pliant fingers. He wore a ring, massively silver, framing a smoking, glowing moonstone.

"Why did you have to—get out?" the man asked. "Where is Ann Regnas? What do you mean by—finding her? Is she sick? Hurt?"

"She's dead," Stacy said, lips dry. "She's been murdered."

"Murdered?" His gray glance sharpened. He repeated the word softly. "Murdered?"

"I'll show you," she offered, eyes wide and defiant.

Perspiration was cool on her body as she paused in the upstairs hall, seeing the man a big featureless blur beside her. No use flunking it now. Her shoulders squared.

"She's in—here," she whispered and opened the door.

The room had been pleasantly warm from the corner fireplace when Stacy had entered it nearly four hours earlier. Now it was cold and repellent; everything in it seeming dingy, too long used. Light came from a shaded oil-burning lamp on the table by the fireplace. The dark gray carpet was worn, but obviously good. There was a single bed against the far wall, a few magazines scattered around, embroidery on a round frame.

The dead woman sat in the low rocker before the fire. The back of her round gray head had been efficiently crushed. There was a curious look of finality to the squat slumped figure, work-toughened hands resting inertly in her brown woolen lap like thick, discarded gloves.

On the floor at her feet lay a statuette of cast metal, perhaps nine inches tall. The head, broken off, stared up with an idiotic expression of childish delight. From the back of the figurine, slim graceful wings were outspread.

"There!" Stacy said in weary triumph. "That's how I found her."

He paused a few feet away, standing easily, without movement. Stacy got the feeling that he was arranging things, mentally examining, classifying them. Then he went to Ann Regnas' side, delicately touched the broken spot at the base of the skull, laid fingers lightly against her cheek.

"What time did you find her?"

"Eight-thirty-seven. I checked it."

He glanced at her approvingly. "Too much to hope that you also checked body temperature?"

"No. The body was distinctly warm. She could not have been dead long."

She was glad that at last she had a definite picture of him. Below that stained dark hair, his face was lean, with strong, out-jutting chin; wide, flexible mouth under a sharply clipped mustache. His eyes were brilliantly clear just now, distinctly gray, and, for the moment, almost terribly impersonal.

He wiped his hands, returned the handkerchief to his pocket.

"Let's get it straight now. Your car stalled in the road?"

"I ran out of gas," she admitted defensively. "Burned a lot running in low between the highway and here."

"And you came in here for help?"

"Among other things. When I knocked, the door swung in of itself."

"The door was open then?"

"It was unlatched. Someone leaving had failed to close it securely."

"You saw someone leaving?"

"Heavens no!"

"Then perhaps you found tracks, something dropped, some indication to furnish a reasonable basis for your conclusion?"

"My conclusion!" she repeated in exasperation.

"Yes. That the door had been left unlatched by someone leaving the house?"

"Well, that's—what I thought," she stammered, angry blood in her cheeks, being unaccustomed to the necessity for stammering.

"Yet in actual truth, you left your stalled car in the road, came to the house, found the door unlatched, and that's really all we know up to that point, isn't it?"

His swift smile was so friendly that Stacy felt her tight body relax, a foolish tremor very like a sob shake her.

"Yes," she answered faintly, "that's all we really know—up to that point." Then on sudden impulse, "Who are you?"

"Who am—? Oh, I am sorry!" He flipped a card from his pocket, and handed it to her.

She held it under the light. It said, *Courtney Brade, Headquarters Division, Metropolitan Police*, and in small print in one corner, *New York City*.

"Oh," she said inadequately, "Mr. Brade?"

"Captain Brade," he corrected, smiling. "I was in the Twin Cities on business connected with my department and took the opportunity to run on to Chippewa City for a visit with my one-time sergeant, Terry Shan."

She made the connection instantly. "Sheriff Shannoloski? I knew he'd worked in the east; that's one reason we elected him. I voted for him."

"Well, you've got a good officer. As to how I happen to be here now, the Sheriff was rather bogged down, and when the report came in of the burning of Miss Regnas' property, I . . ."

"The garage? The car?"

"Yes. I offered to drive over and see what I could pick up. Hit Woodvale first; stopped longer than I realized. Had some trouble in the mud—they warned me about the road in bad weather but . . ." He shrugged the matter aside. "Now let's get on with what we know. No telephone?"

"No."

He frowned. "With our cars nose to nose in that goat track, looks like we're stuck until daylight. Rotten luck. Like to get word to Terry."

Stacy sniffed mentally. "That's what you say! Terry, my eye! You've a nose for murder—can't resist investigating—New York, Woodvale, or Pt. Barrow. You don't fool me, Captain Brade."

"Let's assume for the moment," Brade remarked, "that your conclusion—that someone on leaving the house failed to latch the door—is correct. You saw no one, Miss Lane, nor passed anybody?"

"There was a car on the road."

"Heading out toward the highway?"

"Yes."

"Where?"

"I can't be sure exactly, with the rain and the beastly road. A mile or two from here, I'd say, possibly a mile and a half."

"Any idea what kind of a car, who drove it, how many passengers?"

"Not the slightest. It was just a jolting pair of headlights that I had to pass without going in the ditch. A light car, I believe, and I decided it was trying for too much speed under the circumstances."

"Well, that's something anyway. And now . . ."

"When no one answered the door, I came in. I called. I felt Ann Regnas was here. She's practically never out, you know."

"I understand she was quite a stay-at-home. You know her well?"

"I didn't know her at all. I never set eyes on her . . ." She paused, seeing him standing quite close, looking down at her. She felt his oddly powerful direct gaze going through her. Yet he looked so casual, so friendly, so pleasant. She got in that moment a swift understanding of the danger of the man—danger, that is, to the unfortunate who tried to deceive him.

"He'd get around you," she concluded. "He's got a way, damn him!"

"Then how did you know that her car was a Ford coupe?" he asked, and with the question offered his cigarette case.

She drew smoke into her lungs. "Simple. This time last week, it was my car."

He returned the lighter to his vest pocket. "You sold it to Ann Regnas then?"

"No. I simply turned it in on the one you found in the road. Stupid of me, but I left important papers tucked away inside. When I went after them, I found that my car had been sold to Ann Regnas. Another job took me afield this afternoon and I decided to drive in here from the highway on my way home, pick them up."

"Home?"

"I live in Chippewa City."

"You wouldn't mind telling me the nature of the papers?"

"Not at all. I'm a newspaperwoman. Went in for feature writing a year ago; syndicated stuff. The papers I left in the car were story notes I'd worked like the devil to compile. That's the whole of it."

"That's your story and you're sticking to it?" he suggested, and studied her through narrowed lids.

A slim blade of a girl, young, vibrant, like something growing in a field. Eyes darkly brown with tawny lights in them so at times they looked golden. Hair, fiery red—tumbled red, alive, glowing, a great unruly shock of it disdaining combs and pins, tumbled just now in a turbulent cloud above flaring dark brows.

Not a beautiful face. Too thin, bones showing, nose tilted, too wide as to eye-setting. Not beautiful, but compelling. She wore a trim gray frock, dashes of green at the throat and wrists, a green flag above her heart—the tiny tip of a tiny handkerchief in a ridiculous pocket.

He looked away reluctantly. "Thanks for the details, Miss Lane." He considered the room. "Her bedroom, eh?"

"I suppose so, though there's a bed all made up in a curtained alcove off the dining room . . . to use if she didn't want to climb the stairs, I suppose."

"I'm glad you added those final qualifying words. Let's remember our agreement. You did agree, didn't you?"

She laughed. "Yes, Captain Brade, I agreed. We may only *assume* that the bed in the alcove was for Ann's use if she didn't want to climb the stairs."

"Thank you," he said gravely, and she felt as proud as if she had done him a favor. "She lived entirely alone, I believe?"

"Alone!" Stacy laughed shortly. "And how! You and I are likely the only outsiders to set foot in this house since she bought it—more than thirty years ago. Ann Regnas, the Hermit Woman!"

"Yet someone obviously was here tonight, Miss Lane, unless . . ." He paused, the unfinished sentence hanging in the air between them so Stacy's eyes slowly widened, blood left her face, and her heart pounded raggedly.

"Yes, of course," she agreed huskily. "It's odd, but there aren't any clothes up here." She crossed to throw wide the closet door, exposing two old-fashioned suit cases, buckles rusted, heavy straps worn.

He stirred them with the moist toe of his shoe. "Empty or nearly so. Labels scratched off."

"Brought them with her when she came," Stacy suggested. "When she came to live in this house so long ago." She had a disquieting picture of a younger Ann Regnas lugging awkward cases up the narrow stairs, storing them in the closet, never touching them again.

"What exactly do you know about Ann Regnas, Miss Lane?"

She turned to face him, angry at the unconsciously defensive gesture. "Nothing beyond what just everyone knows."

"And that is?"

"Well, again nothing. I can't remember when I haven't known about her. When I was a child we used to play a game called—Hermit Woman." She laughed ruefully. "Imagine! A bunch of dumb kids amusing themselves with imaginary details about a strange, lonely woman who chose to live by herself in a big old house." Her voice slowed. She stared unseeingly at a worn spot on the carpet.

Brade said suddenly, "Let's see what we can find." He looked about a moment; then, he indicated the broken statuette at the dead woman's feet, shooting his flash on it, studying it carefully, not touching it. "The weapon? She was killed with this, do you think?"

Stacy roused out of her thoughts. "No. With a piece of wood, I believe."

"Wood?" He glanced sideways at the pile of knotty chunks siding the fireplace. "Maybe, though this decapitated Cupid would do the trick. Why do you say she was killed with a chunk of wood, Miss Lane?"

"I didn't say she was killed with a chunk of wood, Captain Brade. I just said I believed she had been. When I came in, the fire was a pile of ruddy ashes, and a fresh piece of wood was smouldering at the edge—you know, as if it had been recently tossed there."

Brade frowned at the black ruin of the fire. "That log—it's burned out now?"

"Yes; about an hour ago."

"How was it when you first saw it?"

"It was burning feebly on the under side, a few flames licking 'round it."

"Experimentation might indicate approximately how long the murderer had been gone," he reflected aloud. "Why do you vote for the wood rather than the God of Love?"

She looked at him tiredly. "It's fairly simple. The broken statuette is at her feet. The blow that killed her is at the base of the skull."

"She was struck from behind, naturally?"

"Naturally."

"Seated in the chair when someone came up behind her . . ."

"Not necessarily. Suppose she was standing before the fire, in front of the chair, back to the room. Suppose the murderer threw the wood."

"Excellent," he purred. "Excellent, Miss Lane. Then how shall we explain the broken Eros?"

She smiled faintly. "I can't answer everything," she admitted, "but suppose she picked it up as a weapon of . . ."

"Defense?"

"Why not—offense? From what I've heard of Ann Regnas she would be capable of attacking anyone sufficiently brazen to force his way into her house."

Brade stroked his chin. The moonstone glowed fantastically. "You suggest then that the wood might have been the defensive weapon? Thrown possibly in an effort to divert Ann until he could get out? Something like that?"

"It's quite possible, I feel." She made a slight apologetic gesture. "I've been here for hours. I couldn't help speculating."

"I understand. It's an interesting theory, Miss Lane. It is not, however, conclusive. The murder weapon may have been neither the statuette nor the wood."

Her brows went up inquiringly. "You suggest . . .?"

"It could have been something which the murderer carried away with him. A heavy walking stick, for example."

She shrugged. "That implies a man, and could you offer a suggestion offhand, as to what man Ann Regnas would invite into her . . . her bedroom?"

"I didn't say she invited him. Maybe he forced his way here."

"Oh," she exclaimed. "That is possible, I suppose. Only . . ."

"Yes?"

"Well, you haven't examined the fortifications of the house. Windows nailed shut, except for a two-inch crack in the kitchen; doors furnished with locks, bolts, chains." She shook her head definitely. "No, Ann Regnas must have admitted her visitor. I believe she had just started dinner when the murderer arrived."

"How do you figure that?"

"Her meal is spread on the table downstairs. Everything arranged, nothing touched. When I found it, the pot of tea was warm. The single slice of bacon was stiff in congealed grease. Her chair was pushed back as if she had risen hastily. It must have been someone she knew."

"Why?"

She said impatiently. "You evidently haven't heard much about her. She never admitted anyone to her house. I've never even heard a rumor of anyone being inside the place, not in all the years she lived here. It's inconceivable that she'd sit down to dinner with the front door unfastened so a stranger could walk in. It's even more insane to suggest that she'd admit anyone she didn't choose to."

He lighted a cigarette, watching her over the flame. "All right, now what do we have? Ann Regnas, a cranky recluse, opening bolts and locks to admit someone around dinner time. Later we find her here, dead; the front door unlatched enabling you to come in." He flicked ashes from his cigarette. "That's the way it happened, isn't it?"

"The way it happened?" Her eyes searched his face. "I don't quite understand, Captain Brade."

"Very well, we'll assume it happened that way. So the unknown killed her. Why? Money? More than one recluse has been murdered for his suppositional cache."

"This one wasn't," she said flatly. "There's practically five hundred dollars in the secretary drawer down stairs in plain sight for anyone to see."

"I take it you've looked around some."

"Yes," she flared, and added, "I didn't disturb anything. I had to do something."

"That how you found the gun you held on me?"

She glanced up in surprise. "Yes. I thought you might be the murderer . . ."

"Returned to the scene of his crime? Things like that have happened. You're convinced then that robbery was not the motive?"

"I don't see how it could have been. The killer couldn't have missed that money."

"Unlikely," he conceded, "but not wholly conclusive. He may have found money elsewhere and been frightened off. He may have been a particularly stupid fellow."

"How do you ever reach a conclusion about anything?" she demanded impatiently. "You're not willing to admit . . ."

"Comfortable though unsupported theories that might be twisted into something passing for a solution?" He laughed agreeably. "I'm confounded well not; but don't be discouraged, Miss Lane. I'm thorough, and crime detection isn't a parlor game."

"No, I daresay it isn't."

"Scarcely. It's largely a matter of arrangement."

Her slim brows puckered. "I don't understand."

"Arrangement of details," he explained and added, eyes twinkling, "Of course, the investigator must first look around and discover the details."

"Then fit them into place? Rather like a jig-saw puzzle?"

"You catch the idea perfectly, but in that looking around process one must be careful not to reach wrong conclusions—conclusions based entirely on surface evidence."

She looked slightly dazed. "I'm afraid I don't follow."

"All right, listen to this." He slumped to a chair arm. "If I am to accept the veracity of surface evidence I'd pick you as the murderer."

"Me!" she shrieked faintly. "You mean you believe I—killed—"

"See?" He laughed good-naturedly. "That's what I mean. You accepted the surface evidence of my statement to the conclusion that I believe you killed Ann Regnas."

She seemed unable to catch the lightness of his tone. "But you said . . ."

"What? That if I accepted things as they looked! See here, Miss Lane, what's the picture? I come into this house in the dead of night, find you here, storm-trapped, car gasless, a woman murdered. Wouldn't it be logical to assume that you did it?"

"But—but—" she stammered, "there wouldn't be any reason. I wouldn't have a—motive."

"As to that I admit that at present I know of no motive, but that's what the investigator has to dig out—what he finds looking around."

"Oh! One of the details you'd have to uncover?"

"Exactly."

She sighed. "Well, it sounds ghastly. I'm afraid you'll have hard luck finding your motive. I didn't know Ann; never saw her in my life. Just the same, I'd be more comfortable if you didn't think I killed her, even tentatively."

He rose, thrusting hands in his pockets. "There you go again. Jumping at conclusions. I didn't say I believe you killed her. I just said—*you could have!*" He turned away, whistling softly, roaming the room, pausing at last before a pile of magazines, stirring them with the butt of his flash, rippling the pages.

"Not excessively literary," he commented. "Happy ending yarns, recipes for cucumber pickles, suggestions for removing rust spots, best way to roast a turkey. Turkey! Lord, I'm hungry."

Stacy's stomach lurched sickeningly. "Food!" she thought miserably. "He would!" Aloud she said, "There are things to eat downstairs." Then, "Have you noticed the pictures?" She indicated half a dozen prints pinned on the walls, obviously cut from magazines, or rotogravure sections of newspapers. "They're revealing in a way. On my second trip up here I forced myself to stand perfectly still, looking at them."

He considered them, eyes narrowed. A field of blowing flowers against an April sky, birds circling, suggestion of a distant church spire. The caption said: *New England Spring.*

A second spoke of lush harvest, bulging fruit bins, heaps of redolent apples, through the medium of an old-fashioned kitchen where a sunny-faced housewife trimmed limp crust from the edges of a pumpkin pie. Across the corner was printed, *Thanksgiving Number.*

Near the mantel was a small, very good print depicting the Landing of the Pilgrims, the figures tiny and lost against the bleak fury of a stormy Atlantic. There was moonlight over an old, winding country road where a covered bridge spanned a meager stream.

Stacy said, eyes tawny-gold, "Don't you see? I believe Ann Regnas was a native of New England."

He said slowly, "Possible, though not positive. This may add weight to your conclusion."

He handed her a piece of embroidery. She spread it out. Plain white muslin, design stamped in thin blue linen, about half of it worked in small, almost childish stitches.

She nodded. "I see what you mean. But don't tell me you know what it is?"

"Eh?" He glanced down at her, eyes crinkled. "Want me to name it? All right, you asked for it. A pillow sham! You spread it over the pillows during the day to pretend they aren't there. I'm not entirely clear as to the psychology prompting pillow shams. An estimable desire to beautify the room . . ."

"Unwarranted conclusion," she interrupted, eyes dancing. "What's wrong with beautifying the room with nice, plump, snowy pillows?"

"What's wrong, indeed? Except that pillows, in some tangled way, have to do with beds, and beds have to do with the unclothed body, and the body, God help us, is in some quarters synonymous with sin and eternal damnation."

"And in what quarter more definitely than New England? New England and the Puritans, witch burning, sin of laughter, crime of playing in the sun."

"You were born in New England, Miss Lane?"

She laughed shortly. "No, but . . . Aunt Susan was."

"Oh, I see. Aunt Susan . . ."

She shrugged dismissingly. "Pardon the personal element. My parents died before I knew them. Aunt Susan reared me. Not my aunt really; my father's adopted sister. I hated her!"

"And she came from New England?"

"Yes. A worthy creature in her way, perhaps, but anathema to me. I used to lie awake figuring out ways of torturing her."

"My dear girl! You suggest a vicious disposition."

"Vicious isn't half of it when it came to Aunt Susan," she said soberly, then looked up at him, eyes golden as a cat's. "I'll be entirely honest. I wanted to kill her!" Breath caught in her throat. "Can you understand that?"

"Perfectly," he assured her gravely.

"She was so damned virtuous. She denied me everything I ever wanted as a child. She was always standing between me and my desires." She turned away, groping for a cigarette. "Let's forget that. It's not important." Then she said over her shoulder, "I'm still inclined to the notion that Ann Regnas came from New England."

"Anything else to substantiate that belief?"

"Nothing definite. Just the feel of the house, I guess. But it's like an eyeless face. It tells no more about Ann Regnas than Ann told herself."

"At first examination, no. Perhaps if we look further . . ."

"Oh, I've been all over it, but then you'll likely find something I've missed."

They went into the narrow cheerless upper hall, into one after another of five sizable rooms, all barren of furniture, all swept and scrubbed clean as a new-laid egg, then down the stairs into the first room off the hall.

As Brade reached to open the door, Stacy said, "Here's something odd," and picked a crumpled, soiled cloth from the floor back of the bare hall-tree. "When I came back after trying to walk to Woodvale, my shoes were clogged with mud. I scraped them as best I could outside, then looked around for something to finish off with. I found this." She spread it out. "It smells of furniture polish; evidently been used as a dust cloth, but examine it, please."

He touched it lightly, pressing a fold between sensitive fingers. "It's silk, isn't it?" he asked.

"Yes. Very old silk. If you'll look at the hem . . ." She held it out, a largish square, with a deep fringe of tattered, delicate lace, "you'll see it's hand-hemmed, the stitches beautifully fine. And . . ." she drew a deep breath, "consider that lace."

"Lace?"

"Definitely. Now why would Ann Regnas have a thing like this for a . . . a dust cloth? Fine silk, hand-hemmed, gorgeous, tattered lace?"

Brade took the square from her hands, examined it carefully. Then he folded it, thrust it into his coat pocket. "I'd like to know," he told her and then they went into the front room.

He shot on his flash. A featureless room, the scant furnishings cheap, plain, uncomfortable. Stiff varnished chairs, luster dimmed by years; a square table exactly in the room's center.

"You see," Stacy pointed out, "not a picture or book, except the Bible there on the table; not a decoration of any kind. Nothing to ease the severity or to add beauty. It's all like that." She led him to the closed double doors which he opened with some difficulty.

"The light was burning when you came?"

"Yes. And there's the meal. Two slices of buttered bread, canned tomatoes, the bacon, tea."

"And here is the chair." He frowned at the quaint, cloth-padded rocker sideways to the table; glanced at the tall, hearse-like secretary in the corner. "The money there?"

She pulled out the top drawer, disclosing a pile of bills held together by a thin rubber band. He counted them, put them back.

"Nothing," he said after a few minutes search. "Nothing here but the money. It's amazing. Where are the things people keep in such a contraption? They're normally stuffed and bulging with odds and ends; old letters, papers, tax statements."

She said soberly, "There isn't anything. Nothing at all in the house to tell anything about Ann."

He straightened, dusting his hands. "Notice anything else?"

"Yes. She didn't have a coat."

"No coat! In this country?"

"Here's her wardrobe." Stacy drew back a thin, faded curtain. He lowered his tall head, looked in. Two dresses hung limply from hangers. Looking at them, Brade got a clearer picture of Ann Regnas. Two dresses for a lonely woman who had been murdered out of the dark stormy night; one black, decent, plain, without a touch to brighten it; the other dark blue, lighter material, for summer wear likely.

There they hung mutely—limp, homely garments, pathetically charmless like the stout, unromantic shoes that waited patiently against the wall; the flat, uninspired black hat on a low shelf.

"There ought to be something," Stacy whispered. "You know, a touch of something—about them. You'd think maybe she'd put on a buckle—a dab of white—a dangle of lace."

"Yes. It's only normal to seek expression through personal adornment. She was a strange woman." He made the statement softly, almost, Stacy thought, as if he were licking his lips.

She felt him there beside her, big, purposeful, direct.

There was comfort in his presence, a strange sense of protection.

He said, "Regardless of everything, I'm devilishly hungry. Did you say there was food in the house?"

She smiled wanly. "Yes. May I serve you?" She turned, letting the curtain fall on Ann's wardrobe, and led the way to the kitchen.

CHAPTER TWO

THE LITTLE TOWN of Woodvale cuddled under its blanket of snow, spirals of blue, fragrant smoke lifting in the cold, sunny air. Two dogs frolicked insanely under the stimulus of cold; venturesome chickens ruffled protestingly, glaring in red-eyed indignation at the strange, new world.

The door of Anson Brandt's General Store opened cyclonically. Olie Hansen burst out, a package of bacon and a can of baking powder clutched in mittened hands. He ran in long striding leaps, small geysers spurting behind, blue eyes bulging, plump boy's cheeks puffed out with his frantic breathing.

The dogs looked up to bark ecstatically, and took up the chase. Grandpa Erickson, tottering along on stiffened legs and a stout stick, backed hastily to the security of a board fence and called defensively:

"Hey, young 'un. You crazy faller . . ."

Olie didn't waste a glance as he churned by, enveloping the old man in a miniature snow storm. Over his shoulder he called, "Ann Regnas is dead! The Hermit Woman's been murdered!"

"You tank dar ban a fire?" Grandpa complained queruously, then his old eyes popped and he exhaled noisily. "Eh? Eh?" he called weakly. "What you say, Olie? Kilt? The Hermit Voman?" He straightened, still muttering, and started an uncertain, jog-trot toward town and the general store.

Mrs. Hansen turned from her hunched position before the open oven door, staring blankly at her snow-caked young son.

219

"Olie!" she gasped. "Where'd you hear . . .?"

Olie danced excitedly. "At the store. They was all talkin' about it. The man was there. I saw him with my own eyes."

"What man?" Mrs. Hansen availed herself of a convenient chair. "Tell it to me straight, Olie. They're sayin' Ann Regnas is dead? That she . . ."

Olie nodded eagerly. "Gosh, mom, it's true. This man . . ."

"Olie, for Heaven's sake, what man?"

"Name's Brade, someone said. Outsider. He found her. She'd been . . ." Olie stopped for breath and said, "murdered," in a small, uncomprehending voice.

"Dearie me," Mrs. Hansen sighed. "I always knew somethin' bad would come of it. Olie, you get right over and tell Mis' Olcutt, then stop by and tell Mis' Henning, and Mis' . . ." Olie was already gone. Faster than his flying ten-year-old feet sped the news of Ann Regnas' death. Over the little, snow-wrapped town it hovered in the bright cold air, burst like an exploding shell, fragments penetrating every house, every store, every warm and homey room in Woodvale. The news hummed like a giant dynamo. Voices called from one snowy porch to another.

"Say, Christine, heard the news? Ann Regnas is dead! They say murdered."

"Oh, help us! I never heard the like. She was a queer one, all right."

And on street corners—"Say, we ain't never had no vilence round here. Less'n you count that fight the Leffler boys had with the Axelsons, seven year back."

"Reckon it was some hobo. Dangerous, woman livin' alone like that. Look what happened few nights ago. Her barn was burnt."

"Oh, that was some of the young roughnecks right around here. The kids've always tormented Ann."

"Who's this man Brade that found her?"

"Dunno, exactly. Heard somethin' 'bout him bein' a big policeman from back east, but I guess that's just talk."

"Likely, and if he was he wouldn't be messin' into our killin'. Ann wasn't nobody special."

"Howda' you know? She coulda' been 'most anybody, I guess. Whatever made her live like she did? Why, I remember . . ."

And so it went until the normal humdrum topics of conversation were crowded out before a growing momentum of surmise, reminiscence, and hearsay concerning the strange, uncommunicative woman who had been a negative part of Woodvale's community life so long she was all but forgotten.

Rebecca Olcutt assumed, by unquestioned priority, position of arbiter of the last court of appeal concerning Ann Regnas. For, nearly thirty years ago, Mrs. Olcutt had personified the acme of social integrity in Woodvale, hitched old Barney to the surrey and driven out one warm June afternoon to call on the new owner of the Herb Altman place.

That classic visit, long embalmed in Woodvale's memory, dusty and unnoticed, was brought out and considered in the light of tragedy. The feminine citizenry of Woodvale gathered at Becky Olcutt's that crisp November morning and listened again to her account.

"She'd been there better'n two months," Becky related, "and I thought some of us ought to call. It was a Wednesday, I recollect, 'cause my washin' and ironin' was done and I figured I could take the afternoon. It was hotter'n Tophet and I thought a glass of ice tea or lemonade would be mighty welcome when I got there."

Ann had received Mrs. Olcutt on the front porch, not inviting her into the house. She had dutifully supplied a cold drink, not joining her guest—not doing anything, in fact, except just sitting immobile in a rackety rocker, speaking in monosyllables when she couldn't make a head shake or a nod do.

When Mrs. Olcutt's attempts at friendliness, not unmixed with curiosity, grew too pointed, Ann announced tonelessly she "didn't aim to have comp'ny. She didn't want any. She wasn't aiming to come into town much so why should she need a rig? She was living quietly, minding her own business . . ."

"I was that put out," Becky admitted, "after drivin' out there in the heat and all."

"Where'd she come from?" young Dilcy demanded. "Seems like no one ever said."

They pitied and excused Dilcy. After all, she was a newcomer, Bert Strange having brought her home as his bride only a little over a year ago.

"Lands sake, honey," Grace Wickham chided, "nobody knows *where* she come from. Word got 'round one day that the old Altman place was sold and . . ."

"That's right," Becky firmly mounted her rightful throne again. "We found out later that Ann bought it from a firm of real estaters in Chip' City. Seems she come to them saying about what she wanted and they found this place for her."

"What'd she look like?" Dilcy insisted. "I've never seen her, you know."

"No one's ever seen her much," Grace admitted. "She used to come to town once a month maybe. Walked both ways, pullin' a little boy's wagon after her to carry things, but she quit that a long time ago. She's got a car and some chickens. I hear her garden does real good."

Mrs. Olcutt's one attempt to establish normal relations with Ann, and Ann's consistent unfriendliness, had settled the status of the newcomer. If Ann Regnas didn't want to "mix in" they weren't going to bother her. Gradually the mild attempts at friendliness on Ann's rare trips to town ceased. Gradually Ann Regnas achieved what she evidently desired: complete isolation.

Woodvale wondered through a number of years. Woodvale gossiped. Young folks concocted stories about her, something that would answer their own need for mystery and excitement and glamour, though it was hard to find anything glamorous about plain Ann Regnas.

Little boys had their season at tormenting her, stealing her apples, pelting her lonely house with stones in the early dusk of long summer evenings. Ann took no notice as far as could be seen, but, about that time, she did get a great fierce dog, half Collie, half something or other, that snarled and snapped and took uncomfortable chunks from the seat of young Woodvale's pants and Ann was again left alone. The dog disappeared years ago, and had no successor. By that time Woodvale had learned to let Ann Regnas alone.

"I'm not bothering anyone, am I?" she demanded one evening when a bunch of young hoodlums had stoned her from behind a vacant building and Anson Brandt had stepped from his store to interfere. "I'm not meddling in your affairs. I'm just living as I want to live. Can't you let me alone?"

Looking down at the squat, powerful woman in her bundling woolens, coarse dark hair wadded tightly in a lump under her queer, out-dated hat, Brandt was struck with a sense of frenzy about her—a kind of savage, back-to-the-wall attitude that must invariably come to anyone who dares to brave group-condemnation by being different.

He said kindly, "Well, ma'am, I got to admit you don't bother us none and I guess you got the right to live's you like. I promise you, Ann Regnas, that from now on you can come into town's often as you like and we'll see that these young thugs don't hurt you. I promise."

Ann's pale eyes bulged slightly. She wet her lips, moved uncomfortably on large flat feet. She said, "Thank you, sir," and marched away, broad shoulders erect, head high.

Anson was as good as his word. He called a meeting of responsible townsmen, laid the case before them.

"It don't seem fittin' that we should let our younkers mud-ball a lonely woman just because she lives different'n us. It's a free country, ain't it? Now I got the names of the boys . . ." The boys who had stoned Ann on that long ago September evening were grown and married now, fathers of boys who again lurked behind vacant buildings to torment the "different," but the men of Woodvale were strong, unimaginative citizens and Anson's appeal got results. There were stinging trousers and blistered back-ends next day and after that Ann Regnas came and went as she wished in Woodvale, which was seldom enough.

Several years ago it got around that Ann had a car. Woodvale realized then that it hadn't seen her literally "in years," and decided she must drive to Chip' City to do her trading. Chippewa City, forty-five miles south, was sufficiently sizable to permit Ann's indifference to pass unnoticed.

So for close to thirty years Ann Regnas had lived in the old Altman place, and its few acres of tall pine and stately spruce remained the only uncut spot in the surrounding country.

The old house grew grayer and gaunter with the passing years. Momentary interest was aroused one fall by a report that Ann had been seen shingling the house, but Woodvale had long ceased to question what Ann did.

When it became known that Ann's out-buildings had been burned, Woodvale unhesitatingly brought in the verdict of "young hoodlums", and the Sheriff's office was notified. Now Woodvale tried to link the two crimes; the burning of Ann Regnas' property, the taking of Ann Regnas' life. Two such dramatic happenings, in Woodvale's opinion, just had to be of a piece.

"I GUESS THERE could be a connection," Sheriff Terrence Shannoloski admitted cautiously, facing the interested group who had awaited his arrival at Brandt's General Store. "Sorry boys, nothing to tell you. Haven't dug out enough facts."

He lounged against the counter, pushing his hat back from thick yellow-blond hair. Terry Shan was a big man, and laced boots, mackinaw and broad brimmed Stetson did not appreciably diminish his stature. He lighted a cigarette, keen blue eyes appraising the group over the flame in his cupped hands.

Funny, Terry thought, how a guy could fall for life in the sticks after knowing the Big Town and being a part of it.

Terry was glad he'd listened to Nora and come on out to Minnesota when her grandpa died and left her that farm. Glad, even if it had meant quitting the Force, leaving Court. Pretty nice place for the kids to grow up! Pretty swell! Lots of outdoors, sunshine, open places. . . .

"Think a hobo done it?" a querulous voice demanded and Terry roused out of his mental wanderings.

"Hobo?" he repeated judiciously. "Well I dunno, Talbot. It don't pay to figure things in advance. You just got to go along, reach your conclusions from what you can prove."

The group was obviously impressed, taking a personal pride in the profundity of Terry's observation. After all, he oughta' be good, hadn't he? Not very many counties could boast of having a former New York policeman in their employ.

Luke Talbot removed his shabby cap, scratched his thinning hair. "Well, it beats me," he admitted. "What'd you find out about her, Terry? How about letters, papers she had tucked away?"

"There weren't any papers," Terry said. "There wasn't a darned thing to tell us about Ann Regnas."

There was a general, discontented group movement. Here they'd wondered about Ann for nigh onto thirty years. Surely now that she was dead. . . .

"Who's them two that found her?" a lanky number demanded. "This here Breen—Brail?"

"Brade," Terry said, eyes glinting. "Captain Courtney Brade, Hawkins. He's caught more murderers than you've shot pheasants without a license, so chew on that. The lady is Miss Stacy Lane, a newspaper gal from Chip' City."

"Looks like she was mighty quick gittin' on the ground," Hawkins insisted. "Says she came in, found Ann just after it happened. Y' can't believe everything you hear. Mebbe she come just . . . before . . . it happened."

Terry straightened slowly, settling big shoulders, hooking thumbs in his belt. "That's just next door to an accusation, Hawkins," he said quietly. "I'll thank you to keep your lip buttoned. Loose talk's stirred up a lot of trouble before now." Hawkins' thin cheeks colored. He glared defiantly at the Sheriff. "Okay," he growled, "but just the same it's a free country. I got a right to my opinion, ain't I?"

"Sure," Terry agreed, "sure, Hawkins, but I'd advise you, friendly like, to damned well keep it to yourself."

He nodded shortly, yanked his hat over blue eyes, stalked toward the door. Then he paused, swung a friendly grin over his shoulder. "See you later," he promised and went out whistling.

The air was tingling, the sun warm, the sky blue. Blue it was, as April. April! Ann Regnas had come to the Woodvale vicinity in April—almost twenty-nine years ago. Now she was dead, murdered in the black night and he, Terry Shan, had to figure out who killed her.

"Great cats!" Terry reflected. "It's a hell of a case. The boys think I can do it, there at the store. That's swell of 'em but gosh-amighty . . ." Then suddenly he laughed and began whistling. "Court's here," ran his relieved thoughts. "Oh boy, am I glad Court ran out to Minneapolis on that Dan Rivner blackmail case. Am I glad!"

CHAPTER THREE

BRADE LEANED BACK in the shabby old Morris chair, long legs stretched toward the fire. The Palace Hotel boasted two *extra* rooms. The extra pair had to do with slight additional footage, windows overlooking Main Street and, most satisfying, small wood stoves. Brade had taken one, Stacy the other.

It was getting on toward evening. The brilliant sun had worked devastation with the snow. It still lingered in spots but ditches ran bank-full, water dripped from overhanging branches, pattered patiently against the small, dingy windows. A raw wind had sprung up. The night would be one for a snug fire.

Brade said, "Still it *could* have been a hobo, Terry," and gazed speculatively at the stained ceiling.

Terry scowled, drawing impatiently at his pipe; sprawled across the bed.

He said, "Nuts, Court. I tell you it's not so. Now look here." He sat up, stabbing the air with the pipe stem. "You wouldn't understand, coming from the city, but this countryside is hobo-conscious. Been a lot of petty thieving, one or two more serious offenses, thanks to bums, and it's got so a travellin' gent can't so much as show his nose without word getting around. I been hunting for news of a stray bum all day and there just haven't been any. Like I say, you wouldn't savvy coming from the city and all." Terry rested his case, leaned back.

Brade said with deceptive meekness, "I'll take your word for it, Sergeant," and they both laughed at the old familiar word. "We'll count the hobo out for the moment, though, mind you, I'm not entirely eliminating him."

"You wouldn't!" Terry growled, "Just the same, I tell you . . ."

"All right, all right, let it pass. If a hobo didn't kill Ann Regnas, who did?"

Terry grunted. "Don't I wish I knew," he muttered. "But one thing, Court, the lad in the car Miss Lane passed didn't."

Brade glanced up quickly. "That ironed out?"

"I'll say. The car was a Chevrolet coupe, driven by Ted Felton from Chip' City, salesman for a novelty company, pretty well known around these parts. That dirt road passing the Regnas place takes about seven miles off the distance between Woodvale and Chip' City. Okay in dry weather. Maybe he was in a hurry and decided to chance it. Miss Lane said he was trying to make too much time. He went in the ditch just before he hit the highway. Fairly deep cut and he just slid off and piled up. Car smashed to thunder; Felton badly hurt. In the Chip' City hospital, unconscious, pretty near through."

"Who found him?"

"Some guy stopped to change a tire on the highway. Shooting his flash around, he saw the car below him in the gully. About midnight it was. The clock in Felton's Chewy was smashed at eight-fifty-nine. Guess that's when it happened."

"Likely. Miss Lane met him around eight, or a little later. He was in a hurry to cover those better than seven miles in less than an hour, but the point is, Terry, he was near Ann's place somewhere around the time she was killed. If we could talk to him he might, just might, give us a tip."

"Yeah." Terry's brows drew down in a frown. "Guess you're right. No chance now, but if he comes out of it . . ."

"Keep it in mind and have a try at it."

"Yeah," Terry agreed, "sure." He stirred impatiently. "That's the devil of this business. No one around to notice anything. No neighbors, no nothing."

"What about the neighborhood filling stations?" Brade asked. "Your boys . . .?"

"Covered 'em, of course. Storm shooed folks off the highways early. And just to make it good, Arnie's Independent station at the Woodvale intersection sports a sign on the door, *Alaska or bust*. Can you beat it? The thing's a jinx."

Quick humor rode Brade's glance and he said, "Where have I heard that phrase?"

"Sure, I know," Terry grumbled, tousling his hair. "You love 'em that way but this thing happens to be in my lap." Then he asked irrelevantly, "Where's Miss Lane?"

"Out for a breather. How does she strike you, Terry?"

"And how!" Terry muttered appreciatively; then seriously, "Nice gal. She's out, I'd say."

Brade laughed. "Terry, old son, the wide open spaces have softened you. I don't recall you as so wholesomely unsuspecting in other days. After all, we've got to suspect someone and Miss Lane is most definitely *not* out."

"No?" Terry asked, unconvinced. "Why'd she . . .?"

"Kill Ann Regnas? I haven't the ghost of an idea. Just the same she could have done it, and I'm not marking her off by a long shot." He laughed unexpectedly, leaned back. "She's worried, Terry, and I'm sorry. I do dislike annoying nice girls by suspecting them of murder. I've a suspicion that she's out now trying for what she can dig up. Double incentive: her natural love of a good story, and her desire to clear her own skirts."

"Okay," Terry said irritably, "we'll chalk Miss Lane up as suspect number one, then set about solving the mystery of who killed Ann Regnas. What the devil do you make of it, Court?"

Brade stretched hugely. "Just one thing I'm sure of, Terry, and that is that there may be a perfectly simple explanation. We've got to walk easy," and Terry sighed with satisfaction at that we, "and guard against being carried away by the oddity of the situation, the seeming mystery."

"Ann Regnas was a mystery herself," Terry said slowly. "Near thirty years ago she came out here, and no one knows from where or why."

"The fact that she chose this place to live does not necessarily constitute a mystery," Brade objected. "Maybe it just appealed to her."

"Maybe," Terry agreed without conviction. "But she never had a visitor, never received a letter far's we can find out. She never wrote to anyone, never spoke if she could avoid it. She lived alone . . ."

"You see?" Brade interrupted. "We're liable to let those facts blind us to the obvious truth. Maybe Ann Regnas wasn't a mystery. Maybe she told the truth. Perhaps she just liked to live as she did. Her antagonism may have been one of the necessities of her way of life—what she had to do to keep the curious at bay."

He paused, staring blankly at the dimming square of window. Terry regarded him in silence for a moment, then—"Nuts!" he said and yawned.

Brade did not seem to hear. "Maybe," he continued, "she didn't have any folks to write to. Maybe she had enough money to live on, used it living as she liked. I tell you, Terry, there doesn't *have* to be a story in the life of Ann Regnas."

Terry wriggled uncomfortably. Court has a way with him, no getting around that. He was the very devil for talking you into things—or out of them. As he put it now, you could very well believe . . .

"Now that that's taken care of," Brade said as if following a definite line of thought, "we'll consider what we have to go on. First, what do we know—not imagine or surmise—but know about the murdered woman? She was, the doctor suggests, around fifty, strong as a horse, in good condition. That's about all the physical mechanism tells us. Except," he glanced at Terry, "that she was killed by a blow on the head from a piece of pine wood."

Terry turned slowly. "Well, we knew she died from a blow on the head, but we . . ."

"Weren't sure what instrument was used? Correct. However, the wound yielded microscopic bits which on examination proved to be fragments of pine bark. They were buried in the blood-matted hair, not visible to the unaided eyes. I've seen the coroner's report and there's no doubt about it. Ann Regnas was struck, not by the metal statuette or a heavy walking stick, but by a piece of pine still carrying its bark. So we know that. The house in which she lived for over a quarter of a century tells us . . ."

"Not a confounded thing," Terry interrupted petulantly.

"The house," Brade pointed out, "is delightfully revealing."

"Revealing?"

"Exactly. It fairly shouts at you. Here's what it says: Ann Regnas was a capable, intelligent woman. In no other way could you explain the *entire absence* of any normal clues to her background and personality. Everything that might give a hint to her origin has been obliterated. From what we can pick up and handle, we conclude that she was a dull, unimaginative woman lacking in any sense of beauty or desire for it in her surroundings. There was no softness in the house. Nothing to ease the harshness of her life. She plodded through the years, working like a mule, carpentering, gardening, doing her own fall butchering and yet . . ."

He paused, stared narrow-eyed at Terry, then took from the mantle a small paper-wrapped parcel.

"This belonged to Ann Regnas," he said. "Consider it. It came from behind the hall tree in Ann's house." He extended a square of soft, rose-tinted silk. "Miss Lane used it to polish her muddy shoes. I bribed the landlord's buxom daughter to launder it for me. It discloses itself as fine old silk and it is edged with genuine rose-point lace."

Terry sighed and laid the thing down. "And Ann had this tossed into a corner."

"Yes, too soiled and shabby to be recognized except by a sensitive touch. The whole point is, how does it fit in with what we know of Ann Regnas? Obviously it's been in her possession for a long time. Likely she brought it with her when she came. A number like that can't be purchased from a mail order house of general store. Now, are we justified in assuming that Ann might at one time have lived in a stratum of society where such things were not unusual, or that she might have known someone who so lived?"

Terry was studying the silk again.

"What's it for?" Brade chuckled. "Ladies used to wear such things over their heads in the evening; sort of a graduated fascinator. You remember fascinators, Terry?"

"Knew one once," Terry admitted. "A blonde . . ."

Brade brought the conversation back promptly. "Aside from my contention that the absence of clues offers a clue, this is the only

tangible thing we have. Rose-point and Ann Regnas make an incorrect picture, just as the dull cloddish creature who waddled into
town on Saturday nights dragging a child's wagon, does not fit into
the pattern of the woman who was intelligent and capable enough
to blank out her past . . ."

He glanced up at a sharp knock, Stacy Lane came in flushed
and excited, dropped into a chair, accepted a cigarette.

"I've got a clue," she announced. "That is," she explained when
their silence made her uncomfortable, "I've found out something.
Ann Regnas once had an out-of-town caller."

Terry's big body gathered into a tense knot as he leaned forward. "Who was it?"

"Well, naturally, I don't know," Stacy protested.

"When was it?" Brade demanded.

Stacy flushed. "Fifteen years ago," she admitted meekly. To her
relief neither man laughed. She said valorously, "I couldn't rest. I
just had to get out and prowl around. I heard all the stories. I followed one. It led to Uncle Peter Harmon. Seventy-two he is,
crippled with rheumatism, but he ran the hack in Woodvale for
thirty-five years—and that's how he took this 'toney' gent to Ann
Regnas' house that night."

"Good work," Terry said under his breath.

Brade asked quietly, "If Uncle's telling the truth, Miss Lane,
how is it that the civic body has been kept in ignorance of this happening?"

"You'd have to know Uncle Peter to understand that, Captain
Brade. Uncle is the soul of honor. You see, the mystery man gave
him ten dollars to keep dark his arrival and visit to Ann."

"Ten dollars!" Terry exclaimed.

"And you mean that Uncle Peter kept his ten-dollar word? That
for fifteen years he never let out a peep about the matter?"

"That's exactly what I do mean," Stacy said seriously. "He told
me, 'This pore woman's been kilt without kith nor kin and mebbe
the story'd help, though land knows it was a time ago.'"

"A 'toney' gent," Brade said reflectively, fingering the square
of silk with the rose-point edge. "Anything more specific?"

Stacy flipped open a small note book. "I took it down just to be sure," she explained. "Here's how it goes: 'He was a thin man like a crow, speakin' like a college professor, and dressed scrumptious. His face was pinched and white as whey. He had a big beak nose, small bright eyes behind nose spec's, set clost each side. He checked his bag with Billy Winters, the station agent, statin' he'd be back in an hour or so for the eastbound. He never said nothin' all the way out though I made a try at friendly talk. He tuld me to wait, front of Ann's house. Well, it was mid-December and too consarned cold to just sit, so I got down and stepped around some. That's how I see the way Ann Regnas acted when she come to the door.'"

Stacy paused, crushed out her cigarette, went on. "'This man marches right up to the door, knocks, and Ann opens it. There was a light in the hall; it was well into dusk, and I guess it showed on his face, cause sudden-like she lets out a squawk and I heard just one word. 'You!' He said somethin' and at once she went quiet, and stepped aside so's he could come in.'"

"Well," Terry grunted, "at least we got proof that someone was once admitted to that house. Go on, Miss Lane."

"That's about all," Stacy admitted, closing the book. "The man stayed more than half an hour, come out, climbed into Uncle Peter's hack, was driven back to the station, where he caught the eight o'clock train back to . . ."

"Where?" Brade demanded.

"Minneapolis," Stacy admitted dispiritedly, recognizing an anti-climax when she met it.

Terry asked, "That bag the professor left with the agent? Any hope he got curious?"

"I thought of that," Stacy told him, faintly reproving, "and yes, Billy Winters was curious and looked the bag over. He got the man's name . . ."

Terry whooped, jerked upright on the bed.

"Who was the man?" Brade asked softly.

She said, "Uncle Peter couldn't remember. He thinks Billy told him but . . ."

"Uncle Peter forgot," Terry pointed out, "but how do you know Billy Winters did?"

Stacy blinked. "Well," she admitted, "I just . . . assumed . . . that Billy forgot too." Her guilty glance met Brade's. "You see, Billy didn't know where Uncle Peter took the stranger. There was nothing to make him remember."

Terry was on his feet, struggling into his mackinaw. "You city people," he grumbled, "don't understand small-town folks. Me, I know 'em, and I'm telling the both of you they don't forget unusual happenings."

"But a name written on a grip label—fifteen years ago," Stacy protested.

"I know Billy Winters," Terry said grimly. "I'll see what I can dig up."

Stacy looked rather helplessly at Brade as the door slammed behind the sheriff.

"Think there's any hope?" she asked.

"Slight, I'd say, but if anyone can dig out that man's name, Terry Shan's the boy. How does it strike you, this yarn of Uncle Peter's?"

She jerked off her hat and the ruddy waves of her hair coiled round her thin, rather tired face.

"One could make anything he chose out of it, I suppose. Another piece of the puzzle that doesn't fit in, like the . . ." Her eyes lighted on the square of silk. She lifted it gently. "Beautiful!" she said softly. "How ever did Ann Regnas come by a thing like this?"

She laid the silk down, glanced at him under the long curl of dark lashes. "Still not willing to give me a clean bill of health?" she asked with a slight smile.

"My dear Miss Lane, I have never accused you of killing Ann Regnas. I merely said you *could* have done it."

She sighed, ran fingers through her hair. "The slight distinction fails to comfort me," she said; then added, "I happened on a minor yarn."

"Yes?"

"A car skidded into the ditch last night just before it hit the highway. The driver was badly injured . . ."

"Novelty salesman, name of Felton?"

"Oh, you've heard then . . ."

"The Sheriff brought the news. Likely the car you passed."

"Yes. Guess there's no hope for us there unless Felton happened to have noticed something. He's as solid as the Bank of England and the chances of him having killed Ann, well, there just aren't any."

"I suppose not, though I insist that all comers be considered as . . ."

"Suspects? Yes I know, Captain Brade. Felton will be small comfort to you unless, in passing the place, something attracted his attention."

"Possibly but unlikely. It was dark, snowing . . ."

"No," she corrected, "raining. The snow came later. You came in the snow," She paused, swinging one slim, nervous foot. "I'll be disagreeably frank, Captain Brade, and completely cheeky, but I believe you had some interest in visiting Ann Regnas aside from the very laudable one of lending a helping hand to Sheriff Shannoloski."

He did not reply for a moment, then, "Why do you say that?" he inquired, not looking at her.

She said defiantly, "You acted like . . . like you'd known her," and moistened her lips because the statement sounded so ridiculous.

He said evenly, "Sorry, Miss Lane, I did not know Ann Regnas. However," he sat up abruptly, facing her, "you are correct in saying I had an interest above the burned car in visiting her place. I first heard of Ann Regnas last spring. The story's simple and is pretty well told in half a dozen lines. Here they are."

He drew an envelope from his pocket, extracted a folded slip of paper, handed it to her. She spread it carefully, a small section cut from a newspaper column.

If Prudence Sanger is still alive and reads this notice, something may yet be saved of two ruined lives. She was last seen in the vicinity of Woodvale, Minn.,

April 6th, 1917. Anyone having information please
communicate with Rodney Grange.

Stacy looked up, eyes puzzled. "An address in New York City.
Where did it come from?"

Brade returned it to its envelope. "Sheriff Shannoloski sent it
to me. It appeared in a Minneapolis paper. Terry's been intrigued
by the story of Ann Regnas ever since he came out here. He read
this and thought of her."

"For heavens' sake, why? That she might be Prudence Sanger?"

He glanced at her oddly, a humorous twinkle in his eyes, restrained by the set grimness of his compressed lips.

"Well," he hazarded, "the line says 'last seen in the vicinity of
Woodvale, April, 1917.' The best minds in Woodvale, according to
Terry, set Ann's purchase of the Altman place at a 'mite less'n thirty
year ago.' I have it on unquestioned authority that Ann arrived in
the Spring of 1917."

Stacy nodded, twitching with excitement. "Who," she wondered,
"last saw Prudence Sanger in the vicinity of Woodvale and who . . ."

The door opened. Sheriff Shan came in, head lowered slightly,
hands buried in the side pockets of his mackinaw. He closed the
door carefully, leaned against it. His glance went instantly to Brade.
It was as though sparks leaped between them.

Brade said tersely, "Okay! Who was Ann Regnas' visitor?"

Terry said, "His name was Sanger! Artemus Claude Sanger!"

Stacy barely restrained a cry. "It's the name in the clipping.
Prudence Sanger! Artemus Claude Sanger!"

"Yes," Terry said, and all at once it was apparent how excited
he was. "What do you make of that, Court?"

Brade answered nothing for a long moment, then a hard twinkle
rode his glance as he twirled the moonstone ring.

"Make of it, Terry? Why, plenty—when I consider the name of
the woman who was murdered last night. Regnas. Try spelling it
backward!"

Chapter Four

Stacy was the first to break the stupefied silence.

"Regnas," she said faintly. "Regnas—reversed is—Sanger!"

"Good Lord!" Terry exclaimed. "Regnas—Sanger! I'll be damned!"

"But she *wasn't* Prudence Sanger," Stacy insisted irritably. "She was . . ."

"How do we know she wasn't?" Terry demanded, zipping his hat to a chair, shrugging out of his wet jacket.

"Why . . . why . . ." Stacy began and stopped, staring wide-eyed at the Sheriff. "How *do* we know?" she finished weakly.

"We don't," Terry stated flatly and sat down, fumbling for his pipe. "What we do know though," he added, "is how and why her barn was burned."

"That settled, eh?" Brade glanced up interestedly.

"Yes. One of my deputies washed that one up. Got the report as I came in. About like we figured it. Bunch of useless kids, other side of the creek, thought it'd be fun to smoke Ann out. Five of 'em—we got their names and a signed confession—started a smudge with old casings in the lean-to shed, expecting her to come runnin', then the darned blaze got away from them. They been so scared they didn't dare show their heads but the killing last night did the job. They told their folks and they got in touch with my office."

"I'm glad," Brade said gravely. "At least that angle's cleared up."

He looked at Stacy. "No, we certainly don't know that Ann Regnas was Prudence Sanger. There are, however, some intriguing

237

angles. When Sheriff Shannoloski happened on the newspaper clipping he wrote to Rodney Grange, suggesting that if he could furnish definite details there might be news for him." He glanced at Terry. "Right?"

"Exactly. A long shot but the only hint of a clue I'd ever heard of concerning Ann. So I wrote Grange . . ."

"Yes," Stacy urged, wriggling with excitement as he paused to get his pipe going. "He answered? Sent you a description of Prudence Sanger proving . . .?"

"The letter was returned," Terry said, "with one word written across it. 'Deceased'!"

"Oh!" Stacy wailed and felt her stomach muscles collapse.

"That's where I came into it," Brade took up the account. "Terry sent the information on to me, suggested that I try for Grange's background. In my position, it wasn't too difficult. Rodney Grange was an American, fifty-six, slim, dark, hair nearly white, an artist, never having travelled very far at it, though as a youngster great hopes were held for him. Died as result of gas poisoning working on murals in badly ventilated room; bad lungs, tricky heart. No relatives we could locate, no friends who could throw light on his life or the reason back of his advertisement. We were, in short, straight up against a stone wall."

"Yeah," Terry growled, sucking at his pipe, "until you turned the trick."

"The name Sanger," Brade continued, "may seem uncommon but the list in the New York City directory gave me pause." He glanced at the Sheriff. "This will interest you, Terry. I've never furnished details. I poured my troubles into old Doc' Blucher's lap, He's a good friend of mine and not far behind Bob Ripley in collecting odd and interesting facts, though he confines himself to the history of medicine, with early American families as a side line.

"'Sanger!' he shouts. 'Straight from the deck of the Mayflower. Three branches—Boston, Plymouth, and Reddington. Boston strain pinched out. Plymouth—can't be sure, only—hold on. If this Rodney Grange was doing the Cape Ann coast in those murals, that spells

Essex county and Reddington.' And that," Brade said, "is how I happened on the Reddington Sangers."

"Good work," Terry muttered.

"You see," Brade informed Stacy, "I never do any work myself if I can induce someone to do it for me. John Arden was my next victim. Another friend, highly valued. An artist like Grange, except that John's going somewhere."

"John Arden," Stacy said softly. "What a nice name!"

"I talked to John about Grange. He didn't know him personally but Grange had once done something that hangs in a gallery somewhere which John passionately admires. The fellow's story, what little we know of it, interested John and the upshot is that he accepted what I hope was my subtle suggestion that he take a spot of vacation and see what Reddington was like."

Terry said slowly, "This is all news to me, Court."

"Hadn't got around to discussing it with you, Terry. But John went to Reddington and instead of the day and a half I'd mentioned, he stayed a week. The place seems to have fastened onto him."

Brade drew a letter from an inner pocket. "Here's what he wrote me."

It's an old town. Something left over from another age. Off to the side, passed up by highway and railroad, though there's a branch in here as you know.

It has mossy, sunken stone walks, mighty trees and the houses are old, dignified and rheumatic. There's the Commons, a nice old church at one end, the post office at the other. The hotel, God save us, is the OLD COACH!

That's just the outside, Brade. That's Reddington as you walk through it. There's another Reddington— one you can't actually see, but do most definitely feel. A mixture of aristocracy, hide-bound prejudice, intolerance and cruelty. Of witch burnings and soul savings. The air prickles with it. I get up in the night,

stand by the narrow window in my room at the Old
Coach—but pardon me. After all, you sent me up here
to do a job.

So here's the dope. The Sangers could fit into the
sketchy pattern you gave me; they confounded well
could. Old, old family. Old, old people. Two of them,
at least—Mr. Sanger and his wife—though in actual
years they're not tottering on the brink, I'd say. Their
daughter, Elizabeth, ought to be some younger but
doesn't seem to be. Queer stiff people, repressed
until they're like to pop. Artemus Claude . . .

Stacy shrieked faintly, clapped a hand across her mouth. Terry,
pipe forgotten, hunched forward, one blonde lock tumbling into
his eye. "Good night!" he muttered.

Brade resumed without comment:

Artemus Claude is a stringy old goat, stiff as a boiled
shirt, elegant as an 18th century print. I was taken
to the Sanger home by the charming old parson
whom I captured by an interest in New England furniture. He insisted that I MUST see the Sanger place,
and just off the record, it's worth seeing.

Big double parlors, tall windows with gorgeous
red velvet drapes, thin Madonnas in the garments
of sin. A black marble fireplace, two delightful
whale-oil lamps with crystal prisms and gold leaf
ornamentation. Couple of genuine Chippendale
chairs, a Hepplewhite wall cabinet containing some
fine china; on top, a candelabra of Waterford glass.

The townspeople are achingly close-mouthed but
I got a few things which will interest you. There was
a Prudence Sanger; her father, elder brother to
Claude. The Sanger fortune, including the old house,
fell to her on her father's death, Claude acting as
guardian until she was twenty-one. The only catch

is—Prudence died. All neatly interred in the Sanger lot in the village cemetery.

I stood in waning sunlight beside her grave. Nice, that old burial ground. Green-black pointed spruce and firs, interspersed with maples that in autumn would be gold and crimson. Weathered tombstones, gray with years, respectable, highly respectable decay.

I read: Prudence, beloved daughter of William Bennet and Constance Sanger, born May 10th, 1899—called to her reward, April 3rd, 1917.

Brade's voice, deep, rich, oddly sympathetic in reading lines, slowed. He leaned back.

"That's about it," he said. "All John was able to dig up about Prudence Sanger. She died almost twenty-nine years ago."

A brief silence broken by sound of voices, stamping of muddy boots in the Palace lobby.

Then Stacy said musingly, "Prudence Sanger died in April, 1917. She was eighteen years old."

Terry scowled at her in concentration. "Ann Regnas bought the old Altman place in April, 1917."

"Yes," Brade said, "and according to Rodney Grange, deceased, Prudence Sanger was seen in the vicinity of Woodvale, April 6th, 1917."

"May be only coincidence," Terry argued, "s'pose you could figure out a lot of things."

"Well, we didn't figure out that Artemus Claude Sanger called on Ann Regnas fifteen years ago . . ."

"Or that she lived as a virtual recluse for better than a quarter of a century," Brade added, "and was murdered for no reason that seems obvious from where I'm standing."

"All right, all right," Terry grumbled. "I'm spoiling to be convinced. It's just that . . ."

"By the way, Sheriff," Brade interrupted amiably, "what do the prints tell us?"

Terry scowled and blinked. "Prints? Well, there's plenty of 'em. Ann's, of course and . . ." he glanced apologetically at Stacy, "yours, Miss Lane. Pretty well scattered over the place. Found 'em all over that old black sec'etary in the dining room."

"I was looking for a weapon," Stacy said coolly.

"How about the murder room?" Brade asked.

Terry's hesitation was so slight as to seem imaginary. "Just one or two of yours, Captain; the rest Miss Lane's."

Brade glanced up quickly. Stacy got the impression that he licked his lips.

"Just mine and Miss Lane's in the room where Ann was killed?"

"Yes," Terry admitted, looking unprofessionally bothered.

"He's a pet," Stacy decided. "He doesn't believe I killed Ann Regnas." Then she thought, "Well, Courtney Brade doesn't believe it either. He just said I *could* have done it, damn him!"

"Not one of Ann's prints in the whole room?" Brade insisted.

"Nary a one, Court, which means . . ."

"That the murderer cleaned the room before he left," Brade concluded and looked at Stacy, brows puckered.

She felt a distinct stir of triumph. "That ought to pretty well let me out. Unless he figures that I polished everything up, couldn't get away, and made the prints when I came back with him."

"In all the house," Terry said slowly, "we found just one set of strange prints."

Brade's head jerked up. "Yes? Where?"

Terry looked at him oddly. "You'd never guess. On a little metal spice box set back on a shelf in Ann's kitchen cupboard."

"Huh!" Brade grunted, eyes puzzled. "Did the job thoroughly, didn't you, Sheriff?"

"Yeah, Captain, thoroughly. Ann's prints are on the box, which is proper; then there are three stray prints: first and second fingers and the thumb, nice and clear." He sighed heavily. "God knows how long they been there. The thing was tucked way back with a lotta other spice cans."

"What spice did it hold?"

"Cloves. Half full of cloves. Now make something out of that if you can."

Evidently Brade couldn't at the moment. He scowled at the pine knot sputtering in the fire, the stove door being slightly ajar.

The others followed his glance. Stacy shivered and, after a moment, said, "I'll always remember Ann Regnas when I look in the fire, I suppose. It was just such a knot . . ." she hesitated, then continued, frowning, "It just doesn't seem logical that Ann Regnas would invite any man into her bedroom."

"As I pointed out earlier," Brade reminded her, "she may not have invited him. She certainly would not invite anyone unless she knew him very well."

Stacy laughed a bit uncertainly. "I'd appreciate a list of men, or women, for that matter, with whom Ann was on intimate terms."

Brade said slowly, "How about Artemus Claude Sanger of Reddington, Massachusetts? He enjoys the distinction of having been, at one time of which we have knowledge, invited into the house."

Stacy's heart skipped a beat. "Yes, he was. Now why would he come all the way from Massachusetts to see Ann Regnas, I wonder?"

"So do I, Miss Lane. All right, how's this? Suppose her uncle forced her to turn over to him the Sanger fortune which John Arden says she inherited on her father's death. There might be ways. Suppose for the sake of discussion that Claude had knowledge that would endanger Prudence with the police. Suppose he promised to keep quiet if she did as he said . . ."

"Blackmail!" Terry exploded. "Well, after all . . ."

"Suppose," Brade continued implacably, "whatever it was, is finally cleared up and Prudence discovers that it is. Suppose she threatens to expose her uncle's action, demand return of her money . . ."

"But it can't be," Stacy cried suddenly. "Prudence Sanger is dead. She's been dead nearly thirty years."

Brade leaned back, laughed soundlessly. "I was wondering how long you would allow me to romance before hitting on that." Then he sobered. "There is, according to Arden's statement which is to be trusted, a gravestone in the Reddington cemetery which states that Prudence Sanger died on a certain date. We, however, have no certain knowledge that she did die on that date—that she did not die last night as a result of a blow on the head."

For all that the notion might have been a shadowy suspicion in their minds, Brade's bald statement of it was a jolt. Stacy made a futile gesture of smoothing her riotous hair. Terry stirred so the rickety chair creaked.

"But, Court," he protested.

"Hold it, Sheriff. I don't say it's true. I only say it—might be."

"How're we going to be sure?" Stacy asked. "How does one go about finding out?"

Brade lighted a cigarette, inhaled, eyes crinkled with a kind of impish mirth. "Sheriff, that question is directed at you. It's your case."

"What!" Terry swung around violently. "My case! Good Lord, Court, I can't . . ." He checked himself. After all it wouldn't do to assert his incompetence in the hearing of one of his supporters. He swallowed, swabbed at his brow with a crumpled handkerchief, gave up all attempts at face-saving. "Confound it, Court, you've got to lend a hand. I need your help."

Stacy admired him for his frank plea.

Brade said, "I'd be glad to help, Terry, but I don't see how it's possible. After all I've got a job, you know. I'd be more than willing to do what I can by way of suggestion . . ."

"This case can't be solved by suggestions," Terry said emphatically. "I want you to take over, unofficially if you like, but I'm asking you to find the murderer of Ann Regnas. I'll be the one to help, be under your orders . . ."

He paused, looking big and appealing and terribly in earnest.

Brade glanced across at him under tilted brows and was silent a moment. "Okay, Terry," he said at last. "I'll solve your Ann Regnas murder case for you," and Stacy gasped at the monumental egotism of the man. "It will require a little phenagling at Headquarters but I can manage it. I'll be getting straight on back . . ."

"But, Court," Terry wailed, "the murder happened out here."

"I know that, Old Timer," Brade grinned, "but unless we're willing to accept the wholly obvious, for which at present there appears little substantiation, we'll have to agree that the motives for murder lies in another quarter."

"Reddington?" Stacy questioned softly.

He nodded. "I've ten days belated vacation coming. I've wanted to visit Reddington ever since John Arden put it on the map for me. I'll run along up, look things over."

"Oh, Lord," Stacy thought, "don't I wish I could go too!"

"But first," Brade went on, "I want something more definite about Ann Regnas. I believe it's there."

"Where?" Terry demanded.

"The only place it could be. In the house where she lived for twenty-nine years."

"But, Court, we've looked . . ."

Brade gestured impatiently. "We're going to look again—one place we haven't even considered. The attic."

"There isn't any . . ."

"I know, Sheriff. We couldn't find access to the attic. You won't deny there *is* an attic, will you?"

Terry hitched at his belt. "It sure looks as if there ought to be one, but there aren't any stairs, ladder or—anything."

"That's not an accurate statement, Terry. You mean we didn't *find* stairs, ladder or—anything. Now here's what we'll do." He rose suddenly like a spring released. "Get an early start, run out to the Altman place and see about the attic. And you, Sheriff—do it yourself or have it done—get along over to Chippewa City, dig out the real estate firm that sold that place to Regnas—the individual who sold it, if possible. Get his story, anything he can remember, bring it out by the roots, then we'll see."

Terry's eyes were gleaming with satisfaction. He saluted smartly. "Yes sir, Captain Brade," he said, swooped up hat and coat, turned toward the door. "I'll have the report in as soon as possible. Good night, sir."

"Good night, Sergeant," Brade replied, eyes twinkling.

Then Terry turned at the door. "Good night, Miss Lane," he smiled; scowled toward Brade. "S'long, Court," he said and went out.

Brade chuckled comfortably, strolled to the window, hands in pockets. "Great lad, Terry," he commented, half to himself.

Stacy was collecting hat, coat, purse. "He worked with you a long time?"

"A long time. Never had a better. Terrence Shannoloski . . ."

"Such an odd name."

"Isn't it? Irish mother, Polish father." Then, abruptly, "Care to come along in the morning?"

Stacy's oxfords plopped to the floor as she swung around. "Oh, Captain Brade, I'd love to. May I?"

"I was intending that you should," he remarked, and she felt about six inches tall, face hot with quick anger.

"He acts like he owns me—like all he has to do . . ." and then she reflected sensibly, "After all, he's the officer in charge of this murder investigation. I'm a suspect." She stood up primly.

"Yes sir, Captain Brade," she said, and restrained an impulse to salute as Terry had done.

CHAPTER FIVE

LEANING AGAINST THE WALL in the room where Ann Regnas had died, Stacy watched Brade. It was half-past eleven. They had been at the house nearly two hours. Sheriff Shan was not present, having left the night before for Chippewa City.

The house was shabbier, gaunter, than Stacy had remembered it. She was filled with a sort of incoherent wonder that any human being could live in such drab surroundings. The wonder had grown as Brade had unlocked the front door and they went inside. It was not that the place was rackety, run down. It was, to the contrary, in excellent repair, everything snug and tight. But so gray, so utterly devoid of stray touches to relieve its dark plainness!

Brade seemed unaware of her. He prowled the downstairs rooms not touching anything, just looking—seeming to sniff, Stacy thought. She tagged after him, cold, uncomfortable, remembering her misery and discomfort all too vividly; learning nothing at all of what he discovered, if anything; wondering, impatiently, why he had brought her along. Then abruptly he paused at the foot of the stairs.

"Let's look at the second floor," he suggested amiably.

He devoted the longest time to the room in which the woman had died and here, to Stacy's shivering thankfulness, he built a fire. He hunched now on a stool beside the fire, smoke trickling through his nostrils, literally drinking in the room—appraising the faded, rather delicately patterned wall paper, the worn gray carpet, the thick dark hangings at the prisoned windows. He took in the narrow bed, the clean, coarse sheets, flat pillow, the shapeless slippers underneath.

"Ought to be something," he muttered. "Something to give a hint about her. This could be any woman's room—any woman, that is, who was insensitive to beauty, felt no interest in personal adornment, had no desire to . . . entice." He shrugged, laughed abruptly. "Well, let's find the attic entrance," he suggested briskly and went into the hall. "The Sheriff and his men are on the record that there is no access to the attic but they can't deny that there *is* an attic and since the attic is, I maintain there is an entrance to it."

"Sheriff Shan and his men hunted everywhere," she began.

"Without finding an entrance. Yes, but I refuse to accept the evidence when my intelligence refutes it. Now we'll start at the beginning. This big room on the front."

He opened the door. The sun, struggling to soak up moisture, shone feebly and the room was so bare it reminded Stacy of a skeleton exposed to sun, rain and wind until it gleamed. A bulky dresser was the only piece of furniture, hulking defensively against a wall.

Stacy said in exasperation, "Why is it all—everything—so damned clean?"

"In my opinion, Miss Lane, Ann Regnas came here to lose herself, beyond the possibility of finding. She intended that her past life, everything connected with it, should be completely obliterated. She must early have formed the habit of clearing out, discarding anything that might have offered the slightest gleam of light. It must have become a habit, continued long past the point of necessity. If you kept it up for twenty-nine years . . ."

"Yes, I see. You'd end up by having a clean house."

He nodded, carefully running fingers over the wall paper.

"The attic entrance may well have been closed and papered over. Take the north wall, please, Miss Lane." Stacy obeyed, though the process seemed wholly unintelligent. You could tell just by looking at the walls that there wasn't anything there. But she worked carefully, the action warming her, dispelling the creeping chill of the unheated room. Her fingers grew almost painfully sensitive, aware of every slightest irregularity. Brade worked swiftly, soundlessly.

She cried, whirling to face him, "There's something here! Behind the dresser!"

He was beside her instantly. "Where?" He tugged the heavy piece aside, explored the uneven surface, had his knife out, picking at the seam in the paper, yanking it away in thin strips.

"Is it anything?" Stacy pleaded. "If it is, what . . ."

"It's a door." He was on his knees tearing the old paper from the bottom, rising, pulling a long, wide flap with him. A wooden door was partially disclosed.

"There isn't any way to open it," she said breathlessly. "No knob."

"It's nailed shut. I need a hammer."

"There's one in the kitchen. I'll get it."

The door was fully revealed when she returned. He was examining the fastenings. "Ann Regnas nailed this door shut," he said, "that is, if she nailed the windows. They are identical. Now why," he wondered, taking the hammer, "would she seal it so carefully unless . . ."

He removed the nails with difficulty, examined the lock, and, drawing a bunch of keys from a pocket, selected one. It required nearly five minutes, then the door was opened protestingly, spilling a shower of dust and powdered plaster.

"Oh!" Stacy gasped. "It's a—it doesn't lead to the attic after all."

Brade's flash swept round the sizable closet with the one deep shelf, the row of empty hooks. "Just a minute. There's a ladder." The light shot up. "Take a look," he advised, and she craned upward seeing the outline of a large trap. Brade set the ladder in place, tested it, mounted. The trap was wedged and stubborn.

"Is it nailed?" Stacy asked.

"No, just stiff. Hasn't been opened in years." The trap squeaked, groaned, gave slightly. Brade rested, breathing hard. Then he set his shoulder in place and gradually forced the door back.

Stacy stared up helplessly, seeing his head, shoulders, upper body, finally his legs, vanish into the black maw of the attic. Watching, fascinated, she felt suddenly the stirring of the old house as if in protest—a curious kind of groaning, a sobbing sigh, that she knew well enough was the wind in the pines, the natural creaking of ancient timbers, but which seemed to her excited imagination to be the tortured struggles of a heavy body rising to prevent this desecration.

She choked and scampered up the stringy rungs. She clambered up with some difficulty, clutched a handy studding and pulled herself to her feet, seeing Brade prowling soundlessly at the far end. It was a very respectable attic, floored, sided, everything finished except overhead where the skeleton of the house was revealed.

"Ought to be a window," Brade muttered, then grunted, bent down, yanking free heavy layers of paper, admitting light from a narrow grilled pane set close to the floor under the sharply slanting roof. "Now we can get somewhere."

"Where?" Stacy demanded disappointedly. "I don't see anything." Then, "There's a rug on the floor over there."

"Right. Before this old divan."

"Divan?" She was beside him. "I didn't see it here in the dark. Sofa pillows—three of them—stuffing falling out. Mice been busy."

"How did they get it up here?" Brade asked. "Did Ann Regnas . . .?"

"She must have. Old man Altman lived here alone for almost twenty years after his old woman died and the kids went away. I have it on the best Woodvale authority. Well, I can't see the old man lugging that thing up here, or wanting to. Ann must have done it."

"Why?" Brade asked softly of no one in particular.

Stacy said excitedly, "Oh, look! There's a bookcase in the corner behind the divan. Now we'll find what Ann read besides the Home Comfort magazine."

She was on her knees tugging at thick layers of newspapers nailed over the face of the home-made shelves. Brade came to help and as the old papers gave crackingly, dust settled over their hands in thin gray layers. Again Stacy felt guilty, as if they were clawing their way into a tomb.

There were three shelves, approximately four feet long, filled with books—excellent as to quality of binding, printing, paper—arranged with loving exactness.

"Shakespeare!" Stacy said unbelievingly. "A complete set. Read too; passage marked. Why, she must have loved Shakespeare."

"Poems of Passion," Brade commented. "Ella Wheeler Wilcox." He turned the pages slowly. "It's marked too. Nice custom, neglected these days. Gives one looking through the book an idea as to what has appealed to you. Now this, listen . . .

> I am tired tonight and something,
> The wind maybe, or the rain,
> Or the cry of a bird in the copse outside
> Has brought back the past and its pain."

His deep voice was resonant, flexible, playing the words like the keys of an organ . . .

> "—the hand of an old dead June
> Has reached out hold of my heart's loose strings
> And is drawing them up in tune."

Stacy vibrated to his voice, hearing the wind, the rain, the crying bird . . .

> "And I seem to be newly lonely,
> I, who am so much alone—
> And the hand on my heart strings thrums away,
> But they have not the same old tone."

"Stop it!" she cried. "It's too—too—vivid!"

"Well, that's the last of that one; the marked part, that is. Now I wonder . . ." He bent forward, frowning at the page. "Something written here—pretty faint—but—yes, that's it." He read slowly, "'O, my dearest, my dear,'" and over the edge of the green silk, silver-stamped volume, his eyes met hers.

"Oh, my dearest, my dear," he repeated and the way he said the words changed them from faded characters on a yellowed page to a despairing cry aching out into the windy night and the rain.

Brade closed the book with a soft plop. "Now shall we go on?" he asked.

Stacy's fingers were unsteady as she examined the books. "Novels, history—Gibbon's Decline and Fall—Guizot's History of France—complete works of William Harrison Ainsworth—but have you noticed each volume, at least the ones I've looked at, has had a name and date written in it and carefully scratched out?"

"Not this one," Brade exulted. "This one was overlooked. It reads . . ." he bent toward the light, "'To Prudence Sanger on her 15th birthday—from her father.' But Prudence Sanger is dead," Brade said. "She died nearly thirty years ago."

"You don't believe that!" she cried. "You don't believe it any more than . . . I do."

He laughed. "No. I don't see why Prudence Sanger should voluntarily give up her rightful place in society, her inheritance, and go into hiding here; but I do see that there's something mighty queer about it. That's why I'm going to Reddington as soon as I can."

A few minutes later Stacy gave a stifled exclamation as she lifted a large tattered straw hat from a nail. "Look!" She held it out carefully. "Can you see Ann wearing this, a long time ago?" Brade bent his head examining it. It had been pale yellow, a kind of gay, laughing color, as disclosed by the inside of the soft crown. The floppy brim was laced with moth-eaten wreaths of small cotton flowers, thick with dust, almost indistinguishable as to color. "Blue, I believe," Stacy said, fingering the ruin. "See, here underneath. Yes, the yellow hat was trimmed with blue forget-me-nots." Her voice broke. "A garden hat. The kind a girl would wear on a summer morning—in the rose garden."

Brade nodded, touching the crumbling fabric and again she got that feeling of a monstrous satisfaction about him. Stacy did no more prowling after that. She was abruptly tired. The dusty reaches of the attic oppressed her. She sat down limply on the floor by the open trap, not caring what ruin was wrought on her nice gray frock.

Brade, over by the window, rustling through the crackling news-papers, looked up suddenly.

"Here," he said, "is the notice of Prudence Sanger's death."

She went quickly to stand beside him. He read with difficulty:

> Reddington was saddened today by news of the death of one of its fairest daughters. Prudence Sanger, only child of the late William Bennet Sanger, passed from this life in the Quintelle Hospital in New York City, following a brief illness. The news comes as the greatest shock. We extend our sympathies to the bereaved family of Prudence's uncle, Mr. and Mrs. Claude Sanger, and their daughter, Elizabeth. Interment will be in the family lot.

"Then she didn't die at home," Stacy said as Brade paused. "Brief illness?"

He was slashing black lines in a leather-bound note book. "Never heard of the Quintelle Hospital but we'll check it. Wait a minute." He straightened the paper, squinted at the faded date line. "April 5th, 1917," he read and looked up at Stacy. She nodded. One by one disjointed bits were falling into place. Tiny buried flakes of information, gathered painstakingly, delicately fitted into the yawning gaps presented by the strange life of Ann Regnas.

Prudence Sanger dying in a New York hospital in early April, 1917. A mystery woman giving the name of Ann Regnas, appearing as owner of the old Altman place outside Woodvale, Minn., in April of the same year. An unknown artist, Rodney Grange, crying through the columns of a big city newspaper for news of Prudence, who, he said, was seen in the vicinity of Woodvale in April, 1917.

"What is left of two ruined lives," Brade muttered, staring at the dusty floor; and like an echo, "Oh, my dearest, my dear!" ran through Stacy's mind from the pages of an outdated volume of love poems.

"Whatever made Ann Regnas come here," she said, "she was determined to blank out her past. She did it rather well, only . . ." her brooding gaze swept the attic, the old divan, the fragment of rug. She bent, fingering it, velvety soft, the texture rich, somehow ancient, ruined by moths and mice, but unmistakable as to quality. "Oriental," she whispered. "Here's something that ties in with the rose-point lace."

"Yes. Two fragments linking Ann Regnas with a wealthy past. A small Oriental rug, some inches of handmade lace. Why didn't she destroy them, also?"

"It would be difficult, I believe," Stacy told him, "no matter what one's determination to completely blot out the past. Wouldn't you cling to just one or two things, especially at first? Wouldn't you, if you'd been Ann Regnas, ease the terrible wrench by, say, fixing up this place? Bringing up a divan to rest on, books you had loved, a rug you valued?"

"And then," Brade took up the pattern, "as time went on, wouldn't you close the attic, nail the door shut, paper over it, bury the room and everything in it because, after all, it did no good?"

"It was closed a long time ago," Stacy guessed. "You can tell by the dust, the ruin. She never came here again, did she?" Unconsciously her eyes rested on the crumpled garden hat in the refuse of years. "No, she never came after she sealed that door. She was a terribly strong woman, Ann Regnas."

She thought of the thick, clumsy figure in the rocker before the dying fire, the coarse gray hair, the work-reddened hands. She remembered the years of isolation, self-imposed, which Ann Regnas had lived in this house. How many winter evenings had she sat before a meager fire, reading the Home Comfort magazine instead of the Shakespeare she loved? How many spring mornings had she worked in her vegetable garden, her body thickening with the lonely years, hunched over onions and cabbages instead of bending slimly above heavy-headed roses?

Stacy looked up at Brade and said in a rather tired young voice, "It will be fascinating—finding the story behind the life of Ann Regnas."

"Yes," he agreed, "and finding who killed her."

Stacy's eyes flared wide. She felt dizzy, unfooted. For more than an hour now, she had forgotten that this man insisted rather definitely that she, Stacy Lane, *could* have murdered Ann Regnas.

Chapter Six

THE INQUEST HELD the day following the visit to Ann Regnas' house was totally unproductive of results. Beyond establishing that the woman had been murdered, a fact permitting of slight argument, nothing was accomplished.

Stacy told her story and was grateful, though not convinced, when it was not questioned. She felt Brade watching her, but whenever she looked at him, his eyes were elsewhere.

Listening to the sketchy bits of information offered, she was appalled at the task Courtney Brade had so readily taken on.

"Okay, Terry," he'd said, "I'll solve your Ann Regnas mystery for you . . ."

"Oh, Lord," she reflected, "does he hate himself!"

Yet that evening when she sat with Sheriff Shannoloski and Captain Brade in the latter's room at the Palace, she had to admit that there was no suggestion of super-egotism in his quiet efficiency.

"That chap, Felton, who took the ditch the night Ann was killed—how's he making out, Terry?"

"Still alive but not yet conscious. They're figuring on operating, I've heard."

"Well, remember if he does come out of it, try for a talk with him."

Terry promised, then plunged into an account of his investigations in Chippewa City.

"Finally dug out the firm that sold Ann the Altman place. *Scanlon and Weaver—In Business More Than Forty Years.* That line was my tip. Young Scanlon's taken his dad's place and arranged for me to see the old man. He remembered well enough the day Ann came in looking for a certain kind of property.

"Not a lot different than now, though naturally she was younger, slimmer, not so weather-beaten. A rather good-looking young woman, Scanlon described her, but what he knew about her was exactly nothing. Wouldn't talk to him any more than she would to the others. He took her to the Altman place. She examined every-thing very carefully, questioned him as to the likelihood of neigh-bors, if he thought she could have a garden. Then she said she'd take it, paid cash for it, moved in and that's about the limit of his knowledge." Terry sighed and knocked out his pipe. "Only one other point. A week or ten days later, Scanlon happened by and dropped in to see how she was making out. He found the place locked like a bank vault, Ann gone."

Brade glanced up quickly. "Gone?"

Terry nodded. "Scanlon had a large business deal that held him in the Woodvale vicinity for about two weeks. He was driving 'round a lot and stopped by now and then out of curiosity but she seemed to have vanished. Then on the 22nd of April—he remem-bers because old Harvey Watson bought the Kellerman farm that day—Scanlon found her home. He didn't get a warm welcome. She was touchy, unfriendly, finally insulting, trying to get rid of him. So much so that Scanlon became suspicious."

"Of what?" Stacy inquired. "It is hard, isn't it, just to live alone and mind your own business!"

"Well, all he could tell me was that he thought there was 'some-thing funny going on there.'"

"Basing his conclusion, I suppose, on Ann's unwillingness to tell him her business," Brade surmised.

"I suppose so, though she did tell him she'd been East."

"East?"

"Yes. An accident, her saying it I guess. She was all upset, Scanlon says. Evidently just got home the night before; seemed tired and half frantic."

"Odd," Brade commented, "to think of her like that."

Again Terry nodded. "Well, that's all I got from Scanlon. The sheriff's office is mighty anxious to trace Ann's connections not only because it might help find who killed her, but because she left nearly twenty-five thousand dollars in a checking account in the Chip' City First National."

Even Brade was jolted by that one. Terry looked immensely pleased. Stacy felt certain that it was generally Captain Brade who made the announcements.

"The records show," Terry went on, "that Ann made sizable deposits regularly four times a year and never drew out a penny. They tried to talk her into a safe investment once or twice but it was no use."

"Where did she get that much money?" Stacy asked.

"It seems probable that someone was paying Ann Regnas to live as she did," Brade told her.

"The money came in quarterly installments," Terry said. "At least that's the way Ann deposited it. Always in cash."

"The bank has no information concerning Ann Regnas?"

"Not a smidgin. Nor anyone else, far as I can find out."

Brade rose abruptly. "Okay, Terrence my boy, that'll just about wash things up out here for the present. I'm leaving first thing in the morning. After a few hours, a day at most, in New York, I'll go on up to Reddington." One slim, vital hand, absently stroking his chin, dropped, rested lightly on the chair back. He looked at the sheriff, eyes faintly crinkled.

"I can't guarantee results," he said. "The answer may rest in some deeply hidden chapter in her early life and if so, it most certainly will not be easy to uncover. It may," his glance rested briefly on Stacy curled lithely at the foot of the bed, "lie in some fairly simple, wholly obvious motive which to date we've failed to catch. While we're checking up in Reddington we won't forget this other possibility.

"You're to keep in touch with me. Report immediately any new development, any slight variation of an old one. I'll send you frequent notations as to what I'm doing." He smiled companionably, looking again at Stacy. "Let Miss Lane in on them. She holds a peculiar position, right from the first. I know she understands that what she learns this way is not for publication—at present."

"Thank you, Captain Brade," Stacy said quietly. "Yes, I understand that, of course. But when it's all cleared up, when the answer is found, I hope that I can write the story."

"Who would be better equipped?" he asked and took her hand in a warm, strong clasp. "It's been a real pleasure knowing you, Miss Lane. I hope we'll meet again. If your interest overcomes your common sense, take a vacation and look in on me in Reddington, at the Old Coach."

LATER IN HER own room Stacy sat before the wavy mirror and brushed her flaming hair with the indifferent equipment she'd purchased at the City Drug Store. Brade and Terry were still talking, murmur of their voices reaching her faintly. She brushed the short length of her hair thoughtfully, studying the thin, pale face it framed.

"I might at that, Courtney Brade," she reflected. "I might look in on you at the Old Coach. Who knows?" She sighed tiredly.

It had all been rather ghastly. She was glad it was over. Her eyes flared wide. Over? Not yet! Not until that charming, casual, entirely ruthless man next door had settled beyond any question the identity of the murderer of Ann Regnas.

On the other side of the wall Sheriff Shan was saying, "Mean that, Court? Want me to show Miss Lane your reports?"

Brade grinned. "Why not, my lad? She'll enjoy details immensely, and, after all, she's entitled to some recompense for the uncomfortable time I've given her."

"Uncomfortable time? Why, I didn't know you'd . . ."

Brade's laugh was pleasantly spontaneous. "You're entirely right, Terry. Miss Lane hasn't been beaten with a rubber hose once. I really haven't done a thing to make her unhappy, yet you can see she's been simply bedeviled wondering just when I was going to arrest her."

CHAPTER SEVEN

A FORMIDABLE ARRAY of letters, phone calls, memoranda, awaited Brade on his arrival in New York. He glanced through them impatiently, sighed faintly at one, laid it tenderly aside. John Arden had been phoning at regular intervals.

Brade lost no time in calling him, grinned appreciatively at his excited recognition.

"Brade! I've been in a state since last night. They admitted you'd wired you were arriving today, omitting to say just when . . ."

"Never like to commit myself," Brade chuckled. "What's on your mind, John?"

"Well, that ad we ran, remember? Asking information about Rodney Grange? I got a reply last night."

"Good stuff! Anything important?"

"How'm I to know? The chap said he's laid up and if we want the dope, we can come and get it. His letter came too late for action last night; besides I thought you'd want to be there."

"Check. See you in an hour."

In less than the time mentioned, Brade was pressing the bell of Arden's apartment. The door opened instantly. Brade regarded his friend with satisfaction, noting the vital strength of his long, powerful body, the excited light in his eyes, set of his dark head, purposely avoiding notice of the shortened left leg, the limp, the slim dark cane. Arden was a gifted young artist, as Brade had told Stacy, making his living by commercial art while he studied and labored toward a different goal.

259

Brade slumped to the divan before the fire, accepting the cigarette Arden offered.

"Yes, I had a fine trip, John, a really magnificent jaunt. Got my business all ironed out, had a couple of days with Terry," Arden nodded, having heard plenty about Terry Shan, "and then to top it," Brade finished, "happened in on a perfectly top-hole murder."

Arden laughed. "As I live, Courtney Brade, you're positively sadistic."

Brade chuckled. "Maybe so, maybe so, but don't let's get sidetracked on that. What's the dope on this lad who knew Rodney Grange? See him tonight?"

"He said any time. What say we run along over. I'm set on hearing what he's got."

Brade rose. "Let's be going. I'll tell you about my prize mystery on the way. What's the chap's name?"

Arden handed him a folded piece of note paper.

If you want information about Rodney Grange, come and see me. I knew him plenty but I'm sick and can't get out. Any time's okay. I figure what I know is worth about fifty bucks. Peter Leeds.

The room was small, scantily furnished, disheartening. A weak electric bulb was draped by a tangled cord over the head of the single bed. A man sat up in bed, papers and pencils scattered over a writing board, a disreputable portable typewriter on the table beside him. He had a monstrous mop of tannish hair, gray-tarnished, though he was not old. His face was wasted, lined and savage. Blue eyes of fathomless intensity burned rebelliously.

"Resentment," Brade decided instantly. "He's consumed by a terrible sense of wrong." But his voice was polite as he inquired, "Mr. Leeds? I'm Brade. This is John Arden."

Peter Leeds studied them carefully, mouth twisted to one side. He had thin, knowing hands—sensitive and suffering, delicate fingers blunted by manual labor. His blazing, perpetually angry eyes went slowly over his visitors.

He asked abruptly, "You friends of Rod? You knew him?"

"Knew him!" Arden said. "No. Sorry. Only wish I had."

Brade said quietly, "No, Mr. Leeds, we did not know Rodney Grange. We are interested . . ."

"Sure, I know," Leeds cut in. "Interested in prying into his life, finding out all you can—now they've murdered him."

"Murdered!" Arden exclaimed. "He wasn't . . ."

"I know, I know," Leeds agreed wearily. "No one put a gun at his back and pulled the trigger." He coughed with sudden violence, blunted fingers fumbling at his chest. "No, they didn't do that. They just broke his living heart."

"And who," Brade inquired, "are they, Mr. Leeds?"

The crisp tones roused Leeds. He said sullenly, "Skip it. I was just talking. Rod wasn't murdered, of course." He sighed, leaned back, hands defeated and hopeless among the littered papers.

Brade's intensive glance settled unerringly on a small canvas obscured by corner shadows—a bleak headline, a lone twisted pine, sweep of gray water, flash of white gulls flying. There was a simple reality about it, a magnificent loneliness so one could almost hear the crash of breakers, the gulls mewing.

"Rod's work," Leeds said. "Give you an idea of what he had to start with. Should have been one of the finest. Was too, until their damned cruelty ruined him."

"Grange was a friend of yours?" Brade asked.

"Friend! I'll say. We started out together. Studied in Paris, London—starving along, making out somehow. Tough at the time, but fine—strong and real. We had ambition, Rod and I. Used to sit up all night cooking up tales of what we meant to do."

"Where'd Grange hail from?"

"Eh? I don't know. Midwest, I think. What does it matter? Background! Tribal instincts! Barriers! Shackles! Harnessing a man to the past. Got to get free of them—break loose and rise above them." He hunched forward, hands against his chest, the ruined shell of a man who had battered his life away against hostile barriers. "Just what are you after?" he asked huskily.

Brade studied his linger tips carefully. "Why did Rodney Grange want to find Prudence Sanger?"

Leeds' head jerked back. His eyes widened, blazed out at them savagely. Then he collapsed, gathering himself into a queerly defensive gesture.

"Prudence—?" He wet dry lips. Then abruptly, "Say, I have but little idea and less interest as to what my information means to you but fifty bucks will clear me of this hole and it's costing you that to hear me sing."

"Very well," Brade told him, "I'm willing to pay but . . ."

"You want to judge as to its value? Well, listen mister, you can take my proposition or get out. You said—anyone having information. You didn't specify the *kind* of information. How about it? Do I get the cash?"

Brade drew out his wallet, extracted two twenties and a ten, laid them on the writing board. Leeds snatched them up hungrily.

"Thanks," he said, and for a moment relaxed, eyes closed. That way there was a kind of beauty about his face, something that touched a chord of understanding in Brade.

"Poor broken devil," he thought. "Born to be a purveyor of beauty—beauty no one wanted. Or maybe," he amended, "his translation was faulty." He asked, "Can you tell us why Grange wanted to contact Prudence Sanger?" Leeds' eyes opened, black with a kind of monstrous despair. "Sorry," he mumbled. "Better pocket the cash. I can't tell you anything about Prudence Sanger. My information was to be about Grange."

Brade was deeply disappointed but he had to admit the truth of Leeds' statement. "Keep the money," he said. "Tell us all you can about your friend."

LATER IN THE APARTMENT they talked over the visit.

"I never met a man more completely, bitterly savage," John Arden said thoughtfully. "If that boy had his way, he'd burn at the stake—slow fire preferred—every citizen who had more than enough cash for the next meal. He's convinced that the curse of national wealth has ruined his gifts . . . and those of Rodney Grange. A number of disconnected facts. Youthful ambition, ideals, desires, years of study abroad, favorable mention by the big-wigs, but . . .'"

"Exactly. Not one thing to help us on our case. He swears he never heard of Prudence Sanger, doesn't know whether or not Grange spent any time in New England, though he thinks it likely judging from some of his subjects. Hadn't seen him for months; learned of his death through the papers."

Arden didn't answer for a time, staring thoughtfully at the fire. "Brade," he said at last, "in my opinion, you pretty well wasted your money. Leeds was lying."

"Yes," Brade agreed with satisfaction. "My conclusion exactly. I believe first, that he did know the Sanger girl; second, that he knows exactly why Grange wanted to find her. I think, in short, that Leeds pretty well holds the key to the whole situation, if he'd talk."

"Why the devil wouldn't he? He certainly needed cash. He could have held you up plenty."

"It's possible," Brade said carefully, "that Leeds is playing for bigger stakes. Maybe there's someone who'd be interested in what he knows who would be willing to pay him more than I could."

"Yes—only it's not much a question of being willing to pay as being compelled to pay."

Brade's head snapped up. "You've put your finger on it! Look here, John, when I leaned over to lay the money on the board I caught the address on the letter Leeds was writing. 'Mr. Artemus Claude Sanger, Reddington, Mass.'"

John whistled. "So that's the line. Blackmail, you think?"

"Possibly. If he's got information that's not healthy for the Reddington Sangers."

Arden leaned forward slightly as Brade paused. Brade looked up. Their eyes met. Arden's asked a question; Brade's recognized it.

"I didn't tell you about my top-spot murder case on the way over, after all," he said. "Too much rush and, racket. All right, you'll get it now. It might, just might, you understand, offer an explanation of Leeds' attempted blackmail of Claude Sanger, if he *is* trying it."

He told Arden about the old house in the pines, outside Woodvale; the Hermit Woman; the car that blocked his journey; the bolted door that was opened by a flour-faced girl with burning hair, tawny eyes static with terror; of the squat figure in the rocker upstairs.

He told of the sealed attic, the inscription in a volume of Ainsworth's novels, the rose-point lace, the crumbling Oriental rug, the faded yellow hat. He told him last of all of the amazing riddle of the backward reading name.

Arden sat without moving, one leg crossed over the other, head thrust forward, dark eyes fixed somberly on Brade. When Brade pointed out that Regnas in reverse was Sanger, he exclaimed sharply, straightened.

"Incredible! That woman, Regnas,—she is—she must have been Prudence Sanger. Why would she bury herself out there? But," as Stacy had done, he came suddenly against the inescapable evidence, "Prudence Sanger's dead! I saw her grave!"

"Correct, John, but did you, by any chance, contact a citizen who actually saw Prudence Sanger in her coffin?"

"Saw her? Oh, I see. The charming old custom of mourners strolling by to view the remains? You mean, is it possible to produce witnesses to the truth of Prudence Sanger's actual death?"

"That's exactly what I mean. She didn't die at home."

"No. At the . . . say, where was it?"

"The Quintelle Hospital."

"Never heard of it."

"Nor had I, though I've been around here a fairish time. However, I contacted the unquenchable Doc' Blucher as soon as I landed. He steered us onto the Reddington Sangers, you remember. Well, he remembered the Quintelle, and how! It was a shady place—one of those private institutions, run by a professional yegg named Thaddeus Quintelle who got by with murder according to Blucher."

"Odd place for the daughter of a wealthy New England family. Of what exactly does your doc' accuse his professional brother?"

"He told me in a torrent of expletives that Thaddeus Quintelle 'would do anything for money.' Able man to start with, I gather, but his gifts became perverted. Was kicked off the staff of a reputable institution, finally barred from practice, then started up this private racket with a sufficiently decent front to get by. Old warren of a place, the hospital; all sorts of unpleasant things are alleged to have happened there. Public disapproval finally got around to doing something about it, and Blucher was one of the boys who helped close her up. Quintelle dropped from the picture—never heard of again."

Arden shifted slightly, easing his injured leg. "Places of that sort were common enough at one time, I suppose, and are not wholly unheard of now, but what strikes me is that the daughter of the Sangers should have died there."

"If she did," Brade told him, and added, "Blucher offers to check vital statistics."

"Yeah? You're letting him?"

Brade's right brow twitched. "I never quench enthusiasm, my boy. The doctor's on the job. Remember my interest in this business is . . . unofficial."

"And you're really going to Reddington, Brade?"

"Yes, principally to assist Sheriff Shannoloski. Terry's a good sort. I'm fond of him; want to help him out . . ."

Arden's laugh was genuine and hearty. "My eye! All for good old Terry—just to help the lad along. He running for re-election? Not a penny's worth because you're just palpitating to ferret the thing out! Was Ann Regnas Prudence Sanger? Whose the hand of mystery that killed her?" He hesitated, then said slowly, "This girl you mention—Stacy Lane. Think she did it?"

Brade laughed then. "Don't look so alarmed, old man. It would be a shame to spoil our number one mystery by anything so simple."

"What's so simple about it? You mean . . ."

Brade said, "I've got to be running, John. What I mean—it would be something of a let-down, wouldn't it, if this nice little girl from Chippewa City should turn out to be the killer?"

Arden glowered moodily. "Oh, I don't know. She sounds intriguing with her brush-fire hair and tiger eyes. Witness will answer the question put! Think she did it, Court?"

Brade was slipping into his coat, reaching for his hat. "Not for a moment, John, not for a moment! I only point out to you, as I did to Miss Lane herself—hers *could* have been the hand!"

CHAPTER EIGHT

OUT IN CHIPPEWA CITY, Sheriff Shannoloski said to Stacy Lane as he faced her across the pleasant width of her apartment living room, "How does this Peter Leeds strike you, Miss Lane?"

Stacy, effective in dull gold lounge slacks, curled slim legs under herself on the divan and looked at the Sheriff. His phone call had come as a surprise and a faint shock. She hadn't really believed Courtney Brade when he'd promised to keep her advised, through Terry Shan, of how things went.

She said, "I believe he was lying—that he knows about everything we want to know."

Terry was not aware that Brade had come to practically the same conclusions. Brade's report on Leeds had included no surmises or opinions, merely a bald statement of fact.

"Yes," Terry said, smoothing crisp curly hair. "Court's doing a good job, like he always does. Got himself all settled in at the Old Coach, getting to know some of the folks. Wouldn't surprise me if he got himself invited to the Sangers before he gets through."

Stacy thought maliciously, "It wouldn't surprise me if Courtney Brade got himself invited straight into the front gates of Heaven— if he set out about it." But aloud she said, "Captain Brade is a capable officer, certainly. And I do thank you for remembering me, Sheriff Shannoloski. You have no idea how interested I am." Her eyes twinkled. "I seriously hope to write the story of Ann Regnas when it's possible."

"There wouldn't be any law against writing it, far's' I know," Terry said and rose. "I'll be on my way. Nora's promised me corned beef and cabbage for supper." He grinned boyishly, looking immense in the distinctive femininity of Stacy's quarters.

When he'd gone she sat down, stretched slimly toward the fire. A mean night! Comfortable to be securely housed, safe, unafraid. She yawned, stretched again, laughed gently. It was nice to be getting bulletins on the Ann Regnas murder case—straight from headquarters.

Brade's letter was vividly before her. After it had disposed of Peter Leeds, it had said:

There is at least one citizen of Reddington who holds it as his conviction that there was "something between that little girl and that painter feller." He refers, of course, to Prudence Sanger and Rodney Grange. My informant, old Darius Sheffield, unburdened himself to me as we stood beside Prudence Sanger's grave. He'd come on me there, paused for a spot of gossip.

"I minds her when she was only a tot," Uncle Darius said, motioning the grave, "and I knew her father before her. She growed up here in Redd'nton but young folks get curious ideas sometimes. She wanted to leave. Wanted to go to New York, and darned if she didn't"

Then it was that he voiced his suspicions that there was "something between," etc. I could get no details. He didn't rightly remember the pitcher-paintin' feller's name but, comparing a sketchy description with what Leeds told us, it was unquestionably Grange. He came in the fall, according to Uncle Darius, remaining not more than a month. Prudence ran off within a week after his departure.

Darius assured me, "We all knowed she'd come to a bad end and she did, pore little gal!" The bad end, I take it, was death in a New York hospital more than a year later. "And here," says Uncle Darius, "she's a' lyin' for good and all."

I longed to ask him if he was sure she was lying there. I did inquire as to the nature of Pru's illness, but he was vague and said a fever or somethin' he thought, or mebbe she just went into a dee-cline.

So what do we have now, Terry? Maybe Prudence never returned to Reddington. Maybe she took another name and buried herself for some thirty years in Minnesota. If Ann Regnas was Prudence Sanger, who killed her? And why? And if Ann wasn't Prudence and we're way off the track, why was Ann killed? Brade.

Stacy stirred, laughed unhappily. Nothing made any sense, even by implication. Even the posies on the yellow hat were all wrong. Forget-me-nots? When all Ann's mature life had been built with the express purpose of forgetting and being forgotten.

She yawned, brushed ruddy hair from her brow. Bed would be welcome, tonight. She'd been tired of late, ever since her experience at Woodvale—unable to get enough rest.

She decided to write to Brade and chuckled impishly, toying with the idea. Would he be glad to hear from her? She'd nothing important to tell him. Only—and she'd forgotten to mention it to Terry Shan—according to a brief newspaper account, Ted Felton, the salesman injured in the car wreck the night Ann Regnas was killed, had died without regaining consciousness.

Early the following week Sheriff Shannoloski received the following from Courtney Brade:

Dear Terry: Things happened at the Sangers tonight! Here is a report of the evening in chronological sequence.

My invitation to the fine, gaunt old house came to pass through John Arden's "delightful old parson" the Rev. Thomas Winship. The household consists of Artemus Claude Sanger; his wife, who must have once been a beautiful woman; and their daughter Elizabeth, who should also have been a real beauty.

In addition to the Rev. Winship and myself, there was another guest, Benjamin Grannis, the family lawyer. Large and competent fellow—quite the opposite in looks from the anemic Sangers.

I finally got the conversation around to the family and Claude commented briefly about his brother William's death, but he choked up a bit when he tried to talk about his niece, Prudence. Rev. Winship helped him out, saying, "Prudence died. She was Mr. William's daughter."

Elizabeth started violently at the mention of Prudence's name and remarked faintly that she had died "a long time ago."

Then came the shock of the evening. Claude gave a breathy squawk, staring at the window pane opposite. He tried to say something, pointed, took one step forward and crashed to the floor.

The doctor came in a hurry. Heart attack. Claude's had them before. Restoratives were administered and Sanger came alive, propped on the divan, looking like the devil. He said, "The window! I thought I saw . . ." and gave it up.

I'd noticed Sanger staring at the window. I went out as soon as I could, decently. A terrace ran along the front of the house. It was heaped with snow and, under the window, the snow was tramped down as if someone had stood there.

Couldn't tell a thing about the tracks. They led off the terrace by the side entrance, through the fairly deep snow, making a continuous furrow as if someone had run crazily. Lost the trail at the corner of the grounds, right inside the fence where someone had climbed over. Saw where he landed on the other side, but the snow had been recently cleared from the walk.

Back in the house, I found that Sanger had been put to bed. Grannis and the parson were with him and Elizabeth was standing like an anemic ghost in the center of the big room. I tried to say the conventional things but she just stood there in her out-of-date dress, staring at me, and suddenly I knew the poor creature was just naturally scared to death.

She whispered, "It's awful! I don't know what to think. I'm afraid. Afraid to go to bed . . . because I'll lie there and . . . think . . ."

I asked her what she was afraid of and she promptly said, "Prudence Sanger!" Before I could get my balance after that, Grannis and Winship came in and it was time to leave.

They walked back to the Coach with me and Grannis and I had a drink in my room after the parson left. Grannis seemed worried about Sanger. Said he was likely to pop off in such a spell some time. He's been the Sanger lawyer for close to forty years.

Spoke freely of Prudence. Said she was a lovely girl but high-strung, impressionable and rather went off the deep end following her father's death. She ran off to New York. Some sort of an idea of studying art. Died from pneumonia after a few days illness.

I asked him what it was Sanger saw at the window that laid him low. Said he couldn't imagine— probably an hallucination caused by the reflection of the fire.

And then we went on to talk about his recent trip to the coast. I kept mum about the tramped snow on the terrace, but what was it Claude Sanger saw, or

believed he saw, at the window? And why is Elizabeth afraid of Prudence Sanger, snug in her grave
nearly thirty years?

Brade.

Stacy gave a long shivering sigh not unmixed with satisfaction.
The letter was fascinating and exciting. She exhaled breathily,
leaped up, started a swift, restless pacing. Terry Shan had not personally delivered this second letter. She had found the typewrit-
ten copy in her mail box, with a note from the sheriff saying he
was leaving on business connected with his office.

Now she paused, frowning down at her portable on its stand in
the alcove, the stack of blank white paper beside it. She hadn't been
able to write a decent line since Ann Regnas had been murdered.
She laughed impatiently, turned away.

"I know why," she told the silent room. "I can't write any story
but Ann's. If I could write the finish to that one . . ."

She shivered, wandered back to the fire, lit a cigarette, and
collapsed into the deep chair, staring moodily at the yellow licking
flames.

"WELL, AT LEAST," Brade reflected, walking briskly through the black New England night toward the lighted church, "it's something I've never done before—attended a church bazaar."

He pulled his coat collar tighter, jammed hands deeper into warm pockets. Snappy all right, yesterday's snow crackling under foot. Black figures, muffled to the ears, were streaming through the open door into the vestibule, on into the Sunday School room where the bazaar was flourishing.

"Yes, my first church bazaar," Brade grinned as he went in. "Smells good, all right. Warm and bright and crowded." Booths had been built along the walls, tables set at intervals for the display of wares offered.

He glanced up then, saw Claude Sanger, his wife and daughter standing by the handkerchief booth. Elizabeth was staring at him— a thin figure in a dark defeated coat, flat unbecoming hat, eyes simply crawling with terror.

It was so apparent, even at some distance, that Brade frowned slightly, and went toward her. He said, "Good evening, Miss Sanger. Your father . . ." and followed the flick of her eyes to where Mr. and Mrs. Sanger had passed on a dutiful journey of the booths.

There was a crisp smell in the air, like gingerbread. Brade sniffed appreciatively and at once felt guilty. How could he be interested in gingerbread when this pale woman was so terrified?

"Father's all right," she said. The words were like tiny exploding shots. "That is . . ." Her hands clutched convulsively. "Captain

273

Brade, I've got to talk to someone. I don't know you, but you're the only one . . ."

He heard her dry tongue clicking against the roof of her mouth. He heard small talk behind him; a woman saying, "I knew Lizzie Wardell took in roomers but to get one this time of year . . ."

Brade said quietly, "I'd be glad to help, Miss Sanger. Can't we find a private place to talk?"

She nodded swiftly, head jerking back and forth on her taut, thin neck. "The church room," she said, moving past him. "Don't come with me. Follow."

Brade strolled after her thinking, "Grotesque! She doesn't dare walk out of this room in my company," and became oddly self-conscious, imagining a strained silence—that people stopped talking, were turning, staring at him as he went through the door.

Elizabeth was sitting well down front as if proximity to the altar offered sanctuary. He could see the sharp bones of her narrow shoulders making humps through her coat. There was a feather or something on her hat. It quivered slightly as though she were sobbing, or shivering. But she was rigid, eyes dry, as he sat down beside her.

"Well, this is better," he began, thinking to put her at her ease. "It's quiet here and . . ."

"A man came to see my father two nights ago," she told him. "My father's been like a dead man ever since. I think the man means to kill him."

Brade rested one hand loosely on the back of the seat. "Who is he, Miss Sanger? You know him?"

"I never saw him before. He's staying at the Old Coach." Brade glanced up quickly. He lived at the Old Coach. He hadn't seen any strangers. Then he recalled that he was outside, or in his own room most of the time. He used a side exit, not wishing to attract special attention, and took his meals in his room.

She went on in a kind of desperate urgency. "I opened the door for him. He's a thin man, looked ill—has lots of light colored hair like straw."

Wires clicked in Brade's mind. Peter Leeds! He said, "Did he give his name?"

"No. He asked to see my father. Father came into the hall from his study just then. He stopped suddenly, made a queer sound. He said, 'Show the gentleman in, Elizabeth,' and went back to the study."

"How long did the man stay?"

"Nearly an hour. My father didn't come out after he left. When I called him for dinner, he told me to go away. He stayed in there till after midnight. I passed the door a number of times. It sounded sometimes like he was . . . sobbing." Her voice slowed, dropped as if she were shamed. "Or choking," she added. "I heard him pacing the floor for hours. I am afraid of that man. I believe he means to kill my father."

"Why do you think that?"

She stared at him from wide, hypnotized eyes. "I listened. No use saying I didn't mean to—that I just accidentally . . ."

"You had a right to listen if you feared for your father. What did you hear?"

She relaxed slightly. "Very little. My father said, 'No, for the last time—and be damned to you!' Then after a moment, 'You can't prove anything.' The stranger laughed. 'That's what you think. What I can prove will be the death of you—get that, the death.'"

Brade's hand moved toward the solace of a cigarette, checked sharply. The church room was cold, the steeply pitched roof far away and icy. A fitful wind ghosted along the floor, flickered down from the bleak dimness above. "This was day before yesterday, Miss Sanger?"

"Yes. Since then he's been like a . . . dead man. I can't explain— he moves, speaks, but it's like everything inside him was dead."

"I believe," Brade told her, "that your father is being blackmailed, Miss Sanger—that this man has information which would be unpleasant, if not actually dangerous to your father, if it were made public. He's probably demanded money to keep still."

"That is blackmail?" she quavered.

"That is blackmail. Didn't you ever hear of it before?"

She shook her head with a curiously pathetic movement. "But what . . ."

"I believe it's something about your cousin, Prudence. Something your father would not want known."

She made a little wailing sound, crumpled forward, face buried in her hands. The silly feather twitched spasmodically with her frantic efforts at control.

Brade said, "Do you know anything, have you any suspicions in connection with your cousin Prudence, that might be used as a means of blackmail? If you'll tell me, I might be able to help."

She lifted her head slowly, face drained of color. "I know nothing," she said stiffly. "My cousin Prudence died long ago. Her name is never mentioned in our house."

Brade recalled how Claude Sanger had stuck over it the other night.

"Why?" he asked.

"You mustn't speak of it," she said harshly. "Prudence is . . . dead. She . . . was . . ." Elizabeth made one last desperate effort at control, lost, and began sobbing—low, hopeless sobs like tepid water trickling from a nearly dry container.

"You were girls together, you and Prudence?" Brade asked after a moment.

She dabbed at her eyes, let her hands fall inertly. "Yes but . . ."

"She was older than you?"

"Six years older."

"You were fond of her?"

Silence while the wind rustled uneasily in the distant loft and voices from the bazaar rose and receded like lazy waves on a sunny shore.

"I . . . loved . . . Prudence," Elizabeth said stranglingly.

"You grieved deeply when she died?" Relentlessly Brade turned the probe in the covered wound. The surface had been broken, the probe inserted. He had to twist it, force it down, touch that raw, throbbing layer of consciousness that all these years had been securely hidden.

Elizabeth Sanger lifted her head slowly, looked straight at him. Light from the distant vestibule touched her face. It was the face of an old, exhausted woman, stark agony streaming from every pore.

"She *is* alive," Brade exulted. "She's alive inside somewhere . . ."

She said, entirely without inflection. "I'm not sure my cousin Prudence *did* die. Naturally, that is. I think she was murdered!"

A bomb shell exploded in Brade's head. "My God," he muttered, and then Elizabeth said, still in that flat expressionless voice:

"I believe my father killed her—to gain her inheritance."

CHAPTER TEN

BRADE WAITED UNTIL he was in his room at the Old Coach before opening the letter he had found waiting for him on his return from the bazaar. He did not, however, wait until he had removed his overcoat. The note was from John Arden.

> Dear Brade:
> There is no record of the death of Prudence Sanger, in the year 1917. Blucher called me tonight, incoherent at what he evidently considers more phenagling on the part of the esteemed Thaddeus Quintelle. He's sending along details in the morning, but I couldn't resist shooting you a line straight off.
>
> How's it going up there? I can't get the damned tangle out of my mind. Maybe I might as well knock off and run up. Could I lend a hand, or would I be a nuisance? J. A.

Brade's fingers were slightly unsteady as he carefully folded the letter, returned it to its envelope, then turned at a light tap.

He crossed and opened the door. Peter Leeds stood in the shadowed hall, hair foaming over his head, face thin and desperate as Brade remembered it. He wore an obviously new flannel robe over dark trousers and a light shirt, tagging himself as a guest of the hotel.

He said before Brade could speak, "Hello, Brade. May I come in?"

Brade stepped aside, eyes narrowing slightly, and closed the door behind Leeds. Leeds dropped into a chair by the fire and lit a cigarette.

"Saw you tonight for the first time here," he said, not looking at his host. "Knew you'd nose me out sooner or later. Decided to hit right at the center of things." His head lifted. He looked straight at Brade. "What're you here for?" he demanded.

Brade strolled to the fire. There was a smouldering look in his cloudy gray eyes. He leaned on the mantel, set a foot on the low hearth.

"Frankly," he stated pleasantly, "I don't see that it's any of your business. How about clearing out of my room into which you were never invited?"

Leeds' head snapped up in that fiery, intolerant way, eyes blazing in quick fury. "Don't be an ass," he said ungraciously. "There's only one reason for your being here. You're sticking your nose in things that don't concern you. Take a tip. Leave Reddington to its ghosts."

Brade brought a bottle and glass from the dresser, poured a drink, set it beside Leeds. "Better get outside of that," he advised. "Might make you think clearer."

For a moment Leeds seemed on the point of refusing, then he snapped up the glass, drained it at one gulp. It was as if he swallowed liquid fire. His pale face flushed deeply scarlet; he clutched at his chest and went off into a shocking paroxysm of coughing. Seeing the man jerked and torn as by tangible outside forces, strangling for breath, Brade felt a quick, intense sympathy.

"Lord, Leeds," he exclaimed. "I'm sorry. Really I am. I had no notion . . ."

"Skip it," Leeds croaked. "Not a baby—didn't have to take it." He sucked in a deep breath, sat a moment, face buried in trembling hands. Brade saw his emaciated body through the flannel robe, the sharp shoulder bones that reminded him of Elizabeth Sanger.

Then Leeds said angrily, "Wanted a drink, damn it! Sure, I know how it acts but I take one now and then anyway. Forget it!"

Brade sat down opposite. "Better now?"

Leeds lifted a face white and drenched with perspiration. "Yes, better now. You'll be leaving Reddington soon? Tomorrow, maybe?"

Brade studied the tip of his cigarette. The wind was rising, setting up strange, tired noises in the old building.

"Sorry," he said curtly. "I haven't the slightest intention of leaving . . . before I'm entirely ready."

Instead of the expected outburst, Leeds eased himself on the chair, clasping his hands loosely between spread knees. "Well, that's settled," he admitted with a glint of grim humor. "What the devil do you want here, anyway?"

"Just by the way—what do *you* want? I don't expect you to tell me. Not that it matters. I know."

"Like hell you know."

"Okay. You're here to blackmail Claude Sanger because you have, or mean to convince him that you have, information about his niece, Prudence, who allegedly died in a shady institution in New York, in 1917. Not that she did, of course." Watching closely for the effect of that statement, Brade was frankly disappointed. Leeds' lips tightened slightly, his eyes flicked. That was all.

"Smart guy," he said under his breath. "Who are you, anyway? What's your game? Trying for a touch yourself? Blackmail's a serious charge without pretty good proof."

"Yeah? I'll take my chances. And why not stop sparring like a couple of ham pugs and come out in the open. Might be to our mutual advantage. Why, for example, would your information mean death to Claude Sanger if it were made public?"

"How did you . . .?" Leeds checked himself. "I don't know what you're talking about. I won't deny that I'm up here to conclude a business deal with old man Sanger. We've been corresponding for some time but there's nothing crooked about it."

"What have you got to sell him?"

Leeds grinned. "Don't you wish you knew?" He shifted slightly on the low chair. "Well, he's going to buy and if you try any blackmail charge on me, you're likely to singe the seat of your pants. Sanger'll back me up; have you thrown bodily out of town."

"My risk," Brade said curtly. "But look here, Leeds; if I spill a bit of my business, what's the chance of you coming across with some information? How about a trade?"

Leeds considered, deep puzzlement in his eyes. He obviously didn't know where to place Brade. "All right," he said at last, "only you've got to let me judge the importance of what you tell me."

"Why?" Brade inquired, rising to throw wood on the fire. "Your position's not savory, Leeds, for all your bluff. Elizabeth Sanger has told me certain things you said to her father night before last— threats you made. She was all for direct action; set to call in the local constabulary. I got her promise to hold off a bit but . . ."

"Say," Leeds exploded, "who the devil are you? How come you have such a stack around here? Seems like I've seen you or . . ."

"I'm Brade," Brade said simply. "Captain Courtney Brade."

Breath whistled through Leeds' parted lips. He looked as if he had been lustily whacked. "Oh!" he said. "Brade? Sure, that's it. Courtney Brade—a policeman."

"Yes," Brade grinned comfortably. "A policeman. How'd you miss it?"

"Don't know," Leeds admitted, slumping back. "I sure don't know, only you don't specially look like a copper, a dick. Shoulda' got it, when you came to see me in town, but then I've never seen you. Pictures in the paper, I guess—read about you." He brushed futilely at his unruly hair. "But say, what're you up here for? Think I'm going to spill my business to a copper?"

"I don't know," Brade admitted. "Are you?"

"Not by a damned sight."

"That's too bad. I'll be forced to align myself with Miss Sanger and her direct methods. I'd thought we might, you and I . . ." He paused, holding a lighted match to his cigarette, inhaling deeply, staring thoughtfully while the match burned out.

Color stained Leeds' cheeks. He wet his lips, moving uneasily. "She can't do anything," he argued. "Her old man . . ."

"I wouldn't count too much on Mr. Sanger's control over his daughter," Brade suggested. "She's terribly upset and believes you are threatening her father's life."

"Threatening his life? She's crazy. I never said anything . . ."

"Did you tell him what you had would be the death of him?"

"What?" Brade was becoming accustomed to Leeds' habitual questioning exclamation with which he groped for time. "No, I didn't. That is, only . . ."

"Look here, Leeds," Brade swung around facing him squarely. "I'm not going to sit up all night arguing with you. I'm convinced you're blackmailing Claude Sanger. Blackmail happens to be a pet aversion of mine. I'm fond of tripping blackmailers and I'm good at it. Now if you're innocent, you've nothing to fear. I'll give Miss Sanger the nod first thing in the morning and we'll let daylight into your activities. If I'm wrong, you'll have the fun of thumbing your nose at me. If I'm right . . ." he leaned back, staring at the fire. "The first train's out tomorrow afternoon. You'll have no luck getting a taxi. I'm sure you won't walk . . ."

In the warm silence he heard the faint chattering of the man's teeth.

"I thought," Brade suggested casually, "that you and I might . . ."

"Okay. Might what?"

"Well, just sort of pool resources. I'm glad of help wherever I can find it and I'm not ungrateful. I'm here investigating murder."

"Murder!"

Brade nodded, ignoring Leeds' half hysterical cry. "The murder of a woman out in Minnesota whom we've pretty definitely traced to a beginning here."

"Prudence dead?" Leeds cried and threw out his hands as if Brade would strike him.

Brade's heart did a quick flip-flop. "Yes," he said carefully, "Prudence is . . . dead. Murder. Killed by a blow on the head the night of November 15th."

"My God! Just a spot after Rod died. They went out . . . almost . . . together. How fitting!"

"Rodney Grange? Why was it fitting that they should go out so nearly together, Leeds? What was the connection between Grange and Prudence Sanger?"

For a moment Leeds looked like a man stunned by a heavy blow.

"Grange?" he said blankly. "Prudence?" He brushed at his tumbled mop of hair. "She was so lovely—Prudence. Tall and slim and lovely." Then, rousing from his temporary hypnosis, he said distinctly, "What was the connection between Grange and Prudence Sanger? She was his wife. They were married in New York, years ago."

BRADE CLOSED THE DOOR after Peter Leeds, crossed to the high narrow window on the front, lifted it, leaned out, breathing deeply of the cold, fresh air. The moon was hidden now and thick white flakes blotted out the darkened street just below him.

Yet light from the moon still lingered somehow and Brade saw the leafless branches of the old trees 'round the square twisting like dark knotted veins through the smothering whiteness.

After that one statement about being present at the marriage of Prudence Sanger to Rodney Grange back in 1916, Leeds had shown no inclination to talk further. Brade had curbed his impulse to get hard, convinced that he'd go farther by easy travelling. It had been a difficult business, trending the uneasy conversation, skillfully lessening Leeds' suspicion, making slight friendly overtures, putting him at his ease—playing him.

Then just before he left—"Well, we're even so far," Leeds told him, "I know you're a dick here trying to figure out the murder of Prudence Sanger and . . ."

"Just a moment, Leeds. I said I was investigating the murder of a woman in Minnesota whom we figured stemmed from Reddington. What made you leap to the conclusion that she was Prudence Sanger? In fact, her name was . . ."

"Sure, I know—living under another name. I'll tell you this and then I'm through. I was the one who tipped Rodney that Prudence was in Minnesota. For nearly thirty years he'd believed her dead. When I told him I'd seen her . . ."

"You saw her? When?"

"Not recently, for a fact. It was in April, 1917, that I saw Prudence Sanger sitting in a railway station, in Minnesota."

April, 1917! Brade remembered Terry Shan saying, "It was the 22nd of April Scanlon found Ann in. She said she'd been east."

He heard Leeds saying, "My train had stopped. I was looking out of the window and through the open, lighted station window I saw her. I couldn't get my sights straight for a moment. I'd lost track of her and Rod more than a year before, shortly after their marriage. By the time I got my wits together, the train was set to move. I stuck my head out of the window, shouted her name. 'Prudence,' I called. 'Hey, Prudence!' There wasn't time for any more."

"You sure, Leeds? Sure about it being Prudence?"

Leeds' glance was hostile. "Oh, nuts! I knew Prudence Sanger. Besides, she lifted her head when I called, stood up, leaned out. That's the last picture I have of her, standing there with her head out of the station window looking after the train."

"How did you hit on Woodvale? You couldn't have gone through there on the train at that time."

"I know. It was the best I could do for Rod. I didn't remember the name of the town, but I did remember the big farmery-looking fellow who was worrying everyone to death because he'd failed to get off back there and drive over to Woodvale. So I figured it must be in the vicinity of Woodvale."

Brade considered these amazing facts. Grange had dropped from sight when Leeds reached New York. He had continued his rebellious way and it was not until late last winter that the two friends had met again—Grange seedy and frankly licked; Leeds little better, but still fighting.

Their eager reminiscences had included Grange's story of the death of his wife, and Leeds insistence that he'd seen her in Minnesota in 1917. Although the trail was so old, so seemingly hopeless, Grange had sent that advertisement to the Minneapolis paper.

Although Brade had probed pitilessly, he had been unable to get further details. A mystery woman near the spot in Minnesota where he'd seen Prudence, a woman connected even remotely with

Reddington, to Peter Leeds, could only be Prudence. Why she should have been there, why the moss-veined stone in the Reddington cemetery bore her name, Leeds could not or would not explain. Brade thought Leeds knew and decided shrewdly that this knowledge formed the basis for his attempted blackmail of Claude Sanger.

Leeds was not so simple as to attempt to sell Captain Brade on the legitimacy of his efforts in that direction, but in little ways he let it out. Sick, exhausted, fighting desperately for a chance to regain his health, Leeds had no compunction in forcing the money from Sanger if he could. He avoided direct reference to it again and Brade did not press the point. Just now, he reflected, he had more important business to attend to than the fleecing of Sanger. He wanted information from Leeds and had no hesitancy in using any means at hand to get it.

He snapped off the light, stretched on the clean, fresh-smelling sheets. The darkness was pleasant; relaxation welcome. He heard the gentle crumbling of withered coals, whispering of snow against the windows, bleak whimper of the wind through the black, snow-smothered night.

WHEN HE ROUSED he did not know whether he'd slept hours or minutes. The room was dim and very cold. There was wind in the chimney, odor of frying bacon, someone knocking frantically on his door.

He groped for his robe, curled bare toes against the cold floor as he crossed and opened the door. William Sloan, proprietor of the Coach, stood there, meager face colorless.

"Hello," Brade greeted sleepily. "What's up? Someone want me?"

"Oh, yes sir, Captain Brade. It's a terrible thing. Everyone's so upset. She's asked for you—she said if you'd come at once . . ."

"Just a minute! What's happened? What's awful? Who's asking for me?"

Mr. Sloan responded nobly. He swallowed audibly, thrusting out his head on his stringy neck like a startled old bird and said distinctly, "Miss Elizabeth Sanger, sir. Mr. Claude shot himself to death! Mrs. Claude found him. The shock nearly killed her. Miss Elizabeth says would you please come, sir."

CHAPTER ELEVEN

ELIZABETH SANGER SAID again, "I don't know who it was, Captain Brade. My father went at once to his study when we reached home. I heard him tell mother he'd be busy for a while."

"This was approximately what time?" Brade questioned patiently.

Elizabeth, whose mental processes had become so thoroughly congealed with the years into definite, accustomed patterns, was like a bewildered child stumbling helplessly among the monstrous confusion resulting from this tragic toppling of her world.

Propped by pillows, she half-reclined on a couch in her upstairs sitting room. She wore an old-fashioned "wrapper," though Brade could not have named it—a long, concealing garment with high neck, wrist-length sleeves. She looked so thin lying there, her body starkly apparent through the voluminous folds of the garment designed to conceal it.

He'd come to her at once on arrival, passing quickly through the group of shocked, excited townspeople milling about the place. For a time he had encountered only incoherencies, but with quiet patience he was getting a few facts. Chief among them was that Claude Sanger had had a caller the evening before.

"I saw you leave the church," he persisted. "About ten forty-five, I think. Would it have been something around eleven when your father went to his study?"

"It was ten minutes past eleven when I came to my room," she told him. "I stopped to fix mother's warm milk when . . ."

"And how long after you came upstairs did this person arrive?"

"Possibly half an hour. I heard the side door open, and close."

"The side door?"

"Yes. I was in the upper hall. If it had been the front door I could have seen who came in."

"Any special reason for you being in the hall?"

She turned her heavy head to look at him, a faint flush coloring her white cheeks. "I was worried. I thought when father stayed down there that maybe that . . . man . . . was coming."

Leeds! Brade nodded shortly. Possible. Leeds hadn't come to his room till a little past midnight. There would have been time for his call on Sanger previous to that.

"You didn't see anything at all, Miss Sanger?"

"No. I heard the side door open, heard my father return to his study. It never occurred to me that he was not alone; that is, not until I heard him speak."

"Speak? What did he say?"

"He said, 'Go in, please.' Then the study door closed. I returned to my room."

"You can't see the study door from the top of the stairs?"

"No. It's under the stairs. The side door is beyond the double parlors. You have to cross the hall, of course, to reach the study. If I'd been leaning over, looking down—but I wasn't. I was just standing on the landing. I didn't hear father go to the side door. He must have been there, waiting. When his visitor came he brought him back, though I didn't hear him."

"Just a minute, please. You heard your father's steps clearly enough, but not those of his visitor?"

She nodded. "I never dreamed anyone was with him until he spoke at the door. By the time I got to the railing, looked down, they were inside."

Brade's eyes narrowed slightly. "I don't remember—is the lower hall carpeted, Miss Sanger?"

"Carpeted? No. There are rugs in summer, but mother has them taken up because of snow and . . ."

"I see," Brade said softly. "So you heard your father's footsteps, among other reasons, because he crossed the hall to the study, walking on bare boards."

"Yes."

"That being the case, why did you not hear the visitor's steps on the bare boards?"

Her eyes widened pathetically. "I don't know," she quavered.

"Don't worry about it. Just go on with the story. Later you went down, tried to hear what they were saying?" Brade had garnered a few bits of information from the earlier jumble. "But you were unable to catch anything. Couldn't tell anything about the visitor's voice. Not even if it were a man or a woman."

Her eyes flared wide in shocked disbelief. "Oh, it was a man! It couldn't have been a woman!"

"Why?"

She lay back, mouth working soundlessly like an exhausted fish. Behind the disassociation of her eyes, he caught a flicker of logical reasoning, something, he suspected, that Elizabeth Sanger had seldom indulged in.

"Why couldn't it have been a woman?" he insisted. "Aren't you just assuming that it was a man because, well, because it *seems* impossible to you that your father could have had a woman caller, under the circumstances?"

After a moment she nodded slowly. "I suppose that's right, Captain Brade. My father! Why should a woman . . .?"

"That's what we're trying to discover. Why a woman, or a man, should call on him last night and why, following that visit, he should take his own life. Now—why should he? What's your theory?"

"My theory?" she whimpered. "I . . . I haven't any . . . theory."

"Then why," he asked practically, "did you send for me? I'm a stranger. There must be others closer to you whose sympathy . . ."

"I don't want sympathy," she spit, sudden fire burning the vagueness from her eyes. "I've had sympathy all my life. Since I was a child, people have been feeling sorry for me. First, because I was just a poor relation, living in my uncle's house. Because my

cousin was richer, gayer, more beautiful than I. Because I would
never be able to . . . catch a husband."

The outburst cost her great effort, the words forced through
the barrier of long-restrained emotions. There was pale agony in
her eyes, but she held her glance steady on him.

"Pity for poor Elizabeth Sanger," she choked. "Pity for the poor . . .
old . . . maid," and her flaming eyes challenged him to deny the fact.

He said matter-of-factly, "I have only the deepest admiration
for you, Miss Sanger. You are potentially a beautiful, charming
woman. There isn't the slightest reason why you shouldn't 'catch a
husband' any time you wanted to, if you'd break loose here and get
back into the world where husbands grow."

His smile was so warm, so friendly, his words so honest and
understanding that she stared at him in dazed wonder. Then breath
went out of her in a sharp puff; she collapsed, eyes closed, mouth
sagging. But he noticed that her hands were quiet, and suddenly
she looked at him from dark blue, comprehending eyes.

"Thank you, Captain Brade," she said simply. "As to why I sent
for you, I am convinced that whatever caused my father to take his
own life is something that must be uncovered. I've no one to talk
to, no one who pays any attention, considers me . . ."

When she could not continue, he said, "I understand, Miss
Sanger. I appreciate your confidence." He paused, turning the
moonstone slowly. "I feel that I must be entirely honest with you."
His glance lifted, met hers frankly. "I am not just a chance visitor
to Reddington. I am a police officer, and the unravelling of mysteries is my business."

She did not seem to understand. Her fine dark brows contracted
painfully. She moistened dry lips.

"Police!" she whiskered and he saw the instinctive withdrawal
in her eyes.

He smiled genially. "That's right. Police. Always been afraid of
'em?" He laughed, lounging back comfortably. "Not so bad. Look
at me now. You're not afraid of me?"

She looked at him gravely and he wondered why he had thought
her vague.

"No," she said abruptly, "I'm not afraid of you, Captain Brade. Naturally, I know nothing of the . . . police, but I'm terribly glad you're here. Will you help me?"

"Yes. If you'll help me."

"Help you?"

"That's right. I can't get the answer alone. You'll have to tell me everything you know, anything at all, that might be of assistance. You'll have to agree to answer questions as honestly as you can. How about it?"

She drew a long, deep breath. "I promise. What do you want to know?"

Brade felt slightly dizzy. There were so very many things he wanted to know, but training held him to the point. He wanted all she could tell him concerning the last night of her father's life, details connected with the finding of his body.

The story, in essence, was simple. The first intimation of trouble had come about seven-thirty that morning, with Mrs. Sanger's stricken cry. Elizabeth, finishing her toilet, rushed downstairs, into her father's study. He was seated before the desk, upper body sprawled across it, the gun, his own, on the floor beside him. Her mother was senseless on the couch. She had not yet regained consciousness.

At Mrs. Sanger's insistence Caleb, the Sanger's one male servant, had tried to break down the study door when he found it locked. Claude had not come to bed at all and Mrs. Sanger, remembering his heart attacks, was badly frightened. Unable to force the door, Caleb had gone outside, smashed a window pane, lifted the catch, climbed in and admitted his mistress.

"No one heard the shot?" Brade asked,

"No. Martha and Caleb sleep at the back. Our rooms are all up here. The house is large, the walls thick. If mother had heard anything I know she'd have wakened me." This opinion was confirmed by old Martha Warmser, Caleb's wife. Neither she nor her husband had heard the shot that killed Mr. Claude. Mrs. Claude, Martha was sure, had not heard it either. She'd been unable to sleep and finally taken a fairish dose of sleeping medicine. It had seemingly not occurred to the poor woman to attempt to discover what was detaining her husband. Or more likely, Brade decided, she would not have dared.

Caleb testified to the securely locked study door. He'd known the house too well, he stated, to try and break the thing down, but made a pretense to please the mistress. Later, he'd done what he'd known would be necessary—broken the window and entered that way.

It was well into the afternoon by the time Brade finished his talk with the servants. He wanted a look at the study before returning to the hotel. The doctor was upstairs with Mrs. Sanger. Friends, acquaintances, had been calling all day but for the present the lower hall was deserted. Coming through the big dining room from the Warmsers' quarters at the rear, Brade crossed the hall and noiselessly opened the study door.

The room was dim with fast-fading winter sunlight entering meagerly through a row of high, narrow windows opposite. It struck him fully in the eyes and for the moment he did not distinguish the man on his knees before the low bookshelves in the corner.

Benjamin Grannis rose swiftly. "Captain Brade?" His words were more question than greeting.

"Oh, Grannis! Sorry if I intruded."

Grannis came slowly toward the table. His naturally pleasant, florid face was drawn and gray.

"That's quite all right, Brade," he said. "Looking for something? Can I be of help?"

Brade was uncomfortably conscious of his position, which he realized could appear as nothing but unwarranted intrusion.

"Oh, just wanted to look around," he admitted, and, meeting the lawyer's suddenly bleak eyes, added, "It's not curiosity. I've been retained by Miss Sanger to investigate the cause of her father's suicide."

"Investigate?" Grannis asked sharply.

"Yes. Naturally a man does not shoot himself without reason. Miss Sanger is interested in discovering that reason."

Grannis was silent a moment, then he sighed and drew a hand across his eyes. He sat down heavily. "Poor Elizabeth. Naturally, it's been a shock. But I admit I'm surprised at what you tell me. I had not thought she had the . . ."

"Initiative?"

"Well, yes." Grannis grinned faintly. "And why you?" His eyes went over Brade appraisingly.

"Why should I be selected?" Brade supplied when he paused. "That requires explanation." He extended his card.

Grannis accepted it, turning slightly so the waning light from the window struck it. He grunted and glanced at Brade.

"Courtney Brade, eh? Odd I didn't hit on it. I've heard of you, of course, but I didn't make the connection. Are you here on . . . official business, Captain Brade?"

Brade hesitated, then made a quick decision. "I might say I'm here on official business, unofficially. Here's how it is."

Briefly he told Grannis of the death of Ann Regnas in Minnesota, the curious, buried facts which, unearthed, had led him to Reddington. Grannis listened intently, brows drawn down, eyes narrowed and puzzled.

"And you believed that this strange woman could have been Prudence Sanger?" he asked.

Brade lighted a cigarette. "Claude Sanger called on her once," he pointed out. "Regnas in reverse is . . ."

"What?" Grannis snapped. "Regnas backward . . . Good Lord! As I live! Regnas reversed is Sanger. My God!" He stared at Brade blankly, then sat back, breath going out of him in a deep puff. "I can't believe it! It's incredible. You must be mistaken, sir."

"Mr. Grannis, as Sanger's attorney, have you any facts concerning Prudence Sanger's runaway trip to New York back in 1916? Was it really to study art as you suggested the other night, or do you know of . . ."

"Heavens no!" Grannis was on his feet, striding nervously. "Prudence just . . . ran away. One evening she was here. The next morning she was gone."

"Did she leave a message? Anything at all to explain?"

"If she did, Claude never told me. It hit him like an avalanche. He merely told me that Prudence had left, then he closed up like a bank vault. I naturally wondered a lot, as did everyone else. Claude never spoke of it again." He paused, staring at Brade. "To the best of my knowledge Claude Sanger never mentioned his niece's name directly from that moment to the hour of his death."

"Why?" Brade asked shortly.

"Why? Good Lord, man, I don't know except that he was like that."

"I see. Did you ever hear of a quarrel which preceded Prudence's leaving?"

The lawyer shook his big silvery head. "Not a word. In time it was forgotten, at least on the surface. Then . . ."

"Yes? Then . . .?"

"Well, one day Claude came to my office, told me his niece had died in a New York hospital from pneumonia. I was deeply shocked. I'd known her from infancy. She was a . . ." he turned abruptly, "sweet girl," he added in a muffled voice.

Brade waited in silence. After a longish pause Grannis went on.

"Her body was returned here for burial. I don't wish to speak ill of the dead, Brade, but the fact is, Sanger acted like the poor girl had died of the plague. The coffin was not opened. The services were so brief as to be indecent. She was buried, a stone erected—and that's all." He ended explosively as if glad to be done with an unpleasant subject.

Brade asked slowly, "Has it ever occurred to you, Grannis, that Prudence Sanger did *not* die at the Quintelle Hospital in New York?"

"Did not die?"

"Correct. That the services here were a fake, that Prudence went on her own to a spot in Minnesota, buried herself in a lonely old farm house, lived the recluse for almost thirty years, receiving quarterly allowance from Sanger until she met death mysteriously ten days ago?"

The lawyer's face gleamed faintly with moisture. "Captain Brade! What you suggest is . . . monstrous. Why, I ask you, should Prudence Sanger, heiress to a considerable fortune, young, with all of life before her, do such a mad thing? Your suggestion of an allowance from Sanger implies . . ."

"Exactly. That Sanger paid her to remain there. Or brought some pressure to bear which caused her to remain there. How about it? You've been legal adviser to Claude Sanger for a considerable time. Can't you offer a suggestion?"

Grannis walked uncertainly the length of the room, head lowered in thought. Then, "I can't," he said. "I knew the Sanger affairs well, all the way through. I can't think of anything that would make your suggestion in the remotest degree possible. If you want my honest opinion, it is that the whole thing is a monstrous mistake. There is not, can not be, any connection between the dead Prudence Sanger and this strange woman you mention."

"Sanger came to see her once," Brade objected.

"Eh?" Grannis' brows jerked. "So you say. Well, I don't know. Maybe he did, but for the life of me . . ."

"And her name spelled backward is Sanger."

"Yes, yes, I know." Grannis sat down heavily. "It seems absolutely mad, but I'll admit that may be because . . ."

"Because you never considered such a thing. Very well. Let it slide for the present. Why did Sanger shoot himself?"

Grannis laughed shortly. "Talk to Dr. Bronson if you want the answer to that. He had an incurable heart ailment and suffered intensely. I suppose he just . . . got tired."

"Did you know he had a visitor last night?"

"A visitor?"

"Yes. One he admitted through the side door."

"Who told you this?"

"Miss Sanger." He related Elizabeth's story.

Grannis grunted. "Well, that's a new one on me. She is telling the truth, you feel?"

Brade frowned, realizing that he had accepted Elizabeth's story rather easily.

"I'm not saying she isn't," Grannis put in quickly, "but the fact is she's a bit queer at times, Brade. You know how it is, living here with her parents, little outside interest, deeply self-centered. She didn't see who it was, you say?"

"No, she didn't. It's a pretty puzzle."

Grannis rose impatiently. "And one that I can't answer. Maybe something will come to light. What particularly did you hope to find here?"

Brade roused out of deep thought. "I scarcely know. Just wanted to look around."

"Well, let's get to it. I was starting a preliminary checkup of some of Claude's papers. Getting them in order. I'll continue with my work. You go right ahead with your investigation."

He drew back the chair before the desk, sat down, pulled out a drawer, began swiftly sorting through an already orderly pile of papers.

"Elizabeth and poor Mrs. Sanger are quite beyond this sort of thing," he commented.

Brade considered the large silvery head bent above the desk. "This trip you made west, Mr. Grannis," he began.

Grannis glanced up. "Yes? I drove to the west coast a few weeks ago. Business connected with an estate I'm handling."

"Go by Minneapolis?"

"Minneapolis? Let's see. Yes, I did. Stopped over night there. The Nicolet hotel, I believe."

Brade sat carelessly on the desk's edge. "Just there the one night?"

"Yes. Left the next morning. No, come to think of it, didn't get out until after lunch. Car trouble."

"I see. Well, Grannis, this town of Woodvale near which Ann Regnas lived, is within possible round-trip driving distance from Minneapolis in, say, one night. You didn't, by any chance, run out to see Ann, have an argument with her and . . .?"

"Oh!" Grannis said softly, eyes faintly narrowed, the suggestion of a smile on his rather grim lips. "Working at your job, aren't you, Brade? Trying to determine if I could have killed your recluse. Well, I'm sorry, but it's no use. In the first place I didn't know her. I never dreamed of her existence or that her name, reversed, was Sanger. There would have been no reason for me to visit her."

"You might have done it at Sanger's request."

"Yes, I might . . . if he had requested it. But he didn't. If he had knowledge of this woman he never mentioned it to me. If what you suggest is true, he wouldn't. No, I assure you, Captain Brade, that I did not leave Minneapolis."

Brade excused himself shortly after that and hunted up Caleb to settle one point to his satisfaction. Sanger had not accompanied his visitor to the side door when he left. The door had been unlocked this morning, Caleb said, adding that it was never left unfastened even in daytime. Certainly if Sanger had gone with his caller to the door, he would have locked it automatically.

Chapter Twelve

Brade left the house without seeing Grannis again and walked straight to the hotel. He was hungry. He had answered Elizabeth's summons without breakfast and had only eaten a sketchy luncheon at the house. It was dusk and the lights of the Old Coach shone pleasantly through the chill evening air. He swung into the lobby, paused to collect his key, started toward the stairs and stopped in blank amazement.

Hunched companionably over a small corner table in the dining room, Brade saw John Arden and Stacy Lane! The captain literally rubbed his eyes. Arden's lean, eager face was twitching with laughter, eyes alive and glowing, hands expressive. Brade had seldom been so glad to see anyone in his life.

Stacy Lane was stunning in a wood-brown wool suit, a short, extremely swagger cape tossed carelessly over the chair back. The smart carelessness of the outfit gave her a reckless air, the rich brown deepening the bronze shadows of her unbelievable hair where it glowed beneath a soft crushed felt, rearing rakishly on one side to the accent of a long devil-may-care green quill.

"Looks like a gypsy," Brade thought, "A very modern, sophisticated gypsy."

Stacy glanced up, thin, vivid face absolutely radiant. Even at that distance Brade caught the fire in her tawny eyes, the scarlet of her sensitive lips, sensed rather than heard her exclamation as she half rose. Arden turned, saw Brade, and was instantly on his feet.

Brade went toward them slowly, took their extended hands, one in each of his.

"Miss Lane! John! I am speechless and . . . delighted!" They were all talking at once. Brade felt as if he had been swept bodily into a whirlpool of tumbling enthusiasm, breathless excitement. He caught stray sentences, incoherent explanations, piecing out a reasonable pattern with difficulty.

"—same train out of New York—didn't know each other—just by accident—asked the time—"

Brade nodded gravely, aware of John's excellent Bulova which he had given him last Christmas, seeing Stacy's fragile watch against the slim whiteness of her wrist.

"Of course," he agreed, "the time—naturally."

"—found we were both coming to Reddington—"

"You'll forgive me, Captain Brade," Stacy pleaded. "I swear I couldn't do a thing out there but sit and think and wonder . . ."

"I'm delighted you came, Miss Lane."

"I've news for you. Sheriff Shan is in the hospital."

"Terry? The hospital?"

Stacy lifted a hand. "It's going to be all right. There was a filling station hold-up. The Sheriff was chasing the bandit's car and they blocked the road on a sharp turn . . ."

"How badly hurt?"

"Not dangerously. I saw him in the hospital the day before I left." She drew a long breath, eyes glowing.

"Look," Arden cut in, "can't that wait until we're in a better spot to talk? Have you eaten, Brade?"

Brade hadn't and they insisted he join them.

"Excuse me," he urged. "I'll catch something later. Now, it's a bath, a shave, a moment to get my breath. You've swept me off my feet, the two of you."

He heard their joyous, subdued laughter as he went toward the lobby. Half way up the stairs he paused. A door had closed hurriedly, almost furtively. Brade stopped, flattening against the wall. Peter Leeds appeared at the stair head, lugging a suitcase, carrying hat and overcoat. He did not see Brade and the captain felt a

ghoulish satisfaction in the man's appearance. Evidently scared
half senseless.

Brade said softly, "Hello, Leeds. Leaving us?"

Leeds jumped violently, the ungainly case bumping the bannisters. He mumbled something and attempted to pass but Brade
was directly in his way.

"How about dropping in for a farewell chat?" he suggested.
"Some little points I'd like to clear up."

"Can't," Leeds said testily. "Got a fellow waiting . . . going to
drive . . ."

"Sorry." Brade's hand was firm on his shoulder. "We'll get word
to him that you won't be needing his services tonight. Come along,"
and before Leeds realized what was happening he had been herded
up the stairs, directly to his own room.

Brade closed the door, snapped on the light, faced him. "All
right, let's have it straight. What do you know about Claude
Sanger's death?"

Leeds kicked savagely at his luggage and slumped into a chair.
"Not a damned thing. Don't want to know anything. All I want is to
get out of this place. Me, I've had enough."

"Not quite that simple. Sanger's dead with a bullet in his brain."

"Yeah, and from his own gun. What've I to do with that?"

"Nothing, possibly," Brade assured him equably, "but you were
here to blackmail Sanger." He silenced Leeds' protest with a gesture. "Elizabeth Sanger heard you threaten her father. She is determined to get to the bottom of this thing. If she cares to prefer
charges, to go on the stand and tell . . ."

"Well, what do you want me to do?" Sweat stood visibly on Leeds'
brow. "I tell you I don't know anything about the old gent's kick-off."

"You called on him just before you came to see me last night,
didn't you?"

Leeds' surprised stare was sufficient answer. "Lord, no! I've
only seen him once since I came. I was waiting until he, well, until
he put things in order and . . ."

"Got the money you demanded," Brade finished. "How much
were you asking, Leeds?"

Leeds squirmed, eyes seeking escape, finding none. He sighed and gave in. "Five thousand," he muttered sullenly.

Brade whistled softly. "And what were you offering him for this?"

"None of your business."

"Okay. We'll let matters take their course, only you won't be leaving Reddington. I'll see to that."

Leeds said savagely, "What the hell you buttin' in for? What's it to you? You may be a big-shot copper in your own home town, but here . . ."

"It's nothing to me, really," Brade said lazily, "but there's a question lacking an answer arid I believe you have information that will help. That's what I'm after."

Leeds blinked. "About that business out in Woodvale? Pru' Sanger's murder?"

"Check. And by the way, do you know that a gravestone bearing her name is standing in the Sanger lot here? That the town thinks of her as dead almost thirty years?"

Leeds' eyes were suddenly sly and triumphant. "What you think I was dickering with Sanger for? Sure I know it. Like I know that the body of Prudence Sanger no more rests in that grave than mine does."

In spite of his own convictions, Brade's heart skipped a beat. "Then—whose body?" he asked.

"My God. I don't know." Again Leeds' blankness was convincing. "Maybe no one's. I only know Prudence wasn't buried here in April, 1917. Why? Because I saw her later in April, 1917, better than a thousand miles from here. That's good enough for me."

"What was your approach with Sanger? How did you get under his guard?"

"I wrote him that I knew his niece didn't die as proscribed— that she'd run away to marry Rodney Grange—and that I knew what he, Sanger, had done about it, the old buzzard. Then for good measure I claimed to know where Prudence was. Not literally true, but good enough."

Brade sat down. "Reddington doesn't know that Prudence married?"

"No. Nothing wrong with a girl marrying far as I can see, but old Claude acted like she'd gone to join the leper colony. Raised heaven and earth to locate her. Worked at it 'most a year. When he finally found her, he whisked her away. Rod was out one afternoon. Claude arrived and Prudence went away with him. Rod never saw her again."

"Lord!" Brade ejaculated involuntarily. "How do you know this?"

"Rod told me last spring. He and Pru' realized it was useless to try for her uncle's consent to their marriage. According to her father's will, Claude was to have charge of everything, including Prudence, until she was twenty-one. When Rod left here, Prudence had plans all made to follow him. They were married, moved into a little flat and were getting along swell. Rod was nearly crazy when he came home and found her gone. The neighbors tipped him about the man she'd left with. Rod went around like he was wild for a while, I guess. Came up here to beat the truth out of Claude. Didn't get anywhere. Old Sanger just stood on his dignity, said he had no notion what the young man was talking about, no knowledge of his erring niece, no idea where she was. What's more, he didn't want to know anything about her."

"And Prudence never appeared again?" Brade asked slowly. "From the time she left that flat in company with her uncle, she just vanished?"

"That's right," Leeds said seriously. "I'll be frank with you, Brade, and you can think what you like of me. I did want that money, but all the same I didn't mind one bit causing old Sanger some bad moments. He ruined that girl's life—he ruined Rodney Grange—no matter what happened later, he killed them both."

There was something oddly impressive in Leeds' words. Off the record, Brade was inclined to agree.

"Then he staged her fake burial up here," he speculated, "and inherited the Sanger fortune?"

Leeds nodded. "It's a dirty deal, Brade. I don't know the details beyond what I've told you, but there's something black and ugly behind it. I don't wonder Sanger shot himself."

"But who called on him previous to his suicide?" Brade wondered and saw that Leeds knew nothing of that. No one but himself and Elizabeth Sanger knew of it, aside from the visitor.

Leeds' eyes narrowed sharply. "Called on him? Don't get you, pal."

Brade regretted his careless words for a moment, then took a chance. "Well, here it is. See if you can make anything of it," and he told him what he had learned that morning from Elizabeth. Leeds listened intently, eyes sharp with concentration.

"Now we're getting some place. If we can find who that was . . ."

"Yes, but the chances seem about a million to nothing. I thought it might have been you."

"I can see how you would, but I give you my word, Brade—if that means anything—I wasn't there. No reason for it. Sanger told me he'd get in touch with me soon's he got the cash. I was lying quiet until I heard."

The words were surprisingly direct and frank. With the telling of his story, admission of his purpose, much of the antagonism had dropped from Leeds. There was no doubting his real interest in the problem, aside from his own involvement. Sitting there, he looked thin and tired, but, for the moment, quite a normal human being. He glanced up suddenly, a half smile giving him a wistful charm.

"Look, Brade, you've been pretty decent. That fifty bucks you slipped me in New York got me up here and then some. So far you haven't tipped the authorities about anything, so I'll come clean. Tell you all I know. There's just one other thing." His hand went to an inside pocket and came out holding a large manila envelope. "Rod showed me this the last time I talked to him. After his death, I sneaked it from his effects. Read it."

There was a second envelope inside the first—worn, yellowed, the address in strong square characters, all but illegible. "Rodney Grange"—a street number he could not read—"New York City." Wonderingly he drew out the letter. The ink had faded; the fine spidery writing had a curious other-age look. Studying it, Brade remembered the sealed attic in Ann Regnas' house, the volume of poetry, the words written on the side, words like a cry—"Oh, my dearest—my dear." It was the same writing!

"It's the one communication he ever had from his wife," Leeds said. "It shows why he stopped his efforts to find her." Brade carefully spread the paper under the light. The message had faded until reading was difficult. He made out the date as November 17th, 1916.

> My Dearest
> What I am asking will seem hard, but I am praying that you will accept and try to understand. Our life together is at an end. I can see now that what we did, in defiance of all wisdom, was wrong. How terribly, wickedly wrong, I pray you will never know.
>
> If I live to be a hundred I can never really recompense for that awful sin I committed when I married you. If you cared for me, and I know you did, my prayer is that you will bury memory of me in your heart, and let grasses grow on the grave. I cannot go on living, unless I can feel that you will do this. Forget me! Let me go! It cannot be. It should never have been.
>
> For what I have done, may God forgive me. I can never forgive myself.
>
> > Prudence.

"My God!" Brade gasped.

Leeds' smile was bitter. "That's all Rod ever got, poor devil. No other answer, no other explanation. The following spring he heard of his wife's death. He tried to get details, but the trail was blind. If I could only have met him then! But when I got back to town he had vanished and left no trace."

"There was no return address on the letter, of course?"

"No. It had been mailed in New York, to the old address where he and Prudence had lived."

Brade tapped the envelope. "If Prudence Sanger wrote this letter, she did not write the address."

"Wondered if you'd catch that. Rod had no answer. The letter was in his wife's writing. The writing on the envelope he'd never seen to his knowledge."

"Claude Sanger? No, it's a woman's writing, I believe."

"Yes. If Prudence was in an institution, at the hospital where she supposedly died, a nurse, an attendant, could have addressed the envelope."

"Why? To both suggestions. If Prudence wrote the letter, surely she could have addressed the envelope. And then, why should she have been in an institution? She was in good health when she left?"

"Perfect, and that's what drove Rod half out of his mind. Her death in a hospital a few months later suggested it, I suppose. You can imagine . . ."

"I certainly can," Brade agreed grimly. "But it still seems incredible that Grange should have given up, even after getting this."

"It is odd, knowing Rod. But he worshipped that girl, Brade. Her slightest wish would have been his law, even if it . . ." Leeds made a futile gesture. "Prudence was advanced for her time, judged by Reddington standards. A girl of character and determination; but her background—well—all you have to do is look at Sanger's daughter to see what Prudence had to overcome. Rod had a devil of a time convincing her that they had a right to life together. No telling what terrors pursued her because of her act of disobedience. How strong the pull was is shown by her leaving with her uncle whom she hated and feared. Yet she walked straight out of her husband's home when the old devil beckoned. What pressure he brought to bear to get her to write that letter; what . . ."

"Sin!" Brade exclaimed. "What sin did she commit in marrying Grange?"

"I don't know," Leeds acknowledged. "God only knows what Sanger told her, what he threatened, but it's evident he convinced her she'd done a terrible thing, got her to . . ."

"Give up her name and personality, go out to Minnesota, live like a hermit for thirty years on money which he sent her quarterly."

Brade rumpled his hair irritably. "It's insane! But who killed her? Who came that night? Someone she knew! Someone she admitted—into her bedroom."

Leeds grunted, eyes narrowed and bright. "Someone she knew," he repeated. "It had to be someone she knew."

Brade grinned mirthlessly. "Yes, if she admitted him voluntarily. Suppose she opened the door at a knock and found a gun barrel under her nose. Suppose someone marched her up the stairs . . ." He paused, frowning at the fire.

CHAPTER THIRTEEN

SOME HALF HOUR LATER, after Leeds had left, Brade had a quick tub, dressed and was ready when John Arden and Stacy arrived. To his entire satisfaction, they brought a plate of sandwiches and a pot of coffee.

"Knew you'd never stop to feed," Arden explained, setting the things down, "not if you ran into something. I figured you'd run into something when you didn't come back."

"Wrong in your original premise," Brade objected, sandwich in hand. "My devotion to my art does not drive me to the point of neglecting my groceries. No sugar, thank you, Miss Lane. As a matter of fact, I did run into something rather good. I didn't return because I couldn't get away."

Arden laughed. "There! You see?" He appealed to Stacy. "Didn't I tell you how he was?"

Stacy laughed, too, snuggling into the nice, old-fashioned Morris chair. She had changed into a tweed skirt, a slim green sweater and looked about twelve years old with her hair tucked behind her ears.

"Captain Brade will likely throw me out, but all the same I'd love to know . . ." She slowed, glancing at him uncertainly.

Behind her lightness Brade sensed an intense interest, an almost hungry eagerness for details. Well, why not, he reflected. She'd been a principal actor in the Ann Regnas case. After that, she was a newspaperwoman.

He said, "All right, Miss Lane, I'll bring you up to date." And with a brilliant sparsity of words, he drew for them the happenings since his arrival in Reddington. Their individual reactions were distinctive and interesting.

Stacy said, "Peter Leeds. I'm intrigued with Peter. He knew them, Prudence and Rodney; was present at their marriage. I'd like to . . ."

She stopped at a tap on the door. Brade rose to answer, held a short conversation with someone they could not see, and closed the door.

"Meet him?" he suggested, smiling at Stacy. "I believe it can be arranged." Then he said, "Sorry, you'll have to excuse me for a while. Miss Sanger has sent an urgent message. I must go to her at once, but in my place I will give you . . . Peter Leeds."

When, some twenty minutes later, he started for the Sanger house he left the three of them grouped around the fire in his room, cigarettes fuming, Stacy's suitcase percolator humming comfortably. He was somehow deeply satisfied as he walked through the cold, crisp night. Leeds had agreed readily to coming in. Brade had been pleased at the changes a few hours had worked.

Head a bit higher, shoulders straighter, eyes more direct. In brief glimpses Brade thought he saw the Peter Leeds of the old Paris days. He sensed comfortably that his treatment of the man had worked the change. Leeds, for all his questionable position, had been accepted, taken in, made a part of the group.

It was near midnight when Brade returned. John and Stacy were still in his room. Leeds had left shortly before. They looked up expectantly as he tossed his hat to a corner, shucked his coat, strolled to the fire.

"How about it?" John demanded. "What's the Lady Elizabeth got on her mind now?"

Brade, recalling Elizabeth Sanger as he had last seen her, sat down wearily. "Mrs. Sanger died about seven," he said shortly.

"Oh!" Stacy gasped sympathetically.

John said, "Brade, I'm sorry. Sorry I . . ."

"Skip it," Brade advised. "Elizabeth is convinced that someone's out to do in the whole family, one way or another. The whole family now is—just Elizabeth. She insists that I move in, live there for a time, under proper chaperonage, of course," he ended with a quirked smile.

"That badly scared?" John inquired.

"Absolutely. Can't say I blame her, in a way. Here's what finally did for her mother." He laid an envelope on the table between them. "Martha, the old servant, found it on the hall table this evening and not using ordinary common sense, took it to her mistress. Mrs. Sanger read it, gasped once, died before anyone could reach her."

"What in heaven's name?" Stacy reached for the note and read aloud:

> God is not mocked! Neither is life. You cannot shut
> life off by the closing of a door, the turning of a rusty
> key. Eventually it forces its way out, and when it
> does—the debt must be paid!

"Good Lord!" Arden exclaimed, reaching for the paper. "Where'd it come from? On the hall table, you say? Who put it there?"

Brade lit a smoke, tossed the match into the fire. "Miss Sanger believes that the murderer put it there."

"Murderer? I thought . . ."

"Yes. Claude Sanger committed suicide. Mrs. Sanger died from shock. Yet their daughter feels, not without justification, that whoever called on her father the night of his death, whoever wrote this note, murdered them."

They were silent, considering. Claude Sanger fired the shot that ended his life. His semi-invalid wife collapsed and died in a matter of hours. Men do kill themselves—women do die of shock. Statistics prove it.

"Elizabeth thinks," Brade's quiet voice stated, "that this person is at present concealed in the house."

Stacy gasped. "The house?"

"Ridiculous, of course," Arden snapped, "that anyone should be hiding in the house."

"Why?" Brade wanted to know. "What's ridiculous about it?"

"Well, after all . . ."

"For a fact, it is ridiculous—not that anyone could not have been hiding there, but to think that he is now. I went all over the place, cellar to garret, with old Caleb as guide, and there is no one concealed there."

"Then how did the letter get on the hall table?" Stacy asked. "The door wouldn't be standing hospitably wide open this time of year, so a chance passerby could carelessly drift in . . . like smoke . . ." and immediately her own words sent chills racing up her spine.

A murderer drifting in and out of places—like smoke! Like the gray tenuous wisps of cigarette smoke that curled and wavered ghost-like between her and the light.

"No, the door wasn't open," Brade told her. "The hall wasn't deserted a moment, and, if you think about it, there is an explanation, though I couldn't make Elizabeth see it. The note wasn't there at 5 o'clock. I've definitely settled that. It's practically dark by then. Someone just took advantage of the callers, slipped in unobserved, left the note and . . . drifted out." His eyes met Stacy's, twinkled slightly.

"The message isn't written," John pointed out. "Printed—on cheap tablet paper. Doesn't make sense, either. What sort of gibberish is it? Life shut off by closing of a door, the turning of a rusty key?"

"It's a good idea," Brade advised him, "to qualify our statements at times, my friend. You say the message doesn't make sense. It doesn't make sense to you because your information is incomplete. It makes perfect sense to me."

Arden glanced up in surprise.

Brade said, "The possibility of error is as wide as the range of human experience. It's possible that we have made a very serious error in this case, that the pattern of our thinking has been predicated on a false premise to begin with."

"I'm afraid I don't follow you," John admitted.

"Pay no attention to me. Indulging myself in a bit of whimsy, I suppose." Brade turned, looked out of the window. Suddenly he jerked from his thoughts and said over his shoulder, "I forgot to tell you. You're both invited to be guests of Elizabeth Sanger, along with me, as of tomorrow."

"Guests?" Stacy cried.

"Of Elizabeth Sanger?" Arden echoed, and Brade laughed, swinging around to face them.

"Don't take it so hard, my children. She wants me to come. She can't have me . . . by myself." He grinned beneath his mustache. "Not in Reddington. She was at a loss; didn't want anyone in town, so I suggested two friends who were visiting me. It was simple. She insists you come."

"Why on earth does she want you so desperately?"

Brade said, seriously, "I told you, Miss Lane. She is scared out of her senses. Insists that someone's hiding in the house."

"Someone in the house." Stacy repeated slowly. "Someone whose visit caused Claude to kill himself. Whose mysterious message, left on the hall table . . ."

"Say, let's see that thing again," Arden exclaimed and Brade handed him the note.

"Go on," he urged, eyes twinkling. "You're perishing to, old man. Go on and read it."

Arden read:

> God is not mocked! Neither is life. You cannot shut life off by the closing of a door, the turning of a rusty key. Eventually it forces its way out, and when it does—the debt must be paid!

"I wonder," Stacy said, teeth chattering from emotional exhaustion, "if the key in that door upstairs was . . . was rusty!"

CHAPTER FOURTEEN

ELIZABETH SANGER SAT in a thin, tight huddle before the fire in her room. She wore a negligee of pale turquoise satin, thick and rich, with long endearing folds, soft fountains of lace spilling from the low neck. On her slim, fine feet were blue satin mules, gay frothy pom-poms foaming over the high arched instep. Her hair, thick and brown, fell in a dark cape around her shoulders, carefully arranged so the gray would not show.

Elizabeth had owned the negligee, the mules, for nearly a year, and this was the first time she had worn them. She had secretly purchased them on a rare trip to New York, hidden them in a locked drawer in her closet, never taken them out except when alone in her room at night.

Now, with both her parents dead, the shadow of mystery and terror darkening her life, she had put them on, loosened her tightly bound hair and sat down before the fire.

The house was very still. She had lived in it so long she knew it with an intimate understanding. She knew it in summer when the intense heat seeped through the strong walls, tempering the chill rooms—in autumn when early frosts sapped the faint summer life from its old joints.

She knew it best, perhaps, in winter. The winters were so long, Elizabeth thought, so cold, so dark, so bitter. It seemed that all her life had been spent in winter. She had read of places where it was always summer—where the skies were blue, the air warm; where happy, careless people ran and leaped and laughed on the shores of a blue ocean, where crisp cold sea water received hungry bodies. Yes, she had read of places like that.

She shivered, huddling nearer the fire. Some undeveloped sense of humor twitched her lips at her scant attire on such a night. Her long, thin arms, white as the lace of her negligee, flaccid and unresisting against all that had happened to her, curled 'round her meager body as she sought warmth.

There was no one in the house tonight except herself, and old Caleb and Martha in their rooms behind the kitchen. They could not help her in any way . . . if anything happened. She caught her breath, turning slightly, staring at the door, locked and bolted.

What could happen? Her eyes ached on the door handle. Was it turning? Was the door opening, regardless of keys and bolts? Impatiently she rose, walking feverishly, trailing rippling blue satin. Foolishness! She must be going mad! She stopped, a cry choked in her throat. Mad? Why had she thought of that?

Angrily she returned to the fire, opened a small box on the mantle, took out a cigarette. Defiantly, inexpertly, she lighted it, inhaled, half-strangling but persisting. She wanted to smoke; she wanted to taste a cocktail. She wanted to dance. She wanted to feel a man's arms about her.

"Mad?" she said aloud, smoke haloing her head. "I'm saner than I've ever been in my life." Although it was her first cigarette, it was strangely soothing, giving her a kind of courage. "I'm going down," she said under her breath. "There's nothing to be afraid of. Captain Brade and Caleb went over the house. There's no one here. I'm going downstairs and look through father's papers . . . see if I can find . . ."

She crushed out the cigarette, removed the negligee, slipped a thick warm bath robe over her narrow whiteness, then, without pausing to think, unlocked the door and stepped into the hall. At once she was conscious of the wind like a stealthy cat prowling the house. A small light burned at either end of the hall, making everything seem more cavernous, bringing her shadow smokily on the pale walls.

From the stairhead she snapped on the light in the lower hall. She could not keep her eyes from the black oval of glass in the door, staring through its thin veiling of net. She could not refrain from glancing at the hall table. There was nothing there! Certainly there wasn't. How could there be? Only there had been—that evening!

She leaned against the door of her father's study, eyes closed, so frightened she was without any other feeling. She couldn't go in! Not into that room that had housed childish terror of punishments and reprisals—that had seen every faintest blossoming of hope crushed ruthlessly. Then she lifted her head, stared at the smooth blank panels.

"He's dead," she said aloud. "He can never hurt me . . . or anyone . . . again." She drew a long strangling breath. "I'm glad," she whispered. "I'm glad, glad, glad!" Then she opened the door and entered.

She snapped on the light, went at once to her father's desk and drew out a tiny bunch of keys. She knew where her father had kept the duplicate keys for his desk; had wasted no time getting them.

She sat down, unlocked the middle drawer and began rummaging through the scanty contents. There was absolutely nothing of importance. She really hadn't expected that what she sought would be lying around loose, but, one after another, she went through the drawers.

When she finished, she sat back tiredly. Well, there was nothing here. Somberly she studied the room. Her father had a secret hiding place here, for certain very private papers. She had come in once as a child, without knocking and had seen him at it. Well she remembered the punishment that intrusion brought. It was a long time ago. She'd all but forgotten, yet she sat limply, eyes blank with effort at remembrance.

The wind was rising. Bare branches snarled against the house. She heard the cold like a tangible beast stalking the night. It penetrated the room, ate into her body, to the marrow of her bones. She started violently, half rising, clinging to the desk. Something had moved in the hall! Her heart thudded against her flat chest so

that she was unsteady. Then she forced herself to control. Imagination! No one was in the house!

And suddenly she remembered the location of the hiding place.
She ran to the corner beside the fireplace, knelt before the book
shelves, began hurriedly yanking at them. The books heaped
around her knees, tumbling over her hands that were so cold and
clumsy. Her fingers, groping over the smooth wood behind, touched
a small metal ring. Then she froze, crouching against the wall.

The handle of the door was turning! Fascinated too completely
to move, she hunched there, staring at it. Why hadn't she locked
it? Then with courage she did not recognize as her own, she was
on her feet, crossing the room, opening the door. Cold air swept in
from the darkened hall. She was faintly outlined against the light
behind her. She stared into the dimness, then deliberately closed
the door, turned the key and leaned against the wall.

There had been no one there, of course. The opening door had
been sheer imagination. She returned to the bookcase.

The metal ring was in a tiny door that opened easily. There was
a small compartment where dusty papers rustled under her fingers—two bundles of letters, held together by rubber bands. She
pulled them out, closed the door, replaced the books. The letters
slipped from her lap, thudded to the floor, the band around the
largest bunch breaking, so that the letters scattered like snow over
the dark rug.

Sobbing with strain and terror, Elizabeth groped for them,
crushing them angrily, stuffing some into her pocket, finally collecting the bulk into one package held by the good band. Then she rose,
tucked them under her arm, and with a final glance, went to the door.

Useless wishing she was upstairs, in her own room with the
door locked and the lights on. Lights on? As she pulled the door
shut behind her, she understood!

She had snapped the hall light on from the upper landing. When
she opened the study door and looked into the hall, it had been
dark. Someone had cut the light!

She stood perfectly still for a moment, body cold as ice, mind
crackling with a terrible lucidity. She thought, "I'll walk quietly

the short distance to the stairs, find the switch, see that nothing, no one is here. I'll go upstairs."

She felt the bare cold boards through the thin soles of her slippers as she walked, saw faintly the darker dark of the door glass. She grasped the newel post, set her foot on the first step and reached for the light switch.

Behind her, something moved with a rustling sound—the hiss of carefully restrained breath. Elizabeth tried to run, to cry out, but the world descended on her head in a sickening crash. She knew pain, splintering light that went all through her, then oblivion as she crumpled forward and was still.

How much later she could not say, Elizabeth drifted back to a sick consciousness, moaned, tried to sit up. The darkness, shot with jagged blades of light, reeled crazily around her. She lay still for a time.

There was, strangely enough, no break in her mental processes. She remembered instantly and clearly everything that had happened. She struggled to a sitting position, hanging valiantly to the newel post. A heavy blow had crashed on her head, behind the right ear. It was a dull, throbbing area of agony. She realized that in all likelihood her heavy hair, which she had knotted carelessly before coming down, had saved her life. She got to her feet, found the light switch. The hall was empty save for herself. She leaned against the wall for a moment gathering strength, then walked to the telephone on a little table at the stairfoot, called the Old Coach and asked for Captain Brade.

It seemed an endless time before he answered. It was really only a few moments. Brade had not gone to bed, and had only to run downstairs to the phone. The Old Coach frowned on the modernity of room instruments.

He said, "Yes? Courtney Brade speaking."

Elizabeth's fingers ached round the receiver. Behind her, all around her, all through the big, silent house, she felt danger.

Brade said again, sharply, "This is Courtney Brade. Who is it, please?"

She found her voice then. "Elizabeth Sanger. Can you come at once . . . please? I've been attacked. There was . . . someone in the . . . house . . . after all."

"Be there in ten minutes," Brade said. "Can you hold on that long?"

"I'll try," she whispered. "I'm . . . terribly . . . frightened . . ."

"Yes, I'm on my way." The receiver clicked.

Automatically she replaced the instrument and turned, seeing the tall narrow hall, knowing the shadows beneath the stairs were hiding places where her attacker might be lingering. She thought, "I can't endure it. I can't stay here . . . waiting . . ." and heard the wind whistling icily through the leafless trees.

Then she shut her lips hard, slumped weakly to the third step, head falling back to rest against the bannisters.

Here Brade saw her as he stood on the porch squinting through the filmy net curtain. He tapped lightly and she rose unsteadily.

He called softly, "It's Brade; let me in, Miss Sanger," and she moved slowly to unlock the door.

His eyes swept over her in one quick, comprehensive glance. "Bad hurt? What was it? Not a bullet?"

"No. I was struck on the head as I came out of father's study."

"It's terribly cold here. Is there a fire anywhere? You need warmth."

She replied mechanically. "The only fire in the house is in the room upstairs."

"That's fine," Brade assured her. "Let's find it."

He assisted her up the stairs, steadying her by an arm around her waist when she slowed halfway and swayed dangerously. The room was pleasantly warm, though the fire was low. Brade removed his hat and overcoat, tossing them to a chair. Then he immediately transferred them to another because of the shimmering blue satin garment that draped the first. He glanced at it curiously—at Elizabeth—came to the fire and stood looking down at her.

"Now," he said, "why were you in your father's study?"

Her eyes jerked open. She gazed at him dazedly. "I'd forgotten," she said limply. "The letters . . ."

"Letters!"

"I thought they might be there. I remembered where father used to hide things. I knew he always kept everything."

Brade lit a cigarette, watching her intently. "Want me to call a doctor?" he asked abruptly.

"Heavens, no!" Her hands went out protestingly.

He said after a moment. "How bad's the head? Better let me examine it," and before she could speak, he was behind her chair, strong vital hands encircling her neck, sensitive fingers exploring, touching at last the ugly swelling contusion behind the ear. She sat rigidly, tense with unconscious resistance, but he continued to massage gently until gradually the tension lessened, her head fell forward, she sighed deeply and began to cry.

"That's better," he said. "I think a cold compress . . ."

But she interrupted him quickly. "Thank you, no . . . It's greatly improved. If I could have a cigarette . . ."

"Do pardon me," he begged, without a flicker to indicate that the request had rocked him on his toes. He extended his case, held a light, strolled to the window, whistling softly under his breath, and she was grateful that he did not witness her inexperience.

He said, not turning to look at her, "What was the nature of the letters, Miss Sanger?"

Her voice was muffled. "I don't know. I can't remember. I think they had something to do with the death of my cousin, Prudence."

"What makes you say that? Why can't you remember?"

"It's been so long ago . . . so long ago since I saw them. I walked into my father's study. He was stooping in front of the bookcase. He didn't see me or hear me at first, but I saw him . . . with some letters. I tiptoed up behind him, touched him, and he screamed!" She shuddered, then added matter-of-factly, "I was punished, severely."

"What makes you think the letters had to do with your cousin Prudence?"

Elizabeth met his concentrated gray regard without flinching. "I told you, Captain Brade, that I have believed for nearly thirty years that my father murdered my cousin so he could inherit her money. He had never kept me out of his study before. He had never acted like that to me before. I was just a young girl. It happened just after my cousin Produce died. I was never allowed in the study after that."

Brade sat down opposite her, carefully adjusting a flaming log. "You never saw the contents of those letters?"

"No. That was what I was hunting for tonight." She doubled over suddenly, arms hugging her thin body hysterically. "I found them, too."

Brade's head jerked up.

"Whoever struck me . . ." Her teeth started clicking faintly.

"Your assailant stole the letters?"

"Yes. I realized it as soon as I regained consciousness. I thought the study door opened slightly while I was searching. I looked out, but no one was there. At least, I didn't see anyone. Later I knew the light had been switched off."

"You saw no one at the time of the attack? Heard no one?"

"No. It was dark. I heard nothing until a slight movement behind me gave warning. It was too late then. The blow crashed on my head; I lost consciousness."

"And you can't even offer a guess as to whether is was a man— or woman?"

"Woman?" She shrank back a little, lips quivering. Then she said, "No, no, I don't know. Only . . . whoever it is . . . was in the house, Captain Brade."

He shook his head. "If so, he came in after I left, shortly before midnight, Miss Sanger."

"That is impossible. I went with Caleb to check the fastening of each door and window."

"Windows and doors have been forced before this," he reminded her, but in his heart he did not believe it.

She asked timorously, "You will remain the night, Captain Brade? You won't leave me here alone?"

"I certainly will not. And you're to get to bed, and to sleep. I'll take care of things outside—in the house. Lock your door after I leave. Nothing will disturb you. Tomorrow I move in officially."

He smiled at her engagingly. "I am bringing my two friends, Miss Lane and Mr. Arden. That suit you?"

"Oh, I shall be so thankful. Tomorrow is the funeral of my parents."

"Yes, and you will be unable to attend if you don't get some rest. I should like something done about that hen's egg . . ."

"That what?" she gasped, and unconsciously her fingers caressed the bump. "Hen's egg?" she repeated, then comically her face reflected what her fingers told her. She began to laugh. "It is like that, isn't it? A perfect hen's egg. Not so large . . ."

"Yes, a nice smooth Buff Cochin egg."

"Buff Cochin? What do you know about . . .?"

"About eggs? And hens?" He rose, reaching for his things. "And other odd and curiously assorted things? My dear girl, you'd be surprised. Now where shall I bunk?"

Girl! Color swept her pale cheeks. Years dropped from her as if my magic. She looked, in that moment, as if she belonged in the blue negligee. "The guest room at the end of the hall, Captain Brade. It's cold, I'm afraid, but there's firewood."

"Never mind. I'll be on the prowl most of the time. You'll try for some sleep."

"Yes, I'll sleep now." Then abruptly, "The letters! I'm sorry about that."

"So am I," he told her gravely, "and on an off chance that your attacker might have missed them, I'll take a look in the hall."

She listened to his steps down the hall, the opening and closing of the guest room door. A dreadful weight slipped from her with the knowledge that he was there. She thought fleetingly of Caleb and Martha and people who would come in. What will they think? Then her head lifted, she glared defiantly at the blank walls, through them to every dry-as-dust conservative in Reddington.

"To hell with them," she said distinctly and slipped off the wool robe.

She stopped as something thudded softly to the floor. A crumpled bunch of letters, held together by the fierce pressure of her fingers there in that moment by the hidden safe. She'd jammed them into her pocket—forgotten about them.

She seized them eagerly, turned toward the door. Stopped. She wouldn't disturb Brade tonight. There were only six or seven, not the entire lot. She'd give them to him in the morning. Tonight she'd lock them securely in her dresser. Halfway across the room she slowed and turned the letters curiously.

Should she read them first?

CHAPTER FIFTEEN

ARTEMUS CLAUDE SANGER and his wife, Rosamond, were buried in the family lot in Reddington cemetery after services held in the great double parlors of the Sanger house, attended by practically every able-bodied adult in town.

It was a cold razory day, marked by intermittent flurries of snow and unseasonable bursts of pale sunlight when the winter-stark trees, the crusty snow, the warm, tight houses, stood out with unreal intensity.

For a brief time during the services at the house, the sun shone brilliantly, almost gayly. "Practically indecent," Stacy thought where she sat rather dejectedly on an uncomfortable folding chair in the corner, watching the shoulders, hats and bald heads of Reddington's citizens as they listened with suitable gravity to the shaken, rather quavery voice of the Rev. Winship saying all he could of praise for the deceased.

John Arden and Courtney Brade sat uncomfortably a few feet from Stacy. Elizabeth Sanger was not present. Her absence was attributed to shock. Stacy knew from Brade what had happened the night before—that Elizabeth was in bed, really ill.

At Elizabeth's request, Stacy had looked in for a moment of greeting. Memory of that pale, tormented face, those beautiful dark eyes, the thin fragility of the hand she clasped briefly, stayed with her. Elizabeth had thanked her for coming; asked her to be as comfortable as possible.

321

Later, during the brief services at the cemetery, Stacy's reporter's soul could find no objection to the atmosphere. The sun had gone. Clouds, light at first, growing soggier with unshed moisture, moved sluggishly before a high wind.

Behind the clouds sunlight lingered. It was light up there, Stacy thought, shivering inside her coat, in the group beside the open graves. Down here, under the thick cypresses and firs, it was dim, cold, airless.

She hadn't noticed Leeds at all until he tapped her on the shoulder. "That woman over there," he whispered, "there's something peculiar. . . ."

She followed his pointed finger to a rather tall woman, in a dark coat and a small hat with a veil. Stacy stirred slightly, investigating the possibility of moving to a better vantage point. A spinsterish woman beside her glanced at her malevolently and Stacy subsided.

"Dust to dust. . . ." Reverend Winship was intoning, and Stacy, without actually looking, saw a piece of crumbling earth fall from his fingers.

"If I could see her face," Leeds was saying. "It's so darkish here—that damned veil."

Stacy was only mildly interested. But, like playing a game all alone, she said to herself, "I won't take my eyes from her."

"I DIDN'T," SHE ASSURED Brade and Arden that evening at the house. "I swear I didn't look away for a moment, yet when I was free to move, she was gone! She just vanished—like smoke!"

Brade said, "I know. I saw her also."

"You?"

"Yes. I was standing almost directly opposite you. This woman was between us, at the point of the triangle. I had exactly the same experience. She did literally vanish like smoke." He smiled slightly, eyes narrowed and thoughtful. "Of course," he added, "what happened was just that we both lost her in the crowd."

"Of course," Stacy agreed without conviction. Then, "Leeds called my attention to her. Why did you notice her at all?"

"Because," Brade answered casually, "I have ideas of my own."

"You don't mean to say you think she might have been . . ." Stacy was wide-eyed.

"Yes, I do. A very serious error has been made in this case. We have been working on a completely incorrect premise, assuming from certain reasonable deductions that the woman calling herself Ann Regnas was . . . Prudence Sanger."

Stacy cried, "But she was Prudence Sanger!"

Brade said, "She was no more Prudence Sanger than you are!"

"Not . . . Prudence . . ."

"No. It's apparent when you think of it. If you remember, Elizabeth told me 'people pitied me because I was poor, because my cousin was richer, gayer, more beautiful.' Peter Leeds speaking of Prudence Sanger said she was 'Lovely. Tall and slim . . .'"

"Yes," Stacy, said faintly. "Yes, I see. Ann Regnas by any name she called herself was *never* beautiful. She couldn't have been tall and slim and lovely."

"Leeds gave me the final tip. An old battered diary he found among Rodney Grange's things after his death. He said he 'hooked it' along with the letter he showed me earlier. The entries were disconnected, fragmentary, written largely in pencil. Couldn't make much out of it. It was evidently a sketchy record of Rodney's search for his wife. The one significant passage—I copied only a few lines . . ."

> . . . makes no sense. All I can think of is that Annette must be involved. Hard to believe, but she's never forgiven me.

"Annette?" Stacy said breathlessly when Brade paused.

"Yes. Leeds didn't know who Annette was, but Annette could be Ann, couldn't she? Rodney feels that Annette must be involved in his wife's disappearance. Hard to believe, he finds it, but adds that she's never forgiven him, which implies a score that she might be willing to settle by somehow depriving him of his wife."

Arden said, brow wrinkled, "But how does that explain Ann's thirty year residence in Minnesota?"

"In the simplest manner possible," Brade assured him. "Consider the facts as we know them. Ann Regnas appeared in Chippewa City in the spring of 1917, bought a piece of property, moved in, and a week later is gone. When she returns, she says only that she's been east on business. Now what was her business?" He answered his own question before either of his listeners could hazard a guess. "Prudence presumably died in a New York hospital of questionable reputation in 1917, though no official record exists to that effect. Presumably, she was buried here in Reddington. Very well, I say *she did not die* but was taken from the hospital by Annette, whoever she was, transported to Minnesota . . ."

"Oh, my God!" Stacy whispered, hands at her throat.

"You're suggesting that she—that Prudence—was kept prisoner in that house . . .?"

Brade registered her frantic protest by a glance, but went on relentlessly. "It explains how Leeds saw Prudence through the station window—probably in Chippewa City. If Ann got that far with her charge, if Prudence was sitting in the station waiting until Annette arranged transportation home . . ."

"But, Brade," Arden interrupted, "why should a normal woman, in possession of her senses, sit quietly waiting while someone arranged . . ."

"How do we know she was in possession of her senses?" Brade asked and for a moment they could not speak, staring at him.

"So you mean," Stacy persisted, "that Prudence Sanger was kept a prisoner in the old Altman Place for almost twenty-nine years, no one seeing her and no one having an inkling that she was there?"

Brade curled arms around his knees as he hunched on a corner of the hearthstone. "Not necessarily, Miss Lane. I only suggest that it *could* have been that way. It would explain Ann's way of life, her unfriendliness, her refusal to admit anyone to the house. It lends sanity to the attic room, the silk headpiece, the Oriental rug, the Shakespeare. If Prudence lived secretly in that house all those years, either she remained voluntarily, or was mentally incompetent to the point of being unable to manage her escape."

The picture he brought before them of a woman demented to the point of helplessness in that lonely house in the pines was not pretty. Stacy's face was white as whey.

"It . . . would explain . . . Ann's death," she said weakly.

Brade caressed his chin, eyes half closed. "Now how would you work that out, Miss Lane?"

Stacy shaded her eyes from the fire. "We thought the open door meant that Ann had admitted someone to the house, that someone from the outside had killed her. Maybe we're completely wrong. Maybe it meant that someone living in the house killed Ann . . . and left that way, not bothering to latch the door."

"You imply then, that Prudence, for what reason we do not know, sufficiently regained her senses to realize her position, killed her jailer and left?"

Stacy nodded wordlessly.

"You will recall," Brade pointed out, "that the night Ann was killed was jet black, with rain and snow, the road all but impassable. A woman who had been shut up in four walls for twenty-nine years, whom we are assuming is of unsound mind, would find it rocky going, don't you think?"

"Yes; but I also think, Captain Brade, that such a woman might get along better than one who was normal and fully realized the difficulties."

"I agree. You will remember also, Miss Lane, that the only clothing we found belonged to Ann. Since our imaginary prisoner certainly didn't go around unclothed, we may assume that the only garments she had were the ones she was wearing. She left in those. It's unlikely she'd have taken luggage."

"Do you remember," Stacy asked eagerly, "that Ann's wardrobe held no coat?"

Brade had forgotten for the moment. He saw quite clearly the dull garments on their hangers, the broad-toed shoes, the flat hat. He nodded, eyes narrowed on Stacy.

"Now that you mention it, yes. So if we're building this picture correctly—if Prudence Sanger killed Ann Regnas and walked out of that house—she wore Ann's coat."

"But where," Stacy asked, "would the poor thing go?"

Brade drew a bulky envelope from his pocket. "This report from Sheriff Shan came in on the last mail. He apologized for being late with it—but that accident of his, you know. I stopped in the hotel to read it before coming up. Remember the salesman who was injured in a car wreck on Ann's road that night?"

"Of course; he died without regaining consciousness."

"Sorry, but that report was incorrect. Felton was fully conscious for more than an hour before his death. The operation did it likely, though it could not save his life. However, the sheriff was there and got his story. He sent it to me." Brade flicked open the paper, read carefully:

> I was dumb to take the cut-off, but the sales manager was meeting a bunch of the boys at Chip' City and I didn't want to miss him. I was driving faster than I should, the road being what it was, saw someone weaving along in the car lights. I stopped, offered a lift. It was a woman. She didn't pay any attention at first. I gave her the horn. She came over and climbed in. Didn't say much only that she was going somewhere. I had all I could do to keep the crate in the road. Then we hit a wash and the bus took the ditch . . .

"Good Lord!" Arden said softly. "Where did he pick her up?"

"Wasn't very specific," Brade explained, tapping the report, "except to say he'd passed the house on the left where 'that crazy old woman lived.' He believed, it seems, that it was Ann Regnas he was helping."

"What did she look like? Couldn't he give any kind of description?" Stacy asked.

"He was very weak, and Terry had to take what he could get. This is everything by way of description Felton gave." He read from the second sheet.

> She was kinda skinny, didn't seem to be dressed very well. Had on bedroom slippers. She wore a kind of

big shapeless coat. Gray I think. She was bare headed. Hair very light; blonde, I think, bleached or something.

"But what became of her?" Arden asked. "When the car went in to the ditch the driver passed out—where would the woman go?"

"The most logical explanation—and we have no proof—is that she might have got over to the highway—it was not far—and caught the bus. Terry is checking that angle. She evidently escaped injury since she wasn't found there and didn't show up anywhere around."

"But look here," Arden said excitedly, "if we've figured it straight so far, if Prudence was kept a prisoner in that house, got next to herself one night, caught Ann napping and smacked her from behind . . ."

"She called her from her room upstairs," Stacy interrupted. "That would explain the obvious haste in which Ann left her meal."

"She must be balmy," Arden said. "Bad wreck, man knocked out, and she never even reports it. Just goes on her way, leaving the chap who gave her a lift to die in the snow."

"Sounds rather callous, doesn't it? If we are right, Prudence Sanger must have been, must be not wholly sane. If she did kill her jailer, ended her long imprisonment by striking out in the night . . ."

"How could she go anywhere?" Arden demanded. "Where would she get the cash?"

"Ann Regnas may have had another cache beside the money in the secretary drawer," Stacy told him. "She might have had cash on her person. Certainly Prudence had to have money to get any- where, find lodgings, buy clothes. She couldn't travel around like that." She stopped, head lifted, eyes wide. "Travel?" she repeated. "And you mean . . ."

"Exactly. I think," Brade told her softly, "that Prudence Sanger would follow a natural instinct and . . . come home. Come straight to Reddington, Mass."

John Arden made a futile gesture toward the match jar, let his hand fall, sat back. "That woman—the one you both saw at the fu- neral . . ."

"*Could* be Prudence Sanger."

"Yes, I suppose so." Stacy frowned at the fire. "But this woman was well dressed."

"Well dressed, yes, but I don't find that conclusive in proving that she isn't Prudence Sanger. If she had money and reached Minneapolis, say, it wouldn't be difficult to find assistance in selecting the correct garments."

"No," Stacy agreed, "nor would it be difficult to travel even after her long imprisonment." She glanced sharply at Brade. "What made her change from, presumably, a manageable prisoner into a murdering . . ."

"I don't know, Miss Lane. I'm not an authority on mental affliction. The one thing I am sure of, is the unpredictable quality of many of the ailments. It's possible that whatever pressure Claude Sanger exerted that caused Prudence to leave her husband a year after their marriage resulted in grief and shock that threw her off balance. Perhaps physical illness resulted and she eventually attempted escape from what she found unendurable by unconscious refuge in mental blankness—a blotting out of what had hurt her, a return, perhaps, to the docility of a child where it would be possible to do with her as one wished.

"If this occurred, and she suddenly or gradually returned to reality, I would conclude that something happened to rouse her. She came to, so to speak—she understood—realized all that had happened. She would remember those years in the old house, perhaps as one remembers a dream, with no clear perception of the time that had passed. Perhaps she thought all she had to do was to get out—return to Reddingon—find her husband . . ."

He made a brief gesture, turned away. Through the slightly parted curtains he saw the dark street of Reddington, the great trees, the white blur of snow-covered ground.

He thought, "Something pierced through that wall—touched memory. What? Something connected with that buried time, surely. Who? Not Ann. She had seen Ann every day for twenty-nine years without making the connection."

Chapter Sixteen

STACY AND JOHN ARDEN sat before the fire in Stacy's sitting room, on the second floor of the Sanger house. Stacy was tremendously relieved that Arden was there. Brade was occupied with Elizabeth. They apparently spent long hours in conversation. He had reported Miss Sanger much improved this evening, when he brought her regrets that she could not join them at dinner.

It had been a rather dismal meal, served by Caleb in the dark paneled dining room. Stacy concluded that Captain Brade was dining with Miss Sanger, since he was not present. She wondered rather irritably what in heaven's name they found to discuss at such interminable length. She wished rather lonesomely that she was back in Chippewa City. Just then she looked at Arden and something warm and healing flowed over her, so she felt suddenly light and incredibly happy, as if she had wings and could fly.

Arden said, "It's an amazing complication, isn't it?"

"Incredible! I'll make a confession." She glanced at him through gold-flecked lashes. "I came here on the most unprincipled mission. I'm callous enough to be trailing this case from the writing angle."

He looked up interestedly. "What's callous about that? The story'll be worth writing, I believe."

She sighed, relieved that he had agreed with her. "If we ever get the answer."

He said very quietly, "Don't worry, young lady. We'll get the answer."

"Yes? You are very sure."

"So would you be if you knew Courtney Brade as I do."

Color stung her cheeks. The constant reminder of Brade's supreme worth annoyed her.

"Naturally I'm handicapped there. I'd never heard of Courtney Brade until a few weeks ago." She added uncomfortably, "At our first meeting."

He slid down in the chair, resting his head against the back, staring at the ceiling. "Lord, I'd hate to have old Court drop in on me bending over my victim."

"John Arden," she cried indignantly, "I think that's horrible."

He straightened swiftly. "It was, and I'm ashamed of myself. This is nothing to joke about. I couldn't help thinking . . ."

"Yes, I know." she interrupted, still angry. "I know it's tantamount to the electric chair just to have Brade glance your way if you've . . ."

He laughed endearingly. "Stacy, please don't be like that. Let's not quarrel, please. I haven't been so happy in years—please let's don't spoil it."

Her heart started racing.

He said, "You'll have to pardon my feeling for Courtney Brade. I owe him a lot."

Her lip curled faintly. "Terry Shan owes him a lot, too. He told me so."

"Eh? Shannoloski? Yes, I guess he does. Just a dumb flat-foot until Brade . . ."

Stacy rose impatiently, cheeks hot. "Oh, yes, I know. Until Brade cast his Jovian eye in his direction, lifted a finger—and presto! The world was changed for Terrence Shannoloski, for John Arden. They have the priceless privilege of working with Courtney Brade, of playing errand boy for him, of listening when he speaks." She checked herself abruptly. "At least Terry Shan had that privilege."

Arden laughed, sparks dancing in his eyes. "It goes for me also."

He glanced up at a knock. Brade entered in answer to Stacy's summons, competent and handsome in dark grey tweeds.

Low fire burned in Stacy's eyes as she looked at him. "There ought to be a law," she reflected, greeting him pleasantly. "No one, man or woman, has the mortal right to be so . . . so damned sure of himself."

Brade sat down, crossed long legs, lighted a cigarette, smiled at them through smoke. "How's it going?" he inquired.

"Judge for yourself," John Arden said. "I've been telling Stacy the story of my life."

"Oh," Brade said softly, "like that, eh?" and his grey gaze encompassed them so that Stacy felt her cheeks flame. "Well, that's good, my children, that's good. Elizabeth's been telling me the story of *her* life." He leaned back comfortably, arms crooked behind his head.

"Does it help in our mystery?" Stacy asked.

"Definitely. Here are the salient points. Prudence and Elizabeth were close friends. Elizabeth adored her older cousin, admired her tremendously because Prudence always had the character and courage to do the things that Elizabeth wanted to do, but didn't. Annette Sanger was living here the fall Rodney Grange wandered into Reddington with his paint brushes in his pocket."

"Annette . . . Sanger?"

Brade nodded. "Annette was a cousin removed an indeterminate number of times. I have a description, by the way. A short, heavy young woman, broad face, pale, rather prominent eyes, straight mouse-colored hair."

"Oh," Stacy shivered, "you do present a terribly plain picture, Captain Brade."

Brade chuckled. "Elizabeth's words, practically verbatim. To the contrary, Prudence Sanger was a beautiful girl. Tall, slim, brown hair." He flicked ashes carefully. "Dark blue eyes, well though conservatively educated, love of literature, poetry . . ." He paused, squinting at the fire. "So it's not hard to guess which girl the young artist chose as the object of his affection," he finished.

"Chose?" Arden question. "He had a choice, then."

"Yes. I know now what it was that Annette never forgave Rodney. She was cruelly in love with him. I use the term advisedly, gathering from Elizabeth's account that Annette Sanger with her unenticing appearance, unyieldingly Puritanical nature, took the emotional storm which swept her cruelly indeed. If Grange had returned her fierce affection, all might have been sufficiently well, but, blind in love with Prudence, he unwisely rebuffed Annette, not bothering, I take it, to soften the blow particularly."

"And the cream curdled?" Stacy inquired. "Annette probably hated his . . ."

"Undoubtedly she believed she did," Brade agreed, "and when his love for Prudence came to her knowledge, she *knew* she hated *her*."

"Grange guessed correctly then," Arden suggested, "in believing that Annette had something to do with his wife's disappearance."

"He did, but Annette had disappeared also. Claude Sanger's reaction to his niece's elopement—that is what it amounted to—is interesting. Everything in him, apparently, rebelled against the girl's breaking of precedent, daring to go against established custom. Behind it, I conclude, was working at the same time a sly, growing determination to turn it to his own advantage. He covered this by his bitter railing against what he termed her 'sin.' He built very creditably a monstrous defense for what he intended to do—if he could.

"It took him nearly a year to locate her. Rodney Grange evidently figured his wife's uncle might make trouble, and took pains to hide their trail. Elizabeth learned of her father's activities indirectly, much later. He went to the city, called on his niece when her husband was absent and took her away with him."

"I can't see," Stacy objected impatiently, "for the life of me, I can't see why she just went with him."

Brade glanced at her oddly. "My dear girl," he said gently, "you are fortunate in that you were not born in Prudence Sanger's generation or environment. It would be, I believe, practically impossible for you to understand how she was reared—how trained and educated—to what degree strict obedience was ingrained in her nature. However, that unfortunately was not the whole story. Sanger evidently convinced her that she had a background of hereditary insanity."

"My God!" Arden gasped.

"Yes. That since this was the case, she had committed a terrible sin in marrying."

"'For the awful sin I have committed,'" Stacy quoted, "'may God forgive me. I can never forgive myself.' The unspeakable brute!"

"Exactly. The whole ugly structure was found on nothing more genuine than a gaunt spinster aunt who in the last years of her life became 'queer'—unquestionably, as the rejuvenated Elizabeth explained, because of the kind of life she had led, stifled and prisoned by the shackles of her unwholesome upbringing. Elizabeth added that her father had used this club over herself and her cousin since she could remember. She, herself, has lived for years in intermittent terror of insanity."

Stacy sighed and relaxed. "He was a . . . a monster," she said not very steadily.

"He returned from New York that April of 1917," Brade went on, "with the statement that Prudence was dead. He gave Elizabeth and her mother no explanation, nor any details, and they did not dare question. The body, presumably, was brought to Reddington for burial. However," Brade's sensitive forefinger outlined the pattern on the carved chair arm, "Elizabeth *did not see* her dead cousin. Nor did anyone else. The casket was not opened. Grannis mentioned that point. Elizabeth confirmed it."

"Ah!" John Arden said on a deep breath.

"Elizabeth told me that Annette had left shortly after Sanger went to New York. She never returned, Elizabeth had no idea what became of her, until I told her."

A knock interrupted him. Old Caleb came quaveringly to announce that a man he didn't know wished to see Captain Brade.

Just then Peter Leeds said behind him, "Brade, I've got to see you . . ." shoved Caleb aside and came in.

"It's all right, Caleb," Brade soothed the indignant old man. "Mr. Leeds is a friend of mine." He closed the door, turned. "Okay, Leeds, what's on your mind?"

Leeds was deathly pale, hair seeming to stand erect, and to Stacy he represented perfectly her childish idea of an apparition.

"It is Prudence! Prudence Sanger!" he said. "I saw her. Met her face to face. She's . . . she's . . ." he stopped there, tongue clicking against the roof of his mouth.

Brade said. "Well? She's what, Leeds?"

Leeds swallowed, blinked, came to himself. "Here!" he said, and sat down suddenly.

Stacy thought later, "Well, we all knew it, didn't we?" but at the moment it had the effect of a stunning blow. She felt herself go slightly dizzy, so the room swayed bendingly and she feared she would retch.

Then Brade laughed! Quietly, pleasantly, normally. He said, "Okay, Leeds, light up and let's have the details. Where did you meet Prudence Sanger?"

Leeds sighed, relaxed, accepted a cigarette. "I'd been for a tramp," he said defensively. "Couldn't stick that place any longer, wanted action . . ." he paused, drawing smoke into his lungs.

"Which way were you walking?"

"Don't know the names of the streets. Out past the old school house . . ."

"Straight out?"

"Yes. Clear to the end of the street. Too sloppy off the walk, so I turned back. Prudence passed me about halfway to town. I knew her instantly."

"Just a moment," Brade said softly. "When did this happen, Leeds?"

"Oh, an hour ago maybe. I tramped around some."

Brade glanced at his wrist. "About nine-thirty then. Dark, of course. How did you know Prudence Sanger? How did you recognize her?"

A moment of stupefied silence followed, while Leeds sat like a man temporarily relieved of his senses.

"How did you recognize Prudence—in the dark?" Brade persisted.

Leeds wet his lips. "I don't know," he said thickly.

Brade's gray glance was narrow and glinting. "Haven't got a cat's eyes?" he questioned pleasantly, and Stacy decided she had never heard a more gently vicious remark.

"Cat's eyes?" Leeds stammered. Then, "A car! The headlights of a car . . . swinging 'round the corner, across the street. That showed her to me. I knew her instantly, the way she walked, how she carried her head."

A definite tension went out of the air. Brade sat down. "Very well. Go on please."

Leeds mopped his brow. "It knocked me goofy for a minute. I knew she wasn't dead—at least I knew she wasn't buried here. Just the same—well, anyway, I spoke before I had time to think. I said, 'Prudence! Hey, Prudence!'"

"Just as you called to her through the station window?" Brade suggested, and Leeds nodded.

"She stopped instantly. I turned, went up to her. I said, 'Prudence, where'd you come from?' and I got the queerest feeling. Like . . ." he groped for words, "like she wasn't there, after all. I mean . . . *she* wasn't there. Her body, yes, but not Prudence inside it."

Brade caressed a slim stiletto-like paper knife on the table beside him. "That is quite possible," he admitted. "What did she say?"

"She said, 'Who are you?' I told her, 'I'm Peter Leeds. Remember me, Prudence? I was best man at your wedding. I was your husband's friend—Rodney's friend.' She made a queer sound then, and put her hands over her mouth. I was used to the dark and could see her eyes as big as lakes. 'Rodney?' she said, not very loud, 'Rodney?' and then, she turned and ran." Breath went out of him in a noisy puff. "My God! I thought I was going nuts. One moment I was standing so near I could have touched her. The next, she wasn't there, and I heard the sound of her footsteps racing away from me into the dark."

He hunched forward, face in his hands, thin shoulders shaking. Brade made an involuntary movement toward his flask, but recalled the effect of the one drink he had witnessed and let his hand fall.

"Prudence ran which way, Leeds? Back toward town?"

"No. Toward the open country. I went a way trying to find her, but . . ."

"Trying to find her? Where did she go?"

"I don't know. She just vanished!"

"Like smoke!" Stacy finished mentally, and shivered in the warm room.

Brade rose, paced slowly, head lowered. There was a subtle sense of excitement about him that his casual manner did not wholly hide.

"Now think carefully, Leeds," he said directly. "When Prudence ran from you along the walk, you distinctly heard her steps?"

"Yes, for a time."

"How long a time?"

Leeds tormented his hair. "I don't know. I just heard her running . . . and then . . ."

"You didn't hear her running any more?"

"That's right."

"We may conclude, then, that she had passed beyond your hearing. Out of ear-shot, as the saying is."

Leeds stirred uncomfortably, brows puckered. "I think that was part of what got me so. The sound didn't last long enough. It didn't die away, grow fainter, as she put distance between us."

"No?" Brade paused. "Tell me as accurately as you can, how it was."

"She turned and ran. I heard her steps distinctly. Stood there listening to them, clear and sharp tapping the bricks, then, just all of a sudden, I didn't hear them any more. It was like . . . like she just went up into the air."

"Yes," Brade said with intense satisfaction. "Up into the air, so you no longer heard her steps. Now we will decide definitely that Prudence *did not* take wings and fly away. Since you heard her steps one moment and the next you did not, what conclusion shall we reach?" He did not expect any answer, quite obviously having one.

"The only possible explanation is that Prudence left the brick walk where her steps were audible for a medium where they were not audible. She ran off the walk, onto soft ground. In other words, she stepped into someone's front yard."

Leeds drew a long breath. "That must be it. I went a way looking for her, like I say, without a sign. I didn't know what to do, so I . . . well, I finally came here."

For the third time that eventful evening, there was a light tap on the door. Brade opened it. Elizabeth Sanger walked in. She wore a becoming dark red velvet house coat, gracefully full about her slimness, a stunning collar uprearing at the back framing her delicate whiteness. She came toward the fire and the group gathered around it.

She said, "I hope you'll pardon me," and smiled with sudden graciousness. "I have committed the unforgivable sin. I was passing the door and I heard voices I did not recognize. I listened." She looked at Brade. "This man . . ."

Leeds was on his feet.

"Miss Sanger, Peter Leeds," Brade said, and Elizabeth looked at Leeds in a long, slow survey.

Leeds' head lifted slightly as he looked at Elizabeth. He said, "I apologize for coming uninvited into your home, Miss Sanger. Certain happenings made it necessary for me to see Captain Brade at once."

"I understand, Mr. Leeds. I heard what you said. I am glad you came. There seems little doubt, Captain Brade, that my cousin Prudence is alive and . . . here . . . in Reddington?"

Brade glanced briefly at Leeds. "I believe there is little doubt, Miss Sanger."

Elizabeth's fingers locked in the folds of her red skirt. "Then she . . . escaped from that house . . . in Minnesota . . . where she had been held . . ."

"That would be my opinion," Brade stated gravely.

Elizabeth's eyes were wide and dark in her colorless face. "It was doubtless Prudence who called on my father the night of his death."

Brade nodded. "Prudence undoubtedly spoke to your father here in your house."

Elizabeth rested an arm on the mantel as if for support. "And after that talk—after learning all that had happened—he . . ."

"You mean," Brade asked, "discovering that Prudence had escaped and returned to Reddington, that the whole ugly story would become public . . ."

"Father . . . shot himself. She left the note that ended my mother's life. She was—she must have been—in the house last night. She struck me and stole those letters . . ."

"Why would she want the letters?" Brade demanded.

"Don't you see? They would furnish proof."

"She got *all* the letters, Miss Sanger?"

His level tones checked her rising hysteria. "How did you . . .?" she quavered, then hid her face in trembling hands.

"I saw the tips of the envelopes protruding from your bathrobe pocket," he told her. "It was a chance I had to take, letting it ride as you told it."

She looked at him then. "I didn't know I had them when you were there. I had forgotten about putting part of the letters in my pocket. I decided to wait until morning to give them to you. Then . . ."

"Then you read them and decided you couldn't give them to me. That, and not the blow on the head, made you ill today. I do understand, believe me, but now, *what did those letters disclose?*"

She looked straight into his eyes, tall and slender in her brave crimson velvet. "They were letters from Annette to my father," she said. "Prudence had a child. That was how they were able to get her away. My father convinced her that she must let him . . . dispose of it!"

"Dispose?" said Brade. "Do I understand . . .?"

"No, not what you think. But they gave the baby away. Father and Annette left it at a foundling home in the city. The child, a boy, died when he was a year old."

"You did not guess," Brade asked, "that Prudence had borne a child?"

"No, Captain Brade. I see now that it might have been the explanation of the one letter she ever wrote me."

Brade stroked his chin. "Yes, what did that say?"

"That she was the . . . the happiest girl in the world."

"Ah!" Brade said softly. "And this was . . ."

"It was in October, 1916. I burned it at once so my—so no one would find it, but I have never forgotten a word."

"And it was in November of 1916, wasn't it, Leeds, that Prudence went away with her uncle?"

Leeds nodded shortly. "So Rod told me. It was November, if you'll remember, that he got the only word he ever had from her, begging him to . . ."

"Yes, I remember. He was to think of her as dead because of the awful sin she had committed." He laughed briefly, unpleasantly. "That makes sense now. Sanger convinced her of her sin of bearing a child, with her background of mental unsoundness."

Elizabeth said with difficulty, "It comes out in Annette's letters—scraps you can piece together."

"Yes, I see," Brade said gravely. Then to Leeds, "Grange had no notion about the child?"

"Apparently not. He never even suggested such a thing."

"It would appear . . ." Brade began, and stopped at the sound of swift, frantic pounding on the downstairs door.

They heard it open, heard Caleb's quavering voice and deeper tones; then hasty, stumbling steps on the stairs and Brade opened the door to admit Benjamin Grannis, face gray, bluish lips twitching.

"Elizabeth," he managed, "Captain Brade." His eyes flicked over the three strangers.

Brade said, "Sit down, Grannis. Tell us what's wrong. This is Miss Lane, Mr. Arden, and Peter Leeds. Don't mind them, they're all friends."

Grannis took three uncertain steps, collapsed into a chair by the table. He was bare-headed and his full brow gleamed with moisture. His eyes sought Elizabeth's.

She said quietly, "Yes, it's all right, Uncle Benjamin. Tell us what's wrong."

He drew out a large handkerchief, mopped his face. His hands seemed clammy, stumbling, as his feet had done in mounting the stairs—the hands of an old, broken man.

He said, "I'm sorry. I didn't mean . . . it is so unbelievable . . . I had to come. I thought you should know . . ."

Elizabeth walked toward him slowly, the edge of her gown trailing redly against the fine, worn rug. "Do you mean something about Prudence?" she asked clearly. "Was she at your house this evening?"

"Yes." Grannis said thickly. "Prudence Sanger. My God! It was like . . . she's been . . ."

"Dead?" Elizabeth finished, "You mean, don't you, that Prudence has been in her grave all these years—or so we've thought—and then suddenly she's here—among us—alive? It would be a shock."

Grannis covered his eyes a moment, let his big clumsy hand plop heavily into his lap. "It's incredible," he whispered. "I was alone . . . in the library. The servant brought word that a woman wished to see me on . . . She would give no name."

"Did you recognize her?" Brade asked.

"No! That strange hair. Her sort of ravaged face. Naturally I never thought . . . She waited until the door closed, then told me who she was. She told me . . ."

Brade poured whisky into a glass, handed it to him, "Drink it, sir, then let us have the story. What did Prudence Sanger want?"

Grannis accepted the drink. He seemed incapable of shaking off the shock. He struggled with the necessity of accepting as living, one believed dead.

"It can't be true," he insisted, "what she told. It isn't possible. The woman's mad."

"Did she give signs of mental unbalance aside from insistence on the truth of her story?" Brade asked patiently. "Isn't that what prompted the belief she was off the track?"

Grannis blinked, setting down the empty glass. Vaguely one hand strayed to his vest pocket, fumbled a moment, went to his lips. "I suppose so," he admitted, "though she seemed a little queer."

Elizabeth cried shrilly, "If you'd been shut up in a lonely farm house for thirty years, you'd be queer too."

Grannis sighed and made a futile effort at smoothing his wet, disheveled hair. The whisky seemed to have steadied him. "I guess you're right, my dear," he said in a more normal voice. "But did you know . . . ?"

"Yes, we know, Mr. Grannis," Brade said. "For almost thirty years Prudence Sanger was an unsuspected occupant of a house out in Minnesota, owned by Ann Regnas. Two weeks ago Ann was murdered. Miss Lane here stumbled onto the tragedy. At that time we had no idea that another woman lived there. Our investigation eventually seemed to prove that Ann Regnas came from Reddington. We came here. Then it was that the existence of Prudence Sanger began to be apparent. It was only tonight, shortly before you arrived, that Leeds, who knew her as a girl, met her." He stopped abruptly. "That's where Prudence went, Leeds. I've just remembered where Grannis lives. When she ran from you and disappeared she simply stepped onto the Grannis grounds. What time did she visit you, Grannis?"

"Oh, an hour ago—maybe a little more. She told me an incredible story. Said she ran away to be married. That her uncle, Claude Sanger, took her almost by force from her husband's home and held her practically a prisoner in a New York apartment with Ann Regnas as her jailer. Later she was taken to a hospital, where her child was born. After that, she's vague. Speaks of living in a big lonely house—of being unable to remember what happened, except fleeting glimpses that apparently grew fainter as the years went on. Then she . . . remembered . . ." He paused on a quick breath.

"What caused her to remember, Mr. Grannis?" Brade asked.

"I don't know. She just said she remembered. Recalled her husband, her baby . . ."

"Yes," Brade urged, "yes, go on, please."

"Then she . . . ran away."

"Did she say how she managed it? How she got away from Ann?"

"No, she didn't say. Her story wasn't too coherent. Eventually she reached Reddington. She was afraid she'd be sent back if her identity became known. So she came here under another name, took a room . . ."

"Where?"

"At Miss Lizz Wardell's."

"She returned there after leaving you?"

"Yes. That is, I suppose she did. She ran from me."

"Ran?"

"Yes, when I convinced her I knew nothing about it—her husband or her child! She seemed to believe I could tell her where they were."

"And you couldn't?"

"My God, no! I knew nothing of it."

"Claude Sanger did not take you into his confidence?"

"He did not, Captain Brade," Grannis said soberly. "Through all the years I acted as his legal and confidential adviser, he never allowed one hint of this dreadful business to slip out."

"You believed Prudence had died in New York, as was reported?"

"Naturally."

"So all this story Prudence told you tonight came as a complete surprise?"

"Yes. I didn't even know the man she claimed she had married. I never set eyes on him, to my knowledge!"

Brade rose, walked to the window. "So what Prudence wanted," he asked over his shoulder, "was information concerning her husband and child? She said nothing about her inheritance? The Sanger fortune?"

"Inheritance?" Grannis' voice arched with surprise. "Good heavens! I'd forgotten that for the moment. *Claude had her money.* No, she said nothing about that. Just her husband and her son."

"And you told her . . ."

"All I could tell her. That I knew nothing about them."

"And that is when she ran away?" Brade faced him.

"She left me," Grannis admitted tiredly. "She just turned and ran from the room. I called after her. I went into the hall—out doors. But she was gone. I went to the corner but could not see her. I returned to the house and thought it over. I had to see some-one—tell what I knew. I came here."

He lifted his head slowly, looking at Brade. "What should we do?"

"Get to her as soon as possible," Brade said. "Come on, let's go to Miss Wardell's place." He was already at the door. John Arden was on his feet, Stacy half risen. Brade said, "You come, John, and you, Grannis. That will be enough. Leeds, stay here with Miss Sanger and Miss Lane. We'll be back soon."

Chapter Eighteen

BRADE OPENED THE GATE and walked up the path between frozen skeletons of summer flowers. A curtain of icy vines rattled against the porch post. He knocked, the sound sharp and summoning in the winter stillness.

After a moment he pounded louder. There was no response but under his hand the door swayed slightly, and he frowned, remembering Stacy Lane saying, "When I knocked, the door swung in."

"Miss Lizzie ought to hear us," Grannis muttered. "She couldn't sleep that soundly."

Brade pushed the door back and peered into the hall. "Miss Wardell," he called, "Lizzie Wardell." The sound of his voice returned dully. "Well, let's see about it," he snapped, and stepped inside.

The tiny cluttered front hall was pleasantly warm. A meager stair led to the second floor. There was a closed door on the left, an open one giving on a room where a lamp burned low on a small center table. A large gray cat blinked golden-eyed in sleepy contemplation. There was no sign of Lizzie Wardell.

"Board meeting," Grannis said. "That's it. Miss Lizzie's a member of the school board. They're meeting tonight."

Brade opened the door on the left. Icy air rushed out, the feel of a room seldom used. "Must be up here," he muttered and climbed the steep narrow stairs, Arden and Grannis at his heels.

Faint light cut through the dimness from the narrow crack of an unlatched door at the front. Brade pushed the door open, halted abruptly, said, "Oh, please pardon me . . ." then was inside in a quick lunge that carried him across the room to the bed under the dormer windows.

A woman lay on the bed. She wore a soft gray woolen dress with touches of white at wrists and throat. She lay very quietly, in a most orderly manner, long slim body stretched out neatly, one hand trailing beside the bed, the other across her breast. Under the fingers that touched the floor lay a snub-nosed automatic; under the fingers that crushed into a froth of white on her breast, blood had oozed redly.

"Good God," Grannis gasped. "Prudence! She's killed herself."

John Arden said something under his breath. Brade did not speak, standing there beside her, faking in every slightest detail; the quiet composure of the body, the orderly arrangement of the garments; noting the wet soles of her trim brown oxfords, the soft beauty of her white gleaming hair, the delicacy of her features, the thinness of the cheeks, the sad, defeated look on her dead face.

"Didn't make it soon enough," he said, and, laying a hand against the pale cheek, glanced at Grannis. "She must have left you, come home . . ."

Grannis was sickly white. "Yes—and shot herself. She was in a highly emotional state."

Brade was standing by the small table against the wall near the door. On it lay a smooth brown purse, a pair of crumpled gloves, a solitary key on a shiny key ring. The brown coat with the fur collar, the chic veiled hat, were tossed carelessly on a chair. A new dark red blotter, desk size, covered the table. Brade touched a dark stain at the front edge, examined a bottle of ink, picked up the purse. It was obviously new and pathetically empty. A fragile handkerchief, a stub of pencil, a coin purse containing several folded bills, a little silver, then a crumpled sheet of tablet paper.

He spread it out under the light. The message was printed and he immediately remembered the note that had been left at the Sanger house. It said:

I am tired of everything. Rodney is dead, my baby gone. There's nothing to live for now. I killed Ann Regnas. I'm not sorry. This is the end.

Prudence Sanger.

Grannis said at his shoulder, "What is it, Captain Brade? Did she leave a message?"

Brade handed it to him without a word. "Get downstairs and call the constable, will you, John?" and Arden nodded and went out.

Grannis laid down the printed message, looked at Brade. "Well, it's finished," he said. "This is the result of Claude Sanger's work, may the good Lord forgive him. Do you have any idea why he did it, Brade? I mean, why he took the girl from her husband—held her . . ."

"My opinion, though I can't prove it, is that Sanger wanted her money. If she'd stayed at home until she was of age—well, he likely couldn't have done anything about it. But when she defied him, ran away, married, it gave him his chance. From what little I knew of him, Grannis, I'd say that to successfully commit a crime—and that's what he did—he would require some sort of moral alibi. His insistence that Prudence had committed a sin in marrying, due to the instability of her mental background, gave him what he needed. He must have hugged that fabrication to his heart all these years." He paused, frowning thoughtfully at the blotter, caressing it absently with a sensitive forefinger.

Grannis said huskily, "It's hard to accept. I knew Sanger as a—well—a near man, as we say—a mean man in some respects; but I always thought of him as rigidly honest—almost painfully upright. That he could do such a thing . . ."

Brade was over by the bed again, bending over the quiet body of Prudence Sanger. The arm supporting the stained white fingers above the wound had slid down slightly.

He stooped closer, hard eyes searching. With an infinitely gentle movement he steadied the slim left shoulder and, without lifting or disturbing the body's position, leaned far across and sunk a knuckled fist deep into the supporting softness of the bed. For a moment he peered at the space between the body and spread, and then he straightened.

Chapter Nineteen

STACY SAT DEFEATEDLY in a shadowed corner of her room at the Sanger home, drenched eyes seeing imperfectly the group before the fire: Leeds, Elizabeth, Grannis, John Arden and Courtney Brade. The moment Brade came in she'd somehow known what his news would be. He'd told them quietly, concisely, and Elizabeth had moaned once and covered her face. She still sat that way, not moving or speaking.

"It might seem logical to assume," Brade's level tones recounted, "that Prudence Sanger, roused from her long somnolence, killed her jailer, left the house out in Minnesota, and eventually arrived here—that she had wit enough to hide under an assumed name, keep her true identity hidden from everyone but Claude Sanger and, tonight, Mr. Grannis. It seems obvious that her one desire was to find her husband and child. That incentive evidently kept her going brought her all that distance, under circumstances that must have been difficult after her long isolation.

"Whether or not she recognized her part in her uncle's suicide or her aunt's death from shock we will never know now. Tonight she called on the family lawyer, whom she would, of course, remember."

He paused and Grannis said not very steadily, "Yes, Prudence and I were always . . . good friends."

Brade nodded, eyes hard. "She called on Mr. Grannis, making no reference to her rightful inheritance, but only seeking information concerning her husband and child." He considered the tip of his cigarette, tossed it into the fire with a sudden impatient gesture, "Mr. Grannis, by his own statement, had no knowledge to give her and was able only to tell her that . . ."

Again he paused, and Grannis said, "What could I tell her? I knew nothing."

"So," said Brade, "apparently hopeless, with the last trail closed, Prudence returned to her room and shot herself."

He was silent a moment, and they all sat motionless looking at him. Brade continued slowly, "In her purse I found a signed confession, in which she named herself the killer of Ann Regnas. There is seemingly no reason to question its authenticity. It bears no resemblance to the one sample of Prudence Sanger's handwriting which I have seen, but it is not written; it's printed. It is apparently similar to the note left at this house which caused Mrs. Sanger's death. Expert attention will confirm this point, if it is true.

"We shall then have an answer to all our questions . . . with one exception. We shall know the story behind the strange life of Ann Regnas in Woodvale. We will have solved the mystery of her imposed isolation. We will have traced the near-invisible facts we were able to discover to their beginnings, and, accepting the statement of Prudence Sanger presumably made before she ended her life, we will know who murdered Ann Regnas."

Elizabeth raised her head then, face pale and ravaged. "It will be over," she said faintly. "It will be . . . concluded."

No one spoke for a moment, and the crumbling of a coal in the grate was clamorously loud. Brade said, a faint smile edging his lips, "Yes, it will be concluded—if the facts in our possession are to be accepted as true!"

It was as though an electric current had vitalized the air. Leeds' head snapped up. John Arden paused with a lighted match half way to his lips. Elizabeth gasped faintly, put out a thin hand, let it fall. Grannis big head lifted. He looked at Brade, dazedly.

"Be accepted as true?" he questioned. "Is there any doubt . . .?"

"That Prudence Sanger killed Ann Regnas?" Brade finished for him.

"She confessed to it," Stacy ventured, and Brade's eyes rested on her briefly.

"Let that go for a moment," he suggested. "Prudence, after remaining in submission for twenty-nine years, so far as we know, suddenly rouses, attacks Ann, and kills her by a blow on the head. We cannot definitely state that such a procedure would be impossible. Personally, I doubt that she would have had the strength to hurl the heavy knot of wood which we believe killed Ann.

"I do not set myself up as an authority on mental illness, but I would suggest that some untoward incident would have been necessary to bridge the broken span in Prudence's memory—to cause the stream of consciousness to once more flow evenly and coherently, so she would be able to remember, to realize what had happened to her. However, let that rest. Both contentions are opinions."

Stacy drew a cold hand across her eyes. She was, for the moment, monstrously confused. She remembered, in what seemed another lifetime, saying to this same man, "I don't see how you ever arrive at a conclusion. You aren't willing to accept. . ." and he had cut in, "Comfortable though unsupported theories that might be twisted into something passing for a solution." But this was not a theory; it was not unsupported.

"I give it as my conviction," Brade said pleasantly, "that Prudence Sanger *did not kill* Ann Regnas!"

Stacy choked a cry, hands against her lips. Well, it was what he had been implying, wasn't it? Saying Prudence wouldn't have the strength to hurl the piece of wood!

"Who did . . . kill her?" She heard her own voice, thin, high, insistent.

Brade flicked ashes from his cigarette. "You killed her, Miss Lane," he said.

She fought to keep her mental balance, not to be swept away in a flood of sick terror. She heard Leeds' sharp exclamation, the breath that puffed out of someone, John Arden's protest. She heard her own stumbling denial.

"I . . . didn't . . . do it! I didn't even know her. Why should I . . . kill her?"

"There are," Brade informed her, "myriad motives for murder. Some are obvious, blatant. Others are tawdry, cheap, rising from shallow surface emotions. Then there is another kind of motive, inobvious, its roots deeply buried, its origin far below the surface of objective consciousness, sometimes the murderer strikes without in the least understanding *why* he strikes.

"I say, Miss Lane, that this kind of motive prompted you to hurl that piece of wood at Ann Regnas. You know, when she waddled over to the fireplace and grabbed that statuette. You told me you called at her place to get some story notes you'd carelessly left in your car, which Ann had later purchased. A simple, reasonable mission. If Ann had been a normal person, she would have told you the truth—that the car had been burned. But she didn't tell you the car was destroyed. She raged at you for intruding; was bitter and vindictive. She likely just refused to let you get the papers." He took three short steps before the fire, then returned to his original position.

Stacy still struggled helplessly in a morass of unreality. He couldn't really believe what he was saying. It was insane. She was conscious of a slight movement beside her. A hand closed over hers, strong, warm, protecting. She gasped faintly, glanced around. John Arden had moved his chair closer. His face was pale, his eyes angry and glinting, but he looked at her and smiled and for a moment sobs struggled in her throat and she wanted to hide her head on his shoulder.

Brade was speaking again. "I contend, Miss Lane, that when Ann Regnas refused to allow you to take the papers without giving you adequate reason—when she laughed at you when you told her how hard you'd worked compiling those notes—when she inserted her broad bulk between you and something you wanted—in that moment, I say, she ceased to be Ann Regnas and was for you . . ." He leaned forward a little, eyes holding her, ". . . Aunt Susan," he finished softly.

Her low cry echoed his words. She shrank back, face paper white.

"Aunt Susan?" she whispered.

"Yes. The woman who reared you, whom you hated, who kept from you everything you desired, who took the joy out of life for you as a child, who caused you to lie awake nights figuring out unique methods of revenge—the woman you longed to kill. In that moment of emotional stress, Ann Regnas was Aunt Susan to you, and those deeply buried impulses took possession of you—controlled your muscles—caused you to snatch the piece of wood from the floor and hurl it . . ."

"My God, Brade," Arden rasped harshly, "of all the idiotic lines I've ever heard . . ."

Brade did not seem to hear him. His eyes were on Stacy's colorless face.

Grannis too sat staring at her, visibly attempting to clothe the horror in his eyes. "It's . . . it's unbelievable, Captain Brade, but complexes, fixations can do strange things to people." He pursed grave lips. "On the face of it there was small reason for Ann Regnas to take Miss Lane upstairs to Prudence Sanger's room. Of course, as you suggest, Miss Lane must have followed her . . ." He paused, spreading his palms, then turned. "Much might be done, Miss Lane, particularly with so much hypothesis, entering a self-defense plea." He nodded judicially.

Brade exhaled softly. "How did you know, Mr. Grannis, that Ann Regnas was killed in Prudence Sanger's room?"

Startled, the lawyer turned. "How did I . . .?"

"How did you know that Prudence Sanger's room was upstairs? That there *was* an upstairs?"

"Why . . . why . . . you said so."

Brade laughed softly. Moisture gleamed faintly at his temples. "I believe not, sir. Very little has been said about Ann Regnas' death, beyond the fact that it did occur. No mention has been made of the kind of house it was, or where the crime occurred. Will you answer my question? How did you know?"

Grannis stared at him blankly, "Why . . . why . . ." he began, and Brade said levelly:

"I will tell you. You knew that Prudence's room was on the second floor because you went to that room with Ann Regnas the night she was killed. It was the sound of your voice, the memories it stirred, that roused Prudence to conscious memory. When you and

Ann came upstairs to visit her she watched her chance and slipped away from the house. You knew Ann Regnas was killed in that upstairs room because *you killed her there*. Correct me if I'm wrong."

"Wrong?" Grannis was on his feet, "You're making a damned fool of yourself. You're trying for a grandstand play for your startling and, you hope, brilliant deduction which will set aside the simple and entirely logical solution we found tonight in Prudence Sanger's purse." He paused breathlessly, mopped his broad, gleaming face.

Brade watched him through narrowed lids. He said, "You have lied nobly and with reasonable efficiency, Grannis, but it's no good. I'm sure Miss Lane will pardon my ruthless methods. I had hoped for a damaging admission from you and I got it. Now you listen to me.

"You know as much about what happened to Prudence Sanger as her uncle did. You knew Claude Sanger's appropriation of his niece's fortune and have doubtless benefited by it plenty. When Ann grew weary of her life, demanding relief—when she flatly said that if some other disposition was not made of Prudence she'd pack her up, bring her back to Reddington and leave her on the Sanger doorstep—it was you whom Claude Sanger sent to try and talk sense into her. Your trip to the west coast took care of that. You went to Seattle all right, but en route you stopped in Minneapolis for the night, drove to Woodvale, settled Ann Regnas for good and all—and returned."

"Why this is preposterous. I checked into the Nicolet Hotel in Minneapolis and remained there all night."

"The Nicolet would scarcely be able to say where you went after you checked in, Grannis. But even if they could definitely say you were not in your room all evening, we wouldn't need their word for it—not in the light of the more absolute proof of your presence in Ann Regnas' house that night."

"Proof?" Grannis faltered. "You're out of your senses."

Brade smiled thinly. "I think not. The proof you left is unbeatable. Your finger prints!"

Stacy lifted her head then, still too stunned to fully comprehend what was happening. But she remembered the absence of prints in that bleak old house—of any prints but hers.

"You carefully removed possible prints," Brade went on, "but one set you entirely forgot. Those were discovered, but at the time pointed to no known person. They appeared on a small metal container in Ann's cupboard. The can held cloves. I sent a sample of your prints to the sheriff in Minnesota and today received confirmation. You like cloves, don't you, Grannis? Always munch them, don't you? When I gave you a drink earlier tonight, you involuntarily reached into your vest pocket for a breath-killer. I submit, being short, you asked Ann for some, and she handed you the box from her cupboard shelf. You helped yourself, she returned the box, and you quite naturally forgot all about it."

Grannis was staring at him, head lowered a little, eyes narrowed and quizzical. "Interesting, if true," he commented, seemingly quite in control of himself now, "but you forget, sir, the signed confession which you found, before witnesses—more than one, I'm glad to say—in Prudence Sanger's own purse tonight. That puts quite a different face on matters."

Brade shook his head. "Just another link in an already broken chain, Grannis. Just for the book, a certain Arnie Lund set out for Alaska or bust. Fortunately or unfortunately, depending on the point of view, Arnie apparently busted and he's back at his old job now. You wouldn't know him by name, Grannis, but he just happens to be the station attendant who sold you seven gallons of gas at the Woodvale intersection of the Minneapolis highway the night Ann Regnas died."

"Gas—" sputtered Grannis. "But—but he couldn't know . . ." He passed a shaking hand across his eyes.

"That you had just come from killing the woman?" prompted Brade. "No. But Arnie Lund just happens to remember many things about you because you were his very last customer before he closed up his shop and started for Alaska. He recalled you as digging a sliver from your hand that night, when a Bay District officer showed him your photograph. Pure coincidence, was it, that Ann died from the blow of a rough pine stick?"

Grannis wet dry lips, attempting to speak, but Brade lifted a hand. "The game's up, Grannis," he continued. "You followed

Prudence Sanger to her room tonight—accompanied her possibly, being old friends—and you shot her to silence her. You arranged her body on the bed neatly, a shade too neatly, I might say, and yourself printed that note I found in her bag. You were not too naive to imitate her handwriting, but there was her printed note left at this house for precedence, and printing . . ."

Grannis said angrily, "It's gone beyond mere discussion, Captain Brade. It's entered the realm of fantasy."

"The killing of Prudence Sanger was a totally useless one," Brade kept on, as if he had not heard, "and not nearly so cleverly executed as the first. She lay on her bed carefully composed for death but there was no vestige of stain or powder burn on the white fissure at her breast as there must have been had she turned the gun on herself. And though the bullet pierced her body, there was no hole in the spread beneath. Had she shot herself elsewhere in the room it is questionable if she could have reached the bed, to say nothing of the peaceful arrangement of limbs and features. Not with a bullet through the heart.

"No doubt you had to get those letters—the ones she took from Elizabeth Sanger—because those letters, written by Annette to Claude Sanger, might well have implicated you. Another link in the chain of evidence, Mr. Grannis! For while we know Prudence took those letters, they were nowhere to be found in her room. And probably the only reason she wanted them was—not for proof of the terrible wrong done her, as Miss Sanger suggested—but because she thought they might lead her to her husband and baby."

Grannis' eyes flicked around the room, returned, tormented. He spoke through twitching lips. "I refuse to listen further."

"You are under arrest," Brade told him, "arrest for murder. As a special deputized officer, I must inform you that anything you say may be used against you."

Breath went out of Grannis in a noisy puff. His chest seemed to collapse, his whole body to shrink. "It's—incredible," he mumbled, "incredible. I'll . . . I'll . . ."

"You'll go with Constable Manners," Brade assured him. "He's waiting my call. John," Brade did not take his eyes from Grannis, "if you'll step down stairs and phone Manners . . ." John left the room quietly.

LATER BRADE SAID to Stacy. "Will you believe I regretted doing what I did, Miss Lane?"

Stacy lifted her tired eyes. She, John and Brade were the only ones remaining in her room. She looked at his lean, intelligent face, his cloudy grey eyes that could be so blindingly brilliant, the quirk of his mouth beneath the clipped dark mustache.

She said, "It's all right, believe me, as long as you didn't really think . . ."

"You murdered Ann Regnas?" he asked. "But of course, you must understand that for a time . . ."

She laughed suddenly, naturally. Unconsciously her hand lifted, fingers curling round Arden's resting on the back of the chair. It was a warm, endearing touch.

She said, "Oh, yes, I know. You did think I *could* have killed her. Isn't that it, Captain Brade?"

His glance touched the clasped hands and slid away. "Yes," he agreed, "Just as I might say you and John Arden *could* be in love."

"You see, Stacy," said Arden joyfully, "there's nothing the man doesn't know."

COACHWHIP PUBLICATIONS

NOW AVAILABLE

**VULTURES
IN THE SKY**
A HUGH RENNERT MYSTERY

TODD DOWNING

Vultures in the Sky, by Todd Downing
Introduction by Curtis Evans
ISBN 978-1-61646-149-2

COACHWHIP PUBLICATIONS

COACHWHIPBOOKS.COM

THERE IS
NO RETURN
THE ADELAIDE ADAMS MYSTERIES
ANITA BLACKMON

There is No Return, by Anita Blackmon
Introduction by Curtis Evans
ISBN 978-1-61646-223-9

COACHWHIP PUBLICATIONS

COACHWHIPBOOKS.COM

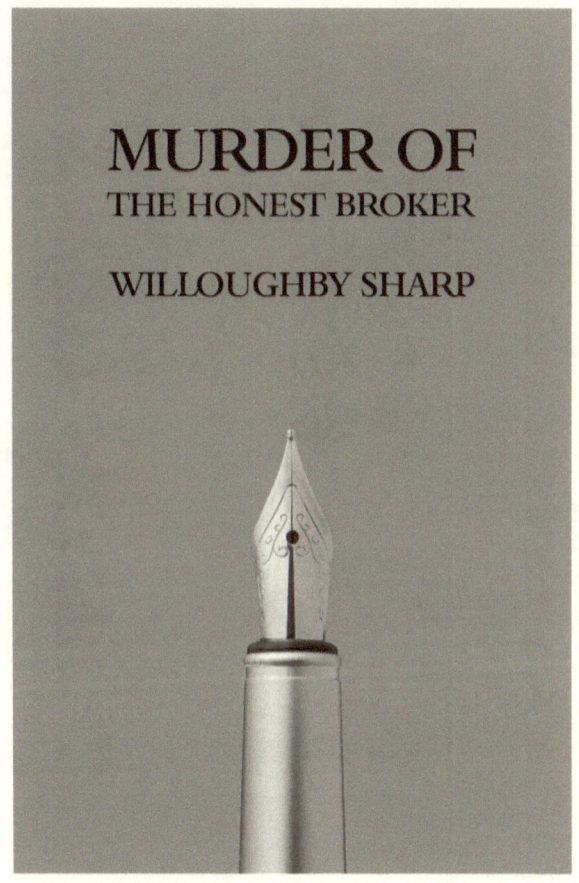

MURDER OF
THE HONEST BROKER

WILLOUGHBY SHARP

Murder of the Honest Broker, by Willoughby Sharp
Introduction by Curtis Evans
ISBN 978-1-61646-211-6

COACHWHIP PUBLICATIONS

COACHWHIPBOOKS.COM

Murder Ends the Song, by Alfred Meyers
Introduction by Curtis Evans
ISBN 978-1-61646-298-7